6/10/15

Bob,

Thank you for all of your help. Hope you enjoy the read.

Frank

Thirty Days Hath September

Cover and book design by Joseph Perrone Jr.

ISBN-13: 978-1470167257
ISBN-10: 1470167255

FIRST EDITION

This is a work of fiction. Names, characters, places, and incidents are either the product of the author's imagination or are used fictitiously, and any resemblance to actual persons, living or dead, business establishments, events, or locales is entirely coincidental.

Dedication

This book is dedicated to my parents, Judith C. and Frank B. Robinson. I am immeasurably fortunate.

Acknowledgements

The path for this book has been quite long. I was lucky enough along the way to receive guidance and support—otherwise this work may never have come to fruition. I would first like to posthumously thank Barbara Hyatt and Pete Shiflet. Each was a pillar of encouragement and I will remember them always. I would like to thank Wendy Stephens, who for the past three decades has been both a friend and stalwart supporter. I would like to thank Mickey Coleman for her insight and attention to detail on this project.

I would also like to thank Joe Perrone, Jr. for his guidance in bringing this book to publication. Lastly, I would like to thank all of the people who over the years asked, "How's your book coming along?"

Chapter 1

Black Creek, North Carolina
September 24, 1976—1:57 a.m.

The kid was stoned.

Not the *"...I dig the colorful clothes you wear, and the way the sunlight plays upon your hair..."* kind of stoned. He was all the way on the other side of the dial—Paranoid City—where ominous shadows line both your path and your mind. The place where no one hears you scream—and even if they do—no one cares.

Alex Madrid and his companion watched him from the shadows—silent and statue-still. Hard and unblinking, they seemed oblivious to the cold rain that had encapsulated Black Creek for most of the last three days.

In the darkness, the kid felt his way along the uneven sidewalk—approached Black Creek from the shabby end of town—where the tax base was low, the street lights non-existent. The water-logged cuffs of his flared-legged jeans hung from his lanky frame, scraped the concrete as he walked. The sound—like a poorly-calibrated metronome—marked him in the darkness.

The throbbing in his head was like a wild-assed monkey wailing on a timpani drum. The pot and the alcohol he could handle. This was something else. He thought back to the party, to the girl with the tight t-shirt and no bra. She'd handed him something—offered him a wink—told him to take it—said he wouldn't be sorry. A short time later she had vanished—and now all that remained of her was confusion and a sense of dread.

The kid sloshed his way towards the pair—maybe forty feet away.

In the darkness, Alex Madrid and his companion tracked the kid, like hawks on a bunny. Fifteen feet away.

Ten feet. Three steps from the darkness to the sidewalk. The pair could cover that distance in just over a second. It would take only another moment to.... .

But the silent hawks let the stoned bunny pass. And that should have been the end of it.

An archaic phone booth stood just a few feet beyond the boundary of the run-down park. As the kid stepped next to it, the phone jangled a shrill scream—the effect like shards of glass on exposed nerves. The kid yelped, stumbled back off of the sidewalk—fell hard and awkwardly into the empty street. Yelped again.

The phone rang a second time.

Sprawled in a puddle of cold water, the kid stared wildly, tried to fight through the fog in his head. *Who is calling me? How the hell do they know where I am?*

A third ring—no less piercing. The kid watched the pair float from the shadows. Each scarier than the other—a man and a beast—a big freaking beast whose breath was like smoke in the cold air. The man's face remained hidden beneath a wide-brimmed hat. The kid heard a sound—something between a whine and a whimper—like a scared child, or a trapped animal. Then the slow realization—the pitiful utterance belonged to him. The phone rang again.

From beneath the hat, the man spoke. His tone was icy—undiplomatic. "Take off," he growled.

The kid struggled clumsily to his feet, stumbled—caught himself. The asphalt tore a chunk of skin from the palm of his hand. He stood, teetering like a man on a tightrope—then he began to run. In reality—little more than a spastic jog. He tried to focus on the sparse street lights a couple of blocks away. Over his shoulder, from the darkness, he heard the phone ring one last time.

Alex Madrid stepped into the booth, placed the cold, wet receiver next to his ear. *Dial tone.* He clinched his jaw, cradled the receiver—waited. It seemed like a long time. After a couple of minutes, the phone jangled back to life. Madrid picked up after the second ring.

There was a pause, then a male voice—cautious.

"That you?"

"Yeah," Madrid answered.

Another pause—this one a bit longer. Then the voice, small and scratchy, said, "The Wizard is loose." Syrupy anxiety coated each syllable.

Madrid closed the glass door of the booth—triggered an anemic overhead light. Writings and doodles, like modern-day hieroglyphics, were scratched and scrawled over much of the cubicle. "Loose how?" Madrid asked, as he looked over one of the messages. If he was interested in the best blow job in town, he should call Debbie. Someone had been thoughtful enough to leave her number.

"Es-es-escaped," the voice replied.

The caller was Nick Vorcheck. And Nicky was easy to read. He stuttered when he needed drugs, which was almost always. The more he stuttered, the more frustrated he became. When that happened, his well-developed vocabulary whittled down to mostly four-letter words.

"Escaped how?" Madrid asked as he continued to read the graffiti in the booth.

Vorcheck's reply was rapid-fire. "Who-the-hell knows? If anybody knows, nobody sa-sa-saying. He v-v-v-anished. Like a g-g-g-ghost or somethin'."

"Take a deep breath, Nicky," Madrid said with vague encouragement. "Just tell me what you know—easy on the drama."

"One minute he was there. Th-th-th-then he isn't. That's what I know. They got d-d-dogs on the ground and helicopters in the sky."

"Anybody else escape?"

"N-n-not that I heard about. Guy's supposed to be some k-k-k-kind of genius, ya' know. That's why they call him 'The Wizard'."

"Yeah, that's what I hear," Madrid replied. He had finished his reading. Most of the other names in the booth were guys—offering basically the same service as Debbie. "Anybody get hurt?" he asked.

"I d-don't know." Vorcheck answered in an annoyed tone.

Madrid snapped back. "It's important, Nicky."

"I-I-I didn't hear about no-no-no-body getting' hurt," Vorcheck responded defensively.

Suddenly claustrophobic, Madrid cracked open the door of the booth. The overhead light flickered to darkness. He stepped outside, the receiver still in his hand. The rain had eased to a steady drizzle. Madrid looked down Middle Street. The kid was long gone. He took a deep breath of cool air—let it out slowly. Two o'clock in the morning—he had Black Creek to himself. It wasn't the first time Madrid had experienced this small mountain town at that hour. But the last time was twenty years ago. He wondered if Black Creek had been any less dreary then, or simply his perspective brighter.

Madrid held the receiver by his side. From the other end of the line, he could hear Vorcheck's voice patter along, distant and tinny. He raised it back to his ear in time to hear Nick say, "You don't sound so worried."

Madrid thought for a moment, then replied. "I try not to worry too much about yesterday or tomorrow."

"Pr-pr-probably goin' to kill you," Vorcheck said, his voice up nearly half an octave. "I-I m-mean, you-you know—he's probably goin' to *tr-tr-tr-try* to k-k-kill you."

"I get where you're going with this, Nicky." Madrid reigned in his irritation. He wasn't ready to run Vorcheck off just yet. Nicky might come back into play. Stranger things had happened.

The man on the other end of the line said quietly—apologetically, "I didn't mean to piss you off, Alex."

"You didn't, Nicky," Madrid lied.

"So-so we're ok-k-k-kay?"

"Remains to be seen, Nicky," Madrid countered. "I'm going to check your information. If it's good, the money will be where I told you."

Panic flooded his tone. "G-g-goddamnit. You know its g-g-good, man. This is Nicky. I've never... ."

Madrid cut him short. "Then you won't have a problem when I check," he said in a tone without compromise. "Pick it up at noon tomorrow—don't come early—don't be late."

"Th-thanks, man," Vorcheck said. "I can really use it."

Madrid considered telling Nicholas Vorcheck not to put the payoff in his arm. But Alex Madrid understood the futility of negotiating with addiction. Instead, he said in a hard voice, "Be smart and keep your mouth shut, Nick. *Don't* get greedy and *don't* try to play this from both sides. I'll find out. And I promise you—it *won't* be worth it."

"I'd never do that to you, man." Vorcheck's' words arrived in the dark phone booth without a hint of conviction. "N-n-never even occurred to me."

"I'm sure it didn't, Nicky," Madrid replied, matching Vorcheck's tone.

Almost cheerful, Nicholas added, "You be careful, man."

"Yeah," Madrid answered, not cheerful at all. "You too."

"It was like The Wizard disappeared into thin air, man," Vorcheck said with child-like awe. "Just walked out of that prison—like f-f-fuckin' magic."

Madrid cradled the phone. The deal was done. Fatigue washed over him. He rolled his thick neck from side to side. It sounded like a fat man stepping on bubble wrap.

The big dog sat outside the booth, continued to look down the street, oblivious to the rain. Slowly, he turned—looked up at Madrid, as if expecting to be apprised. Madrid obliged. "The Wizard is like magic, Toto." he said.

The dog tilted his massive head roughly twelve degrees.

"Let's go home," Madrid said tiredly—resisted telling the big mutt "...there's no place like home...."

* * * *

Two hundred miles away, Nick Vorcheck shuffled from one leg to the other. His skin had taken on a life of its own. Itchy—crawling over him like a thousand worms. He rifled through his pockets, finally found the scrap of paper in his dirty jeans. The number, once neatly printed in blue ink—was now smudged but still legible. He fed coins into the phone, let his index finger travel around the rotary dial After the eighth ring, someone picked up—a thick voice laden with sleep and irritation.

"What?"

"It's N-n-n-nicky."

"It's two o'clock in the morning, Vorcheck. What the hell do you want?"

"You said to call when I made contact with Madrid."

"You got the number?"

"Yeah, but I got better than that. I tracked it down. It's a phone booth in Black Creek, North Carolina. It's a little hick town up in the mountains."

"What the hell is Madrid doin' there?" the voice on the other end asked.

Vorcheck answered somberly. "My guess is he's hiding from you."

Chapter 2

September 24th—10:14 p.m.

To the west, beyond the crest of the Blue Ridge Mountains, a thunderstorm gathered power. On the small porch, in a chair with a sagging cane seat, the woman rocked slowly. The decking boards under the chair creaked in protest of her substantial weight. From above, red neon washed her in a hellish glow. Her eyes stayed fixed on the horizon, her large pupils like watery black pits. The neon had once spelled *OFFICE,* but the last three letters had burned out. The effect was a little like the closing shot from a B-grade horror movie.

A cool breeze snaked through the valley, rushed over ~~the~~ her corpulent bare arms. A shiver triggered from deep inside her. Above her head, wind chimes tinkled urgently—a tardy warning—too late to be of use.

The woman lifted her plastic mug—vodka flooded her mouth. The alcohol, warm in her throat, did nothing to relieve her dread. She had been sober for three years, three months, fourteen days, and six hours. Then Alex Madrid had walked into the motel office. The silver bell attached to the door had remained strangely quiet. She had been watching the local news, waiting to see who was going to be on with Johnny Carson—wishing she had the cash for a color TV. He'd stood motionless, watching her from the far side of the worn Formica counter. A lyric from a Kris Kristofferson song had flashed in her head—flashed as clearly as the lightning she now watched *"...hidin' intentions of evil, under the smile of a saint..."*

Words were passed—money changed hands. It had only taken a few moments. Madrid had been neither forceful nor threatening with his request. It was more cash than she'd seen in a long time—Ben Franklin and a bunch of dead presidents. An hour after the exchange, her sobriety had evaporated. That had been a week ago, almost to the minute.

Through bleary eyes, she spotted another flash—a moment later, heard the faint, angry rumble of thunder. Clearly a sign—an apparition of doom. It had visited her before—three times in her thirty-six years. It always began differently—always ended the same. The vision was a prelude to trouble—the kind of trouble where people died.

* * * *

Dicky Padrick hadn't picked up on the approaching storm—but he didn't pick up on a lot of things. Dicky Padrick was slow—short-bus slow. He switched on his Boy Scout flashlight, sent the beam around his dark bedroom. The light washed over the poster of a red swimsuit-clad Farrah Fawcett. There was a set of bunk beds. Dicky slept on the bottom bunk—no one had ever slept on the top. The beam came to rest on the framed pictures of his family hanging on the wall. His mother and father were standing on the beach smiling back at him. They were dead. Dicky liked looking at the picture, but it made him sad. There was also a picture of his older sister. She was pretty, but she had moved away. Dicky missed her, too—maybe missed her the most. There was no picture of Dicky's older brother in the collection. But two doors down the hall, he was sleeping.

Dicky switched off the light and waited. From the hallway outside his door, the grandfather clock ticked along, dividing time onto neat, equal segments. The flashlight was on again. He inventoried the equipment he'd laid out on the floor. A Boy Scout pocket knife; he might need it for protection. A small pair of binoculars he had "borrowed" from his brother; they would be good for looking in windows. Dicky had included his inhaler—in case he got "too excited".

Quietly, Dicky loaded the pack—shrugged it onto his soft, round shoulders. With practiced touch, he slid open his bedroom window—poked his head outside. The wind offered a cool greeting. Once on the ground, he wished he had worn his jacket. He considered going back inside, putting an end to the adventure. But now the desire was too strong. Dicky's sister had called it "natural sexual interest". A sheriff's deputy had called it something else.

He worked his way through the neighborhood, traversed backyards until he reached the edge of the woods. Then he adjusted his pack and started down the wooded path toward the Black Creek College campus.

* * * *

Miranda Toliver stopped dancing; the music continued to pound. She checked her watch again. Under the strobe lights, Mickey Mouse's hands took on an epileptic quality. The Black Creek College Homecoming dance swirled about her like a human vortex—bodies gyrating—a brightly-colored, kaleidoscopic mass. Bell-bottom jeans and leisure suits; patches of the *"Keep on Truckin"* guy and bandanas affixed to a variety of appendages ; tie-dyed tee shirts, platform shoes, long dresses and really-short skirts.

Miranda was wearing her faded hip-huggers with a peace sign embroidered on the butt; a white peasant blouse was pulled down over tanned shoulders—just a hint of cleavage. A wide suede belt was knotted below the exposed naval of her flat stomach. The large room was warm, the residual effect of stage lights and moving bodies. Miranda felt a trickle of sweat slide down the curve of her spine. She began to thread her way toward the perimeter of the room. No one seemed to notice.

No one except Andy Frazier. On the perimeter of the manic energy, Andy Frazier studied her with obsessed fascination. In the shadows, on the other side of the room from the band, he felt himself growing hard.

Miranda was Andy's vision of female perfection—thick blonde hair and deep blue eyes—an athletic body—a dimpled smile—with just a handful of freckles sprinkled strategically over an impish nose. Andy sat near her in two of his classes—but not too close—and always a couple of seats back. The first quarter was nearly a month old and he hadn't yet worked up the courage to speak to her. He'd heard her laugh once. The sound had been intoxicating, like music from a rare instrument. The kind of instrument guys like Andy rarely got a chance to play.

"How can anyone so damned beautiful be dancing by herself?" For a second—a fleeting instant, Andy latched onto a delusion. He could step from the darkness. *"Miranda is waiting for me,"* he whispered, not loud enough for anyone else to hear.

It was the logic of an obsessed mind and from the safety of his dark corner, the concept seemed marginally plausible.

From the small stage, the local rock band continued to hammer on his dream. Self-loathing replaced the vision of Miranda's body.

The darker side of Andy Frazier's obsession began to claw to the surface of his psyche. *"This wasn't the time,"* he lamely assured himself. If he was going to take a chance, it would be a high risk—high reward.

His eyes followed Miranda as she wound her way through the crowd. Miranda reached the double doors at the back of the Student Center. They led to a hallway, to a flight of stairs, and to the rear entrance of the building. The band did their best to cover a Grand Funk Railroad tune. "....*I can feel the hands of a stranger and they're tightening 'round my throat. Heaven help me, heaven help me...* ". Andy watched the doors close behind her.

Chapter 3

September 24th—10:49 p.m.

The town of Black Creek was named for..., well, Black Creek. But the body of water that separated the town of Black Creek from Black Creek College was not Black Creek. It was the Pisgah River. Black Creek, which emptied into the Pisgah River was actually about a mile north of the town and the college. It was confusing.

On the "college" side of the Pisgah River, the Black Creek College campus was scattered across the valley floor—a smattering of brick and stone buildings. Most of the buildings had slate roofs—none were over four stories high. In the past hundred years, the college had seen good times and bad. The pendulum was currently arced deeply into the negative end of the cycle. Black Creek College was a small school. *Intimate* was the term recruiters most preferred—and getting more intimate every semester.

Near the center of Black Creek College campus a perfect circle of brick driveway surrounded a smaller circle of neatly-trimmed grass. Some of the red bricks were inscribed with the names of financial donors—most were just bricks. In the center of the grass was a shabby-looking fountain—three tiers of badly-stained limestone. Water cascaded unevenly over two banks of multi-colored lights—reds, yellows, blues, and greens. Seven years ago it had been really groovy—a sentiment that had lasted about three days.

Parked on the drive, next to the fountain, Alex Madrid sat behind the wheel of a 1964 Ford Galaxy 500. The car looked like someone had lovingly rolled it off the set of *The Andy Griffith Show*—then spent the next twelve years neglecting it. Sun and time had faded it almost white—the big magnetic logos on the front doors declared it a Black Creek College Security vehicle. The same logo adorned the back of [redacted] Madrid's Navy-blue nylon jacket.

Madrid had been on the job for less than a week. He'd seen the ad while thumbing through the local paper—had called the number on a whim. The job had served as a limited escape from boredom and isolation. Last night's call from Vorcheck signaled the need for an abrupt departure. Tomorrow morning he would inform the head of security—make if official.

A cherry-red GTO pulled past Madrid and rolled to the front of the Student Union. Steve Miller's *Fly Like an Eagle* was blaring from the stereo. Madrid watched five students climb from the interior, four girls and a guy. Three of the girls were wearing short skirts. Two had the legs for it.

Madrid replayed his conversation with Vorcheck—assured himself the man Nicky referred to as *The Wizard* would not come to Black Creek tonight. He'd been out less than twenty-four hours. He would need time to hook up with Charlie Blades—time to plan—time to fine tune his madness. But Madrid also knew The Wizard could be brilliantly unpredictable—and amazingly brutal.

"Do what they least expect, when they least expect you to do it," the Wizard had told the handsome TV reporter. The Wizard had been wearing an orange prison jump suit that looked three sizes too large on his small frame. His demeanor had been meek and innocuous—his voice little more than a girlish whisper.

The handsome reporter had arranged his face like a serious journalist, had made sure the camera was getting his good side. He leaned forward—focused on the little man. The reporter nodded knowingly, his blue eyes intense, his highlighted-hair perfectly coiffed.

"So you understand what I'm telling you?" the Wizard asked, like a professor might ask a not-so-bright student.

"Yes, I believe I do," the reporter had replied. And then, as if to confirm his understanding, the reporter removed his engraved Cross pen from the inside pocket of his blazer. For dramatic effect, he touched the butt end of his pen to his square chin, lined it up with the clef.

The Wizard sank back into his chair. He smiled his gapped-toothed smile—relaxed and content. He watched the reporter cross his legs and carefully balance the small pad on his knee—made mental note of the perfect crease in his powder-blue trousers.

In what was later described as "the blink of an eye", the Wizard snatched the engraved Cross pen. The first blow was downward and left a deep, ragged track from the cheek bone to the jaw. The second blow was a savage thrust. The pen barely missed the reporter's left eye. The tip plowed through the skin just under the socket and jammed into his nose, breaking it just below the bridge. The Wizard had made sure to get his good side.

*"**Now** you understand," the Wizard had whispered happily. His gap-toothed smile had contorted to a disgusted sneer. His words were drowned beneath the volume of the once-handsome reporter's screams.*

The interview had never aired, but Madrid had been given a copy of the tape. That night, alone in a rented room, Madrid had played it. Played it until he lost count—then had tossed the tape into the burning fireplace.

Now the tape only played in his head.

* * * *

Andy Frazier emerged from the far side of the garishly-lit fountain—the image of Miranda Toliver's supple body still dancing in his brain. He opened the door and slid into the passenger side of the Galaxy 500. Madrid offered him a peripheral glance. Andy, a day student at Black Creek College, worked part-time with campus security to fulfill the requirement for his scholarship. His thick reddish hair was cut short. His uniform didn't fit his chunky body; the pants too loose—the shirt too tight.

"Hey, Alex," Andy said with forced cheerfulness.

"Hey," Madrid answered, scrutinizing the younger man. Something seemed off, but Madrid's mind was spinning on other matters.

Andy Frazier retrieved a bottle of Pepsi and a freshly-opened bag of pork rinds from the floor board. He extended the bag in Madrid's direction. The smell was strong in the car. Madrid mumbled, "No thanks", and rolled the driver's side window down halfway. Cool air and the sound of the fountain entered the old car together.

"What about your dog?" Andy asked.

Madrid glanced over his right shoulder to the big back seat of the old Ford. Spread over most of it was a hundred and forty-five pounds of German Shepherd and Bull Mastiff mix. The dog stared back at Madrid without emotion. The two had been together for just over a year. It remained an uneasy alliance.

"Yeah," Madrid told Andy Frazier. "Toto might like a little snack about now. But I need to give it to him."

The big mutt tilted his head the slightest degree upon hearing his name. After being nearly starved to death, the dog never turned down food. Madrid reached into the bag and selected a couple of large rinds. He knew better than to shove his hand towards the back seat. Instead, he held them up in the air for the dog to see and get a whiff . The massive animal took them gingerly then dropped them on the back seat. He ate them slowly, one at a time.

"Can I give him some?" Andy asked.

"No."

"I think he's beginning to like me," Andy argued.

Madrid kept his eyes fixed forward. He pushed the sleeve of his jacket up over this thick forearm to reveal the scar from the dog's first bite. "I thought that once, too."

Rain began to pepper the windshield of the car.

Chapter 4

September 24th—11:04 p.m.

Cold rain plastered Dicky Padrick's blond hair to his oddly-shaped skull. His big, pear-shaped body rocked back and forth. Dicky was breathing hard.

The young woman before him was beautiful. Maybe the most beautiful girl he'd ever seen—and she was mostly naked. Mostly naked from the pants up. This was the closest Dicky had ever been to a woman so naked. He could see both of her breasts, both of her nipples. They stared back at him like pink hypnotic eyes. Around her neck, was a delicate gold necklace with a tiny flower. Slowly, Dicky extended his shaking hand. He touched the necklace. He jerked his hand back—unsure. But she didn't speak—didn't resist him. Dicky's circuits were overloaded with excitement, confusion, and fear. His breathing became ragged. Lost in the moment, Dicky forgot about his inhaler. Slowly, carefully he laid his hand on the girl's naked breast, as if trying to cradle a delicate bird. He closed is eyes, rocked harder. His lungs made a rasping sound in the hard rain. Later, he would be asked how long he had knelt there. He would be unable to remember. What Dicky Padrick would be unable to ever forget, was what happened when he opened his eyes.

A flashing blue light was slicing through the darkness. Dicky heard the distant crackling sound of a woman's voice on a police radio. A man yelled something at Dicky. Dicky Padrick blinked cold rain from his eyes. The man yelled at Dicky again, louder and more forceful than before. Dicky took one last look at the woman. He slowly removed his hand from her breast, as if not to awake her. Terror raced over him like a thousand spiders. His asthmatic lungs were suddenly on fire. Dicky fell back onto the wet asphalt, flailed as he tried to find his backpack. He struggled awkwardly to rise, lunged and pitched, tried to get his feet under him. He thought he heard the man shout again, but wasn't sure—didn't care. The backpack was just a few feet away, at the base of a small ornamental cherry tree. Dicky took one step, then another. Then he heard the explosion. It was deafening—terrifying. Wasn't like the cartoons that Dicky watched for hours at a time. This was real. "Oh, god," he heard himself yelp. The words sucked more precious oxygen from his aching lungs. Dicky picked up the backpack, clutched it to his chest, fumbled for the zipper. Dicky heard the second explosion. At the same instant he felt his legs fold under him. His body hit the pavement like a soft-boiled egg.

Chapter 5

September 24th—11:05 p.m.

"Backfire," Andy Frazier said after the first explosion.
"Gunshot," Madrid countered tensely.

Andy eyed the last pork rind. "You sure, Alex?"

The second blast reverberated across the small college campus. "Damn," Madrid muttered savagely. A string of mostly-disjointed thoughts tumbled through his head—macabre and disturbing. His movements smooth and practiced, Madrid pulled a pair of .45 automatics from beneath the front seat.

"Call Pete and tell him what's happening," Madrid barked at the kid. "And stay in the car." He glanced into the back seat at the giant mixed breed. The hair had begun to rise on the back of the his neck. A low guttural growl rolled from deep in the dog's throat. "Keep Toto in the car."

Andy nodded—it was all moving too fast for the small-town boy.

Madrid was out of the old cruiser—running. His first couple of steps felt stiff and slow. The rain-soaked grass made footing treacherous, but after a few strides he was at a full sprint. For a guy almost forty, Madrid still had good wheels. The shots had come from behind the Student Union. Madrid raced across the front lawn. A walkway ran between a stone-clad retaining wall and the north side of the building. Madrid reached a side door of the Student Union. He pressed his back to the cold, wet brick.

From inside, he could hear the local rock stars. The bass guitarist thumped an irregular heartbeat. Madrid moved quickly along the wall, stayed low, his silhouette slid in and out of the shadows. His movements were nearly silent; the rain covered whatever sound was left.

The alley ended at eight concrete steps. The run off from the parking lot flowed down them, washed over Madrid's shoes. He eased to the top step, carefully peeked around the corner. The revolving glow of blue light skittered across the back of the building. The cruiser was parked off to his left—on a narrow side road that wound through the back of the campus. A large man with a Stetson hat stood silhouetted in the blue light. He wore the uniform of a deputy sheriff; his eight-inch barreled magnum revolver was drawn and leveled.

Another man was on the wet asphalt—under one of the yellow vapor lights that dotted the parking lot. He jerked violently, both of his hands clutched his left leg. His high-pitched screams struggled through the rain-drenched air. Between the man and deputy, Madrid could see another prone figure. It was a woman—she wasn't moving.

Madrid backed halfway down the steps and yelled, "Campus security!"

The deputy spun in the direction of the alley, the big pistol leveled at the shadows. "Come out with your hands in sight."

Cliché as hell, but Madrid didn't take the advice lightly.

"Show yourself. Come out slow!" the deputy yelled a half a second later. "Come out now or I start shooting!"

"Calm the hell down!" Madrid yelled back angrily. "My name is Alex Madrid. I'm Campus Security!"

Like a giant weather vane in a cross wind, the big deputy swiveled erratically back and forth between Madrid and the man on the ground in the parking lot.

Madrid tucked the .45s into his belt. He walked slowly up the steps to the parking lot. His hands were out to his side, palms forward.

Madrid had seen the deputy a couple of times around town. He was a Sergeant who was running for sheriff in the fall. "Check the girl," he ordered Madrid.

Madrid walked toward her, careful not to get between the downed man and the over-excited cop. The young woman stared up at him, her soft pink mouth open slightly, as if surprised by his visit. Her blouse had been pushed up. A broken strand of gold necklace curled between the swells of her smallish breasts. On one end of the strand Madrid could see a tiny gold four-leafed clover. The irony did not escape him.

He placed two fingers on her neck, felt for a pulse—the exercise academic. Madrid had seen too much death to have hope for this girl. The back of her blonde head had been crushed on the surface of the parking lot.

"What's the story, Madrid?" the deputy yelled.

"She's dead," he answered. Through the drone of the rain, Madrid's voice sounded disembodied. Vaguely, he heard the deputy swear.

In the distance, Madrid could hear a vehicle rapidly approaching. A moment later he saw Pete Wilson, the head of campus security, roar up the narrow side street. The white Ford LTD sliced through the standing water—sprayed it high into the air. Wilson locked down the brakes—slid the vehicle sideways to keep from slamming into the deputy's patrol car. Madrid rose from beside the girl, slipped one of the .45s from his belt, strolled over to the man on the ground.

"Keep that son of a bitch covered, Madrid!" the deputy yelled in a voice crackling with adrenaline. "Check him for weapons. That son of a bitch is dangerous!"

The young man on the ground rocked in spasmodic rhythm. His yelling had subsided to a soft, steady whimper. He continued to hold his leg tightly. Madrid could see the blood oozing through his fingers, down his chubby hairless forearms. He didn't look dangerous. But sometimes, the most dangerous ones don't.

Madrid jabbed the .45 under the kid's soft chin and, in the same voice he would use to order a taco, said "Don't do anything stupid." Madrid patted him down. No weapons. He spotted the backpack a few feet away. Someone had stitched his name on the satchel in bright orange letters.

"Is your name Padrick?"

"Dicky Padrick," the boy on the ground wheezed. Struggled for breath.

Madrid gave the man on the ground a good look. He was a kid, maybe fifteen or sixteen. He had blond hair that grew in every direction from the apex of his skull. He wore blue denim overalls and a red short-sleeved tee shirt, now soaked with rain. His body was large—pear shaped, his eyes Downs Syndrome. They vividly reflected his apocalyptic terror. Madrid rifled through the backpack—found an inhaler in one of the side pockets—handed it to the kid.

Dicky Padrick stared up at Madrid, his focus equally divided between the inhaler and the .45. He tentatively reached for inhaler with his bloody right hand—pumped three shots into his lungs. Some of the blood from his hand transferred to his chin and around his mouth—made him look a little like an obtuse vampire.

"Keep him covered!" the deputy yelled again.

The distant siren of an ambulance began to wash over the parking lot. "Help is on the way," Madrid told the boy. "Let me take a look at your leg."

The boy tried to stop crying. His hands continued to clamp his calf. His eyes remained fixed on the .45. "Please don't shoot Dicky again," he pleaded in a soft, high-pitched voice.

Madrid slid the pistol under his belt. "I wasn't the one who shot you," he told him without emotion, "let me take a look."

The boy slowly removed his hand. "Man shot Dicky with a gun," he said dully.

The bullet had creased the calf muscle. A lot of blood—but maybe not that much damage.

He asked weakly, "Is Dicky going to die?"

Alex Madrid felt a rush of emotion—thought back to the last time someone had asked him that same question. This time he didn't lie. "You're not going to die," he said evenly.

Pete Wilson was a big man with an uneven stride that hinted of knees going bad. He trained the twelve-gauge pump he carried on the boy's head. "Jesus H. Christ," he said between ragged breaths. "What in the hell is going on here, Madrid?"

"I'm not completely sure, but that shotgun is scaring the hell out of him."

"It's suppose to," Wilson growled.

"Please don't shoot Dicky," the kid pleaded.

"He's clean, Pete," Madrid said diplomatically. "If the kid pulls a piece and shoots someone, he can shoot *me—then* you can shoot him."

"Jesus H. Christ," Pete Wilson repeated, then reluctantly moved the shotgun aside. The ambulance arrived with sirens and lights. The two attendants started unloading equipment as a small group of students began to gather at the rear of the Union. Tightly huddled, they stayed near the back door. Another deputy pulled up—more lights and sirens. The shooting deputy told him to get the students back into the building.

When the noise subsided, Wilson said to Madrid, "Tell me *something.*"

"We were parked in front of the building. Heard shots. I told Andy to radio you. I got back here and found this. The kid was on the ground screaming and the girl was dead. You were maybe a minute and a half behind me."

"Do we know who the girl is?"

"No, but I'm guessing she's a student."

"Goddamn," Wilson said miserably, "this is all we need."

"What about *this* guy?" Wilson asked, motioned with his gun to the kid on the asphalt.

"According to what's written on his backpack, his name is Dicky Padrick."

Wilson took another look at the kid. "Goddamn," the big man moaned. "This is Miles Padrick's brother."

The name didn't mean anything to Madrid.

"Padrick's head of the History Department. Miles is a prick—thinks of himself as some great academic that somehow got waylaid to Black Creek College. His brother here's the village idiot. Kinda' ironical, huh? "

"I guess," Madrid mumbled.

Wilson looked back at the girl. "God, there ain't no *tellin'* what happened here."

The ambulance attendants had already given the girl a cursory look, confirmed what Madrid already knew. They began to look over the boy as another deputy's car pulled onto the scene—lights flashing, siren blaring. Dicky Padrick began to sob uncontrollably.

From behind him, Madrid heard a familiar voice. It was Andy Frazier's, but he sounded ten years young.

He stood above the dead girl, hands gripped tightly to the sides of his head. He spoke in a horrified voice. "It's Miranda," he said, choking on the words. "Oh, Jesus. It's Miranda."

Chapter 6

The North Georgia Mountains
September 24th—11:52 p.m.

There was no signage inside or out, and it was known by a variety of names. To some it was the local bar; to others a private club with unspecified membership. To most, it was an ominous-looking shack in the middle of nowhere—on an acre of land where few laws seemed to exist. Some folks called it *Harley's* because of the half-ton pig who often roamed freely among the patrons. Some called it *Scatter Brain's*—a veiled reference to an alleged incident—a sawed-off shotgun and a couple of bikers no one ever saw again. Others called it *The Hole in the Wall.* That had less to do with the ragged façade and more to do with the sepia-toned poster of Paul Newman and Robert Redford; the last scene of *Butch Cassidy and the Sundance Kid.* The desperados frozen in time—hopelessly outnumbered—Hollywood handsome—guns blazing. The poster hung behind the bar under the Pabst Blue Ribbon sign. The shrine ablaze in blue neon.

Whatever one called it, it was a low-slung building on wooden pilings capped with a tin roof. A sagging front porch ran along the front. The windows were few and barred. The glass had been painted black. A single naked bulb glowed dimly over the front door. The unlit parking lot was wrapped on three sides by large deciduous hardwoods. The lot was half full—motorcycles—mostly Harleys, a custom chopper and an old Indian. The rest of the vehicles were mostly pickup trucks in varying stages of demise. A black Cadillac with tinted windows was parked near the back door of the bar.

In the furthest, darkest corner of the lot a VW microbus was tucked between two maples. It was white, four years old. The vehicle was chosen to be inconspicuous, but in the parking lot outside of *Scatter Brain's* –it was anything but. A pair of yellow smiley faces were plastered on the back windows, their beady black eyes and maniacal grins barely visible in the gloom.

Charlie Blades sat motionless in the VW—scanned his surroundings with predatory eyes. His massive hands rested lightly on the steering wheel. Blades was a big man with a laundry list of disproportionate body parts—big hands, big feet, and a big head with a prominent thick nose. His thick hair was coarse and unruly. His face was a mask of scars—the testimony of a man who'd fought his way through life. The overall effect had once been quietly described as man morphing into a troll.

And Charlie Blades was strong—freakishly muscular for a guy who'd never touched a barbell.

Under his stoic, scary-as-hell, exterior, anxiety and suspicion churned. Nervous energy nibbled on edges of his logic. *The Wizard hadn't contacted him directly? He was careful, but why send word through some piece-of-shit street junkie like Nick Vorcheck? Why meet here? This was a stupid place to meet—or was it? The Wizard wasn't stupid. How many people walk out of a high security prison and disappear without a trace? Maybe meeting here was some sort of test? Or a set up? It seemed complicated, but much of what The Wizard did—much of what he thought—was complicated.*

A wisp of fog drifted lazily past Charlie's windshield. It looked a little like a ghost—which didn't help his state of mind. He rolled his window halfway down. The sound of the jukebox inside the bar floated inside the van, the noise barely audible through the thick, board and batten walls. Charlie couldn't make out the song, but simply the rise and fall of rhythmic hum. After nearly thirty minutes, his eyes had fully adjusted to the darkness. He swiveled in his seat, surveyed the parking lot again. Charlie adjusted the rearview mirror, but couldn't manage the angle he needed. Reluctantly, he tore his eyes from the darkened lot—turned to the girl on the bench seat behind him. She laid with her back to him, wearing a plain, white cotton dress. The narrowness of her waist and the curve of her hip were silhouetted against the dark upholstery, like the negative image of a photograph. The dress had ridden up her left thigh. He studied her with a mixture of lust and apprehension. As if feeling his eyes upon her, the girl stirred from her meticulously-controlled, drug-induced stupor.

She looked much like the previous two—by design—not tall—not short. This one had bigger tits, but not ridiculous. Her skin was pale—alabaster is what The Wizard called it. Not many freckles—and those green eyes. Charlie had taken her shoes in case she tried to run. This one was a little prettier than the last. Not as sexy as the first—but that wasn't her fault. There could never be another one like the first.

What had The Wizard called that? Three in a row? A trilogy? Yeah, that's what he had called it. A trilogy. Charlie didn't know what you called four in a row—didn't want to know. This girl would be the last. At least *his* last. Charlie Blades was still trying to get his mind around that idea.

He stole one more look at the girl, allowed himself to slide back into time. The memory had been filtered and refined over many years. It was one hour of his life that had influenced every hour that followed—the apex and the abyss of his life inexplicably fused into one event.

Sometimes, like now, he could replay the scene without acknowledging the end. Charlie felt himself getting aroused. He reached into the back seat, ran his hand up the girl's exposed leg. Continued under her dress, caressed her lace panties with his long thick fingers He was about to slide inside the silky material when The Wizard's drawn, ashen face flashed in his brain. Charlie heard himself. An utterance—something between pain and shock. The sound made the girl stir. She turned over—stared up at him through the darkness with unfocused eyes. Slowly, she sank back to the seat, back into the pharmaceutical fog.

Charlie took one more look. The drugs and the sparse light painted her with the illusion of tranquility. Again, he thought about the other two—hoped she wouldn't end up the same way—but knew she would. Charlie turned back around in the seat of the VW microbus—waited for something bad to happen.

As if on cue, a rattle-trap pickup eased into the parking lot, tires slowly crunching over the sparse gravel. The truck nosed into an open area about fifteen feet from Charlie's van. The driver killed the engine, then the lights. Charlie had a clear view of the cab. He could make out three people; two shaped like women. The female shape in the middle raised her arms over her head. It looked to Charlie like she was taking off clothes. The other woman sat motionless staring out of the passenger window, her back to the other two. A couple of minutes passed and Charlie Blades could make out the shapes of bodies moving in rhythm. He could hear voices, mostly from the woman—moaning and guttural commands—like listening to a porn movie without the funky background music. The woman sounded older, her voice deep, the way some women sound after twenty years of smoking. The other woman continued to stare out the window. The people in the truck made it hard for Charlie Blades to concentrate.

* * * *

Cindy Carson had been promised ***a big night out.*** That promise had come from her Aunt Cheryl. Cheryl was thirty-three, thrice divorced, the younger sister of Cindy's recently-deceased mother. Though nearly twice her age, Cindy considered Cheryl her best friend—until tonight.

For the past two hours, the trio had ridden around the county in Buddy's truck. Buddy, Cheryl's new boyfriend, had seemed all right at first. Good-looking—in a kind of greasy, smarmy way. He had a tattoo of a mostly-naked woman on his right shoulder. He said it was Cheryl, but it really didn't look like her. A few years younger than Cheryl, Buddy liked to talk—his motorcycle, his guns, and the slew of fist fights he'd won. Cindy had started out in the middle watching Buddy and Cheryl knock back cans of Budweiser between occasional pulls from a bottle of Wild Turkey. When Buddy wasn't drinking, or stopping on the side of the road to take a piss, he was reaching across Cindy to feel up Cheryl. Cheryl hadn't seemed to mind when Buddy's hand occasionally strayed to her niece. On the last pee break, Cindy had moved to the passenger side of the truck. The next stop had been the parking lot.

Now she was in the parking lot at Scatter Brain's—sitting with her nose pressed against the window while her aunt was having sex just a few inches away.

Cindy felt Buddy's hand on her shoulder. "Come on over here, baby," he said. "Let me see those little titties." More command than request. "Buddy's got somethin' for you."

Cindy felt tears gathering in the corner of her eyes. She shook her head—said nothing.

Aunt Cheryl's approach was softer—a slurred, erotic diplomacy. "Come on, Cindy. It will be fun, baby. Buddy can make you feel *so gooood.*"

Cindy reached for the door handle—pushed. The door of the old truck opened with a loud creak. Cindy felt Buddy grab her hair—yank her backward. She heard something pop in her neck and felt an electric pain shoot through her.

"Where the fuck do you think you're going?" Buddy growled savagely from the other side of the cab..

"Goddamn, Buddy!" Cindy heard her aunt yell. "Take it, fuckin' easy!"

Cheryl was still straddling him on the front seat. Her jeans and panties were wadded on the floorboard of the truck, her shirt pulled over her shoulders, bunched around her neck. Cheryl could still feel Buddy hard inside her, was still drunk enough to enjoy the feeling. Then Buddy's open palm slammed against her face. White light flashed in her head—Cheryl's skull lurched sideways. She was vaguely aware of the taste of blood in her mouth.

"Don't tell me what to do!" Buddy screamed at her, his face only inches from hers. Cheryl felt the spray of angry spittle. "You told me this little bitch would party!"

* * * *

Charlie Blades watched the door of the old truck swing open—saw the girl's head snap back, her splayed legs almost touching the ground. He watched the other woman recoil from the punch to her head. The younger woman slid out the truck—crumpled to the ground. When she struggled to her feet, she was only a few steps from the VW, looking directly at him. Charlie thought she might try to escape to the microbus. The irony did not register. The man who had been in the truck tumbled out behind her, lost his footing, and fell out of sight. Then the girl was jerked from Charlie's view—like the girl in *Jaws* when the big shark took her under for the last time.

* * * *

Cindy felt her body go limp. She poured from the truck, splashed to the parking lot like so much water. From above her, Cindy heard Cheryl cry out, then moan. It was a different kind of moan than the sex sounds—this one a product of pain. She worked to get her knees under her. There was pain in her neck. Fear and indecision bogged her thought process. She crawled a few steps towards the van, then struggled to stand up. Cindy could see the silhouette of a big man in the van next to her. His hair was bushy, his profile grotesque—like something from a fairy-tale nightmare. He turned his large head slowly—stared at her—his eyes like evil black holes. Even so, she wanted to call out to him for help. Then he was gone.

Cindy felt the hand at the small of her back. She felt Buddy's fingers inside the waistband of her hip huggers just before he jerked her to the ground. In a blurred instant, she felt Buddy on top of her, pulling at her clothes, trying to kiss her. She felt her jeans slip over her hips and past her knees. Buddy pinned her to the ground, the damp Georgia clay cold beneath her. Buddy's weight compressed her lungs. She smelled the whiskey and beer—felt Buddy's hard penis pressed against her thigh. Then Cindy stopped struggling. Through a gap in the leafy canopy above her, she could see the filmy light of the three-quarter moon—like a window to a safe harbor well beyond her reach. Cindy tried to focus on the light—attempted to shift her mind into survivor mode.

Cheryl fell out of the truck. She was naked except for the shirt still around her neck and one sock. She crawled across a patch of gravel and got to her knees. She flailed at her boyfriend with small, poorly-aimed fists. Her long slender arms moved like an erratic windmill. Her large breasts gyrated wildly. Buddy caught Cheryl's wrist, twisted it hard. She felt pain shoot through her arm. Buddy came up to his knees—hit her in the face with a straight right. Hard. A small sound, like a yelp from a sleepy puppy, escaped her lips. Cheryl fell back against the truck and didn't move.

Cindy was only vaguely aware of her aunt's feeble defense. But what happened next would stay with her forever.

The hazy moon disappeared—an eclipse of sort. Buddy was still on his knees when a massive hand smashed into the side of his face. He slumped forward, and just for a moment, he and Cindy were cheek to cheek. Then he was gone. Cindy later describe it as if Buddy had been lifted like a piece of paper caught in a breeze. The big man from the microbus had Buddy by the throat. He pulled him away towards the front of the truck. Cindy wasn't sure if Buddy's feet were still touching the ground. Another punch crashed into Buddy's ribs. The big man adjusted his grip from Buddy's throat to the back of his neck. The big man spun Buddy's body and began to slam Buddy's face into the hood of the truck. Cindy lost count—maybe twelve times—maybe twenty—the damage was delivered with metronomic rhythm. The sound like a heavy foot on a bass drum pedal.

Sitting on the wet ground with her pants around her ankles, she watched with horror and fascination. The hairy monster continued to slam Buddy's head. Then the big man stopped—looked at Buddy for just a moment. It reminded Cindy of the look her father offered a fish he was about to throw back into the creek. The big man released his catch. Buddy crumpled into a pile at Cindy's feet. With no sense of urgency, the big man strode back to the van. Cindy heard him adjust the radio, then he slowly drove away. The big scary man never once glanced in her direction.

* * * *

Rex and Flex. That's what The Wizard called them. Rex was tall, a couple of inches taller than Charlie Blades, and a lot better looking. He had dark hair, parted in the middle, that framed his angular face. His dark eyes paired with his one-hundred-watt smile worked wonders on the ladies.

Flex's real name was Tommy. He was half a foot shorter than Rex—looked like the cover model of a cheap romance novel—wide shoulders, thick neck, flowing blonde hair. His tanned, hairless body was the product of copious portions of barbells and steroids. He was brutally strong, maybe even stronger than Charlie Blades. The pair watched from the front seat of the black Cadillac. They were parked in the shadows, near the back door of *Scatter Brain's,* across the lot from the VW microbus. Behind them, The Wizard was tucked into the dark recesses of the back seat.

Flex shifted his mass, turned and asked, "So how long we gonna' wait?"

"Patience," The Wizard replied sternly. "'All things come around to him who will but wait'."

"Yeah, I heard that somewhere," Flex agreed vaguely. "I think my momma used to say that sometimes."

Momma. The word triggered a collage of images and emotion—rapid-fire memories, some actual, others distorted. It was a rush toxic serum—love, hate, lust, betrayal, fury, terror, manipulation, and sadness. The little man in the back seat pulled himself from his psychological nose dive. From the darkness, he forced a canine smile. *Yes,* he thought. *I'm sure your slut whore of a mother got off her back long enough to quote Emerson.* What he said aloud was, "Your mother must have been very well read."

"Yeah," Flex grunted. "I reckon so."

An old truck pulled into the parking lot, stopped next to the VW bus. A country song trailed along, then died along with the head lights. A few minutes after that, Rex leaned over the steering wheel, squinted through the tinted window and the murkiness of the lot. "I think those people in the truck are screwing."

Flex rolled down the passenger-side window. The muffled sound of sex floated across the lot. "Sounds like he's fucking her brains out," he said happily.

A moment later, they heard the squeaky truck door open. Through the darkness, they watched the girl tumble out of the cab—sprawl on the ground. She struggled to her feet. Then a guy tumbled out of the cab—pulled her back to the ground—crawled on top of her. Then came another woman—mostly naked.

"Goddamn," Rex said, a touch of admiration in his tone. "He's doin' two of them."

They watched the man punch the older woman, pin the young girl to the ground.

"We might ought' a get the hell out of here," Rex told the man in the back seat. "This looks like it could get nasty."

"Not yet," The Wizard replied. He drank in the sounds like fine wine. Another set of maternal images played behind the curtain of his closed eyes.

The gorillas in the front seat watched Charlie Blades slide out of the microbus. The darkness, and their line of sight masked the details of what happened next.

Hearing the rhythmic thuds, Rex muttered, "Somebody's killing somebody."

"That would be Charlie doing the killing," The Wizard replied casually.

A minute later Blades rolled past them—in his microbus with the smiley faces—out of the parking lot—into night.

"Guess you were right," Flex said.

"I usually am," The Wizard retorted. But he realized Charlie Blades had changed. And change was not good.

Chapter 7

September 25th—1:20 a.m.

The courthouse in Black Creek sat almost squarely in the center of town—halfway down Middle Street. It was boxy—architecturally unimpressive—two stories of old brick and a bit of white trim. On the lower level, large windows looked out on three sides. The upper level was the jail. The windows on that floor were smaller—vertically divided with heavy iron bars. To make room for additional government, the building had been scabbed onto over the years.

The Sheriff's Department was housed in a low, shabby building at the back of the courthouse, connected by a rusting metal breezeway. In the back of the building were three offices. Two of the offices were small and doubled as interrogation rooms when needed. The third, and largest office, was for the sheriff. There was a brass plaque on the door that said so. But a group of men were meeting there without him.

To the right of the sheriff's desk, in a tight corner of the office, Alex Madrid leaned his straight-backed chair against a wall. The office was paneled with dark laminate that had probably been marketed as English walnut. The dark brown carpet was badly worn at the doorway—a little less around the desk. The furnishings were cheap and old. The lighting was sparse and cast the room is a weak yellow glow.

Sergeant Josh Galloway—the deputy who had done the shooting—sat behind the Sheriff's large oak desk. He leaned back in the chair, one leg propped on the corner. His black leather ankle-top shoes were dull with dirt and rain. On the wall behind him was an American Flag and an autographed black and white head shot of Richard Nixon. Next to the picture of Nixon was another black and white of three uniformed men standing in front of a patrol car. The one in the middle was a robust man with a black handle-bar mustache, a big cigar stuck in one side of his face. Madrid figured he was the sheriff. It took a moment for it to register, but Madrid realized the other two men in the photo were now in the room with him. Josh Galloway and Pete Wilson were older now—each about fifty pounds heavier than when the picture was taken.

Wind-blown rain drummed against the two windows that looked out onto the parking lot. It had been almost two hours since the incident behind the Black Creek College Student Union—since Dicky Padrick had been shot—since Miranda Toliver had stopped breathing.

Madrid placed his empty Styrofoam coffee cup on the floor beside him—then folded his thick forearms across his chest. Conversation bounced around the room. It seemed equally divided between the dead girl and the TV press who had staked out venues around the courthouse . A crew from Asheville had arrived first and had lodged themselves in the arched entry of the building.

Josh Galloway was probably mid-forties, six feet five inches or so, probably twenty pounds south of three hundred. His head was big—*squarish*—his dark receding hair shaped into a crew cut. He wore a neatly-trimmed, military style mustache; his eyes were hard and unfriendly. Madrid figured he was probably smarter than he looked—but probably not as tough as he wanted people to believe.

Pete Wilson stood next to Madrid's chair. He was almost as big as Galloway, but softer. The head of campus security was fidgety—uncomfortable with the company. On the other side of the office was a pair of deputies. A short round one leaned against a closed door Madrid supposed was either to a closet or a bath. A tall lean one was sitting next to him in a chair like Madrid's, his long legs stretched out, crossed at the ankles. Andy Frazier sat in the smaller office next door. The last time Madrid had seen him, Andy was still crying for the girl in the parking lot.

Pete Wilson cleared his throat. "I think Avery ought to be here, Josh." His voice was tight and defensive. "This is a major crime. A murder, for Christ's sake. Sheriff Boyd ought to be here."

"Ain't your call, Pete." Galloway's voice was thick with condescension. "And if you'd seen him in the past few days, you'd be whistlin' a different tune. The Sheriff needs his rest. He's old and sick." After a dramatic pause, he added, "Waitin' on death."

Galloway continued. "You and Madrid are here 'cause I said you could be. Professional (it came out *pro-fesh-a-nile*) courtesy.

Don't press your luck." A cruel smile played at the corner of his mouth. "I could make you two wait out in the other room with the boy."

Madrid watched amusement grow into stupid-assed grins on the faces of the two deputies. He saw Wilson shift his weight. Madrid could hear Pete Wilson breathing—wondered why Galloway was trying to bait him.

The following information had been verified. The girl's name was Miranda Toliver—and she was definitely dead. Until a couple of hours ago, she had been a junior at Black Creek College. She had lived in Mary Thornton Dormitory—had been majoring in psychology. The kid Galloway had shot was Richard "Dicky" Padrick. Padrick was sixteen—village idiot or mentally handicapped—depending on which person in the room provided the description. He lived in faculty housing on the fringe of campus with his brother, Miles Padrick. Miles Padrick was head of the history department at Black Creek College. Josh Galloway offered the motive for the attack.

"He's a fuckin' pervert. Knew that two years ago," Galloway said matter-of-factly. He looked over at the round deputy by the door. "Remember when we caught him up on "Reefer Ridge" lookin' in the girls' dorm?"

The short, fat deputy nodded, as if his head were controlled by a puppeteer. "Sure do, Sarge."

"Yeah, that was about two years ago. I knew we hadn't heard the last of him." Galloway looked hard at Pete Wilson. "Your buddies over at the college made sure we kept it quiet. On account of the kid's brother bein' a teacher there." Galloway added with an accusatory grin, "You remember it, Pete. You had your chance to do somethin' about it then. But you just sat there with your mouth shut and went along with 'em."

Madrid, still leaning back against the wall, spoke for the first time—his tone conversational. His eyes locked on Galloway. "Kind of a big leap, don't you think?"

Galloway adjusted his stare—down and to the right—gave Madrid a hard look. "What'd you say?"

Madrid met the look without challenge. "I said it was a big leap. You're telling us the Padrick kid is a murderer because he likes looking a naked college girls. I mean, hell, *I* like looking at naked college girls." Madrid turned from Galloway and looked out the window. Under the lights in the parking lot, he could see the rain falling harder. Television crew were rigging tarps to keep their people and equipment dry. Still watching the crew, Madrid added, "But liking naked girls, doesn't make me a murderer." He turned back to Galloway—finished the thought. "As far as you know."

The deputy spoke carefully. Some of the animosity evaporated into the gloom of the dreary office. "I got a hell of a lot more than that, Madrid. I saw that retarded pervert choke the life out of that poor girl."

"You saw that?" Madrid asked. The insinuation was clear. *If you saw it, then why didn't you stop it?*

Galloway—now cautious. "I saw enough to know what happened."

"Is that what you're planning to tell them?" Madrid asked, nodding back to the window. *"I saw enough to know what happened?"*

"You need to stop talking, Madrid," Galloway growled.

Madrid knew Josh Galloway was right. His logical side screamed at him to shut up and walk away—but Dicky Padrick's orb-shaped face had already started to haunt him. With no cards to play, all he could do was bluff. "We all saw what we saw." Madrid said quietly.

Galloway's expression made several slow transitions—confidence to anger, anger to confusion, confusion to concern. The unasked question lodged in this throat. In a voice barely loud enough to be heard, he said, "Get the fuck out of here."

In the office next door, Andy Frazier sat on the edge of a worn vinyl sofa. The crying had stopped, but his eyes were still swollen. Madrid said, "Let's go, kid. I'll drive you home."

They walk down the darkened breezeway—threaded their way past the leaks—by-passed the waiting press. Madrid dropped the Black Creek College Security car at the campus office. He and the kid and the dog climbed into his Chevrolet Blazer. Toto spread himself out over the back seat. Andy Frazier gave Madrid directions to his parents' house.

On River Street, Madrid waited on a traffic light. He gave the kid a surreptitious glance. Andy's gaze remained fixed straight ahead.

After they had cleared the light and were rolling out of town, Madrid asked,

"Did you see Dicky Padrick tonight, Andy?"

"Huh?" Andy replied, suddenly back in the moment.

"Did you see Dicky Padrick tonight?" Madrid repeated.

"Yeah, I saw that dopey bastard," Andy replied, a mixture of sadness and anger. "I wish Josh Galloway had shot him in the head instead of the leg."

Madrid let that go. "I'm not talking about what you saw in the parking lot. I'm talking about earlier. When you were out walking around campus. Did you see him then?"

"I...uh,. No. No I didn't see him."

Madrid noted the kid's tone had gone cautious.

"You're sure? This is important."

"Pretty sure." More caution.

"What about Miranda Toliver? Did you see her?"

Madrid's question blindsided Andy Frazier. Panic raced through him as he remembered her body moving to the music—remembered his pathetic fantasy. The panic kept him from looking in Madrid's direction—made his throat go tight. "No, I'm pretty sure I didn't see her."

"*Pretty sure*?" Madrid countered, not exactly friendly.

Madrid left the question hanging, let it mingle with the odor of the wet dog on the back seat. He drove another half mile. "I can see how you might look past Dicky Padrick. He looks a little out of place, but no more than some of the other students."

Andy Frazier shifted in his seat. "Yeah, I guess," he said.

"Yeah," Madrid echoed agreeably. "You might forget Padrick, but you would remember the hell out of Miranda Toliver."

Andy Frazier shifted in the seat, looked everywhere except at Madrid.

"You know her—knew her," Madrid corrected in a quiet voice. "You called her by name in the parking lot, Andy."

"I didn't see her," Andy Frazier repeated, slightly defiant. "Not 'till the parking lot."

Madrid switched his wipers from low to high, turned onto Andy Frazier's street. "You're positive?" he asked again.

"Yes, I'm goddamned positive." The younger man's voice was sharp with emotion.

The dog in the back seat raised his massive head. A low growl rumbled from his broad chest. Madrid grimaced, jerked his head toward the back seat—spoke just above a whisper, "He doesn't do well with a lot of excitement, Andy." Madrid glanced back at the dog, then back at the kid. "I just asked you a simple question."

"And I answered it, Alex." Andy's voice was softer, back in his control. "What difference does it make if I saw Miranda or Padrick? Miranda's dead and Padrick killed her. So what goddamned difference could it make?"

Madrid stopped in front of the address Andy had given him. Andy's parents lived on a street of one-story ranch-style houses. Some of the houses had brick facades and some had detached carports. Andy's house had neither.

Madrid killed the motor which made the rain seem even louder. "It could make a lot of difference. Somebody on that campus saw something. Dicky Padrick and Miranda Toliver didn't just materialize in that parking lot. They were there for a reason, or, more likely, for different reasons. But they got there somehow. One, then the other—or maybe at the same time. And more than likely, someone saw one or both of them."

"I didn't see them, Alex."

"Yeah, that's what you said."

Andy Frazier got out of the Blazer and stepped into the rain. With the door still open, he said, "It's the truth."

"Okay," Madrid said. Then he added, "You think about it some more, Andy. Tomorrow I might ask you the same question." Madrid watched the young man slog though the rain to his parent's front stoop. A light came on as he approached the door—went dark as soon as he was inside.

Madrid started the Blazer—pointed it towards The Paradise Court.

Chapter 8

The Paradise Court
September 25th—6:00 a.m.

Alex Madrid awoke without an alarm clock.

The room that greeted him was sparse and ugly: two double beds with miss-matched spreads, a scarred pine table, a pink ginger-jar lamp, a dented white metal cabinet with a small sink, and a hot plate. And then there was the refrigerator. It was like the one Madrid remembered from his grandparent's house—squatty and rounded at the top. The large chrome handle always made it a challenge to open. This one had been painted a vile shade of green. The compressor was about to flat line, so every time it kicked on, the noise was somewhere between a freight train and a jackhammer. Madrid unplugged it at night.

The only window in the room was covered with heavy vinyl curtains that gapped in the middle. But that didn't matter. The sun wouldn't be up for another hour. Madrid reached up, clicked on the lamp, then squinted his eyes against the depressing yellow light. Toto was sprawled over the other bed, his huge head squarely on one of the pillows.

Still groggy, Madrid thought back to the night before—to Dicky Padrick, and to Miranda Toliver. The first couple of lines of "Sunshine go away today ... " ran through his head. He could think of no reason to be awake this early on Saturday morning. He turned off the lamp—spent the next few minutes futilely trying to doze off again—careful not to move around.

The big mongrel rose from the bed, shook himself noisily. With a single motion, he hit the floor and bounded up onto Madrid's bed—landed like a cement truck on a grape. Both of his front paws were squarely on Madrid's chest. The ancient box springs groaned in protest.

"Damn it, Toto," Madrid said irritably. "I've told you not to get on my bed."

Through the gloom, the big dog stared down at him—unremorseful.

"Hell, you've got a bed of your own," Madrid half wheezed. "With *two* friggin' pillows. How many mutts like you have a bed with *one* friggin' pillow?"

Toto's massive head tilted slightly—as if pondering Madrid's perspective.

"Get your furry ass off of me," Madrid told him, pushing him to one side. Toto slid off the bed and stood by the door of the tired little motel room. Madrid threw the blanket back—felt the chill of the worn linoleum as he tip-toed to the door. He let the big mongrel out to commune with nature—plugged the refrigerator back in—muttered, "This day is off to a lovely start." His words were dówned out by the compressor that rumbled back to life.

A few minutes later, Madrid slipped on a pair of nylon shorts, a sweatshirt with the sleeves cut short, and a pair of New Balance 320s. He attempted some half-hearted stretches among the rusting porch furniture outside his room, then moved stiffly across the parking lot. The small dirty white gravel crunched under his feet. Toto, familiar with the routine, came from the edge of the woods, fell into step on Madrid's left. Madrid carried a thick leather leash and snapped it to the dog's collar. Out on the highway, the red neon of The Paradise Court struggled through the thick fog that had settled into the valley. The pair started west on Old Highway 64. There was no traffic and the first mile was miserable. Madrid made a pact with himself—if it didn't get better soon, he would stop—walk back to the motel. Drink some coffee—maybe go back to bed. Pretty much the same pact he made every morning. He slogged past the sign that read "Welcome to Black Creek". Just below the official greeting, someone had neatly painted in block letters "Gateway to Nowhere". Toto loped along easily by his side, his tongue hung just slightly from his black muzzle. They ran past the phone booth where Madrid had waited for the call from Nick Vorcheck. Kept running.

The town of Black Creek looked different in the daylight—not necessarily better—but different. Fading ribbons, left over from the bi-Centennial parade, still clung to the occasional lamp post. Campaign signs filled the windows of the empty store fronts. Josh Galloway's picture was directly above the caption which read "Best for Black Creek". Like most things political—it sounded good and said nothing. Further down the street Madrid could smell bacon frying. Toto could smell it, too. They came to Carl's Diner and

Madrid gave the leash a quick tug to keep him moving. It was getting light and a handful of people were on the street. Most seemed to be headed to Carl's. Their expressions were somber, their glances suspicious. Black Creek was like a lot of small towns. News traveled fast—bad news traveled faster.

The pair continued up Middle Street—made the turn near the courthouse—crossed the street, and started back. By the third mile Madrid was beginning to feel awake and alert. The fog painted everything gray. Somewhere in the distance Madrid could hear a rooster crowing. A few of the trees were beginning to show the first hints of fall color and there were silvery spider webs slung from power lines and tree branches. It was a tranquil backdrop to the scenes that periodically flashed through his head.

Madrid had seen murder before—sudden and brutal—fueled by money, lust, or rage. Much of the killing had been senseless. But he didn't get that vibe from Miranda Toliver's death. There was an unseen sense of order—of something planned and executed. It was hard for Madrid to insert Dicky Padrick into that theory.

He and the dog stop running after four miles. Madrid checked his watch—just over thirty-four minutes. Not great, but not bad.

He walked the last couple of hundred yards to The Paradise Court. The main body of the motel was tucked about sixty yards back off the highway. It was low, with a flat roof—shaped like a squared-off horseshoe. Just beyond the mouth of the horseshoe was a tall stand of white pines that backed up to heavy woods. Nestled under the giant evergreens were three small cottages. Each had a small porch and a brick chimney, moss-covered shingles. Several seasons of pine needles gave the structures a gnome-like quality.

The office was closer to the highway—detached from the rest of the motel. It was a faded barn-red building with a glass front. Madrid followed the plastic grass carpet up three steps and onto the tiny stoop.

Inside, the motif was no less depressing. Rays of early-morning light struggled through the filmy windows. Several large, broad-leafed plastic plants had been placed on worn indoor-outdoor carpet. They filled most of the small entry—like an artificial, dust-covered jungle.

Behind the plywood registration counter was a rotund woman. Peroxide-blonde hair sprung from her skull at extreme angles. A blue-flowered dress hung loosely over folds of flesh. The first two fingers of her left hand were stained yellow from nicotine. It wasn't yet seven-thirty; she was working on her second vodka.

Behind the woman a new color television barked loudly. Before she handed Madrid his mail, she said in a cigarette-racked voice, "Rent's due tomorrow."

Madrid looked over the envelopes.

"You *are* staying another week, aren't you?" the woman asked.

"Looks that way," Madrid answered. He sensed her relief.

She looked past Madrid. Toto was eyeing one of the big plastic plants. "Your dog ain't goin' to piss on my bush, is he?"

Madrid glanced at the dog, then back at the woman. "I couldn't say for sure."

"I don't usually let dogs stay here."

"You mentioned that when I checked in."

"I don't like dogs," the bleary-eyed blonde said.

"Mentioned that, too."

"Then I guess I'm mentioning it again." A feeble whine from a woman in no position to bargain.

"Good to know," Madrid replied.

"And by the way," she added, when he was almost to the door. "You got a visitor."

Madrid felt his jaw clench. "Who?"

"Didn't say," the big woman replied indifferently.

"What did he look like?"

"It isn't a *he*. It's a woman."

"Okay. What does *she* look like?"

"Not like a hooker, if that's what you're getting at." The big woman gave him a scrutinizing look. "You in some kinda trouble, mister?" Before Madrid could answer, she added, " 'Cause we don't need any more trouble 'round here."

"No trouble," he replied without the effort to be convincing.

The fat woman bit her lower lip, nodded skeptically.

Madrid walked out the dingy motel lobby—followed Toto down the steps. When the pair was out of sight she reached for her bottle.

Chapter 9

Great Smoky Mountains National Park
September 25th—6:13 a.m.

Order. It took many forms. It was the reward of a disciplined mind. Or the byproduct of political or religious fanaticism. Sometimes—simply the mask of insanity.

The Wizard survived on order. Success demanded it—from escaping prison to putting on his socks in the morning. Socks were to be folded—not rolled. The left sock went on first, followed by the right sock, followed by the right shoe, followed by the left shoe. Socks were either navy blue, black, gray, or limited shades of brown. No white socks and no socks with even the slightest pattern. White socks were for rednecks—patterned socks were for fags.

Order.

Order demanded planning. Few people planned more meticulously than The Wizard—a brilliant weave of the simple and intricate. And with each plan, came a back-up plan—and then another back-up plan. No one knew this better than Charlie Blades. So when things had gone to hell in the parking lot of the bar, Charlie hadn't panicked. He had the backup plan.

Charlie had driven most of the night. He wanted to get as far away from the bar parking lot as he could. He doubted the older woman could identify him—doubted the younger woman would even try—doubted the guy with a face full of truck hood had survived. Around three o'clock in the morning, the road meandered through the Cherokee Reservation. Charlie Blades rolled past rows of connected shops with low roofs and darkened windows. Plastic bows and arrows, rubber tomahawks secured to brightly-painted handles, moccasins, postcards and t-shirts, hats and soda pop. Tomorrow morning there would be photo opportunities with tribal chiefs in full head dress. At the edge of the village, two miserable-looking black bears in chain-link fence cages watched him roll past in the darkness.

The transition between the Cherokee village and the Great Smoky Mountains was abrupt—an invisible line between commerce and nature. Charlie Blades watched the lights grow smaller in the rearview mirror of the VW microbus. The darkness of the thick forest closed in ahead of him. He drove until he was somewhere near the North Carolina-Tennessee line. Charlie nosed the VW into a scenic overlook. He tucked the van near the curb. He climbed into the back seat. He woke the girl enough to pour another dose of drugs down her throat. He thought about getting her naked, but he was tired and still thinking about the other girl back in the parking lot. Charlie awkwardly climbed back into the front of the van. He propped his legs on the passenger seat—leaned his head against the drivers' side window—closed his eyes.

Three hours later, he awoke to a transitioning sky—black fading to gray. It took Charlie a moment to put everything back in focus. He swung his legs back under him and looked around. At the edge of the parking area a large wooden sign described what he should have been seeing. The fog and misting rain obliterated any view. He adjusted the rearview mirror—took a look at himself. *Blood.* It was on his hands, arms, clothes. There were small spatters on his face.

He climbed out of the van, planted his heavy boots on the wet asphalt and stretched. His back and neck were stiff from the awkward sleeping position. At the edge of the overlook, he saw a concrete picnic table set next to a trash receptacle. A sign next to the trash can warned of bears. Charlie opened the side door. The girl was facing away from him. He could hear her faint, rhythmic breathing. He took a Coleman stove and some other things he needed—carried them to the table. He went back to the van, found a bottle of aspirin. He shook five of the white tablets into massive paw, tossed them into his mouth—washed them down with a swig of water from a gallon jug. The water had plastic aftertaste. The girl shifted on the bench, settled back down. He watched her—battled his lust. After a minute he walked back to the table.

He filled a battered coffee pot and a shallow metal bowl with the water from the jug. The Coleman was a two burner. He turned on the gas, listened for the hiss, lit a match. Charlie adjusted the flame from yellow to blue then repeated the process for the coffee pot. He waited for the water in the bowl to warm—tested it with his fingers.

He dipped a bar of *Lava* bath soap into the bowl—scrubbed the blood from his face, hands and forearms. He scrubbed hard—masochistically—the little particles in the soap dug into his skin.

Charlie considered washing the shirt. He only had two, and even with the blood, the one he was wearing was the cleanest. If he washed it, it would be wet for the next couple of hours. But the blood was noticeable—really noticeable. He went back to the VW—found his blue jean jacket with the sleeves cut out. He peeled off the shirt and tossed it on the picnic table next to the stove. Surrounded by forest, Charlie Blades looked a little like "the missing link"—big, powerful, and hairy. Massive arms and shoulders—knuckles not quite scrapping the ground. He shrugged on the jacket. It was a size too small so he didn't bother to button it. He opened the jar of freeze-dried coffee—took a deep whiff. Not like the real stuff, but it smelled good. The water in the pot was almost ready, but he wanted to give it another minute. Coffee couldn't be too hot.

Suddenly, Charley needed to take a leak. He walked over to the edge of the woods and unzipped his pants. Charlie had a psychological connection with his dick—even more than most men. It was huge—comforting in his hand. A woman had once told him he should be using it to make porno movies. Charlie liked that idea. Charlie liked the idea of being special—of being admired. If he were a porn star, everyone would know he had a big dick. And that might be enough for Charlie Blades—a little fame, a lot of pussy, and some cash in his pocket. He thought about the girl again—thought about waking her up—showing her his secret monster.

That's what Charlie Blades was thinking when he heard the car engine and saw the headlights struggling through the fog.

* * * *

Darius McCrary was twenty-four years old and loved his life. He loved working for the Forest Service, wearing the uniform. But he loved his wife the most. They had been married for exactly six weeks. And Saturday mornings were always special. Darius was coming off his last shift. Sally would still be sleeping—in their new bed. She would be waiting—warm and eager to snuggle. Soft and firm at the same time. Darius loved the way she looked in the morning. Her long blonde hair would be tousled about her face, her green eyes sleepy and slightly mischievous.

They had waited until after the wedding to have sex. It had been her idea—solely her idea. Not a religious thing, she had assured him—more *spiritual.* It had been a long year. Sally had promised him it would be worth the wait. And now she was making good on that promise. *Damn,* was she making good on it. Darius glanced at himself in the rearview mirror—realized he was grinning that goofy grin.

The first day he had brought the cruiser home she had been there in the front yard. Their white, four-room cottage sat back off a seldom-traveled country road. It was cute and cozy and not close to any neighbors. Sally had come out into the yard barefoot and smelled of something lemony. She was wearing one of his t-shirts, her alert nipples apparent through the thin, white material. She had smiled at him sweetly—a deliciously evil little smile.

Darius had shown her the car—all of the special equipment. It hadn't taken long—maybe thirty seconds. His lovely new wife had slipped off the t-shirt—had wiggled out of the cut offs. The sunlight had played in her long blonde hair—and in the smaller blonde patch between her legs which she had trimmed in the shape of a heart. Darius had wanted to take her inside their cottage. Sally had wanted something else. She had pulled him into the front seat of his new patrol car.

That's what Darius McCrary was thinking about when he saw the VW microbus parked at the overlook on that foggy morning.

* * * *

The overlook was in a curve, so Charlie Blades could see the approaching car taking shape in the fog. At that early hour, he guessed cop. *Critter cops*, he thought. He stood motionless at the tree line, his penis still in his hand—the proverbial deer in the headlights—almost in the headlights. The car slowed down, entered the curve and kept rolling. When the VW was between Charlie and the patrol car, he zipped his pants—headed back for the picnic table. Charlie was no longer in the mood for laundry. He dumped the water onto the parking lot, watched the steam rise in the cool morning air. He thought about dumping the coffee pot, but the water was just right.

Charlie hustled back to the van, got a large metal cup and spoon, once part of an Army mess kit. He dumped an unmeasured, but generous amount of freeze-dried coffee into the cup. The water was almost at a boil. Charlie wadded the blood-stained shirt and used it as a pot holder. He poured water into the cup and watched it turn inky black and steamy. He took the first sip and immediately started to feel better. Then he looked up.

At the edge of the overlook was a man—almost more a boy—standing next to the patrol car, the driver's door open. He was tall—lanky, with red hair cut short. His face was freckled, his mouth not quite symmetrical. It made him appear amused, even when he wasn't. He wore a uniform and a badge. On his right hip was a .38 special—canted forward for a quick draw. He closed the door and headed toward Charlie Blades. His manner was relaxed and when he spoke, his voice easy and pleasant.

"Good morning."

"Mornin'," Charlie Blades replied, trying to match the kid's upbeat tone.

"You know," Darius McCrary said, almost apologetically, "you can't camp in the overlooks." He could smell the coffee—wondered if the big hairy man might offer him a cup. If he did offer, he was going to take it.

"Oh, I know," Charlie said. "Just stopped to stretch my legs and make a cup." He motioned with the tin cup, as if making a half-hearted toast.

"Yeah, it smells good." Darius looked over the microbus with Tennessee tags and the smiley faces. He liked the vehicle—could picture himself and Sally traveling—camping—maybe in a few years with a kid or two. Family stuff. Yeah, they'd need to get a camera—take movies like his parents had—show them to the grandkids in thirty years. That would be fun. "You been driving all night?" he asked, still friendly.

Charlie Blades worked hard to control his face. He saw the kid looking over the van. The sliding door was open, but on the side opposite of the road. He would have to walk all the way around the van to see the girl. Without looking, Charlie wondered if he had gotten all of the blood off of his hands and arms—had an "out damned spot" Shakespearian moment. *"You been driving all night?"* It was a cop question. The kind of question cops asked on their way to other questions. Like it was any of his goddamned business to begin with.

Charlie Blades' expression remained stoic—disinterested—sleepy. Another part of his brain calculated the distance between him and the kid. Maybe twenty feet. A long way to close on a guy with a gun. But Charlie Blades was quick—real quick. And he had the scalding hot coffee. Maybe twenty feet wasn't that far after all.

But that was *last resort* thinking. Charlie didn't want to kill this kid. The guy last night had been different. What had the naked chick in the truck called him? Oh, yeah, *Buddy. Fucking Buddy.* Charlie had known lots of guys like Buddy. They were shit and nobody much cared if they died. And usually, nobody looked very hard for the people who'd killed them.

This kid would be different. He was federal. Kill him and there would be a lot of people looking forever. What Charlie really needed was an answer that would send him on his way. And it came to him—the perfect lie—like a gift from the Devil himself. But what happened next made all that moot.

* * * *

"You been driving all night?" Darius asked. The guy looked tired and Darius was going to suggest a campground just up the road. He was still waiting for the man's answer when he heard the movement from inside the VW. The passenger's side door cracked open about an inch. There was a pause, then slowly the door opened wider, like a curtain on the opening scene of a play. The lead actress stepped uncertainly onto the asphalt stage. She was dressed in a gauzy white dress, her long red hair flowed wildly from her head. She moved slowly, and in the fog, she had a dream-like quality—like someone who had awakened from a long sleep. She took a step towards Darius, and then another—almost as if she were floating.

Darius turned back to the man by the picnic table. But the big hairy man was gone. Darius jerked his head back toward the road—sensed the man behind him—spun on the balls of his feet—reached for his revolver. Darius felt the walnut grip in the palm of his hand. The .38 started out of its holster—then suddenly stopped.

Thirty Days Hath September

The girl from the van spoke. Her voice was soft and hoarse. Darius McCrary wasn't sure what she said, but thought it was "Help me."

Chapter 10

September 25th—5:52 a.m.

Julie Kingston's sports car was parked nose out, in front of Alex Madrid's motel room. She had backed it in next to Madrid's ratty-looking Blazer. The interior section of The Paradise Court was concealed from the two-lane. Time and neglect had caused big chunks of the light-green stucco façade to fall away from the walls of the building. In the middle of the courtyard was a dirty fountain adorned with Cherubs, grapes, and other stuff. The fountain was surrounded by brown weeds—it's murky water as stagnant as hope for the hopeless.

Madrid's room was at the back of the court, precisely in the middle of the squared off "U" the twenty-five units formed. The rooms opened onto a shared covered porch that was supported by rusted metal poles. It sagged in various places. Scattered around the porch were random groupings of mostly-broken lawn chairs. The best two were sitting outside Madrid's room.

Julie Kingston watched Madrid round the corner of the office. He was average height—muscular—thick through the shoulders and neck. Through the fog, she watched him scan his surroundings. Then there was that dog—that huge dog who seemed to float next to him. She noticed just the slightest hitch in the dog's gate—wondered if he'd been injured. She flashed back to the days when she had studied to be a vet. It seemed like a lifetime ago. Now she was here—in Black Creek—at the Paradise Court—for reasons not totally clear.

They continued their approach, both looking in her direction—like a pair of modern-day Medieval thugs. The dog lurched forward and Madrid tugged the leash. The muscles in his left forearm jumped to attention. The dog fell back into stride.

She picked up her pad and pen from the passenger's seat, stepped out of the car, worked up a smile.

* * * *

Madrid spotted the Mercedes SEL 450 convertible parked next to his Blazer. Through the fog, Madrid could only get a sense of the woman behind the wheel. A moment later she opened the door. Toto made a move, and Madrid gave the leash a quick jerk. She unfolded herself from the sports coupe and stood up. The woman was like her car—long and sleek. She had long dark hair and wore designer sunglasses with gradient lenses that made her look exotic—or at least mysterious. Madrid figured her eyes were either green or brown. The sleeves of her white cotton blouse were rolled up to just below her elbows. Her arms were tan, her fingers long and elegant. The blue jeans she wore were strategically faded—slung low on her hips—looked like they had been molded to her body. The motel manager was right—she didn't look like a hooker. She looked like a movie star—but she wasn't.

She was a reporter. Madrid had seen her last night. Actually, he had seen a lot of reporters last night—but she was the only one he remembered.

When he was almost to the car, she said "Hello."

Madrid nodded his reply.

"Nice morning, don't you think?" she added, keeping an eye on the dog.

Her voice had a Lauren Bacall quality—not quite as deep. It made him think of sex—but then everything about her made him think of sex.

"Lovely," Madrid replied without enthusiasm.

"You are Alex Madrid?" she asked.

He walked past her on the way to his room. Over his shoulder he asked, "Who wants to know?"

"I'm Julie Kingston. I'm with the *Black Creek Herald*. I was hoping to talk with you." She was still watching the big dog closely as she tentatively extended her hand in Madrid's direction. She added, "About last night."

Madrid wiped the sweat from his palm on his shirt and extended his arm. Her grip was firm. There were no rings on her fingers.

Toto eased over to the reporter—sniffed her hand. Julie Kingston stood very still, asked in a quiet voice, "Does your dog bite?"

Madrid finished unlocking the door. "Is that going to be part of your story?"

"No," she countered, a hint of impatience in her tone. "I just wanted to know if I should be concerned about your dog."

"You should be concerned." Madrid gave the leash a gentle tug. He opened the door. The dog trotted in and found his water bowl.

Madrid stepped into the room and shut the door behind him.

Julie Kingston stood on the porch deciding whether to knock. From inside the room she could hear some sort of motor come to life. A moment later Madrid stepped back outside with a chilled bottle of water in his hand. "You want something to drink?" he asked. "I've got water, orange juice, herb tea, and beer."

"I didn't figure you for an herb tea guy," she said with a hint of smile. "And it's a little early for beer."

"Just trying to be a gracious host."

Madrid pulled up one of his hand-selected chairs and eased down into it. After the run, it felt good to be off his feet. He took a long drink from the plastic bottle and said, "So you're a print reporter?"

"Yes."

"Wouldn't have figured that," Madrid said casually. "But you must be pretty good."

She asked cautiously. "Why is that, Mr. Madrid?"

Madrid nodded toward the Mercedes. "That's not a small-town reporter's car."

She looked back at the car, as if noticing it for the first time. "You weren't at the press conference last night."

No more car talk.

"No, I wasn't," Madrid answered. "Invitation probably got lost in the mail."

She smiled. It wasn't a dazzler—more the *"oh, you were trying to be funny"* smile. It was still nice.

"So, do you mind if I ask you some questions?"

"You have been asking me some questions," Madrid told her.

"I want to ask you questions about last night."

"Okay."

"There was a lot of excitement," she continued.

Madrid nodded.

"Were you there when Miranda Toliver was murdered?"

Madrid took a healthy pull from the bottle of water. "No," he ~~said~~ answered. "I got there a few moments after Sergeant Galloway arrived."

"Did you see him shoot Richard Padrick?"

Madrid shook his head. "No. But there's not much question that he did."

"Yes, you're right about that."

"Do you know he's running for sheriff?" she asked.

"Galloway mentioned it a time or two last night," Madrid replied. "And his posters are plastered over half the town."

It was Julie Kingston's turn to nod.

"So is Galloway going to win?" Madrid asked.

"Probably," she answered. Then added, "I'd give him the edge—particularly after last night."

"You seem less than thrilled."

She shrugged. "Sheriff Boyd has run unopposed for the past three terms. But he has cancer. It's incurable—I've been told."

"An interesting side story," Madrid said.

"Interesting stories are part of my business."

"How one person's tragedy becomes another person's opportunity?"

"Something like that," Julie replied. She gave Madrid a fresh look—as if she'd found a crack in Madrid's Neanderthal facade. "What can you tell me about last night, Mr. Madrid?"

"Nothing more than I just did," Madrid answered.

"I got up early on a Saturday morning," she said, each word carefully measured. "I was hoping for a bit more. This isn't Atlanta, or New York City, Mr. Madrid. Murder is still a big deal in a town like Black Creek."

"It's still a big deal in Atlanta and New York, Ms. Kingston—depending on who stops breathing."

"I need a little insight here, Madrid." Some of the professionalism had drained from her tone.

"What sort of *insight*?"

"Why don't you think Dicky Padrick killed Miranda Toliver."

"Who told you that?" Madrid could hear the tension in his voice.

Julie Kingston could hear it, too. "Sources," she answered—her tone a mix of defiance and triumph.

"Uh-huh," Madrid replied flatly. He took another drink of water. "You might want to check those sources again, Ms Kingston."

"Yeah, and you might want to spend some time working on your poker face, Madrid," Julie Kingston shot back. "*My* source is good."

She slowly slid her sunglasses down her narrow nose—revealed a wonderful pair of large green eyes.

"Then you don't need me."

"Are you denying what I said?"

Madrid was acutely—painfully aware—he had lost control of the conversation. He looked past her to the dreary fountain in the middle of the parking lot.

"Galloway was the first person there—other than the Padrick kid. Have you talked with either one of them? All I got is speculation. One or both of them will know the truth."

"I already have Galloway's take on record," she retorted, not bothering to cover her cynicism. "And nobody's going to talk with Dicky Padrick until he gets out of the hospital. Dicky's brother, Miles, will have a lawyer in place by then."

"Probably so."

"I want to know what *you* think about last night."

"Why does it matter?"

"You were there," she replied, drumming the pen against the pad with an impatient beat. "You saw the dead girl. You saw Dicky Padrick just after he'd been shot. You tried to help him. You have formed *some sort* of opinion about what happened last night."

"My opinion, Ms Kingston, is that I don't know enough facts to have an opinion."

"Do you think Miranda Toliver's death is related to September Jamerson?"

"September what?"

"September *who*," she corrected. "Jamerson. September Jamerson."

Madrid shook his head. "Never heard of her."

"You *do* work for the Black Creek College Security Office."

"For about a week."

"September Jamerson disappeared two weeks ago." Her tone carried the residue of accusation.

"She's a student at Black Creek College?"

"Yes."

"She lives on campus?"

"No."

"Local girl?"

"Yes," Julie said. "September's a day student. She lives just outside Black Creek."

"Lives with her parents?" Madrid asked.

"Mother and stepfather."

"Have they filed a missing person's report?"

Julie hesitated. "No."

Madrid. "No?"

Julie Kingston. "No."

Madrid. "You don't find that odd, Ms Kingston?"

Julie Kingston skirted the question. "It's odd that a young woman who has lived virtually her entire life in Black Creek would suddenly take off one day—without any of her belongings—and without telling anyone where she was going. Her mother was struggling to make the tuition."

"How do you know she didn't take anything with her?" Madrid asked.

"I've got sources."

"I keep forgetting that."

"September Jamerson took her car and what she was wearing. Her mother thinks she had maybe twenty dollars—no checking account. Certainly no credit card."

Alex Madrid and Julie Kingston remained facing each other—silent and thoughtful. Fog floated along on a light breeze. The air in the courtyard was suddenly chilly.

Finally Madrid spoke, "So that's why you came out here this morning." he said in thoughtful tone. "It wasn't about Miranda Toliver, or Dicky Padrick—it was about this girl. September somebody."

"It was about Dicky Padrick and Miranda Toliver, too. But it was also about September Jamerson," Julie Kingston admitted. "Her mother wants to know where she is."

"She contacted you?"

Julie Kingston nodded. "She didn't know who else to call."

"What about the Sheriff's Department—or Pete Wilson?"

"Pete knows she left the college, but there's not much he can do about it. The Sheriff's Department...well...let's just say family dynamics make it complicated."

"How so?"

Julie Kingston shook her head. A strand of black hair fell across her eyes and she brushed it back with long delicate fingers. Madrid caught himself staring again.

"What would make you think Miranda Toliver and the Jamerson girl are connected?"

"Maybe they aren't," Julie conceded, "but someone needs to pay some attention to this girl."

"Some people don't want attention," Madrid told her. "They leave because they don't want to be found."

"Her mother deserves to know her daughter is all right."

"And if she's not all right?" Madrid asked.

"She needs to know that, too."

"Yeah, I suppose she does," Madrid replied in a somber tone. "So what does that have to do with me?"

"I think you could find her."

It was only six words, but spoke volumes. They told Madrid that Julie Kingston was more than a pretty face. She *did* have sources and apparently knew how to use them. She knew more about him than he knew about her.

"I could pay you," she added, matter-of-factly. "Not the paper—*me*."

"I appreciate the offer, Ms. Kingston, but I'm not for hire." Madrid heard scratching coming from inside his room. He opened the door. Toto strolled out. Madrid caught him by the collar.

Julie stepped closer to the pair, squatted down until she was eye to eye with the big mutt. She let him sniff the back of her hand, then she reached up and ruffled the dog's fur behind his left ear.

"God, I wish you wouldn't do that," Madrid told her. "He's not a very sociable dog."

"I get along with dogs," she answered without looking up, scratched behind his other ear, and added, "better than I get along with most people.

Toto tilted his head to give her a better angle.

"What happened to his leg?" she asked.

"It's a long story."

"I'll bet you have a lot of long stories, Mr. Madrid." She stood up. "I hope you'll reconsider my offer. I'm not rich, but I can pay you well for your time."

Foolishly, Madrid was reconsidering. The images of Charlie Blades and The Wizard were never very far from the epicenter of his psyche. At a time when Madrid needed total focus, Julie Kingston was a beautiful distraction.

No thanks, lady. I've got to keep my eye on the ball. Thinking about you and this September Jamerson girl could get me killed. I might be able to help you, if the situation was different—but it's not. I'm out. And as much as it breaks my heart , I hope I never see you again. That's what Alex Madrid planned to say—succinct—intelligent—decisive.

What he actuality said was, "I'll think about it."

Chapter 11

September 25th—8:11 a.m.

Like most of the luxury appointments at The Paradise Court, the hot water heater in Madrid's room only *sort of* worked. He shaved and showered in lukewarm water—grateful it wasn't the middle of January. He slipped into jeans and a black crew-neck sweater—poured a cup of coffee from an heirloom percolator.

Back on his bed, Toto watched Madrid move to the tiny closet next to the bathroom. He removed the stainless steel bowl from the raised feeding perch, took a strategic measure of dry and canned food from the closet, and mixed it in the bowl. He turned to the big mutt who was thumping his tail against the bed.

"Breakfast is served, your Majesty," Madrid growled.

Madrid drank coffee—watched the dog scarf the mix. He knew enough to keep his distance at feeding time. He cracked open the door of the ancient fridge. Most of the contents had come from Marcy's Holistic Café & Country Fried Grill. Marcy had a thick Scottish accent that was easy on the ears, and a face that was easy on the eyes. She would also let him bring the dog inside the café.

He poured some fresh-squeezed orange juice and slathered freshly-ground peanut butter onto a whole-wheat English muffin. As Toto finished off the bowl, he caught a whiff of the peanut butter—looked at Madrid hopefully.

"No way," Madrid told the beast. "I didn't ask *you* to share."

Madrid sat on the edge of the bed in the dingy motel room—ate his peanut- butter muffin, drank his juice, and thought. He thought about Charlie Blades and The Wizard; he thought about Julie Kingston and September Jamerson; he thought about Miranda Toliver and Dicky Padrick. Madrid let his mind wander to dark places that would do him no good. Depression climbed his soul like a late-afternoon shadow.

An ancient black-and-white TV sat in one corner of the room, along with a rabbit-ear antenna Madrid had scavenged from another unit. He pressed the "on" button—waited for the picture tube to warm up. He used the edge of a dime to loosen the connecting screws for the antenna. After some adjusting, he was able to get one channel—Saturday morning cartoons—*Rocky and Bullwinkle.* Even the cartoons at The Paradise Court were outdated. For the next twenty minutes he and the dog watched Moose and Squirrel match wits with Boris Badanov and Natasha Fatale. When the show was over, and Madrid was certain all was again well in Frostbite Falls, he dialed the Black Creek College Security office. A girl named Angie told him Pete Wilson was out of the office. After that, she told him Dicky Padrick had been released from the hospital.

* * * *

The Sheriff's lobby was dissected by a scarred counter. The citizens mostly stayed on one side; the law mostly on the other. From somewhere in the building, a country station played softly. Loretta Lynn was sporadically interrupted by the crackle of a two-way radio. Behind the counter a young deputy with sandy blonde hair stood ready to meet the public.

"Mornin'," he said with a slow amicable drawl. "Somethin' I can do for you?"

Madrid hadn't seen him last night—took it as a good omen. "My name is Alex Madrid," he told the younger man in ~~as~~ a semi-official voice. "I'm with the Black Creek College Campus Security. I guess you heard about what happened last night?"

"Yeah," the young deputy replied dismally. "I been working here a year and three months. The first time something really exciting happens, I got the night off."

"Yeah," Madrid said empathetically. "That sucks."

"You there?" the younger man asked.

Madrid nodded. "Yeah."

"I heard that retarded boy messed that college girl up pretty bad," the deputy continued in a "just-between-me-and-you" whisper.

Madrid offered a knowing nod.

"So what can I do for you?" the deputy asked again.

"I need to ask the Padrick boy a few questions," Madrid replied casually. "Just a follow up for our report."

"I don't know about you seein' the prisoner, Mr. Madrid."

A deep, hard voice boomed from behind the kid. " I sure as hell know." Josh Galloway stepped into the lobby from a back office.

The deputy's head was on a swivel—to Galloway, to Madrid, back to Galloway, back to Madrid.

"You ain't seein' him, Madrid." Galloway was wearing his Saturday morning civvies: plaid double-knit sport jacket, red shirt with a big, pointy color. Top three buttons open—gold neck chain.

"Why would you care if I talked to the boy?" Madrid countered sardonically. "Your case is made."

"Look, Madrid," Galloway shot back. "You got no right strolling your ass in here acting like you're some sort of cop. You ain't a cop. You're a four- dollar-and-twenty-five-cents-an hour nobody—just like Pete Wilson. What makes you worse than Wilson is you got a pain-in-the-ass attitude. Now get the hell out of here before I throw you in jail."

"Gee," Madrid said drolly. "Just when I thought we were hitting it off."

"Yeah, keep it up, Wiseass."

"I was going to give you some tips on how to run a murder investigation," Madrid continued amicably. " And I thought maybe you could show me how to bake cookies, or darn socks, or something. Or maybe we could just hang out and take turns reading each other poetry. Some Dickinson or Keats."

The young deputy fought off a smile.

"Keep running your mouth." Galloway poked the air with a menacing finger. "I'll close it for you."

"I guess if I were Dicky Padrick that might scare the hell out of me, Josh," Madrid replied, "but I'm not—so it doesn't. I've got this theory about why you don't want me to see Padrick."

The female radio dispatcher had moved into the front part of the office. Her harsh blonde hair was teased high above her scalp. Sheriff Avery Boyd stood behind her, in the shadows of the hallway, leaned heavily on the wall.

"I don't give a shit about your theories, Madrid." Josh Galloway's face was only a couple of shades from his red shirt.

"My theory," Madrid continued, "is that now that after a few hours, you've actually started to think a little. Started asking yourself some questions."

Galloway lifted the folding section of countertop, dropped it with a loud crash, stepped through to the other side. He stopped six inches from Madrid, stared down at him. The veins in his forehead were like ridgelines of an angry relief map. "Don't fuck with me, Madrid," he said through clenched teeth—his voice barely under control. "Get out. I ain't tellin' you again."

Madrid didn't move. The smell of cigarettes and Galloway's cologne filled the small space between them. He looked up and met Galloway's glare—spoke in a quiet voice. "You don't want me to see the Padrick kid just in case you shot the wrong guy. Voters are funny about stuff like that, Josh."

"I shot the right boy...man."

* * * *

Sheriff Boyd was having a rough morning—the pounding in his head getting worse. He thought about the pills in his desk. They were strong, but he didn't like to take them. The pain killers made him sleepy and slow witted. He pushed himself off the wall, waited a moment for his equilibrium to catch up.

"I see no harm in Madrid talking to the Padrick boy." The eyes in the office traveled down the hallway. The sheriff's voice was weak, but steady. "As long as he shares whatever the kid tells him."

Josh Galloway moved his gaze from Madrid to the sheriff. Avery Boyd, on uncertain legs, returned the stare. Boyd wore a uniform that had grown too large for his withering body. Galloway wondered how long the sheriff could physically stand there. Three minutes? He doubted it. Two minutes, he decided. Two minutes at the most. Then he would crumple into a heap. Someone would have to help him to his desk, or maybe call an ambulance.

But that wouldn't help. The people in this office loved Avery Boyd, and now that he was dying—hell, they loved him five times as much. When Galloway got elected, he would need some of them—at least for a while. He stepped back from Madrid—turned to Avery Boyd and said, "Whatever you say, Sheriff." Then to the young deputy he added, "Tommy, take Madrid back to the jail."

"Thank you, Sheriff," Madrid replied without looking at Galloway.

"Remember our deal, Madrid," Boyd reminded him in a hoarse voice.

A black man—maybe in his late sixties nodded to the deputy when he entered the building. The jailer wore a khaki uniform; his matted hair had receded to a point just beyond the apex of his skull. It was the color of iron filings.

"This guy's name is Madrid, Bernie," said Tommy, the deputy. "The Sheriff said he could talk to Padrick."

Bernie turned his copper-colored head towards Madrid. "I'll get the keys." The jailer took the keys from the drawer. "The boy's sister is up there now visitin' with him. You want to go now, or you want to wait?"

"I don't know that I have the option to wait," Madrid said.

"Galloway?" the jailer asked.

"Yeah."

Bernie nodded knowingly.

"Think Padrick's sister would mind?" Madrid asked.

"Don't know. She might tell you to get the hell out."

"I hear that a lot." Madrid said.

"You'd have to go," the jailer said.

Madrid nodded. "I can be charming—if I have to."

Bernie flashed a smile. One of his front teeth had been capped with gold. "Might not be a bad idea."

He used his key on a large barred door at the far end of the room. The two men ascended a narrow staircase without any windows, Bernie leading the way. A naked light bulb hung from a wire high above them; it cast grim shadows on the gray walls. The shadows followed them up, then turned back in the opposite direction when they reached the landing. At the top of the staircase was another barred door. Bernie used his keys again.

Chapter 12

Gatlinburg, Tennessee
September 25th—10:03 a.m.

The Great Smoky Mountain Park ended abruptly. The town of Gatlinburg started a few feet beyond the boundary, waited like an open mouth—ready to swallow the next unsuspecting traveler. Traffic slowed to a crawl. Buildings crowded in from each side of the narrow main street—claustrophobic—an unapologetic display of commerce. The pancake houses and mom and pop motels spewed their patrons onto the sidewalks. The little town was beginning to fill with shoppers, tourists, and teenagers looking for weekend excitement. The VW bus worked it's way down the strip—a repeated series of stops and starts. Sporadic applications of neon light pierced the otherwise gray morning. Charlie Blades rolled his window down about six inches. The smell of onions, peppers, and sausage being grilled in an open air stand floated into the VW. A moment later it was joined by the heavy, sweet aroma of fried funnel cakes. The combination was torturous. Blades felt his stomach rumble. He hadn't eaten since yesterday afternoon.

By the time he was halfway down the street, he realized he'd missed his turn. At the edge of town, he doubled back on a street that was a block off the main drag and ran along the river. There were fewer people, less traffic. A chair lift, filled mostly with kids sitting close, legs dangling, crossed over the road, before it angled up the side of the mountain. A little further up the street, tram cars took a longer route up to the ski slope. Across a narrow bridge that spanned the river, The Mysterious Mansion was tucked into the hillside. It was a two story façade with a turret and a couple of small balconies. Ghoulish figures stared out at the street from darkened windows—a black hearse parked in front. In the light of day it seemed contrived and innocuous. As Charlie Blades rolled slowly past, he heard the muffled, but haunting sound of a pipe organ—wondered why people paid good money to be scared. Charlie knew a lot of scary things that were neither contrived nor easily forgotten.

He glanced in the rearview mirror—saw his image—confirmed the thought.

He found the road that led to the ski slope and the mountainside that overlooked the town. With Charlie's boot heavy on the accelerator, the VW bus struggled up the steep, winding road until he reached the ridgeline. It took him a while to find the house. The entry was unmarked. Tall weeds, bent heavy with rain, encroached on either side. Charlie rolled up slowly—outwardly calm, inwardly nervous. Too much had been crammed into the past twelve hours—the guy in the parking lot—the kid at the overlook.

The house was a small A-frame tucked into a stand of oaks and Frazier firs. The brown board-and-batten siding needed a coat of stain. Once upon a time, the gingerbread trim, the shutters, and the front door had been painted something close to fire-engine red.

There were dead flowers in the window box—the porch littered with a layer of wet leaves—yellows and browns. Charlie stopped short of the house—killed the engine. There were no lights burning—but one of those goofy-assed smiley faces, just like the ones on the back of the microbus, was plastered on the door.

He craned his thick neck, checked the girl on the back seat—she was still asleep. He checked the cylinder of his stainless steel .357 magnum—confirmed what he already knew. Full load. He tucked the weapon into the waistband of his jeans, slid out of the van. The front door was locked. He found the key under the lip of one of the window boxes, but wasn't ready to use it. He peered in through the glass. Under the canopy of trees, the interior of the house was layered with shadow and gloom. Charlie watched—saw no movement. Listened—heard no sounds. He walked around to the back of the chalet. The mountain fell away sharply. A large deck spanned most of the length of the house. It jutted out into gray nothingness. Far below, through the haze, Gatlinburg formed a garish slash along the west prong of the Little Pigeon River. He peered through the windows on the deck, tried the sliding-glass doors. The house was locked up tight. He worked his way back to the front door—used his key.

The house had that smell that houses get when they've been closed up for a long time. The overhead light—a chandelier made from plastic deer antlers—did little to combat the murk. The walls and floors were pine—stained dark brown. The furniture was upholstered with dark bold patterns—faded by time and wear. The art continued the quasi-Bavarian theme. There were prints of snow-capped mountains, of men in lederhosen, of full-figured women with rosy complexions cooking and cleaning. Charlie moved into the hallway—found the narrow door that led to the basement staircase. He pulled the string that activated the dangling light bulb—followed the stairs down. The smell of exposed earth rushed up to meet him.

At the bottom of the stairs, just to the left of the landing, was a door with black metal hinge straps. An open padlock with a key attached hung on the latch. Behind the door was a room—concrete floor, the only window covered with cardboard and duct tape. In one corner, a showerhead angled from the wall over a drain in the floor. There was no curtain. Next to the shower was a full-length mirror built into an oak stand. On the other side of the mirror, a toilet. Against the wall directly across from the door, a metal bed was suspended from the concrete wall with heavy chains. Shackles made from black metal chain and heavy rubber straps were attached to the head and foot rails. Above it, another mirror had been attached to the ceiling. Charlie thought about the haunted house at the bottom of the mountain. This one was real. It was a room where screaming was pointless—where hope could not survive.

"Jesus Christ," Blades muttered under his breath, "here we go again." Then he went back up the stairs—carried the girl from the van.

* * * *

The metal door at the top of the jailhouse stairs was painted a putrid shade of green. Bernie looked back at Madrid—used his key—pushed it open. It was heavy, and creaked on its hinges.

The jail was a big open space with six cells and an "L" shaped hallway. Three of the cells had barred windows. From the far end of the room, in a cell without a window, Junior Jenkins focused on the blonde woman in the cell with the retarded kid. She was sitting with her back to him and he desperately wanted her to turn around. All the best parts of a woman were in the front. Bernie and another man came through the door. The man wasn't much taller than the jailer, but that's where the comparison ended. His face was hard—like he was kinda pissed off at everybody all the time. He looked tough—like a guy who could handle himself.

Junior respected tough. Just over six feet tall, two hundred and twenty pounds, Junior Jenkins looked tough, too—but down deep, knew he wasn't. This was his fourth arrest—one court date away from a stretch in Central Prison.

Junior Jenkins had spent much of the past four days trying to figure a way to escape. His most grandiose scheme played like a movie reel in his head. He would trick the old black man into his cell. Overpower him. Move silently down the staircase, maybe use some karate (which he had never studied), take a gun from one of the deputies. Shoot his way out. Bullets would be flying all around him. He would kill Josh Galloway for sure. And he would kill that judge, too. An unsuspecting Mustang Mach I would be sitting outside the jail, keys in the ignition, motor running. Junior Jenkins would squeal the tires—take one last look at Black Creek in his rearview mirror.

That was Plan A.

Plan B was only slightly more within the realm of reality. It involved the retarded kid on the other side of the cell block. Junior didn't have all the kinks worked out, but his mind continued to clunk along on the details.

Madrid stepped through the doorway—into the middle of the cell block. Of the six cells, four were empty. Each cell was approximately nine by nine, with heavy iron bars. Except for the metal toilets and sinks, the place looked like something out of the last century.

To his far left, a young guy watched him through a veil of long black hair. On the other end of the room, Dicky Padrick sat facing a woman. Padrick looked different than the last time Madrid had seen him. His hair was combed, his clothes dry. He wore a long-sleeved red t-shirt and bib-overalls. He wasn't crying—and he wasn't bleeding. He was sitting on the edge of his bunk, grinning at the woman, eating a doughnut.

On the edge of the other bunk, the woman sat primly across from him. She was pouring hot chocolate from a thermos into a Styrofoam cup. She stopped pouring when she saw the two men outside the cell.

She spoke in a soft, anxious voice. "My time isn't up already, is it?"

"No, ma'am," the jailer answered assuredly. Bernie turned to Madrid and said, "This is Mrs. Thorpe. She's the boy's sister. Come to visit for a spell." His tone was folksy—like they were all old friends who had happened upon each other at a church picnic. Bernie turned to the woman. "This here is Mr. Madrid, ma'am."

"Alex," Madrid said with a nod.

"Elizabeth Thorpe," the woman replied, keeping her eyes on her brother.

Madrid guessed Elizabeth Thorpe was in her late twenties—maybe early thirties. She was a small, well-shaped woman. Her blonde hair was cut stylishly-short. Her eyes were some color between blue and green. When she sat, the hem of her navy blue pleated skirt rode up more than a few inches past her knees. The white turtle-necked sweater followed the contours of her upper body—narrow shoulders and small breasts that sat high on her chest. Elizabeth Thorpe's lips were painted pink, her perfume smelled expensive. She reminded Madrid of a cheerleader he'd had a crush on in high school. Totally, and devastatingly, unrequited.

"You just take your time and visit with your brother," Bernie told her. "Mr. Madrid here was hopin' he might ask your brother some questions. He was there last night, ma'am, when—when your brother—when all that trouble was happenin'."

"What kind of questions?" Elizabeth Thorpe asked. Suspicion tugged at the corners of her mouth.

"Mr. Madrid works for the college," Bernie replied—like it was an answer to her question.

And maybe it was. "Then I suppose that would be all right," Elizabeth Thorpe replied uncertainly. Added in a voice that trailed off to almost nothing, "I guess."

She looked up from the bunk, asked Madrid, "Do you think you could help my brother?"

Nothing was more cruel than false hope. "I don't know," he replied without optimism. "Might be something good to talk about, ma'am," Bernie said.

Madrid offered Bernie an uneasy glance then stepped into the cell. Bernie locked the door behind him—started for the staircase.

"If either of you need me," he said over his shoulder, "just give a holler."

"What about me, old man?" Junior Jenkins yelled from the other end of the cell block.

Bernie muttered something about "scream until your eyes pop out of your head" and started his descent.

Elizabeth Thorpe crossed her arms in front of her, then moved her small hands to the hem of her skirt. She looked directly at her brother and asked Madrid, "You're not with the police?"

"No," he answered. "I work for Black Creek College. Part time—security."

The light of recognition clicked on in Dicky Padrick's Down's Syndrome eyes. "You helped Dicky," he said around a mouthful of doughnut.

Padrick seemed bigger in the small jail cell. Madrid figured him just south of six feet, just north of two hundred pounds—most of it soft and underdeveloped. Padrick's dull blonde hair started high on his forehead—ended in bangs just above his eyebrows—slightly Moe Howard-esk.

"Is that true?" Elizabeth Thorpe asked. "You're the man who helped my brother?" There was a thread of warmth in her voice.

"I didn't do much," Madrid told the woman. "Mainly just tried to calm him down."

"That was a lot, Mr. Madrid," she said, a rush of emotion thick in her voice. "Dicky told me about you. I just didn't know if you were rea...." Elizabeth Thorpe cut the thought short.

Madrid offered a barely perceptible nod. "This won't take long."

"I appreciate what you did for my brother, but I don't know about your questioning him. Shouldn't his lawyer be here?"

"Does he have one?"

"Yes," she said, a hint of pride. "My husband will be defending him. His practice is in Asheville. Nathaniel Thorpe. You've probably heard of him."

"I'm new to this area," Madrid answered diplomatically. "Is your husband here this morning?"

"No. Nathanial couldn't be here," she replied vaguely.

Madrid waited to see if she wanted to add anything. When it became clear she didn't, he said "All I want to do is ask him a few questions about last night. If he doesn't want to answer, or if you think he shouldn't answer—no problem."

She turned to Dicky. "What happened last night was terrible," she said, like a hypnotist to a suggestive subject. "I can't even imagine what that poor girl went through. I can't imagine what her parents must be going through right now." Her gaze continued to bore into her brother. "But my brother had *nothing* to do with it. He was simply in the wrong place at the wrong time. Isn't that right, Dicky?"

Dicky Padrick responded with an exaggerated nod.

The old "didn't do it—wrong place at the wrong time defense", Madrid thought. *Explains why your husband-the hot-shot- lawyer didn't need to show up.* Out loud he said, "So what happened, Dicky?"

Elizabeth Thorpe leaned forward, spoke to her brother in an encouraging whisper. "Tell him, Dicky. Tell him what you told me."

Dicky slid back on the bunk until his back was against the heavy iron bars. He took a pair of deep breaths—let them out slowly. "You didn't shoot Dicky," he said. "It was the bad man who put Dicky in jail." For the first time, he looked directly at Alex Madrid. "Can I get out now?" Desperation flooded his voice. "I promise I'll be good."

Like the ghost of hope, the boy's plea hovered in the cell.

"It's not my decision," Madrid told the teenager.

"Oh," Dicky Padrick replied in a small, capitulatory voice. He worked his hands deep into the pockets of his bib overalls, stared at his sister.

Elizabeth Thorpe sat erect, hands on her knees. Tears began to fill her eyes. She nodded her nicely-coiffed blonde head, forced a weak, encouraging smile.

"I need you to talk to me, Dicky," Madrid said, unthreatening, but firm. "I need to ask you some questions. Questions about last night. Do you think we can do that?"

Dicky shrugged.

Close enough. Madrid thought. "Dicky, the first question I'm going to ask you is important."

Padrick replied with a ambiguous nod.

"Did you kill that girl last night, Dicky?"

Before Elizabeth Thorpe could respond, Madrid showed her the palm of his hand. At this point, it wasn't a matter of legality. Madrid needed to know. Despite what he had seen last night, he wanted to believe this boy was not a murderer.

Dicky Padrick raised his head slowly, offered Madrid an obtuse stare.

Madrid asked again. "Did you kill that girl last night?"

"No," he replied without emotion.

"Tell me what happened last night," Madrid said, glancing at the greasy-haired kid at the other end of the room. He was on his bunk—his back to them.

"The policeman shot Dicky with his gun," Padrick responded, as if reading slowly from a cue card.

"I know." Madrid worked to keep his tone void of impatience .

"I didn't cry, though," Dicky added stoically. "I yelled, but I didn't cry." He spoke in a monotone that belied the seriousness of the situation. "I yelled because I didn't want that policeman to shoot Dicky in the heart." He patted himself on the chest with his chubby hand. "You get killed when they shoot you in the heart."

"True," Madrid agreed.

"Why were you in the parking lot, Dicky?"

"Dicky listens to music back there. They have pinball games inside, but last night they were dancing. Sometimes I watch people dance. But sometimes I just listen to music."

"Did you know there was going to be a dance?"

He shrugged.

"Think about it, Dicky," Madrid said firmly. "Did you know there was going to be a dance when you got to the parking lot?"

"No."

"So what were you doing out there?"

"Sometimes I just walk around."

"You do that often—just go out at night and walk around?"

"Sometimes I do." He took in a large amount of air through his mouth—let it out in a loud puff. "Miles tells me not to go outside after dark. I can go, if he goes with me. But if he doesn't go with me, I have to stay inside the house."

"But you didn't stay in the house," Madrid said.

"I'm not a little boy. I can go out at night if I want," he added stubbornly.

"Miles is your brother?"

Dicky Padrick nodded.

"You live with him?"

"Dicky has lived with Miles since our parents were killed," Elizabeth Thorpe explained. "Miles has been very good to Dicky."

"Why isn't he here?" Madrid asked, trying not to sound accusatory.

Elizabeth Thorpe dropped her blue-green eyes to her lap, then fixed them on the window. Beyond the iron bars, the sky was flat and gray. "Miles is very upset about this whole thing," she said, just above a whisper. Emotion filled her voice. "Miranda Toliver was one of Miles' students. He thought highly of her."

He's not here because he thinks his brother killed her.

Dicky Padrick stopped talking. Madrid watched him retreat into himself. Finally he said, thoughtfully, quietly, "Miles is going to be mad. Are you going to tell him Mr. ... ?

Elizabeth Thorpe looked as if she is about to say something, then changed her mind.

"Call me Alex," Madrid said. "And, no, I'm not going to tell your brother."

"He'll be mad," Dicky mumbled.

Madrid pushed on, "The deputy, the man who shot you. He said you were with the girl on the ground. Do you remember her?"

Padrick blinked slowly, then said, "Yes," in an unsure voice.

"Do you know her name?"

"No," Dicky replied, shaking his head, his blonde bangs moved back and forth across his large forehead. "I asked that girl. But she wouldn't tell me."

"Where was she when you asked her, Dicky?"

"That girl was on the ground," he replied, emphasizing each word. "She was sleepin'. I said *'What is your name?'* and she didn't say anything. I said *'What are you doing on the ground?'* and she didn't say anything."

"Did you put her on the ground, Dicky?"

Dicky shook his head slowly.

"This is important, Dicky," Madrid said firmly. "I can't help you unless you tell me the truth."

The truth was hard to recognize. Madrid had been among liars for nearly half of his life. Some pathologically good—most, not so good. Usually he could tell. Not infallible, but he was right a whole lot more than he was wrong. With Padrick, Madrid couldn't tell how much of what he said, stemmed from nerves, mental handicap—or avoidance of the truth.

Madrid looked down at Elizabeth Thorpe, tried not to stare at her legs. She was wearing white stockings—Navy blue shoes with a two inch heal. Someone needed to talk with her about how to dress for jail visits. She met Madrid's look, turned to her brother, said reluctantly, "Tell Mr. Madrid the truth, Dicky."

"Did you put the girl on the ground, Dicky?" Madrid asked again.

He jerked his head forcefully. "No!" It was between and shriek and a shout. "I—did—not—put—her—on—the—ground!"

Madrid ignored the drama. "Did you see who hurt her?"

And there it was—opportunity.

"Yes, I saw who hurt her," he answered quickly, animation bubbling to the top of his tone. He scooted clumsily to the edge of his bunk. "He was a *big* man." Dicky spread his arms as far as they would reach to accentuate the size. "The big man grabbed her and said 'I don't like you and I'm going to hurt you.' Then he picked her up and threw her on the ground."

Dicky mimicked the action by standing up and lifting an imaginary figure over his head. He posed for a second, his arms over his head—fists clenched, his chest fully expanded. Then slammed his invisible victim to the concrete floor of the jail cell. He followed it downward. He hit the concrete hard with his knees—his face only inches from the dirty cell floor.

Elizabeth Thorpe watched her brother—wide-eyed. His violence—imaginary or not—visibly unnerved her. Dicky's movements appeared primal—and practiced. Forced her to see her brother as less of a boy and more of a man. She caught herself thinking "*what if?*" Almost involuntarily, she glanced up at Madrid. He was staring back at her, as if reading her thoughts

Dicky was back on his feet. "I told him," he continued loudly, pointing to the wall of the cell, "*'You better leave her alone and not hurt her, or I'm going to get you.'*" Dicky turned to Madrid. " And the man said *'I'm not afraid of you, Dicky.'* And I said *'Well I'm not afraid of you neither.'* Then I ran over there and I beat him up."

Dicky continued to choreograph the action. He swung wildly with both arms, stirred the stale air in the cell. His big, loose body wiggled. "Then the big man ran away," Dicky said breathlessly. "He was a big man. He had on a black suit. Dicky beat him up and he ran away. That's what happened."

Dicky fell back on the bunk, physically spent. The metal webbing groaned under his weight. His round face was flushed, his mouth hung open as he tried to catch his breath. Beads of perspiration began to form on his oddly-shaped forehead. Like an actor after an audition, he looked expectantly at his sister, then to Madrid.

Madrid didn't meet his eyes, instead, he looked out the barred window. The patch of sky it offered was gray and depressing. Soon, it would be raining again. Madrid tried to think of the last day it hadn't rained in Black Creek.

He shifted his gaze back to Elizabeth Thorpe. She was still sitting perfectly erect on the edge of the bunk—like she was competing in some half-assed charm-school posture contest. Her eyes glowed like beacons of doubt.

When Dicky Padrick had marginally controlled his breathing, he reached into the bag for another doughnut.

Madrid let him eat half before saying, "I don't think that's what happened, Dicky."

Neither Dicky or his sister offered a rebuttal. The rest of the conversation yielded little. Mostly it was "I don't know" or "I don't remember good."

"Roll up your sleeves," Madrid told the boy.

"Why?" Elizabeth Thorpe asked.

"I want to look," Madrid replied, not answering her question.

Dicky pushed his sleeves up past his elbows. There was a small abrasion on his right hand. A scrape just above his left wrist that was almost healed. Nothing else. Madrid examined the younger man's neck and face. He was about to call the jailer when Bernie appeared at the door.

"You 'bout finished?"

"Yes."

Elizabeth Thorpe said, "I'd like to stay a while longer." She offered an almost imperceptible nod to Madrid. "My brother and I have had little time to visit."

Madrid picked up the gesture. "That's true," he told the jailer.

"Don't matter," Bernie said. "Visitin' time is up. You can come back here tomorrow afternoon, ma'am."

"But, please... ."

"I would, if I could. But I can't," he replied firmly. "Those are the rules."

Elizabeth Thorpe shot Madrid a cool stare.

Bernie unlocked the door. Elizabeth Thorpe stepped across the cell, bent at the waist, kissed her brother on the forehead. "It's going to be all right, Dicky," she told him, forcing a smile.

Tears filled his eyes—rolled down his pudgy face. "Please let Dicky go home," he pleaded to the jailer. "Dicky will be good. Promise. Swear to god. Promise. Dicky will be good. I don't like it here. Please let me go home."

Bernie looked directly at Dicky. "There's nothing I can do, son," Bernie said, his voice a hoarse whisper.

Then Dicky Padrick began to sob uncontrollably.

"You want to tell that cry baby to shut the hell up?" Junior Jenkins yelled across the cell. "I ain't going to listen to that goddamn *re*tard boohoo all day."

"Shut up, Junior," Bernie replied hotly. "You shut your damn mouth, you sorry punk."

Junior sat up on his bunk—grinned at the jailer. "What are you going to do about it, old man?"

Bernie stared at the boy in the cell.

Junior Jenkins grinned some more.

Bernie led Madrid and Elizabeth Thorpe back down the staircase with its villainous shadows. The sound of Dicky Padrick's crying followed them down.

Elizabeth Thorpe left the building without a word or a glance. Madrid watched her cross the parking lot with short, purposeful strides.

"She's mad," the jailer said, mostly to himself.

"Maybe more scared than mad," Madrid replied.

"Nothin' I could do," Bernie said.

"I know," Madrid replied.

Chapter 13

September 25th—12:37 p.m.

The door to the office was standing open, but Madrid knocked anyway. Sheriff Avery Boyd motioned him in with a slow, cumbersome gesture. Though the room was warm, the sheriff wore his jacket. From halfway across the room, Madrid could hear him breathing. As he moved closer, he could smell cough drops mixed with another unidentifiable medicinal odor.

"Shut the door and sit down," Boyd said, like a man used to giving orders.

Madrid followed both commands.

Outside, the wind had picked up. Bands of rain angled out of the sky, peppered the window that looked out onto the parking lot. As it had last night, Madrid's gaze was drawn to the picture on the back wall—the photo of the Sheriff in an earlier day. The then-robust man with a black handlebar mustache and a big cigar clamped between his teeth, standing between his two deputies—Josh Galloway and Pete Wilson.

Madrid shifted his gaze from the photo to the living ghost who sat before him, "Pete used to work for you," he said.

"Long time ago," Boyd answered in a labored voice. "Why you asking?"

"Just making conversation," Madrid answered, nodding to the photo.

Sheriff Boyd spun slowly in the big chair, looked at the image for the first time. "Long time ago," he repeated. He swiveled back to Madrid. "I was a handsome devil, back then."

"I wouldn't go that far."

"Josh said you were a wise ass," the sheriff replied without animosity.

"So far, that's about all he's gotten right."

"That so?" It came out mostly as a wheeze. "Or just your opinion?"

"Both," Madrid answered.

For the next few moments, neither man spoke. Then, Avery Boyd took in a deep breath that exploded into a vicious hacking cough. His thin body convulsed violently. The sheriff placed his left hand on the desk top for support. With his right, he pulled a large, white handkerchief from his jacket—did his best to muffle the attack.

There were spots on the handkerchief that, to Madrid, looked like blood. "You want some water?" he asked.

Boyd waved him off. The coughing continued. It sounded like someone rubbing a brick across a chalkboard—only deeper. Finally, the hacking retreated, but left the sheriff red faced and struggling for breath.

Madrid gave the sheriff another moment. "You sure about that water?"

"No." There was a small, dorm-sized refrigerator on the far side of the room. Sheriff Boyd eyed it—measured the distance, calculated the energy it would take.

Madrid silently watched the process, then walked over and opened the door of the white box. Inside there were three rows of cans stacked neatly on top of each other—all the same brand. "How about a Dr. Pepper?" Madrid asked.

"That's what I drink. Get one for yourself."

Madrid opened the first can—set it in front of Boyd. He opened the second, tossed the pop tops in the waste basket and retook his chair.

Boyd took several carefully-measured sips from the can. Then he asked, "You think the Padrick kid killed that girl?"

The question caught Madrid off-guard. He studied the sheriff. Avery Boyd was dying, but his eyes were already gone. They stared back at him—cloudy glass orbs that revealed nothing.

Madrid answered flatly, "I don't know."

"What did the Padrick kid tell you?"

"Said he didn't do it."

Boyd's drawn face contorted into a tired smile. "I been doin' this for thirty-one years, Madrid." He leaned his frail body across the desk, dropped his voice to just above a hoarse whisper. "That's pretty much what they all say."

* * * *

The heavy smell of fried bologna filled the A-frame cottage. Charlie Blades had laid the thick greasy slices between pieces of white bread—slathered them with French's yellow mustard and Duke's Mayonnaise. He placed the sandwiches on the white plates with tiny blue flowers he found in the cabinets. On top of the sandwiches he piled massive handfuls of potato chips. He found a coffee mug in the cabinet and a glass that once contained grape jelly. Charlie filled the mug with steaming hot coffee—black. The glass was topped off with room-temperature off-brand orange soda.

He transferred the haute cuisine to a small chrome-trimmed dinette set that was jammed in one corner of the kitchen. The chairs were upholstered with shiny red vinyl. Next to the table a sliding glass door led to the deck.

The pair sat at the table staring through the glass—Charlie bleary eyed, needing a shave and a bath—the girl, Anna Marie, wild red hair, wearing her thin white dress and no shoes. Just two folks sharing a mid-day meal—a surreal slice of Americana—like Norman Rockwell on LSD. In the gray distance, they could see the tram cars sliding silently up and down the mountain.

Charlie hoped for a conversation. Just a simple exchange of words with a pretty girl—who, because of circumstances way beyond her control—happened to be sitting across the table from him. Charlie ached for a taste of normalcy. Just a simple friggin' exchange of words about most anything other than The Wizard or Alex Madrid.

But that didn't happen.

Anna Marie didn't speak at all. She sat across from him in a semi-stupor—stared blankly—her mouth slightly open. She took maybe three bites—drank all of the orange soda. Charlie refilled her glass. Then she started to cry. Her tears brought Charlie a mixture of anger and shame. Had he read Tichborne, he might have quoted, *"My feast of joy is but a dish of pain."* But he hadn't—so he didn't.

Instead, he took her back downstairs—put her on the bed—chained her to the wall.

Alone again, Charlie ate two of the greasy sandwiches, washed them down with a half a pot of black coffee, then ate what the girl had left. Charlie closed the curtains so that no one could see inside from the front porch. Then he found the most comfortable of all the uncomfortable chairs in the main room and faced it towards the front door. He double checked the lock—then wedged a straight-back chair under the door knob like he'd seen people do in old movies.

Charlie slumped into the chair, his big feet propped on an orange-colored camel saddle. The .357 was on the scarred end table next to him. Next to the gun was the mug with the last of the coffee, but caffeine and uppers were proving no match for his fatigue. He had been awake for over thirty-six hours. The Wizard would be there soon. Charlie knew he wouldn't be alone.

Chapter 14

September 25th—1:26 p.m.

Marcy's Holistic Café and Country-Fried Grill took up most of the old train depot. It sat between the tracks and the river and was as diverse as the name implied. Marcy served couscous, avocado and bean sprout sandwiches, organic juices, herbal teas, and most anything a respectable hardcore vegetarian might desire. On the other side of the menu were the best cheeseburgers, fried chicken, foot-long hot dogs, home fries, and Texas-style chili Black Creek had to offer.

Marcy Callahan was as paradoxical as her menu. She was a pacifist who had fallen in love with a soldier. They had been married two months before he shipped out to Vietnam. Staff Sergeant Richard "Richie Rich" Richardson had gone MIA in the summer of 1970. Through four cold winters in Wisconsin, Marcy had waited. After that, to salvage her sanity, she had reclaimed her maiden name and headed south.

Madrid sipped coffee, gave some consideration to the menu, and thought about Dicky Padrick. Even after the interview, he wasn't any closer to knowing if Dicky Padrick was a murderer, or just at the wrong place at the wrong time.

Marcy walked up to his table with a pad and pen. She was an attractive woman with curly strawberry-blonde hair, a sharp nose, and a quick smile. She stretched her neck and looked under the table. Toto had managed to maneuver his bulk between Madrid and the opposing seat.

"That a service dog there, Alex Madrid?"

She knew most of her customer's names. Her accent was an odd mixture of Wisconsin and Irish.

"Yes," Madrid answered, noting the amusement in her hazel eyes, "he is, Marcy."

Toto stared up at her like a troll under a bridge.

"And what sort of service does he provide to you?" she asked with a hint of skeptical smile.

Madrid laid the menu down on the red table top, looked into her mischievous green eyes. "When I drop food on your floor, he will pick it up and eat it. Unless, of course, it's tofu. Then I have to pick it up myself."

"Hmmm," she said, tapping the pen against the order pad. "If somebody from the county drops in, you'd better come up with a better tale than that, Alex Madrid."

"I'll get to work on it." Madrid ordered black bean soup and a naked foot-long dog for Toto. There was a pay phone on the back wall. Madrid left the dog under the table, dropped a dime, and dialed the number for Black Creek Campus Security. It was busy. Next to the phone was a window. Madrid watched an older Chevy Camaro pull into the parking lot. It was painted yellow with red flames on the side and a skull painted on the hood. Two men got out—one big and ugly—the other small and ugly. Madrid watched them walk over to his Blazer. The big one kept his eyes on the front door of the café and the other one looked in the windows, tried the front door. It was locked. Madrid caught himself reaching under his jacket to check the .45 that was tucked into his belt at the small of his back. The smaller man walked to the back of the Blazer, wrote down the tag number. Madrid watched them get back in the Camaro. The big one drove. He gunned the engine—squealed the tires. *Inconspicuous*, Madrid thought—wondered if they were scouting for The Wizard or were just local idiots.

Madrid waited another two minutes, then dialed Black Creek Campus Security again. Still busy. Madrid spotted a young waitress carrying his order. He intercepted her before she got too close to the dog. A few minutes later Marcy exited the kitchen and came to Madrid's booth.

"So, how is your soup?" she asked.

"Not bad," Madrid answered.

She raised her eyebrows, cocked her head slightly. *"Not bad?"*

"Okay," Madrid replied, unable to keep a straight face, "pretty damn good."

"Pretty damn good is right, Alex Madrid." She glanced under the table again. "Next time I'll just ask the mutt. Probably get a more intelligent answer."

"Probably," Madrid agreed. "Let me ask you. Do you know a couple of guys who drive a yellow Camaro with flames and a skull."

Any hint of smile left her face. "Yes. What have they got to do with you?"

"Nothing. I've seen them hanging around," Madrid said, nonchalant. "What do you know about them?"

"They're local rabble. Mean. They like to bully. They are into all that Bruce Lee Kung Fu nonsense. You'd be wise to give them a wide path."

"Okay," Madrid said.

Marcy started back to the kitchen, still thinking about her warning to Alex Madrid. At the door, she turned—gave him another look. He was calmly eating his soup, feeding bits of hot dog to that monster under the table. He didn't seem the sort who heeded warnings. She thought about her husband. He had been the same way. She felt a tear gathering in the corner of her eye.

* * * *

The Black Creek College Campus Security office was housed in a small stone building wedged between the campus laundry and the campus post office. Angie was behind the front desk.

Andy Frazier was sitting facing her, his back to the front door. Angie was holding his hand, talking to him in a soft, consoling voice. She removed her hand, said to Madrid in an all-business tone, "The Chief's been trying to call you all morning."

"I tried calling here," Madrid replied. "Line was busy—or off the hook."

"Hi, Alex," Andy said, his voice heavy.

"Hey" Madrid said. "Did you get any sleep?"

"Not much," the younger man replied. "Every time I would doze off I would see Miranda's face." Andy Frazier shook his head violently as if trying to sling the demons from his skull.

"So," Madrid said, "have you thought about what I asked you last night?"

"About seeing Miranda or that retard?"

"Yeah."

"I didn't see them."

He was more convincing than the night before. "Still not sure I believe you, Andy. I might ask the same question again."

"Ask all you want," Andy Frazier replied, emotion rising in his tone. "It ain't going to change my answer."

Angie stared at Madrid the way a mother stares at the neighborhood bully.

"I heard you talked to him, Alex," Andy said. "You talked with Padrick—that son of a bitch that killed Miranda."

"I talked with Dicky Padrick," Madrid replied, purposely stoic. "How did you know that?"

"Sergeant Galloway called the Chief," Angie replied brusquely. "Sergeant Galloway sounded *very* pissed off. The Chief's in his office."

Pete Wilson's office was a dimly-lit, boxy little room with two small windows set high into pale green concrete block walls. The walls were covered with various notices, safety posters, and a calendar with a picture of last year's Black Creek College baseball team.

Pete Wilson had the refuse of his lunch spread on his desk: two cheeseburger wrappers, a large paper cup, a half a package of chocolate mini-doughnuts—a short stack of paper napkins.

"Alex," he said, raking all but the cup and doughnuts into the wastepaper basket next to his desk. "I was just finishing off a little lunch. Want a doughnut?"

"No thanks," Madrid replied.

"Oh, yeah," Pete Wilson said without acrimony, "I forgot. You're a health nut."

"Depends on how you define it," Madrid replied.

"You eat meat?"

"No."

"You drink soda pop?"

"No."

"You work out every day?"

"Most days."

Pete popped a mini-doughnut into his mouth and grinned. "That's how I define it."

Madrid pulled up one of the metal visitor's chairs, sat across the desk from Wilson.

Pete chewed a doughnut, said, "Galloway called me this morning. Said you went to see the Padrick boy."

"Yeah."

"You should have checked with me first."

"You're right," Madrid said. "I should have."

Pete Wilson waved his hand. "Hell, I don't care that you went to see him. I just want to know before it happens. Don't like getting those kind of calls."

"You're right," Madrid repeated, marginally contrite.

"Galloway wasn't too happy."

"Galloway's happiness a big concern of yours?"

"No." Pete Wilson rattled the ice in the bottom of the cup, guided a piece into his mouth and chomped it. "I can say that now, but that son of a bitch will probably be this county's next sheriff." Wilson chased the ice with another mini doughnut. "You find out anything from Padrick?"

"Yeah. He said he didn't kill Miranda Toliver."

"'Did he happen to mention who did?"

"Not specifically—said it was a big guy dressed in black."

"That sound about right to you?"

"No—but I'm still not convinced he killed her."

"Why-the-hell-not?" Pete Wilson challenged.

"Think about it, Pete. Dicky Padrick sneaks out of his house, wanders around campus, stumbles into Miranda Toliver and kills her? "

Wilson reminded Madrid, "He had her half naked."

"Rape?" Madrid asked skeptically.

"You don't think Padrick gets a hard-on for girls like Miranda Toliver?"

"They were in the middle of a public parking lot."

"No one ever accused Padrick of being a mastermind, Madrid."

"Probably not," Madrid conceded. "But he doesn't have any defensive wounds."

"What are you talking about?"

"I checked his hands, arms, face, neck. He's got a small scrape on his hand, but that was probably from when he went down in the parking lot. If Padrick was trying to have sex with her, I'm guessing Miranda Toliver would have run, or if she couldn't run she'd put up a fight."

Pete Wilson picked up the last doughnut, studied it, laid it back of the desk. "Maybe she never got the chance....to fight back."

"Padrick doesn't seem like the stealthy type."

"Yeah," Wilson half conceded.

"Look at it from the other side, Pete. What would you have done if you rolled up on Padrick?"

The question caught Wilson off guard. "I—I don't know for sure."

"You think you would have stepped out of your car and shot him?"

Wilson winced at the thought.

"Does it bother you that Galloway didn't just walk over and pull Padrick off the girl?"

Wilson glanced at the door, lowered his voice. He asked in an anxious whisper, "You sayin' Galloway had something to do with this?"

"I'm not saying that."

"But you're *thinking* it."

"I'm not saying that Padrick wasn't near the girl," Madrid replied. "Maybe he even had his hands on her."

"A hard sale."

"Yeah—I know."

Pete Wilson reconsidered the last doughnut, crushed the empty box in his large hand, tossed it into the wastepaper basket. He sat—chewed—thought about Dicky Padrick and Josh Galloway. He could hear rain drumming on the roof of the building.

Madrid broke the silence. "Julie Kingston showed up at my front door this morning."

Wilson raised his eyebrows a little. "Lucky you."

"She wanted to talk about last night."

"Was she wearing a skirt?"

"What?" Madrid asked.

"Was she wearing a skirt? Sometimes she wears these short skirts. She has great legs."

"She wasn't wearing a skirt," Madrid answered.

"What'd you tell her?" Wilson asked. "About last night."

"Nothing she didn't already know."

"Good," he replied, swallowed the last of the doughnut.

"Then she asked me about September Jamerson."

"September Jamerson?"

"Yeah."

"What about her?"

"Julie Kingston said she was missing. Wanted to know if I thought it might be connected to Dicky Padrick and Miranda Toliver."

"What'd you tell her?"

"That I never head of September Jamerson."

Wilson nodded. "They're not connected. No way in hell." Wilson shook his head impatiently. "I've known Julie a long time. I like her—she's nice. Real nice to look at—but we already talked about that. She was on TV for awhile—reading the news. Then she showed up here. Daddy owns the paper—owns a bunch of them. Family's got money—but she ends up here—in Black Creek, North Carolina."

"So does she really work at this—or just pretend to work?" Madrid asked.

"Oh, hell no. She works at it. Works hard, but sometimes she's like that crazy guy with the windmills."

"Don Quixote?"

"I reckon. The problem is, Julie's always lookin' for the *big story*—even when there ain't no *big story*. She's been bustin' my chops about this September Jamerson kid for a couple of weeks. She just won't accept that the girl ran away."

"Why do you think she took off?"

Wilson lowered his voice again. "September Jamerson lives—until she hit the road—with her mother and this guy, Lyle Holiday. Holiday was working on the farm when September's father was killed. He stayed on—and one thing led to another." Pete Wilson swiveled his hand back and forth. "Then him and Victoria, September's mother, got together."

"How did he die?"

"September's old man?"

"Yeah."

"Fell out of a barn. Broke his neck."

"Huh," Madrid said.

"Farming is a dangerous job—you ever see the statistics on farm deaths?"

"I'd like to see the statistics on how many die by falling out of a barn."

"Goddamn, Madrid. You're a skeptical bastard."

"My momma used to say the same thing—except for the 'bastard' part."

"He fell out of the barn. There wasn't nothing sinister about it. The unlucky son of bitch wasn't watching what he was doing and fell."

"Okay," Madrid said, "he fell."

"Anyway—like I just said—Lyle Holiday stayed on and—I don't know—maybe a year later—he and Victoria Jamerson are a thing. He's one of those holy roller types. Heard he used to live with that Amish bunch up in Pennsylvania. But he got so wacky they sent him packing. Don't know there's any truth to it—you hear all kinds of shit around here. What I *do* know is that September's mother hasn't been to Black Creek for at least six years. Lyle don't like his woman out in public. She didn't even go to the girl's high school graduation. Sheriff Boyd used to send a man around every few months just to see if she was still alive. Victoria Jamerson never once complained to anyone about anything. So, you know...after a while...hell...he stopped checking."

"That's interesting, but it still doesn't tell me why you think the girl took off."

Wilson made a circle with his thumb and pinky—held up three fingers. "One—her mother said she did. Two—Lyle Holiday said she did. Two ain't as good as one, but you put two and one together... . Three—I think the kid had a lot of reasons to go." Pete Wilson picked up a pencil and began tapping it on the metal desk top. "Like I just said, you hear all kinds of shit. Black Creek's a small town—people like to talk."

Madrid waited.

"Lyle might have been...you know...messing with the girl."

"Sexual?"

Pete Wilson raised his eyebrows, tilted his head to one side. "I don't know. Wouldn't bet against it."

"Anyone ever check that out?"

"Yeah. Social Services was out there a few years back. Nothing came of it. The Jamerson girl denied it. When she didn't show up for her classes at the college—I got a call from one of her teachers. I went out to their place—talked to her folks." Pete Wilson tried to remember. "About a week before I hired you."

"What did they say?"

"Lyle said September just left in the middle of the night. Victoria said pretty much the same thing. She was upset—he was more pissed. He said it was between her and God. Josh Galloway went out there the next day—got more of the same."

"How did she leave?"

"Just drove away, I guess. She's got a car. Lyle tried to tell me it was his—that she stole it. But I checked—it's registered to her."

Madrid nodded.

Pete Wilson lowered his voice, his tone fell somber. "What happened to Miranda Toliver last night was a lousy thing, Madrid. Her mommy and daddy spent a bundle to send their little girl to Black Creek College. Hell, they probably sent her here thinkin' it's safer than some big school like State or Chapel Hill. And what happens? She winds up getting killed. It's lousy for Miranda Toliver—it's lousy for her family—and her friends." Pete pauses and looks directly at Alex Madrid. "It's also *real* lousy for Black Creek College."

"A dead coed is bad for business."

Pete Wilson offered a pained expression. "Bottom line—yeah. *Real* bad for business. Now you come waltzing in here—got all these friggin' theories about Padrick not being the killer—maybe another girl involved. Jesus, you need to look at the big picture."

"So what are you saying, Pete?" Madrid asked calmly. "We just leave Padrick sitting in jail?"

"You come up with anything solid that makes me believe someone other than Dicky Padrick killed Miranda Toliver, I'll back you." Then he added, "That goes for the Jamerson girl, too. Otherwise—keep your mouth shut."

"Okay," Madrid said, stood to leave.

Pete Wilson took a pack of Taylor Pride chewing tobacco from the top drawer of his desk, broke a piece off the plug, and stuffed it in the side of his mouth. Then he talked around it. "I've been with the college almost fifteen years. In another five, I can retire. I get a small pension. It ain't much, but it'll help. Anyway, it's a damn sight better than trying to start over at my age."

"I understand," Madrid answered.

Chapter 15

September 25th—3:17 p.m.

Charlie Blades' eyes snapped open—a jolt of adrenaline rocked him from the chair. In a reflexive instant, the .357 was in his big paw, hammer locked back, barrel leveled. His eyes adjusted quickly to the dimness of the room. The house was quiet except for the pendulous tic-tock of the cuckoo hanging in the hall. He could feel his heart thumping in his chest. Then the phone jangled shrill and loud. Charlie dropped his feet to the floor, rose from the chair. His body felt heavy and stiff. Another ring. *In the hall,* he sluggishly remembered. He moved. The pine floor creaked under his heavy boots. Between rings he could hear the rain pounding steadily on the metal roof.

Charlie picked up the receiver of the black wall phone, said nothing.

"Good afternoon, Charles," The Wizard cooed softly.

The voice floated into Charlie's brain like a tranquilizing drug.

"Hey," Charlie replied. "You doin' good?"

"Doing fine, Charles. And you?"

"Yeah, doing alright—I guess." He wanted to ask why he'd been stood up back at the redneck bar, but didn't. "Had a little trouble here and there, but I handled it." Charlie knew better than to offer any specifics over the phone. The Wizard had convinced him that most were tapped.

"I have the utmost confidence in your abilities, Charles."

Charlie Blades stood in the gloomy hallway, the receiver pressed firmly to his ear so not to miss a word. He could feel an inexplicable smile trying to play at one corner of his mouth. The Wizard was judicious—if not downright stingy—with praise. Charlie had just received a heaping spoonful.

"Did our package arrive in good condition?" The Wizard asked, a shimmer of anticipation in his tone.

"Real good condition," Charlie Blades replied. "Perfect."

"I expected nothing less," the voice from the other end replied soothingly. "And as usual, you have not disappointed me."

Charlie felt the smile tug again.

"Have you sampled?" The Wizard asked.

There was a barely perceptible change in his tone, but Charlie Blades heard it. The question sliced a jagged gash in Charlie's quasi-narcotic state of mind. Images of the girl's body flickered through his brain like celluloid on an ancient projector. He struggled for a causal reply. "No," he said tersely.

"Charles," The Wizard continued in the same soothing tone. "It's all right. You did the work—you are entitled to some of the reward."

"I am?" Charlie Blades asked in a quiet incredulously voice.

"But of course. Haven't we always shared?"

"I guess so."

"You *guess* so?" The Wizard asked without animosity. "Think about what you just said. Think about my first offering to you, my friend."

But Charlie was already thinking about the first one. She was never far from his thoughts—from his dreams and his nightmares. And The Wizard knew it, too. Charlie thought about the girl downstairs. He could feel himself getting hard.

"You deserve a sample, Charles."

"I do?" Charlie asked, barely able to contain his relief.

"Indeed. In fact, I insist. But not so that I can tell."

"Okay," Charlie replied. "When are you planning to see the package?"

"Soon," The Wizard answered cheerfully. "Bright and early in the morning. In the meantime, enjoy yourself."

"You're sure about this?" Charlie asked.

"Quite sure, Charles," the Wizard replied. "As you know all too well, life is short—and delicacies such as this don't tend to last very long."

There was a click on the other end of the line. But the words continued to echo in Charlie Blades' freakishly large head.

* * * *

Angie was still at her desk when Madrid stepped outside Pete Wilson's office. Andy Frazier was gone. Angie looked up from her paperwork. "You got a call," she said sharply as she ripped a sheet off a memo pad. "It was some woman." Innuendo was thick in her tone. "She said it was urgent she speak with you. She wouldn't leave her name, just this number."

Madrid took the paper—looked at the phone number.

Angie pushed her glasses back up her nose with her middle finger. "The chief don't like people getting personal calls here at work."

"I'm guessing that's not a problem for you," Madrid replied as he moved past her desk.

Back in the Blazer, he took another look at the number. It was local—but meant nothing to him. Toto was stretched across the back seat. The dog stood lazily, looked over Madrid's shoulder at the piece of paper.

Madrid gently stroked the big dog's head. "Something I can do for you?" he asked.

Madrid gave the number one last look—wondered if it was Julie Kingston's. Reluctantly admitted he sort of *hoped* it was Julie Kingston's.

Madrid drove back to the phone booth where he'd talked with Nick Vorcheck less than two days earlier. The area around the booth looked worse in daylight. Cigarette butts and other trash littered the sparse unkempt grass. A couple of brown beer bottles had been shattered on the uneven sidewalk. In contrast, a large sourwood was beginning to glow autumn red.

Madrid thumbed through what was left of the phone book—looked up Julie Kingston's home number. The number didn't match. He looked up the number for the *Black Creek Daily*. No match there, either. He dropped a dime and a nickel into the slot and dialed. After two rings a woman picked up. In a low, tentative voice she said, "Hello."

"This is Alex Madrid," he told her. "I was given this number to call."

Nothing.

"Hello," Madrid said again. By this time he had scanned everything around him. No one was on the street. The woods around the phone booth were empty for as far as he could see. Then he spotted them, a block and a half away—in front of an empty store front. They were leaning on the hood of the yellow Camaro—the one with the flames and the skull. The big one had his arms folded across his chest. The smaller one had a pair of binoculars trained on Madrid.

Madrid stepped out of the booth, as far as the phone cord would allow. He stared at the two by the car—his best Gary Cooper in *High Noon* stare. He hoped the guy with the binoculars was able to appreciate it. He stepped back into the booth, slipped his right hand into his jacket, rested his palm on the butt of the Springfield Armory .45.

"Hello," the woman said again.

Madrid could hear the tension in her voice. "What do you want?" he asked. Madrid turned away from the two by the car—looked back down Middle Street. *Never rule out misdirection.*

"I don't know," she answered, struggling with each word.

"Look, lady, I don't have time for this. You got two seconds to identify yourself or we're done talking."

Another pause—more than two seconds.

"This is Victoria Jamerson," the woman said finally, her voice just above a whisper. "I am September Jamerson's mother. My daughter is...September is...missing. She's gone."

Alex Madrid felt his pulse click up a notch. He turned back to the pair down the street. They hadn't moved. The connection between the two and the phone call seemed unlikely. "So why are you calling me?"

"You work for the college, don't you?" Victoria Jamerson asked, almost apologetic.

"Yes. At least for the moment."

"I didn't know who else to call." Desperation replaced her tentativeness. "I need to talk to someone," Victoria Jamerson said, her voice still low and tight. "I need to talk to someone about September."

"Okay," Madrid replied without actual encouragement. "I'm listening."

"Not on the phone."

Madrid remembered what Pete Wilson had said about Victoria Jamerson not coming into Black Creek. "Do you want me to come to your house?" he asked.

"No." Victoria Jamerson's answer was quick and emphatic. "You can't come here. If Lyle.... " She decided not to finish the thought. Another pause.

“So if not the phone, and not at your home, where?” Madrid asked. He could hear impatience seeping into his tone.

"There's a state park. Holmes' State Park, I think” she replied, unsure. “I think it's about a mile from my house—or maybe two. I can walk though the woods and meet you there. Would you be able to meet me in about an hour?"

"I'll be there. In one hour,” Madrid replied, then added. “You’re sure this is the best way?”

“I think so,” she said in a tired voice. "If I'm a little late, please wait for me." It came across the line less of a request, more a plea.

"I'll wait," Madrid assured her.

* * * *

Victoria Jamerson cradled the phone as if returning a fallen baby bird to its nest. Lyle, her common-law husband, was napping in the parlor. She offered her God a silent word of thanks. Alex Madrid’s call had not awakened him. She’d been camped next to the receiver—had snatched it up halfway through the first ring.

Nearly silent, she eased through the house—peeked into the parlor. Lyle Holiday was snoring lightly, mouth open. The King James Bible lay open on his lap. From the drawer by the sink, she took her Swiss Army knife—slipped it into the big pocket she’d sewn into the front of her dress. For years, Victoria Jamerson had endured a recurring nightmare. She was in the woods near her house. It was night. There was a man.... . The small-bladed knife was a poor excuse for a weapon, but better than nothing.

Victoria opened the kitchen door slowly—closed it behind her the same way. She picked her way through the early fall leaves on the un-mowed lawn, then waded into the adjoining field with its tangle of weeds and briars. Once she reached the edge of the woods, she looked back. *Past the point of no return*, she thought. Her Timex had been a Christmas gift from September. It informed her she had fifty-seven minutes until she was to meet Alex Madrid. She called to her God again—asked for strength—hoped Alex Madrid would keep his word and be waiting for her. The trail, now poorly defined from lack of use, started on the other side of the field. Before it delivered her to Holmes State Park, it would undulate over two long steep hills and cross the same creek twice. Victoria Jamerson was no longer a young woman.

* * * *

Toto sniffed around at the edge of the woods near the phone booth—searched for the scent of wild game or a hamburger wrapper. Periodically, he turned his massive head to locate Madrid. Standing next to the phone booth, Madrid focused on the pair down the street. They were still leaned against the car with the flames and the skull. The smaller one had relinquished the binoculars to the larger one. He had them trained on Madrid. Madrid pointed to the big one, then made a curling motion with his index finger—*come hither.* The big one dropped the binoculars from his face and said something to the smaller one. They climbed into the car, revved the engine loudly, took off down Middle Street in the opposite direction.

Chapter 16

Gatlinburg, Tennessee
September 25th—4:00 p.m.

The sensation of a thousand needles—only pleasant.

The showerhead spayed the fine, hot mist over her face and shoulders. Anna Marie stood under it, head angled upward—mouth barely open, eyes tightly closed. The smooth cold concrete was beginning to warm under her feet. In and out of sleep, she'd lost track of time and day. The drugs Charlie Blades had given her still blunted her senses, but the fog had slowly begun to lift. She remembered the young red-headed man dressed as a Park Ranger. If she'd had a brother, he might have looked something like that. The giant troll-like man had done something to the Ranger's neck. The smaller man had made only the smallest sound, then melted into a heap on the asphalt. She remembered calling out to him. Or had she? The man who now sat just a few feet away—had he really killed that boy? Anna Marie was *pretty sure* he had. She wondered if anyone was looking for her. Convinced herself they probably were not. And even if they were, she doubted anyone was looking very hard.

She opened her eyes—through the spray surveyed the nightmare that surrounded her. The room was dark—except for the candles. There were close to a dozen in varying sizes and colors. Their collective flicker cast ominous shadows on the unfinished concrete-block walls. Some of the candles had been placed around the edge of her bed. She could see the shackles hanging from either end.

The soap in her hand smelled like lilacs. Anna Marie couldn't remember the last time she'd bathed. She turned away from the light, faced the shadowed corner, began to wash herself.

The predator with cornered prey.

His legs straddled the back rest of the small wooden chair. His thick, hairy arms were folded—resting on ~~the on~~ the top of the slatted back. The point of his unshaved chin rested on his arms. He stared straight ahead—wondered how any moment could ever be better than this. Charlie concentrated, burned every frame into his mind—so that when she was gone—he could replay them over and over.

The water had taken most of the curl from her hair. It stretched just below the mid-point of her back. From there, the water played with the candle light. It glistened down her back—over the delicious curves of her hips and ass. It trailed down the inside of her thighs, past the ticklish curve on the back side of her knees, over her well-shaped calves.

"Turn it back around," Blades told her, voice thick with lust.

"Wash your feet, then your legs—then your titties," he told her. "And do it real slow—we got all day.

Anna Marie felt herself turn towards the voice, as if on auto pilot. Her eyes were still closed.

Charlie watched the slow pirouette, stared hypnotically at the thick patch of red hair between the girl's legs. "Save your pussy for last," he told her. "And open your goddamned eyes."

Anna Marie opened her eyes, faced the man in the chair. He was the embodiment of every monster who had ever lived in a child's closet, or under their bed, once the lights had been turned out. Only no measure of parental reassurance would make this one go away. Anna Marie was still unclear about much of the past two or three days—but of one thing she was certain. The monster under *her* bed was real.

"Look at me," he told her sharply. "Don't look at nothin' else."

She couldn't remember the exact order of Charlie Blade's request, but she got the gist of it. She washed her face, then her feet. The man in front of her sat like a statue, except for his eyes. They followed every movement. She moved the lilac-scented bar over her stomach—made circles until her breasts were covered with a thin film of soapy bubbles.

Charlie was pleased—encouraged. This girl's attitude was different from the last. This one did what she was told. She had hope—false hope, but it all worked the same. *Do as your told and maybe you survive.* But none ever had. Still, she would not have to endure *"the learning curve"*, as The Wizard called it. The last one had been stubborn at first—spit-in-your- eye defiant. She had fought, said that her Uncle Alex would come for her. Said that people would die.

But after less than two days with The Wizard, she had stopped believing. The Wizard was like that—possessed that kind of magic. Madrid's niece changed from defiant to compliant—to desperately compliant.

But then something strange happened—something neither Charlie Blades nor The Wizard had considered. Late one night, when Charlie Blades had been at an all-night grocery shopping for steaks, cigarettes, and duct tape, Alex Madrid had appeared from the darkness. He'd come for the girl. And just as she had predicted—people had died.

Charlie chased the images from his head, focused on the vision before him. Her dark pink nipples stared back at him through the veil of soap and spray. He considered pulling her from beneath the hot shower and throwing her on the bed. But The Wizard had told him only to *sample*. It was a strategic ambiguity which left Charlie uncertain. He left the chair, stepped closer to Anna Marie. The edge of the shower spray dampened the toes of his heavy boots.

"Between your legs," he told her.

Anna Marie watched the man move toward her, then stop at the edge of the shower. He was silhouetted by the candles around the bed behind him—a monstrous shadow that towered above her. She could barely make out the features of his pock-marked face, but his eyes seemed to glow from the blackness. She moved the soap down her stomach. The man worked the heavy buckle of his wide leather belt, unzipped the dirty blue jeans. His penis was just like the rest of him—huge and scary looking. He was fully erect.

"I didn't tell you to stop," he told her, a savagery in his tone. "Keep going. And don't fucking pretend you don't like it. I know you do."

Anna Marie stared at the concrete floor, watched the water swirl into the drain, lathered her pubic hair.

"Tell me you like it," he man told her.

Anna Marie kept her head down, offered a robotic affirmative nod.

"Look at me," the man told her harshly.

She forced her eyes to meet his. He was masturbating furiously. He seemed closer than before.

"Tell me you like it," he told her again through ragged breaths. His gazed bounced back and forth between her face, her breasts, and her soapy hand that continued to rub back and forth over her pubic mound and vagina.

"I like it," she said softly, not taking her eyes from his.

They stayed that way for maybe another minute. Eyes locked, one of them masturbating, the other pretending. Then the man stepped away. His hand pumped furiously up and down his engorged member. Then he made a sound, a cry almost like that of a wounded animal. He ejaculated on the floor. When he was finished he threw is head back, tried to catch his breath.

Anna Marie watched the man's giant cock growing limp. He turned away from her, and when he turned back, he was buckled and zipped.

"You can stop now—if you want," he said, nodding to her hand that was still slowly working between her legs.

She stopped—stood naked under the shower, uncertain what to do next.

"There's a clean towel on the bed," the man told her, his voice back under control—almost soothing. "I found a robe that looks like it might fit you. I'm going to take your clothes upstairs and wash them."

Anna Marie nodded. "Okay."

"You hungry?" The question was casual, like they were suddenly old friends.

She shook her head, almost imperceptibly. From beneath the spray, she answered in a small voice. "No."

The man shrugged his shoulders—made a grunting sound. He flipped the switch that triggered the naked bulb overhead. Whatever ugliness the candles had masked, instantly returned. Charlie extinguished each candle between his thumb and forefinger—gathered her dress and underwear. At the door, he turned. "I'll check back with you in a little while." Without looking directly at it, he motioned to the whitish glob he had deposited on the floor. "Clean that up before I get back."

Chapter 17

September 25th—4:43 p.m.

Madrid pulled a local map from the glove compartment of the Blazer. Holmes State Park was about ten miles outside of Black Creek, just beyond the county line. Madrid called to the dog and Toto bounded between the front seats and into the back. The rain had stopped, but the sky was still close and gray. They drove through Black Creek, circled back a couple of times, tried to catch another look at the pair in the Yellow Camaro. They were gone.

On the way out of town, Madrid stopped at a mom and pop grocery. There were two antique gas pumps out front. High-test and regular. It was the kind of place you could only find in small towns. They sold chain saws and Moon Pies, shotgun shells and baby food. Salted pork hung from the ceiling in burlap bags. Behind the counter was an old Gibson Hummingbird model guitar. The tag said four hundred and thirty-five dollars. Next to the Gibson was a lady named Nell. She had wiry gray hair and store-bought teeth—seemed to call most everybody either "Darlin'" or "Honey". Madrid put some gas in the Blazer, got himself a large cup of coffee, and a six pack of burger-looking things for the dog. He gave Nell a twenty. She gave him eight dollars and thirty-three cents in change. Said, "Thank you, Darlin'. Come back."

Madrid made a vague promise that he would.

Fifteen minutes later he pulled into Holmes State Park. It was smaller than he had imagined. There was a grassy meadow with a walking trail that meandered through young white pines, dogwoods, maple and oaks. Picnic tables with grills were dotted along the forested perimeter of the park. In one of the grassy areas, ten teenagers were divided by a volleyball net. They sloshed around on the wet court, tried to keep the ball in play. Madrid drove past the group, parked at the west end. It was his best guess as to where Victoria Jamerson might emerge from the woods.

Madrid rolled down the windows. He could smell charcoal and grilled hot dogs. Toto could smell it too. Madrid reached into the paper bag on the floorboard. He removed three of the burger-shaped dog servings from the box and pealed away the cellophane wrapper. He broke each one in half and let the big dog take it from his hand. It had taken them a long time to get this far. The dog had nearly starved to death. His instinct for survival was stronger than his loyalty to Madrid.

Alex Madrid was acutely aware of the fact. The dog had bitten him three times—the first attack severe enough to require almost twenty stitches, a tetanus shot, and two rounds of antibiotics. The second and third bites, Madrid was able to close with butterfly bandages.

Madrid continued to break off the small pieces and hand them to the big German Shepherd-Mastiff. He was about to hand over the last piece of pseudo-burger when one of the volleyballers let go a high-pitched scream. Madrid flinched—moved towards the door. Wrong thing to do. Madrid's wrist disappeared into the big dog's mouth.

Toto showed both rows of teeth, offered a savage snarl. It was a controlled grip, but still hard enough to break the skin. A thin trickle of blood slowly trailed across the back of Madrid's left hand. His eyes were locked on the dog's. His right hand slid stealthily over the butt of the .45, his index finger slithered over the trigger.

"Toto," Madrid said with firm diplomacy. "I'm not going to take your goddamn food away from you. I'm the one who bought it for you to begin with."

Toto stopped snarling, but didn't loosen his grip.

Madrid continued. "Come on, Toto," he said, less firmly—more soothingly. "Give me back my arm."

The dog loosened his grip just slightly, but enough for Madrid to appreciate. "Good boy, Toto," Madrid encouraged. "A little more. Let go of my arm. Give, Toto. Give." Madrid's words now a soft plea.

Toto released Madrid's arm—waited. The dog had survived unspeakable pain. Instinct warned him he might be on the brink of more.

Madrid slowly removed his left hand from the dog's grip. His right hand retreated from the .45. He could see two small puncture wounds on the back of his forearm, one bleeding more than the other. Slowly, carefully, gently—Madrid stroked the dog's large head. He talked to the mutt in a quiet voice. It took a couple of minutes before the dog seemed to relax. Madrid reached to the floorboard, retrieved the piece of dog burger he had dropped. Toto took it gingerly.

From beneath the passenger seat, Madrid retrieved a small gray canvas bag with black Velcro closures. Inside was antiseptic, isopropyl alcohol, cotton swabs, a variety of bandages, and some aspirin. Madrid had put the kit together about six months ago. He had labeled it simply "Toto". The dog watched intently as Madrid once again doctored his wounds.

Madrid studied his companion—wondered if one day he would have to kill the dog, or if Toto might try to kill him. Madrid knew the dog was damaged—maybe beyond the point of repair. And knew the same about himself.

As if intercepting the thought, Toto moved to the edge of the back seat, rested his wide muzzle on the backrest near Madrid's head. Cathartically, Madrid rubbed behind the dog's ears.

There was no one in the park Madrid would pick out as September Jamerson's mother. Madrid sipped the coffee. It had cooled but was still drinkable. The bite was beginning to ache. He swallowed some aspirin and waited.

* * * *

Victoria Jamerson struggled along the trail, her flat-soled shoes ill-matched for the steep terrain and treacherous footing. The innermost stretch of the trail had been seldom used in recent years. Nature had reclaimed small sections, literally erasing her path. She tried to remember the last time she had been on the trail. Maybe nine or ten years ago. She and September had hiked to the park to have a picnic and to look for wild blueberries. It had been in the fall—maybe mid-October. The leaves had crunched under their feet. She remembered it as a comforting sound. Her life had been different then. It was before Lyle, when September still had the innocence due a young girl. Victoria longed for those times again. The last time she had walked this trail had been a wonderful day. She couldn't remember any wonderful days since then.

Victoria was more than a half hour late when the trail ended at the large grassy meadow. She had pushed herself hard, was nearly exhausted. She scanned the park trying to find someone she thought might be Alex Madrid—prayed he hadn't abandoned her.

Madrid scouted the tree line—spotted her as soon as she cleared the woods. Madrid told Toto to get back into the Blazer. The dog bounded into the vehicle, stretched out on the back seat. Madrid walked over to the woman.

"Mrs. Jamerson?" he asked.

Her nod was slow, unsure. "You are Mr. Madrid?" A note of disbelief, maybe disappointment, permeated her tone.

"Alex," Madrid replied, studying the woman. He figured she was somewhere in her fifties. She was tall and slender—high cheek bones that tapered down to a sharp chin, a prominent jaw line, a long sharp nose. She was a handsome woman, but her hazel eyes reflected the strain of a hard life.

Madrid's stare made her uncomfortable. She brushed a strand of graying hair from her damp forehead. "Can we sit down?" Victoria Jamerson asked. She could feel the shakiness in her legs—was already concerned about the return trip. "I'm a little tired after my walk."

Madrid thought she looked more than a little tired.

There was a concrete picnic table near where Madrid had parked the Blazer. They walked to it. Victoria sat, faced away from the table. The bench was hard and cold, but it felt good to be off of her feet.

"I have some water in the truck," Madrid said. "Let me get you some."

Victoria Jamerson didn't argue. She watched Madrid move away from the table, saw the massive head of the dog appear in the rear window of the truck. Alex Madrid was not what she had expected—not what she had hoped for. She had pictured the man on the other end of her phone line as tall, with dark hair and piercing eyes. She felt suddenly foolish, realized she had envisioned her own version of Prince Charming. She had wanted a combination of white knight and avenging angel. Alex Madrid appeared to be neither. His short blonde hair showed a hint of gray at the temples. He was neither tall nor short; not exactly handsome. He had the arms and shoulders of a dock worker. He looked more like a thug than a prince.

Madrid came back to the bench with a liter of water and a bag of granola. “You should probably eat this,” he said without further explanation.

Victoria Jamerson felt suddenly awkward. She was unused to strangers—unused to anyone, other than September, doing things for her. "Thank you," she said in a voice just above a whisper, "but I don't have any money to pay you for these things."

"You don’t need any, ma'am," Madrid explained to her. "I usually carry this stuff with me, anyway."

Victoria Jamerson didn't know how to respond. She said nothing. The water was cool, felt wonderful in her mouth. She hadn't realized how thirsty she’d become. She tried the granola. It was oats, nuts, and pieces of dried fruit. She chewed slowly, drank some more water.

"Your dog is very large," she said quietly.

"Yes, he is," Madrid replied.

“Did you raise him from a puppy?”

“No. We’ve only been together for a short time.”

"Does he have a good temperament, Mr. Madrid?"

Madrid smiled. "Not always, Mrs. Jamerson. He’s somewhat a work in progress."

She noticed the bandage on Madrid's left hand. A small spot of blood had wicked to the surface.

Madrid said, "You said on the phone that you wanted to talk to me about your daughter, September."

"Yes," Victoria Jamerson answered with a long, slow nod. She took another sip of water.

"Why did you call *me.*"

"I didn't know who else *to* call, Mr. Madrid. Miss King.... .” She cut the thought in mid stream.

“Julie Kingston told you to call me?” Madrid asked, keeping accusation from his tone.

“I talked with Mr. Wilson from the college,” Victoria Jamerson explained. “He came to our house. He was very nice, but he said there wasn't much he could do. He told me to call the Sheriff's Department and report September as a missing person."

"Did you do that?” Madrid asked, letting the part about Julie Kingston go. “Did you call the Sheriff’s Department?"

"No. But one of the Sheriff's men—a man named Galloway, I think—came the next day. I think maybe Mr. Wilson told him to come."

"Did you report September missing to Galloway?"

Victoria fixed her eyes on a patch of wet grass. Shook her head.

"May I ask why?"

Victoria Jamerson didn't reply.

"Was it because of your husband?" Madrid asked.

She turned her head slowly—for the first time, looked directly at Madrid. It was a mixture of hope and suspicion. "Do you know my husband?"

"No."

She closed her eyes—exhaled a long, tired breath. "Lyle says that September ran away. He says the college has poisoned her against us. Lyle says September no longer believes in the things we believe. He blames the college—and he blames me."

"What do *you* say?" Madrid asked.

"I want more for September," she replied in a tired voice. "I want her to have a chance. To have a life away from Black Creek."

"Do think your daughter ran away?"

"No." She shook her head. "I don't know. I don't think... . No, I don't think she ran away. September wouldn't leave without telling me."

Madrid thought Victoria Jamerson sounded more wishful than convinced.

"If she *did* run away," he asked, " do you have any ideas where she might be?"

"No," Victoria Jamerson answered, shook her head almost imperceptibly.

Madrid stood a few feet away from her. He could see the head of the trail where she had emerged from the woods and the gravel road that led into the park.

"What about friends?"

"Not that I know of."

They both paused--reflected on the implications of her answer.

"Anyone at Black Creek College?" Madrid asked.

"September doesn't talk much about her classes. She goes to the college and then comes back home. When she gets home, she goes to her room. She studies hard. September was never...you know...talkative. Not for a long time, anyway. She's shy, Mr. Madrid. Quiet. Maybe if she'd had more children to play with when she was younger."

Madrid nodded, expressionless. Victoria Jamerson seemed like one of those mothers who took a degree of blame for everything that went wrong in her child's life.

"So what would you like me to do, Mrs. Jamerson?"

"To find my daughter, Mr. Madrid. I was told you are a detective."

"Sort of—used to be."

"Why did you quit?"

"It's a long story."

Victoria Jamerson nodded. "I can pay you some," she said. "I have September's college money."

Second offer today. "Money's not the issue."

As if prodded, Victoria Jamerson sat a bit more erect. When she spoke, there was a spark in her voice. "You're saying you won't help me?"

"I'm saying there are people who could help you more than me, Mrs. Jamerson."

"The Sheriff's Department?"

"Maybe."

The spark in her voice began to smolder. "I realize that I don't get away from my home very often, Mr. Madrid. But I'm not stupid—or senseless."

"I wasn't implying—"

Victoria Jamerson cut his thought short. "I have a telephone—and my daughter."

"I'm not sure I'm following you, Mrs. Jamerson."

"I know what most people think of us," she said, her eyes fixed on Madrid's. "What they think of *me*. Those men at the Sheriff's Department won't take me seriously. Mr. Wilson was polite. That Galloway fellow didn't even bother with that. They think I'm a half-crazy-hermit lady. You probably think it, too."

"I don't," Madrid replied—hoped it sounded sincere.

"It doesn't matter." Bitterness and resignation had doused her spark. Victoria Jamerson's shoulders fell, her fingers retreated into tightly balled fists that rested just above her knees. Her eyes left

Madrid's, her gaze fixed at a point just beyond the tips of her worn, brown shoes.

"I'd like to help you," Madrid told her apologetically, "but I am in the middle of some things. I'll talk with Pete Wilson again."

Tears began to fill her eyes. From the pocket of her dress, she pulled an antique linen handkerchief—blotted her eyes.

Madrid watched the volleyball players pile into cars and head for the park's exit. He knew he had done the right thing—the smart thing. The next few days could determine how many days he had left. Couldn't afford the distraction. But September Jamerson was *already* a distraction. September Jamerson, Miranda Toliver, and Dicky Padrick had all managed to climb inside his head.

"I'm sorry to have taken up your time, Mr. Madrid," Victoria Jamerson said wearily, as she struggled to stand up. Her legs were stiff and aching. She felt lightheaded—waited a moment for the feeling to pass. "I hope you get your matters resolved."

Madrid watched her rise. She stood shakily, brushed some graying strands of hair from her face.

She turned to him, said quietly, "Thank you for meeting me here today. I needed to talk to someone."

The older woman's sincerity was painful—her words an equal mixture of exhaustion, capitulation, and anguish.

"What if I took a look at September's room?" Madrid asked, regretting each syllable as it tumbled from his mouth.

"Why would you want to do that?" she asked with tired suspicion.

"Sometimes you can tell a lot by what someone leaves behind—and what they don't. And if your daughter ran away... "

"She didn't," Victoria Jamerson said sternly.

"But if she did," Madrid continued, "she may have left something behind to tell us where she went."

"Why would September do that?"

"I don't know that she did, Mrs. Jamerson. I don't know your daughter, and from what you've told me, there's a lot you don't know, either." Madrid watched the pain register, like a slap across Victoria Jamerson's drawn face. He tried to lessen the sting. "Your daughter is probably like most kids her age. There are most likely aspects of her life she doesn't want to share with you."

Victoria Jamerson said nothing. She stared at the tree line, then at the grass near her feet. She shifted her unfocused gaze to the dog, then turned to Madrid.

"So you *will* help me?"

"I'll take a look at your daughter's room. I don't want to commit beyond that."

"What if I looked for you?" she asked.

"That wouldn't do. I need to see her room as close to how she left it as possible. Have you been in there much since September left?"

"No." She reconsidered. "Sometimes I go in and sit in her chair. It's by the window. September likes to read there." Her voice cracked as she added, "Sometimes I would find her there—taking a nap—her book on her lap."

"You haven't cleaned the room?"

"No."

Madrid nodded. "Good. What about Lyle?"

"I don't understand your question," she said carefully.

Madrid was blunt. "Has Lyle Holiday been in September's room since she left?"

"No. Not that I know of."

Victoria Jamerson raised her sharp chin, looked up at the graying sky. "It will be getting dark soon, Mr. Madrid. I need to leave now."

"Let me drive you, Mrs. Jamerson."

"Thank you, but no. I'll walk."

"Ma'am," Madrid told her diplomatically, " if you don't mind my saying so, you look pretty tired. If you're worried about the dog, I can secure him in the back of the truck. Besides, I will need to know where you live if I'm going to take a look at your daughter's room."

"I appreciate your offer, Mr. Madrid," Victoria Jamerson forced an anemic smile. "But that wouldn't be a good idea. Lyle would take exception. He will take exception to me talking to you, if he finds out. I'd appreciate it if you didn't say anything about our meeting, Mr. Madrid."

She looked Madrid in the eye—waited for his response.

"I'm not a real chatty sort of guy, Mrs. Jamerson."

"I believe that, Mr. Madrid. I will call you when it is a good time for you to come to our home."

"You're sure about the ride?"

"I'm sure."

Madrid nodded. "All right. I'll wait for your call, Mrs. Jamerson. I'm staying at The Paradise Court on Old Highway 64."

"I remember The Paradise Court," she said, maybe slightly nostalgic. "It's a nice place."

Madrid said nothing. He studied her arthritic gait as she walked towards the trail head. Madrid watched the older woman slip into the gloominess of the woods, disappearing like a ghost into a fog. The only evidence of her visit remained on the picnic table—the empty water bottle and the half-eaten bag of the granola. A familiar feeling of dread enveloped him. He policed the table—waited for the feeling to pass.

But it didn't.

Chapter 18

Jefferson City, Tennessee
September 25th—8:38 p.m.

Saturday night was money night.

Smilin' Sammy McGrady's Traveling Carnival and Freak Show had come to town. Actually, they'd stopped just outside of town. Fewer cops and not as many payoffs. The rag-tag group had set up near the railroad tracks, within sight of the Andrew Johnson Highway. They were spread across the crumbling parking lot of an old textile factory that had run out of orders five years earlier. A rusting eight-foot chain-link fence topped with two rows of barbed wire surrounded the lot. The effect was not unlike a prison yard—the guard tower replaced with a brightly-lit Ferris wheel. The four-story brick mill stood just beyond the lot—large unlit windows stared down like dark, disapproving eyes.

The motley caravan had rolled in three days ago, and the rain had rolled in with them. At the height of the deluge, the parking lot had transformed into a series of tiny rivers that snaked about the rides and streamed under the heavy canvas tents. From the confines of their cocoon-like trailers, the carnies had spent most of the last seventy-two hours staring dismally from tiny windows. Some killed the time by playing cards and drinking. A few of the luckier ones filled the days with sex and weed. Finally, there had been a break in the weather. But just beyond the aura of the neon canopy, the sky was still black and heavy. Threatening.

The guy running the Tilt-o-Whirl was a small, grizzled man that everyone called Toad. Today, like most every day, Toad wore a black denim jacket and matching jeans. Stringy, graying hair hung from the sides of his dirty Atlanta Braves cap. From his elevated platform, Toad's attention was divided between the Tilt-O-Whirl, the weather, and the guy standing next to the fence at the far corner of the lot.

The fence guy looked like some half-fag-muscle-magazine pretty boy—long dyed-blonde hair and lots of tan. Through the fence, Blondie scouted the make-shift parking lot—waiting for something—

more likely somebody. Toad had seen him earlier, with two other guys, over by the Freak Show tent. One of the guys had been big—maybe six-six. The other had been more like Toad's size—only softer. Toad had been inside twice—burglary, then sexual assault—six years, eight months, and two days total. Not much rehabilitation, but Toad had learned to spot trouble. These guys hadn't come for the cotton candy.

He glanced at his old pocket watch—began to slow the ride. The crowd was good, the lines for the rides healthy. Jefferson City was their last stop before they turned south, looking for warmer weather. Tomorrow morning they would break the show down, pack it up, roll on down the road. Barely a memory would remain. Toad forgot about the guy at the fence. He took the tickets, loaded the kids in the ride, checked the line for the next round.

It was Saturday night. And Saturday night was money night.

* * * *

From one of the darkened windows on the third floor of the abandoned mill, the other two members of the trio stared down. Below them, swirling lights and the tops of the red and yellow tents merged, formed a bright splatter on the otherwise drab canvas. The colors reflected off the puddles in the parking lot, reflected again off of the lenses of The Wizard's John Lennon-style glasses. He wore faded overalls and a red flannel shirt. A wide-brimmed straw hat rested low on his small, mostly-bald head. Directly behind him, Rex, the larger member of "The Brothers Grimm," stood motionless.

The top of the Ferris wheel was almost eye level with their perch. The ride had stopped. The young couple at the top of the wheel were necking as their seat rocked back and forth. The boy's right hand worked frantically under the girl's sweater.

The three had already scouted the carnival from the ground. After that, at The Wizard's insistence, they'd bought their tickets to see the freaks—a fat lady, a black midget with a bone in his nose—passing for a wild Pygmy, a bearded girl, a lizard man, and another guy with hands like lobster claws. They were second-rate freaks in a third-rate show, but The Wizard had come away fulfilled. He had looked into their eyes, seen their misery—felt the sense of camaraderie.

Then the three had split up. They left Tim on the ground—next to the fence—a lookout for the man they were there to meet. Rex and The Wizard kept an eye on the lookout.

"Flex has been a disappointment," The Wizard said without taking his eyes from the scene below.

Rex was tempted to say, *"Not to me."* Instead he grunted, "Yeah."

"You told me he was rather obtuse."

"I did?"

"You said he was an idiot."

"Yeah. I said *that.*"

"Actually, you said he was a *mouthy* idiot."

"Yeah."

"You were right—on both counts."

"He likes to talk," Rex replied.

"That's why he's got to go," The Wizard said without emotion. "He'll talk. Probably sooner than later."

"I know," Rex said, a hint of resignation.

"You're up to that—making sure that he's gone?"

"You already asked me—twice."

"And I'm asking again," The Wizard countered sharply. "And I may fucking ask you again tomorrow—or an hour from now. Because I need to know. I need to *hear your conviction,* Rex."

"I'm up to it," Rex answered, still motionless. "I got no problem puttin' a slug in his ear. It's like you said—he'll talk."

The Wizard's tone relaxed. He flashed a gap-toothed smile in the darkness "You are in a rarified position, Rex. I believe in you. I believe you possess the intellect to appreciate your situation."

"Thanks." Tentative.

"Those I believe in—and they are but a few—are handsomely rewarded."

"That's good to know."

"You have no idea, Rex." The Wizard paused, took a cleansing breath, then metaphorically hung the carrot. "If you help me do the things I must—I will change your life forever. But you will have to earn it."

"Just tell me what you need."

"Charlie Blades," The Wizard added—slightest twinge of remorse.

Rex felt his stomach tighten. "I figured it was comin' down to that."

"You figured correctly, Rex."

"You sure that's what you want?"

"I'm quite sure," the smaller man replied with gritty resolve. "I've had almost two years to think about what happened that night."

"Yeah, you're right about that." Rex replied uncomfortably.

"I don't like coincidence," The Wizard declared. "It occurs—I know that. But that was too much to be plausible. One—Charlie goes out for cigars, or whatever-the-hell-he went for. All of a sudden. Two—he's barely out of sight when Madrid shows up guns blazing. Then three—nearly a half million dollars of my money goes missing."

"Damn."

"I lived in a fucking eight by ten cage—like some animal. Do you have any concept what that's like?"

"I was inside," the larger man said quietly. "A year, two months and six days."

"Then you know."

"I know."

"First three months I hear nothing from Charlie—not a murmur—not a peep."

"You sure Blades took the cash? Could have been cops—or even Madrid."

"That's what Charlie said when he finally made contact."

"But you don't believe him."

"It was well hidden. I knew, and Charlie knew. Charlie's got it. But fortunately, there's a lot more that Charlie never knew about."

"Really," Rex said with renewed interest.

"One step at a time, Rex," the smaller man said. "Learn from Charlie's mistake. Madrid—then the idiot down there by the fence—then Charlie."

"I don't know Madrid, but we got plenty enough people to put him down. Timmy I could do in my sleep. But Charlie Blades is going to be a lot harder to kill."

"Leave that to me," The Wizard replied in a tone laced with equal doses of confidence and malice. "Charlie will trust me—at least to a point. Gifting him the girl should get him moving in the right direction."

"What are we going to do with her when this is done?"

"You can have her if you like."

Rex thought, chose his words carefully. "I don't know if I'll want her—you know, after Charlie gets through with her."

Silhouetted by the window, The Wizard's head bobbed knowingly. "Understandable," he said quietly. "I feel somewhat the same way myself. Drawn to her," he said, cocking his head to one side, "but at the same time repulsed." He added, as if an after thought, "I'm sure she's an exquisite sample of young womanhood."

The statement hung in the dark vastness of the room. A moment later Rex asked,

"You think she's a redhead?"

The Wizard turned around slowly—craned his head upward. "Reconsidering my offer?"

"I don't know," Rex replied unconvincingly. "Just something I heard one time—that Blades got this thing for redheads."

The Wizard smiled his gap-toothed smile. "You heard right. This *thing* goes back to when he was little more than a boy."

"Huh."

"Redheads can be so very special." He paused a beat, then added, "My mother was redheaded. Did you know that, Rex?"

The proclamation caught the big man flat footed. He answered slowly—carefully. "No. No, I didn't know that."

"No reason you would," The Wizard replied happily. He dropped his voice and added, *"Natural redhead."*

"Huh," Rex said again.

"Truly a beautiful woman," The Wizard said, almost dreamily, "What I remember most was her eyes. She had these wonderful green eyes, Rex. I would spend my days staring into them—wondering what my lovely mother was thinking. Wonder what she was *plotting*. She was a very shrewd lady—nothing was ever what it seemed. Mother's mind teamed with hidden agendas, twists and turns, plots and subplots." His small, bird-like chest expanded as he took in a lungful of the stagnant air. "Brilliantly manipulative," he said nostalgically. "Sexually manipulative—as only truly beautiful women can be." The dreaminess left his tone—his next words landed flat and emotionless. "Then suddenly—one day—she was gone." He turned his palms to the ceiling. "I never saw her again, Rex. The police came to our house eventually—maybe a week or two after she disappeared. Those idiots asked me the same questions—over and over again."

"That's rough," Rex said.

"Not so bad, really. I've moved past it."

Rex replied in an uncertain voice, "That's good."

"No one ever found her," the smaller man said. A hint of satisfaction had crept into his tone. "Her lovely body simply vanished. Her dark soul most certainly was released into hell. I've always suspected she died a horrible death."

Jesus fucking Christ, Rex thought to himself.

* * * *

Victoria Jamerson's legs ached—quivery with fatigue—her damp cotton dress clung to her legs—made it harder to walk. The wooded path had transitioned quickly—from shadows—to gloom—to darkness. She was beginning to chill. She stopped—wondered if she were still on the trail. Victoria removed the sweater she had tied around her waist, slipped it back over her shoulders. Just ahead, she could barely make out the shape of a large fallen tree—remembered it from the hike over. She was little more than halfway home, but the steepest part of the trail was behind her.

Victoria Jamerson summoned her inner strength, bit back on her fear. She couldn't remember a time in the past ten years when she hadn't been afraid of something. When her husband died, the fear had been of loneliness, and raising a daughter by herself. That emotion had opened the door for Lyle Holiday—the proverbial mirage in her desert of anxiety. For a short time, things were better. There was hope. But hope became doubt—doubt became fear—fear became terror. She needed hope to make the circle complete.

Victoria reached the fallen tree. Not enough room to crawl under and she didn't want to leave the path in the darkness. She felt along the trunk for a hand hold pulled herself up. The rough bark scraped the skin on the inside of her legs. She slid off the far side of the tree trunk, stumbled onto the path, fell face first. Her left knee landed on something hard—a rock or maybe a big root. Sharp pain shot up her leg and into her lower back. She felt dizzy. She stayed crouched on her hands and knees. She could smell the damp earth just inches from her face.

She struggled to her feet, waited for equilibrium. The waves of pain washed over her, each slightly less intense than the last. She forced her aching legs to push forward. In the pocket of her dress, she found the Swiss Army knife. Her cold, stiff fingers fumbled to open the two-inch blade. She was armed, but felt no better. Her mind, as weary as her body, struggled for a plausible excuse to offer Lyle. She was not a practiced liar—nothing came. That was at least as scary as the dark woods that surrounded her.

Up ahead there was another huge tree—an oak growing next to the trail. Its large roots stretched across her path like a gnarled hand waiting to snatch her. Victoria carefully picked her way through the web. She didn't see the man until he had wrenched the small knife from her hand.

Then it was too late.

Chapter 19

Black Creek, North Carolina
September 25th—8:38 p.m.

There was a celebration in Black Creek.

It was a contrived, merchant-driven event. *"The Welcoming of Fall Festival".* Along River Street, leaning against the lamp posts, were bundles of dried corn stalks staged with pumpkins and gourds. Most of the shops were open late and Black Creek's two bars were doing steady business. Street vendors sold hand-made crafts and food. Depending on the direction of the light breeze, the air was saturated with either the smell of barbecue, or sausage with onions and peppers, or freshly-mulled hot apple cider, or popping corn over an open fire. Marcy's Holistic Café & Country Fried Grill had a booth in front of the restaurant. Her fare ranged from curried tofu to deep-fried funnel cakes with copious toppings of honey and powdered sugar.

Along River Street, a flat-bed wagon, loaded with kids and hay bales, rolled slowly behind two large draft horses. At one end of the festival, a local band played traditional mountain music. On the other end of the street another band played bluegrass. To Alex Madrid, they sounded about the same.

His back to the railroad track that paralleled the river, Madrid sat on a park bench. He was dressed in worn blue jeans, a gray tee shirt, and his running shoes. A Carolina blue nylon wind breaker concealed the .45s strapped under each arm.

Toto had just finished off the third of three hot dogs—extra chili, no mustard, no onions. The dog was stretched on the grass beside the bench, content, but alert. Madrid had him on a short leash—figuratively and literally.

Up the hill, Madrid could make out the barred window of the cell where Dicky Padrick was held. A growing cast of characters and scenarios cycled through his head—a continuous loop of which he seemed to have little control. Dicky Padrick and Miranda Toliver. It had been less than twenty-four hours since her death, but it seemed much longer. In the past few hours Madrid had added September

Jamerson, and September's mother, Victoria. Madrid recalled the older woman fading into the tree line. He wondered if she had made it home safely—wondered if their visit had cost her a beating.

Mostly, Alex Madrid thought about The Wizard and Charlie Blades—what the two men had done to his niece. He struggled to sequester his demons. Madrid looked up apprehensively at the darkened sky. Nighttime eventually brought sleep. Sleep cleared the path to his nightmares.

Last night was the third in a row—the dream was always slightly different, but the essence never changed.

Madrid turns. Charlie Blades is there—close. Madrid has his back to a wall—sometimes the wall is stone—other times the wall is earthen and Madrid is recessed into a cavity—as if staring out from a vertical grave.

The Wizard is speaking to Charlie—so softly Madrid is able to hear only the remnants of words. His lips are curled back in a gap-toothed snarl. There are other men present.. They are always shadowy figures. They watch stoically as Charlie Blades' enormous meat hooks form a vice around Madrid's windpipe. Madrid tries to fight. Sometimes he can feel the stone wall pressing hard into his back. He is aware that life is leaving his body. From somewhere in the gloom, a girl appears. It is his niece, Sarah. She is standing just beyond Charlie Blades. Some nights Madrid can see the blood, other times, only her face. She stares down at him—sad eyes and a serene smile. Her five word soliloquy is always the same.

"I'm dead now, Uncle Alex."

Toto growled—a low-pitched throaty noise—like something from the bottom of a tomb.

"You ought to think about obedience school for that mutt," Julie Kingston said—pleasantly—from a respectable distance.

The sound of her voice made the dog tilt his head. Madrid looked up, grateful for the diversion. And Julie Kingston was a first-class diversion. She wore a white turtle-neck sweater. It stopped just below her well-defined jaw line and her silver hoop earrings. Her jeans formed nicely to her long legs. Around her neck was a .35 mm camera with a large flash unit.

Madrid adjusted his expression, studied her for moment. "Toto *has* been to school," Madrid said finally. "I just don't know which schools—or what he might have learned there."

"That's comforting." She motioned to the bench where Madrid sat. "Is it safe to sit here?"

"We're still talking about the dog?"

Julie Kingston almost smiled. "Yes."

Madrid slid over. He didn't tell her that as long as The Wizard and Charlie Blades were alive, it would never be really safe to sit near him. He looked at the big dog. "Behave, Toto," he said in a conversational tone.

"You think that will do it?" she asked, unconvinced.

"No promises."

Julie Kingston sat. Toto repositioned himself on the grass to get a better look at her. *Smart dog*, Madrid thought. "You take the pictures, too?" Madrid asked.

"It's a small paper. I do a little of everything—write the copy, take the pictures, lay it out and proof it. Write the checks."

"Ride your ten-speed around the neighborhood and toss copies on peoples' front porches?"

"No respectable paper boy—paper *person*—rides a ten speed."

"Must keep you busy," Madrid said.

"I'm not complaining," Julie said, looking over the crowd. "I like to be busy—it's better... " She let the thought trail off.

"Better than what?" Madrid asked.

"It's just better," she replied vaguely.

Madrid nodded, changed the subject. "So what's the latest news?"

"You mean about Miranda Toliver and Dicky Padrick?"

Madrid shrugged. "That, or anything else."

"They found the body of a Park Ranger over near the Tennessee line. He was in his patrol car. Someone tried to make it look like an accident, but they're pretty sure he was murdered."

"How did he die?" Madrid asked.

"They're waiting for the report," Julie answered. "He was a young guy. Newlywed."

Madrid said nothing.

"And there are the hurricanes," Julie said.

"Hurricanes are news in Black Creek?" Madrid asked skeptically.

"Not usually," she admitted. "But sometimes, and it's rare, depending on how they track, we get a lot of rain and some decent wind. There are two about to make land. With all the rain we've had already, if either of them end up near Black Creek, we're going to get some major flooding." Julie pointed across River Street. "In '63 the water inside those shops was four feet deep."

"Got any happy news?" Madrid asked.

"Sure," Julie said lightly. "Opie has a crush on Thelma Lou and Aunt Bee's pickles won second place at the county fair."

"That more like it," Madrid said. "How did Aunt Bee take that? Second place?"

"Not too well," Julie answered. "The old girl's got a dark side."

"Always suspected as much," Madrid said.

"So," Julie asked. "Having a good time?"

"Peachy," Madrid answered.

In a sweeping motion, Julie extended her right arm toward the street. "Enjoy while you can. This is just about as raucous as we get in Black Creek."

"I'll pace myself."

"That might be a good idea. You don't seem like the type that gets out much."

In the dim light he could see a smile beginning to play on her lips. He tried to think of a witty retort, but in the end Madrid conceded, "You're right, I don't."

She motioned with her head to Toto. "He must do wonders for your social life."

"He's cuddly—once you get to know him."

"I bet."

They sat—watched the activity on the street. Neither spoke. Madrid drank in the moment like a man whose soul was dying of thirst. The hay wagon creaked past them. The unmistakable smell of horse trailed behind.

"Did you raise him from a pup?" she asked.

The same question Victoria Jamerson had asked. "No," Madrid answered emphatically. "If I had, he wouldn't be this way. I took him from a couple of guys. He was almost dead—beaten and starved." Madrid looked at the dog. "He weighed about half of what he does now—maybe less."

"That's terrible." She leaned past Madrid—gave Toto a fresh look.

The dog's gold-colored eyes were locked on her.

"Don't stare at him," Madrid said. "He doesn't like it."

"Oh," Julie replied and quickly turned her head. "Were you serious when you said he'd been trained?"

"He's been trained—by sadists mostly."

"Trained to attack?"

Madrid nodded casually, "I wouldn't bet against it."

"But, you're not sure?" Julie Kingston asked incredulously.

"Not a hundred percent. That's why I don't try out a lot of new vocabulary around him." Madrid turned back to Julie Kingston. "Never really sure what the "kill" word might be."

"You're trying to be funny." It came out somewhere between a question and a statement.

"If you say so."

She looked back down at the dog—then back to Madrid. "Have you ever *seen* him attack anyone?"

Madrid offered another half smile. "No comment."

"You're not on record."

"Still no comment."

They sat. Julie took an occasional picture, Madrid watched. A small group of local boys walked by. A couple of them wore letter jackets from the local high school. They were maybe sixteen or seventeen years old—carried themselves with the confident swagger of the untested. One of them studied the German Shepherd mix—the rest studied Julie Kingston. She appeared oblivious to their attention. None of them looked directly at Madrid.

"Did you talk with Victoria?" she asked when they had passed.

"Talked with her this afternoon."

"You went to their house?" There was concern in her voice.

"No. She met me at a park near their place."

Julie thought for a moment. "Holmes Park?"

"Yeah. That's where she said she wanted to meet."

Madrid watched Julie's mouth tighten, the muscles in her jaw define. "That's really not that close to her farm. Did she drive?"

"No," Madrid said. "She came through the woods. Walked. By the time she got to the park, she looked pretty tired. After we talked, I asked her to let me drive her home. She wouldn't go for it. Insisted on walking back." Madrid watched Julie process the information. "I offered a ride," he repeated. "Twice."

Julie nodded. “I know. I’m just worried for her—and for September.”

“After talking with Pete and Victoria Jamerson, it sounds like the September had plenty of reasons to leave,” Madrid said.

“I think September would have told Victoria [redacted] that she was going.”

“Why do you think that?” Madrid asked, not quite a challenge.

After a moment, she glanced at Madrid, said in a voice barely loud enough to be heard, “I just do.”

“Maybe you’re right,” Madrid said. “But somewhere—at this very moment—someone is going out for a gallon of milk—or a tube of lipstick, or whatever. And without the benefit of forethought, they’re going to glance in the rearview mirror, see their driveway getting smaller. And they’re going to just keep right on driving. Most of the time they come back, but every so often—they don’t.”

Julie turned, fixed her brown eyes on Madrid. “Do you think that’s what September did—just kept on driving?”

“I have no idea.”

“Is that the end of it?”

“The end of what?”

“You and Victoria.”

Madrid turned. The bench was small. Their knees touched. Madrid caught the faintest whiff of her perfume. There was a sense of intimacy—forced—but still pleasant.

“I told her I needed to see September’s room.”

“Oh,” Julie conceded in a soft voice. “That’s good—I guess.”

Madrid didn’t reply. Another long pause. The distance between them seemed to grow smaller. Then the moment evaporated. Madrid watched it disappear like a bunny in a bad magic show.

Julie turned back to the street and took a picture of the hay wagon as it made another pass. The kids waved frantically. Madrid stood up—the dog was only a half second behind him. Julie turned the camera. Madrid placed his palm in front of the lens.

"I'd prefer you didn't do that," he said without much diplomacy.

"Why not?"

"Toto’s camera shy."

“You’ll tell me what you find out from Victoria?”

“Probably—unless she tells me not to.”

Julie stood up. With the heels on her boots they are almost eye to eye. "So what's your hurry, Alex Madrid? Hot date back at The Paradise Court?"

"It's my bedtime."

"It's nine o'clock," she said without glancing at her expensive watch.

"Yeah, I know," Madrid countered. "It's the weekend—my folks are letting me stay up late."

"You're a funny guy, Madrid."

"I gotta' a million of them."

"One more question," she said quickly, sounding like a reporter. "Why did you rent every room at The Paradise Court?"

"One room for me and the dog," Madrid answered. "The rest are for my imaginary friends."

Julie Kingston took three shots of Madrid as he disappeared into the crowd.

Chapter 20

Jefferson City, Tennessee
September 25th—9:26 p.m.

Nick Vorcheck sat in the passenger seat of the yellow Chevy Corvair—stared out through the filmy windshield at the kaleidoscopic light. He pondered his next move—wondered if there was still time to back out—knew there wasn't.

"You sure you ought a' do this?"

The question snapped him back into the moment.

Rhonda, Nicky's some-time-girlfriend guided a cigarette towards her lips. Her hand was unsteady, her fingernails the color of dried blood. Rhonda was a small woman—not quite five feet. Drugs kept her skinny. Her straight blonde hair hung over her right eye. The rest fell past her shoulders in unwashed strands. It was her eyes that made her face special. They were large and a brilliant shade of blue—provided her the illusion of innocence—of constant amazement. She fumbled with the plastic lighter. It sparked angrily, then produced a short, weak flame. Rhonda sucked greedily—the tobacco began to glow red.

Rhonda had parked in a spot near the fence, just beyond the residual glow of the carnival. She was along because Nick had needed a car—and she had a car—of sorts. She'd want part of whatever he came away with, Nick thought. Overhead. Rhonda was like that.

With no answer to her first question, she offered a second. "Who you gonna' meet here, Nicky?"

He could see the Ferris wheel and the Merry-Go-Round, black and white wooden horses bobbing in rhythm.

"You d-d-d-don't want to know," he answered. His chest tightened as Madrid's words played back in his head. "*Be smart and keep your mouth shut, Nicky. Don't get greedy and don't try to play this from both sides. I'll find out and—then I'll find you.*" Fuck Alex Madrid, he thought. That's exactly what he had come to do. Madrid wasn't stupid, he'd figure it out. But The Wizard was smarter—a *lot* smarter. The way Nick figured it, Madrid would be dead before any of this had a chance to blow back on him. In the meantime, if he played it right—he could double his money. Nick used the thought to comfort himself.

"I know what I'm doing," Nick said, like a line from a mantra. He pulled up on the door handle and pushed. The hinges protested loudly. He forced himself out of the car. Before he closed the door, he squatted on his haunches, looked back at Rhonda. They were almost eye to eye. "Wait here," he said in a tight voice. The confidence he'd felt a moment earlier had wandered away in the darkness. "But if I'm not back in an hour—you need to go."

Rhonda's blue eyes grew even larger. Through the cigarette smoke, she asked, "What are you talking about, Nick? I can't just leave you here."

Nick reached into the pocket of his jeans, came out with a pair of crumpled twenty dollar bills. "Do what I f-f-f-fuckin' t-t-t-tell you," he said, his tone thick with emotion.

Rhonda nodded, big blue eyes fixed on the forty dollars.

"These ain't good people, Rhonda," Nick said softly. "If I ain't back in a hour… ." He paused, took a deep breath, and stood. "I'll s-s-s-see you s-s-soon," he said—mostly to himself.

Nicholas closed the car door softly. He turned on his heals in the soft grass. He walked slowly—with resigned purpose—like a doomed man into a vortex of color.

Flex was still at the corner of the fence. He'd seen the Corvair ease into the lot. It was the kind of piece-of-crap car Vorcheck might have—but the lot was full of old piece-of-crap cars. A couple of minutes later, Flex watched Vorcheck climb out of the old Chevrolet. He squatted, said something to somebody on the driver's side. Vorcheck had been told to come alone. *This would make things more complicated.* Vorcheck threaded his way between the cars. From his jacket Flex retrieved a Radio Shack walkie-talkie, pushed the transmit button. He turned from the crowd behind him, said in a low voice, "I see him. He's headed for the main gate."

Rex's voice crackled softly from the end. "Let him come in—wander around a little. Then bring him around the back of the building. Let us know when you're headed up."

"Okay," Flex said into the walkie-talkie, "but we got a problem."

Rex saw The Wizard's silhouetted shape turn towards him. "What kind of problem?" the smaller man snapped. Problems were not part of the plan.

"Vorcheck brought company," Flex replied quietly into the walkie-talkie.

"How many?" Rex asked.

"Don't know for sure," Flex replied. "I'm guessin' one."

"I'm not paying him to guess," The Wizard hissed angrily. He moved quickly across the darkened room, the old pine floor creaked beneath him. He took the walkie-talkie from Rex, made sure the transmission button was in the "off" position. "I need to know if it's Madrid. If it is—tell the idiot boy down there to stay clear of him. Otherwise, Madrid will swat him like a fly."

"You underestimate him," Rex said.

"I doubt that," The Wizard countered in a condescending tone.

"You think Madrid's that good?" Rex asked skeptically.

The Wizard skirted the question. "Madrid is to die slowly—and in my presence. If Vorcheck brought Madrid along, tell Timmy to stay away. If it's another sort of problem—tell him to solve it. And don't be too descriptive." He nodded to the walkie-talkie. "These things are cheap. No telling who else is listening."

Rex spoke into the plastic transmitter—used generic terms that would result in a specific outcome.

* * * *

Victoria Jamerson struggled with the rope. It bound her hands behind her, tethered her to the trunk of a small poplar tree. The cold bark pressed between her shoulder blades. Her buttocks and thighs ached from where Lyle Holiday had repeatedly slapped her—first with an open hand—then with a clenched fist. "Your just punishment," he had matter-of-factly explained. Her cries of pain had energized his flaccid penis. He'd became hard enough to enter her, but had struggled to maintain the erection. The intercourse had been quick—halfhearted.

Except for her shoes, Victoria Jamerson was completely naked. Lyle had carefully folded her clothes into a neat stack, tucked them under his arm, and had walked away—swallowed by the darkness. Despite herself, Victoria had called after him, begged him not to leave her alone in the woods. Had begged the same man who'd just raped her to come back and save her.

The air temperature had dropped nearly fifteen degrees since she'd left the park. Victoria was cold—her thoughts bogged in hypothermic slush. The rope rubbed her wrists, but the knot was beginning to loosen. Part of her knew she was supposed to escape—not unlike a cat playing with a doomed mouse. Both animals acted on instinct. Victoria Jamerson was a mouse trying to survive the night.

The rope began to release its grip. Victoria stumbled away from the tree, fell onto the path. Near exhaustion, it took all of her fortitude to struggle back to her feet. Through a break in the clouds, the three-quarter moon filtered through the trees, provided just enough light to give her a sense of the path.

The next hour passed like an eternity. She worked her way along the trail. From a cut on her left knee, a thin trail of blood worked down her shin and into her shoe. Victoria Jamerson wanted to cry, but her emotions were too blunted for tears. Most of all, Victoria Jamerson wanted to stop. She thought of September—wondered if she was still alive. If she were positive her daughter were dead, she might simply lie down next to the trail. She would let the cold night siphon the life from her body. But Victoria *wasn't* sure. And it was her uncertainty that fueled the desperate sense of resolve. The uncertainty made her place one foot in front of the other.

When she finally reached the edge of the woods, she had lost all track of time. Across the overgrown field she could see her home in the moonlight. Smoke lifted lazily from the brick chimney. Victoria closed her eyes—could almost feel the warm hearth. She moved stiffly across the field, heavy weeds and occasional briars clawed at her bare legs and hips.

From the steps of the front porch, September's cat, Poncho, curiously watched her approach. Victoria Jamerson trudged across the yard—climbed the three steps that led to the porch. Next to the front door, her shredded clothes were still folded neatly. Next to the clothes three blankets were precisely stacked. Victoria collapsed onto the porch—placed one of the blankets beneath her—wrapped herself in the remaining two.

Poncho jumped down from the porch rail and stood next to her. Victoria opened the blanket. The cat cuddled itself against her chest, began to purr loudly. It was nearly an hour before Victoria stopped shivering.

* * * *

"Step right in!" the barker shouted. "Unless your heart is bad or your will is weak! See the wild boy and the snake man! Step right in, if you dare!"

Thirty yards away, Flex held his position at the corner of the fence. From that vantage, he had a clear view of the parking lot and the front gate. The night was no longer young and the ticket line was dwindling. Whoever had arrived in the car with Vorcheck was staying put. Nick shuffled through the gate, stared vacantly at nothing, talked to no one.

Flex paid no attention to the lithe black man two spaces ahead of Vorcheck in the line.

Flex was content to let him wander for a while. But Nick didn't wander. He stood slumped shouldered, shuffled his feet, his hands buried deep into the pockets of his dirty jeans. After five minutes Flex circled around, approached him from the blind side.

"Vorcheck," Flex said in a low voice.

Nick's head jerked violently, as if he'd been slapped. He stared at Flex, took in the mass of blonde hair, the muscles, the tan, and the cold blue eyes.

"Settle down, man," Flex told him firmly.

Nick nodded uncertainly.

"Let's go."

Nicholas looked around nervously. Panic squeezed his chest, made it hard for him to breath. He thought about running, but his legs felt suddenly heavy. "G-g-g-g-o where?"

The stutter made Flex smile. "Just follow me, Nicky boy. We're off to see The Wizard."

The lithe black man watched them leave.

Nick followed the blonde man past the freak show tent, past the shabby little trailers, into an alley on the side of the old mill. Beyond the mouth of the alley, the shadows were heavy. Flex stopped—Nick nearly walked into him.

"You carrying?" Flex asked.

The question caught Vorcheck off guard. "I got a little weed back in the car."

"No, Dumbfuck," Flex shot back. "I don't give a shit about your weed. You carrying a gun?"

"No," Nick replied emphatically.

"Good. Then you won't mind me checking." Flex patted him down.

They continued down the dark ally. Along the brick walls, Nicholas got a sense of discarded metal work. Broken glass crunched under his feet. They stopped at the back corner of the building. The blonde man looked back down the alley—waited, listened. When he was convinced that no one had followed, they turned the corner—followed a more narrow path along the back of the building. They stopped again. Nicholas watched him remove the chain from a metal door. The blonde man jerked his head, motioned for Nicholas to step inside. The door closed behind them—a heavy clank. The room was completely black. Nick Vorcheck felt the sweat beading on his forehead. He could hear himself breathing.

Nicholas heard the blonde man say, "We're in."

There was a short burst of static, then a disembodied voice replied, "Send him up." It was a voice Nick recognized. "Then take care of the other matter."

From the blackness, the blonde man said in a hushed tone, "There's a staircase—straight ahead—maybe fifteen or twenty feet. He's on the third floor—waitin' to hear what you gotta' say."

The door opened again. There was a wedge of gray light. The blonde man squeezed through the wedge—then it was gone. Nick turned back to where he thought the staircase should be—felt his way along—stumbled onto the bottom step. The tightness in his chest was getting worse. He started to climb. At the landing he stopped—leaned on the railing. He wiped his forehead with the palm of his hand—then wiped his wet hand on his shirt. At the next landing he stopped again. Above, he could see a faint glow, the carnival lights filtering through the windows. He reached the top of the stairs. There was a residual odor of machine oil and old wood. He could see The Wizard silhouetted against the large window. He seemed tiny—but scary as hell.

"Nicholas." The Wizard's voice floated across the room.

It reminded Nick of fingernails on a blackboard.

"Come over hear and lets have a look at you, old boy."

Nick was still holding the handrail at the top of the stairs. Reluctantly, he released the grip. His legs felt heavy. A dull pain was working down his left arm—his legs suddenly unreliable. The old wooden mill floor creaked beneath him in the darkness. Nick stopped when he got near the window—just a few paces away from The Wizard. He could see the carnival-goers wandering about three floors below him. Near the glass were the remnants of a wooden chair. It had no seat and was missing some of the pickets that formed its back. Nick pulled the chair towards him, steadied himself on the wobbly, cannibalized frame. From the shadows to his left, he sensed movement. A large man stepped from the shadows. Nicholas thought it was Charlie Blades, but it wasn't. This guy was taller than Charlie, but not as thick through the shoulders.

"Meet my associate," The Wizard said, with a slow nod. "I would introduce him, but he's the type of chap who doesn't care to have his name bandied about."

The man made a noise, something like an amused grunt.

"Okay," Nick said, not looking at the tall man. Not looking at The Wizard. The pain in his shoulder was getting worse. It felt like someone had parked a bus on his chest.

"You don't look so good, Nicholas," The Wizard said, his tone strictly observational.

"No," Nick replied. He felt a bead of sweat slide off his nose, disappearing into the darkness near his feet. "Maybe got the flu, or something."

"Yeah," The Wizard said skeptically, a hint of amusement in his tone. "No matter. Let's wrap up this happy reunion so everyone can go their merry way." Then his tone suddenly darkened, his next words a command. "Tell me what you know, Nicholas. Be succinct and be accurate. My associate here has no tolerance for—inaccuracies."

His breathing labored, Nicholas told The Wizard what he knew. He told him about the early-morning call to Alex Madrid. Nick had done his homework—had talked with people who knew people—had made phone calls—had even gone to the freakin' public library. Information equaled money. He told The Wizard about Black Creek, North Carolina—Black Creek College—The Paradise Court.

"Madrid's got this dog you might want to watch out for," Nicholas said.

"A dog?" The Wizard asked, in an agitated tone. "Madrid has a dog?"

"Yeah," Nicholas said, leaning heavily on the remains of the chair.

"What sort of dog?"

"I d-d-don't know much ab-b-bout dogs."

"Big dog?" The Wizard asked, spreading his hands out to his side. "Or little dog?" He moved his forefinger to about an inch from his thumb. He held his hand up to his eye, sighted Nick through the gap.

"It's b-b-b-big and m-m-mean as a m-m-motherfucker—they say."

"They say, indeed." The Wizard spun on his heals, turned to Rex. "The son of a bitch stole my dog," he said angrily, spittle forming on the sides of his mouth, his screechy voice getting louder.

The lack of light in the room masked Rex's confusion. "I hear what you're sayin'," he said uncertainly. *Why the hell are we talking about a fucking dog?* "I guess you and this dog were pretty tight."

"I loathed that over-grown half-bred beast," The Wizard shot back, his voice still gaining volume. "That isn't the goddamn point! Madrid stole from me! The goddamn motherfucker stole from me! He's a goddamned thief!"

"Okay," Rex said, raising his arms, showing his palms. "I hear what you're sayin,, but this ain't the time to be getting' loud about it."

Before Rex's last word finished echoing about the cavernous space, The Wizard had regained his composure. He had flipped the internal switch, his small body relaxed—his thoughts flowed clear, like a cool rushing stream.

The Wizard moved to where Nick Vorcheck stood half-slumped against the chair. He spoke in a soft, conversational tone. "Alex Madrid stole my fucking dog, Nicholas. And while I have no particular love for this animal—actually quite the contrary—it still belongs to me. I'm extremely disappointed you did not make me aware of this sooner."

The words came to Nick as if ~~spoke~~ spoken from a great distance, their meaning complex and ambiguous. He raised his head, surprised the little man was so close. The colored lights from the carnival washed over the left side of The Wizards' face, left the other side in villainous shadow.

"He killed the love of my life," he said, as if just recalling the fact. "Alex Madrid did that to me. Were you aware of that, Nicholas? She was my only *true* love. A beautiful woman/child with long red curls. And her skin was perfectly perfect—milky white and not a freckle anywhere on her body." He added with a lascivious twist. "I know this for a fact."

The gap toothed-man was still talking. Nick could hear his voice, distant and scratchy, like an old phonograph. But the words arrived void of meaning. Nick made one final calculation—realized there would be no doubling up today. He was seconds from being tapped out.

"....and ruined my best friend," The Wizard droned on. "Turned him completely against me. Poor Charlie. Totally and completely ruined. To the point I am now going to have to kill...... "

The chair Nicholas had leaned on catapulted away from him. It made a loud echoing rattle as it skidded across the floor. Nicholas landed on his knees, both at the same time—a dull thud. Just for a moment, he held that position, eyes forward—back straight. Then, like a freshly-sawn tree, he slowly pitched forward. Nicholas landed hard, face down on the dark, dirty floor. His last thought was of the forty dollars he'd given to Rhonda.

* * * *

At that exact moment—as Nicholas Vorcheck fell to his knees—wasted his last thought—died face down on the dirty floor—Rhonda was staring at the two twenty dollar bills. She had placed them on the dash board of the Corvair and had attempted to rub out the wrinkles with the palm of her hand. She laid them on her lap, stared at the bills, wondered how much longer she should wait for Nicky. Then she heard the tap on the window. Startled, she jumped, the bills floated to the floorboard. A man was standing next to her. He was blonde and his arms rippled. He smiled down at her, his white teeth flashed in the darkness.

Rhonda found herself rolling down the window.

The man leaned in a little further. Rhonda saw a glint of a thin gold neck chain, caught a faint whiff of cologne. "Hi," the man said in a pleasant voice.

"Hi," Rhonda replied, wondering if this guy could appreciate her blue eyes in the faint light.

"Kinda lonely out here, isn't it?" he said, suggestive, but still pleasant.

"I guess," Rhonda said.

The blonde man came straight to the point. "My wife's got my two boys inside." He tossed his blonde head in the direction of the carnival. "I figure I got about thirty or forty minutes before one of them losses their supper on the rides."

"Uh-huh," Rhonda said uncertainly.

"I saw you counting your money. I was wondering if you'd like to make a little more?"

"Here?"

"Yeah—unless you're married—or got a boyfriend or something." Flex looked around as if suddenly concerned. "Look, if I offended you or something. I apologize. I *really* apologize."

The feigned anxiety achieved just what he had hoped. Rhonda relaxed. "Don't worry, honey," she said softly, trying to calculate how long she might have before Nick returned. "We can work something out. There ain't no need for you to be lonely."

Flex came to the point. "How much?"

Rhonda calculated again—supply versus demand—cost of service in a hick town versus the same service in a big city. She considered the micro and the macro economics of the situation. She thought about the forty dollars lying by her feet—decided to double up.

"Forty," she said with more confidence than she felt.

The blonde man winced. "Kinda high, baby."

Rhonda smiled. "I'm good, baby. It'll seem like a bargain when I'm done with you."

The blonde man stood for a moment, pretending to weigh the offer. He continued the negotiation. "Okay," the man said finally. "But we need to get on with it."

Now it was business. Rhonda said "I need to see the money up front."

Flex handed her two more twenties. Rhonda took the bills, slid them under the seat. Flex climbed in the passenger side, closed the door. Rhonda hoped there wouldn't be much foreplay. There wasn't. Flex reached inside her blouse, groped her tiny breasts, pinched her nipples. Rhonda unzipped his jeans, reached inside. Flex guided her mouth down to his lap. Rhonda bobbed her head up and down enthusiastically.

Flex allowed her to go longer than he'd planned, then said, "Wait a minute."

Rhonda stopped, looked up at him and said, "What's wrong?"

Flex smiled down at her. "Nothing, baby. You weren't kidding about being so good." He brushed her hair away with one hand, and softly caressed the side of her face with the other.

Rhonda smiled back up at him and said, "Told you so."

With the smile still fixed onto his handsome face, Flex replied, "Yes, you did."

"You have the most beautiful blue eyes I've ever seen."

Rhonda smiled again, placed a gentle kiss on the tip of his penis. "Thank you," she replied softly.

"You're welcome," he said, matching her tone.

Flex made a small adjustment with his hands. There was a violent twist. Rhonda's neck snapped. It was an ugly sound that seemed to reverberate inside the car for an inordinate span of time. Flex sat perfectly still, eyes straight ahead. He waited for her to die. Didn't have to wait long. He reached under the seat, found the two twenties—found two more in the floor board. He zipped his pants, stepped out of the car. Flex looked around the darkened lot—pocketed his profit—walked back towards the lights.

Chapter 21

September 26th—8:01 a.m.

Victoria Jamerson stood at the stove, wore a faded floral knee-length dress protected by a red apron. Over a blue flame, thick slabs of bacon sizzled in a heavy black skillet. On the counter was a bag of Martha White flour, a container of blueberries, and a small glass bowl with fresh eggs pyramided above the rim. Behind her, less than eight feet away, Lyle sat at the table, his Bible spread before him.

Victoria had spent most of the last hour in the bathroom, under a shower spray as hot as she could stand. The water had slithered over the bruises on her arms and shins, over the small welts on her thighs and buttocks. Victoria had bandaged the cut on her knee, combed her wet hair away from her face.

At the stove, her shaking hands were anchored on the countertop, her eyes glazed with strain. She struggled to connect simple thoughts with actions. Lyle demanded pancakes on Sunday. This time of year he liked them with fresh blueberries and real maple syrup. Always a side of eggs and bacon. From behind her, she heard the chair scrape on the floor as he adjusted his position. He was getting hungry—impatient.

Lyle Holiday laid his Bible on the table, opened to a page marked with a black silk ribbon. He studied his wife. She was braced against the counter, head slightly bowed—as if in prayer—or defeat. He folded his large hands in front of him—waited patiently—reverently.

Victoria stared into the mixing bowl. *Pancakes,* she thought. Her mother had taught her to make them. She'd made hundreds, maybe thousands since then. *Pancakes.* She studied the items on the white metal counter. There was something else she needed. She struggled to recall the ingredients, the proportions. *Damn it all!* She felt her body flinch, readying for a blow. *Had she screamed that aloud?* It took a moment to realized the screams were only in her head. Victoria moved to the refrigerator, pulled the heavy chrome handle. A weak light was shone over the sparse contents. It came to her. *Buttermilk.* She needed buttermilk.

"Everything all right, Victoria?" Lyle said, from the table behind her. His deep voice seemed to reverberate in the small room.

Victoria flinched again.

Like a dog after a righteous beating, he thought. Another faint smile tugged at one corner of Lyle Holiday's mouth.

"I'm fine," Victoria answered, her voice just above a whisper.

"You should look at me when you speak," Lyle told her, his voice tranquil.

Victoria turned, looked down at him. His smile was still in place. "I'm fine," she repeated. "Are you hungry?"

He nodded, "You know I am, Victoria."

She nodded, turned back to the mixing bowl.

Lyle spoke again, an edge creeping into his tone. "That hike last night left me famished."

Victoria said nothing. She cracked an egg, poured buttermilk into the bowl with the flour. She waited.

"Look at me," he commanded.

Victoria turned, keeping her hands on the counter for support. She forced her vacant stare from the floor to his face.

Lyle felt encouraged. He saw no residue of his wife's sudden, and inexplicable, display of rebellious independence. She seemed back to her old self—the way Lyle liked her—marginally afraid—completely compliant. To reinforce the thought, Lyle picked up the Bible—adjusted the distance for reading. He glanced up at the woman before him to make sure she was properly attentive.

"'....Wives," he read in a clear voice, *"'submit to your husbands as to the Lord. For the husband is the head of the wife as Christ is the head of the church, his body, of which he is the Savior. Now as the church submits to Christ, so also wives should submit to their husbands in everything.'"*

Victoria watched Lyle's mouth forming the syllables. His words tumbled into the space between them—meaningless—undecipherable.

There was a knife in the drawer by the sink—just a few inches from her right hand. The knife had belonged to her father—a long deep blade with a nasty curved tip. The handle ~~hand~~ had been carved from some sort of antler. She rarely used it. It had always seemed more like a weapon than a kitchen utensil. If she could will her hands to stop shaking, she could slip it out of the drawer—conceal it beneath her apron. She would hand Lyle his plate of blueberry pancakes. Then stab him. But where? Stab him in the shoulder? No. Victoria had never heard of anyone dying from being stabbed in the shoulder. Stab him in the chest? Maybe. But he might see that coming. And there were a lot of bones in the chest. She would have to stab him very hard. Stab him in the neck? Yes! Stab him in the side of the neck. The neck was soft—the knife would slide right in. She would stab Lyle in the side of the neck and run. Would that kill him? Maybe—but what if it didn't?

Lyle removed the black silk marker, gently closed the Bible. "Ephesians," he said. "Five twenty-two, twenty-three, and twenty-four."

The knife in the drawer seemed a thousand miles away. Victoria Jamerson looked into the eyes of her common-law husband. "I'm sorry," she said in a capitulatory tone.

Lyle pressed the palms of his hands together, his chin rested on the tips of his index fingers—a prayerful pose. "I know you are, Victoria," he said sanctimoniously, "and I forgive you."

* * * *

"Thumbelina."

She would say the word with a musical lilt in her voice. Like a happy surprise. Like she was discovering the word for the first time. She would draw out the next-to-last syllable—let the "a" die on the tip of her pink tongue. The Wizard did the math in his head. *Jesus.* It had been almost twenty years. *Twenty fucking years.* That was plenty of time for any memory to fade. But this one hadn't. She had been gone for more than half of his life, but it still seemed like yesterday.

"Thumbelina."

The word was like a rotting corpse that floated to the surface of an inky-black pond. And it had floated to the surface almost every day. Each time, it left a putrid taste in his throat. On the worst days the taste never went away.

"Thumbelina."

A haunting, mocking mantra. With every utterance he would see her face—never-changing—beautiful—tragic. Red hair—green eyes—ivory white shoulders. It was the ultimate irony—one he had never seen coming. Once she was finally gone, she never left. At the exact instant Lilly had taken her last breath, her soul had climbed into his head. It lived there, thrived there—often restless and always cruel. The other girls helped. Girls with red hair—and green eyes—and ivory white shoulders. Somehow, their presence kept the real Lilly at bay. At least for a while.

"Thumbelina."

Not "my *Thumbelina."* That term might have inferred the slightest hint of endearment—of connection.

"Thumbelina."

Not to be confused with a term of affection. Mother had made that clear.

* * * *

After Nick Vorcheck's coronary swan-dive, The Wizard had changed vehicles. The black Caddie was gone. Rex had replaced it with a beige station wagon. It was big, with fake wooden panels. Jimmy Carter stickers plastered the rear bumper. Rex had the cruiser barge pointed towards Gatlinburg, the AM radio was broadcasting a ranting Baptist preacher. The Wizard listened intently to parts of three different sermons as the signal came and went. He nodded appreciatively when the preaching turned to fire and brimstone, the devil, Lucifer, Beelzebub—anything to do with hell.

Rex kept their speed just under the limit. Flex was sprawled across the back seat, asleep and snoring. The Wizard had moved up to the passenger seat—his props in place. A large Alabama road map was unfolded in front of him. Freshly shaven, he wore a shoulder-length brown wig and a large pair of women's sunglasses. Around his neck, he had knotted a turquoise-colored scarf. His lips were painted bright pink. They had already passed three cops this morning, two locals and a Tennessee Highway Patrol. No one had given them a second glance. Just good folks out for a Sunday drive.

The Wizard switched off the radio and said, "Johnny Lorenz."

Rex diverted his eyes from the road—surveyed the small man in half drag beside him—silently noted how comfortable he seemed in the costume. "What about him?" he asked.

"Do you know Johnny?" The Wizard asked.

"A little. Seen him around some. Survivalist guy. Came back from 'Nam a little fucked up. Maybe he went over there the same way—I don't know. He's got dogs."

"That right," The Wizard said, not looking up from his map. "He's the dog guy."

"Okay," Rex replied.

"Johnny Lorenz is the guy with the meanest goddamn dogs in five states."

"Okay," Rex repeated. "I guess."

"We need him," The Wizard said definitively.

Rex tapped the brakes. Up ahead, the road crowded a small church with weathered siding and no steeple. It was obvious, at some point, the road had been widened at the church's expense. The ancient graveyard was so close travelers could almost read the names from the sparse tombstones. Three generations of a black family were making their way inside.

"Okay," Rex said, not bothering to hide his confusion. "Mind if I ask why?"

"It's simple," The Wizard said impatiently. "Johnny's the dog guy and we need dogs. He's got dogs trained to work as a team. And they like to kill things."

Rex shifted his hands on the wheel. "We're going to kill Madrid with dogs?" Rex asked skeptically.

"Noooo," The Wizard answered thoughtfully. "But it's an interesting idea." A smile spread across his painted lips. "I need to think about that."

* * * *

At The Paradise Court, Alex Madrid's motel room smelled of wet dog, Alpo, and coffee—but mostly wet dog and Alpo. He stood in the open doorway, freshly shaved and showered. He wore his clothes from yesterday with the addition of a heavy crew-neck sweater over the gray tee shirt. Madrid leaned on the door casing, held the mug in his right hand. The steam from the mug struggled upward into the cool moist air. Over his shoulder, he heard the dog noisily working his way to the bottom of the stainless-steel feeding bowl. In front of him, rain danced in the dark puddles of the parking lot—overflowed the rims of the morose little fountain. The stone was streaked—green, pink and black. Placed back-to-back, three cherubs adorned the top of the fountain. With dark, pitted eyes, they stared out over their bleak surroundings. Prisoners doing life. Madrid sipped hot coffee—stared back at them.

He thought about Miranda Toliver's dead blue eyes—about Dicky Padrick's unlikely story of a big man dressed in black—about Victoria Jamerson's steadfast expression as she entered the darkening woods on her trip back home. Madrid thought about the dream—it had visited him again. Had something been different? He struggled to remember. His mind churned—a hamster on a wheel—growing tired and getting nowhere.

Madrid stepped back into the room. Toto had just finished his bowl, looked up hopefully. "That's it, Pal," Madrid told him, pulling open the latch of the green antique refrigerator. "No dessert on the menu this morning." He extracted a container of fresh pineapple, a honeydew melon, and two Granny Smith apples. He cut the melon into bite-sized pieces, quartered and seeded the apple, tossed in a handful of raisins and a few chopped pecans. He dumped all of it into the only bowl in the room, sprinkled the mixture with cinnamon, then drizzled it with sourwood honey he'd bought from a roadside vendor. Madrid took the bowl back outside under the metal awning. Toto followed him—sprawled on the concrete slab. Madrid considered sitting. His legs were feeling the effect of the run. But rain had blown in on the chairs. Finding a towel and drying one off seemed like too much effort. He stood—stabbed the first bite of melon and pineapple. Then the phone rang.

* * * *

Frustration and anger—separated only by a thin, delicate membrane—on his best days.

Breakfast hadn't gone as Charlie Blades had hoped. Anna Marie had sat next to him, her chair pulled close. She was in her white, gauzy dress—her red curls pulled back from her face with a white ribbon. She smelled like flowers. Around her neck she wore a thin silver necklace with tiny dogwood petals. Charlie had seen it in the market where he'd purchased their food. A bauble, a shiny trinket that hung on a display rack alongside flashlight batteries, Bic lighters, and razor blades. He had presented it to her, carefully placed it around her neck. And that's where the illusion had stalled.

Anna Marie had remained silent—her green eyes fixed on something well beyond the walls of the cottage. She sat perched like a bunny next to a wolf—timid—frozen—waiting to be devoured. She'd barely glanced at the eggs Charlie had prepared. She'd eaten half a piece of sausage—nibbled the edge of a biscuit.

Conversation had never been Charlie's long suite, but he'd tried. Tried to talk with her. He'd asked her questions--conversational questions dipped in normalcy. Her answers had come back in single words, spoken just above a whisper. At one point Charlie thought she was about to cry. After a few minutes, he gave up. Felt foolish for choreographing the charade. He ate the mound of food on his plate—then finished what was left on hers.

They laid on one of the beds upstairs. The room looked out onto a deck that looked out over Gatlinburg, but the town had disappeared below the fog and rain. Anna Marie lay on her side, stared out at the gray wall just beyond the deck railings. Charlie was behind her, his heavy muscular arm draped over the curve above her hip. His hand casually caressed her stomach. He could feel the tension in her body.

He leaned his head next to her ear. "You don't need to be afraid of me," he told her. "I ain't really that bad a guy." His voice was matter-of-fact—as if the information were self-evident.

Anna Marie hadn't spoken—hadn't moved.

"I got a little money—not rich or nothin', but I got a little," he told her.

Silence.

"I ain't that bad," he repeated. This time there was hint of contrition in his tone. "My whole life has been kinda fucked up. It ain't how I planned it—it just kinda' happened that way. You ever have that happen? You not really sure where you're goin'? And then you end up somewhere you never wanted to be?"

Charlie watched the red curls nod, almost imperceptibly.

Charlie Blades looked around the room then back at the girl he was holding. "Yeah, I guess you have," he said in a self-mocking tone.

He pulled her closer, pressed his knees behind her thighs. His mouth was next to her ear. "Anna Marie," he said. It was the first time he had called her by her name. "Some men are goin' to be comin' here." He heard a rush of air escape from her abdomen, as if she'd been struck. "I know one of them. He's a friend of mine—sort of. I've known him a long time. There will be other men with him—I don't know how many—probably two or three—but there might be more."

Another moment passed. Anna Marie rolled over to face Charlie Blades. Their faces were only inches apart. She could smell the coffee on his breath. She spoke. There was terror in her voice—the kind of terror that two days ago would have aroused him. Now it left only a feeling of anguish. "Are these men going to rape me?"

It took him a moment to process the question. *Rape?* It wasn't a concept he could fully grasp. Sexually, Charlie Blades had only known three kinds of women. There were hookers, and occasionally those too drunk or stoned to care—and then there were the few—carefully selected—like Anna Marie. Each had been taken with varying degrees of force. Consent had never been plugged into Charlie's sexual formula.

"No," he told her, suddenly deciding. "I ain't goin' to let that happen—not to you."

"Are you sure?" she asked, unconvinced.

Charlie looked into her green eyes, saw her fear. He could feel the urge building inside him. *Rape.* It was all he really knew. "It ain't going to happen," he said, this time with more conviction.

Anna Marie buried her face into his chest and began to cry.

* * * *

The phone was next to the bed, a heavy black metal instrument with a rotary dial. The bell was loud and insistent. Toto raised his head. On the second ring he cocked his head to one side. Madrid walked back into the room, picked up the receiver. All of the calls were routed through a switchboard in the office. A female voice, groggy and sounding hung over said, "You gotta' call."

"Okay," Madrid said. "Any chance it will be a private call?"

"I'm not a snoop. I got better things to do with my mornin', anyway."

There was a click, then another click, then silence. After a long pause another female voice came on the line—a voice Madrid recognized. She spoke with halting words in a hushed tone.

"Mr. Madrid?"

"Good morning, Ms Jamerson." But her voice didn't sound like it was a good morning.

"Can you come to my house?"

"I suppose I could," Madrid replied. "Is something wrong?"

There was a pause. "No—not really," she finally replied unconvincingly. "You said you wanted to see September's room. That seeing it might help you find her. Do you remember saying that?"

"I do."

"Then you should come now," she said in a rush of words, her tone somewhere between panic and desperation

"Okay," Madrid answered. "But you're sure you're all right?"

"This is not about me, Mr. Madrid," she answered, emotion welling up in her voice. "You must find my daughter."

"I never told you I could find your daughter, ma'am."

"But you have to try. *Somebody* has to try. I don't know anyone else, Mr. Madrid. Will you come here?"

"I said I would."

"Then please come now. Lyle has just left for church. He will be back in exactly two hours and twenty minutes."

Chapter 22

September 26th—10:00 a.m.

Madrid followed the directions Victoria Jamerson had given him. Along the way, he filled the Blazer with gas and a Thermos with coffee. He had expected to be back near the park, but the road had split outside of Black Creek. Madrid and the dog headed east into a farming community. They drove past a series of the small family farms—weathered gray barns—fields dotted with large rolled hay bales—seemingly endless rows of feed corn.

Just past a large tobacco barn, Madrid left the pavement. The gravel road was narrow with pockets of soft mud that required some finesse. After about half a mile he crossed a good-sized creek on a one-lane bridge. The creek, normally little more than a shallow lazy trickle, was moving fast and dotted with white froth. After the bridge, the road became more narrow. A mile past the bridge, Madrid spotted a faded yellow mailbox. The name "Jamerson" had been crossed through. "Holiday" was scrawled in red letters.

The driveway was long. Weeds had claimed the middle ground, but Madrid could see the remnants of recent tire tracks on either side. The approach wound back into a stand of white pines--stopped in front of a white one-story frame house in need of paint. In the overgrown field just beyond the house, Madrid could make out the rusty remains of an old pickup truck. It reminded him of the half-eaten carcass of some prehistoric animal. Behind the house was a large red barn. The doors to the loft were open. Madrid remembered Pete Wilson's story. Victoria's first husband had fallen to his death.

Madrid rolled to a stop, lowered the windows a couple of inches. Toto was sprawled on the back seat. "Don't tear up anything," he told the big mutt.

Sunk into the earth, rounded creek stone created a path from the driveway. The stones led him under a large apple tree with a whitewashed trunk—up to the steps of the covered side porch. In the far corner, curled on a blanket, a yellow cat nervously watched his approach. Madrid knocked on the screen door; it was warped and rattled noisily. The cat bolted, hit the wet grass, did a U-turn, and darted under the porch.

Victoria Jamerson waited in a wing chair next to the window that overlooked the side yard and the driveway. Over the past two weeks, the chair had become her lookout post. She peered through the glass, waited for her daughter's return. Victoria Jamerson had prayed—sometimes half-hearted—sometimes with every shred of faith she could muster. She had begged God for September's safety—had sworn promises of sacrifice and change—had tried her damnedest to broker a deal.

But as far as she could tell, God wasn't listening. Now she was down to this—a man sneaking to her home while her husband was at church—some stranger with a scary-looking dog she had met in a park.

Victoria had watched Madrid's Blazer roll slowly up the driveway. She tried to remember the last person to visit her. *The preacher on the day of her husband's funeral?* That was almost eight years ago. *Could that even be possible? Eight years?* She worked to gather her thoughts. Fear circled her like a starving pack of wolves. She was terrified of what Lyle might do if he found Alex Madrid in his home. It never occurred to her that Lyle Holiday would be no match for the man standing on her porch.

She waited for the knock, rose stiffly from the comfort of the big chair. She moved through the tiny parlor and into the kitchen. She opened the door, studied Madrid through the torn screen. There was an edge about him she hadn't noticed yesterday. In his eyes she sensed an unlikely combination of cunning and compassion. A thought skipped across the surface of her mind. *An avenging angel. The Lord sometimes works in mysterious ways.*

"Come in," she said quietly.

Victoria Jamerson opened the kitchen door, silhouetted by the bright lights in the kitchen. Even in shadow, Madrid could see she was not the same woman as yesterday. Overnight, she had aged a decade. "Come in," she told him, her voice just above a whisper—as if someone were asleep nearby.

Madrid followed her through the tidy kitchen. He could smell the lingering aroma of bacon. The house was small—white plaster walls with simple pine trim. The pine had been stained a dark orange. No pictures on the walls, no rugs on the floor. Madrid saw no radio, no television, and no books. He had already noted the bruise on Victoria's cheek—the small cut on her lip. She moved gingerly and carefully lowered herself into a big upholstered chair.

"I would like to offer you some coffee or tea, Mr. Madrid," Victoria Jamerson said in a meek, apologetic voice, "but my hus....Lyle, doesn't believe in alcohol or stimulants."

Madrid took a seat across from her on one end of the sofa. His eyes didn't move from hers. He wanted to ask, *"What the hell happened to you?"* But, except for the particulars, he already knew. After a moment he said, "Would *you* like a cup of coffee, Mrs. Jamerson? I have a thermos in my truck."

"I... ." Her voice trailed off. "I... ." Again, the thought died.

"I got it at that little Mom and Pop place just outside of Black Creek," Madrid said casually as he rose from the sofa. "It's nothing special, but really not bad."

Victoria Jamerson nodded her head jerkily—tried not to cry.

A few minutes later she was nestling the cup in both hands. Madrid had added just a splash of milk and a spoonful of honey at her request. She took a sip and closed her eyes.

"Thank you, Mr. Madrid," she said.

"As I said yesterday," he said, "I'd like it better if you just called me Alex."

She took another sip from the cup, nodded. "Alex," she said, trying out the name. "Then you should call me Victoria."

"Thank you, Victoria," Madrid replied. He glanced at his watch; it is ten twenty-seven. He figured he might have an hour before she would ask him to leave. "Tell me why you called, Victoria." The answer was blatantly obvious, but he needed a place to start.

She stopped sipping coffee, spoke softly. A measure of resolve had returned to her voice. "I called you because I don't have anyone else *to* call," she replied without apology. "I am desperate to find September. I can't go through what's left of my life not knowing."

"Not knowing where she is?" Madrid asked.

"I think I know what you're trying to say—or trying not to say. I've..... ." Victoria paused, looked out the window—waited for the wave of emotion to pass. She turned, looked directly at Madrid. She spoke—a quake in her voice. "It was a very long night," she said. "But maybe it was a blessing."

Madrid said nothing.

Victoria Jamerson dropped her gaze to the half-empty cup "I've had more time to think," she said. "I realize the... ." She paused. "There could be.... ." Another pause—another stare out the window.

Madrid let her find her own pace.

"Something bad might have happened to September. I know that now," she said finally. "I have prayed every hour of everyday that my daughter is alive. But if September is dead—I still need to know. I can't go on not knowing."

Madrid flashed back to similar conversation, like a fist to the gut. That had also been on a Sunday morning, but in a big house with a wall of windows that looked out over the twelfth green of some golf course. They had sat on a high deck, had sipped fresh orange juice, had watched the carts roll up the path. Golfers in brightly-colored clothing disembarked with club in hand—took their swings—rolled on. The woman had told him that she had prayed for the safe return of her daughter. She had told him there was no one left to turn to. Madrid had agreed. He had found the girl, but the woman's prayer remained unanswered. The daughter was dead and Alex Madrid's sister didn't speak to him anymore.

Victoria Jamerson raised her head slowly—blinked back tears. Like a tall, powerful wave, hopelessness crashed over her. It left her battered—washed away any sense of false courage. She stared blankly at the man sitting next to her—embraced the futility of his presence. Suddenly, she felt foolish and tired.

Madrid sensed the mercurial change. "Maybe I can help you, Victoria," he said, the words out of his mouth too quickly, "but you have to tell me the truth. I need to ask you some questions, and you need to tell me the truth." Madrid's voice was firm—no non-sense. "Not selected truths and not half truths. I'll decide what's important and I'll decided what I need to know. Do you understand?"

She nodded, spoke in a tearful whisper. "I understand."

"Okay then," Madrid said.

"Do you really think you can find September?"

"Like I said—*maybe,*" Madrid replied. He didn't mention the chances of finding her body were greater than the chances of finding her alive.

"What do you want to know?"

"Yesterday you said September had no close friends. Nobody she talked about at the college. No boyfriend you were aware of. I don't suppose any of that has changed?"

"No."

Madrid nodded. "Then let's talk about her life here—in this house."

It was Victoria Jamerson's turn to nod.

"Specifically, I want to know about Lyle Holiday." Madrid watched the tension register in her face and body. The coffee cup became unsteady. She cradled it in both hands, lowered it to her lap. "What was his relationship with September?"

"I'm not sure I know what you mean, " Victoria countered defensively.

Madrid had exhausted his ration of tact, "I think you know exactly what I mean."

"No," she replied, her voice just above a whisper.

Madrid glanced at his watch, changed tactics. "I need to see September's room now. It's going to take me a while to go through her things."

"That would help you find her?" she asked, still hesitant and unconvinced.

"I don't know," Madrid answered impatiently, "and I won't know until I've had a chance to look."

The older woman sat motionlessly in her chair, her long fingers laced tightly around the half-empty coffee cup. "The room is locked," she said finally. "I have a key."

Victoria reached deeply into the pocket of her sweater. When her hand emerged, it held a saw-toothed piece of metal between her thumb and forefinger. She handed it to Madrid, like a secret prize from some perverse contest.

Madrid rose from the sofa, gently removed the key from her grasp. "Which room is your daughter's, Victoria?"

"At the end of the hall," she replied in a sad, quiet voice.

Madrid followed the narrow hallway past a bathroom with a cast-iron bathtub with rusting claw feet. The door was five panel, painted white with a brass door knob and plate. There was a slot for a skeleton key below the knob, but the key Madrid held was for the deadbolt that had been installed sometime later. He used the key, pushed the door open. Madrid noted the deadbolt was keyed on both sides—designed to keep someone out, or keep someone in.

Like the rest of the house, September's room was small, a single window on the north wall. The heavy drape allowed only a thin sliver of light around the edges. Madrid flipped the light switch. Two of the three naked bulbs in the center of the ceiling began to glow, the result no less depressing. Madrid remained in the doorway, sent his eyes slowly around the dreary space. The furniture looked handmade—vintage and substantial. The room arrangement was bizarre. A small bed, made of oak and poplar, was situated in the corner of the room furthest from the window. The rest of the furniture—a small desk, a ladder-backed chair, a chest of drawers, and a single night stand—were grouped tightly around the bed. The access to the bed was unclear; the implication was obvious. September Jamerson had circled the wagons.

Madrid moved the desk to one side, entered the semi-circle. He'd long ago lost count of the number of searches he had conducted. In the beginning, there had been a sense of forbidden excitement—the uncovering of clues and secret vices. But another part of him had often felt a twinge of guilt and hypocrisy. Alex Madrid had plenty of secrets of his own—vices to spare.

But now he felt neither. Just another room that needed to be searched.

Madrid moved through the young woman's belongings with methodical dexterity. He started with the bed—felt the pillows, looked between the mattress and box springs, used a small flashlight and checked beneath the bed. Madrid removed every drawer in the chest nightstand and desk—looked in, behind, and under. In one of the drawers, he found a photograph of September and Victoria. It was in a silver frame, buried beneath some socks and tee shirts. The pair sat primly on a white wrought-iron bench—smiling—staring back at him. The bench was in the middle of a flower garden full of tulips and hyacinths. They wore long-flowing, white dresses. Each wore a pink ribbon in her hair. Madrid figured the photo was nine or ten years old. There was an indisputable beauty in both the woman and the child. They were holding hands. Real or contrived, the photo appeared to capture a moment of serenity.

Madrid stared at the picture, then looked around the dreary room. He thought about the young woman who had slept here, thought about the battered woman standing guard next to the window. A black, toxic rage began to take shape in his psyche. He knew it well—hated it—feared it. But on occasion—embraced it. Madrid removed the photograph from the frame—slid it into the pocket of his field jacket.

In another drawer were two sweaters and a sweatshirt. In another were three bras and six pairs of panties—all plain white cotton. On the floor under the desk, two red bricks served as bookends. Seven books were stacked neatly between them. Six were academic; the other book a Bible. Madrid removed them one at a time, rifled through the pages. Nothing but words. There was a stack of composition books with thin wire rings, each labeled to correspond with her classes. Madrid flipped through each one—found a class schedule. Pocketed it with the photograph.

He checked his watch. He had been in the room for about fifteen minutes. Standing in the center of the make-shift fortress, he closed his eyes—cleared his mind. Madrid asked himself, *Where would* I *hide something in this room?* Certainly not where he'd just looked. He looked up. The ceiling was plaster. It appeared solid and intact. He stepped out of the circle of furnishings—moved around the room—studied the floor. It was oak, roughly three inch planks butted together in a staggered pattern. Finally, Madrid moved to the closet.

Two dresses and a winter coat hung from the rod. There was nothing on the self above. Madrid checked the pockets of the coat. He found a wadded tissue and a gum wrapper—Juicy Fruit.

The walls of the closet were solid cedar planks, still faintly aromatic. Madrid ran the flashlight beam over the closet floor, traced the path of the six-inch baseboard. He paused the light in the back corner. The beam revealed a slight gap between the baseboard and the wall. Two empty nail holes. Madrid knelt in the small, claustrophobic space. He pulled lightly on the baseboard; it fell away easily. Carefully, without any noise, he eased the board away from the wall. There was a small cavity, maybe five inches high and twelve inches long. Inside the hole, was a gray metal box with a black plastic handle. Madrid slid the box from its hiding place. The box was locked; the lock was medium quality. It would take him a few minutes to get it open. He took a final look in the hole before replacing the baseboard. The box was too large to smuggle past Victoria Jamerson. Madrid realized he'd have to make a decision. He could share, or he could lie. Not a hard choice, really. He walked across the room to the window, opened it as quietly as possible. There was no screen, which made the task easier. With the box in his left hand, he reached out the window as far as he could, dropped it the last couple of feet onto the wet grass. He closed the window and spent a few more minutes searching.

Victoria Jamerson was still sitting in the chair next to the window. She turned as Madrid came down the hallway—offered an expectant look as he entered the room. Her coffee cup was empty. Without speaking, Madrid took it to the kitchen, drained the rest of the Thermos, added the milk and honey. He returned to the room—handed the cup back to the beleaguered woman.

She thanked him.

Madrid nodded. He perched on the edge of the sofa. Their knees almost touched. *Intimacy by design.*

"Did you find anything?" she asked.

"Yes and no," Madrid answered. "And maybe."

"I don't know what that means," she said.

Madrid offered a smile that reflected neither joy or warmth. "You know more than you're saying, Victoria," he said with a firm skeptical tone. "You've seen her room."

Victoria turned again to the window.

"Look at me," Madrid said brusquely in a hard voice.

Victoria Jamerson flinched—a defensive convulsion. The sudden movement sloshed a measure of coffee onto her dress. Her head snapped towards Madrid. Fear register in her eyes, her upper body cowered perceptibly in the big chair.

Madrid watched her reaction with a sickening realization. He'd seen it before—women beaten and sexually abused. Their will for self preservation nearly drained, their sanity teetered like a ~~like a~~ tiny bird in a wind storm.

Was Lyle Holiday bedding September? Did he assure their secrecy through threats and isolation? Did he play the safety of the daughter against mother, then flip it the other way? Did he beat them when the threats weren't enough? Madrid's questions would remain unasked—their answers, he already knew.

"I'm sorry, Victoria," he said in a consoling voice. "I had no right to speak to you that way. I know this is hard, and I just made it harder. That was wrong."

With the slightest movement, she nodded. But her eyes still had that thousand-yard stare.

"You don't have to live this way," Madrid continued. "You can leave now. Pack some of your things. You can leave with me now."

Victoria struggled to focus. Tears filled her eyes. She blinked them away and they rolled down her cheeks. "You don't understand," she replied, barely a whisper.

"I understand more than you know, Victoria," said in a soothing voice.

With little more than a tremor, her head moved back and forth. "No." She mouthed the word, but the sound stayed inside her.

"I can protect you from Lyle," Madrid said. "Lyle Holiday won't hurt you again."

Her tears began to flow. "God sent you to me, Mr. Madrid. I prayed and he sent you to me."

"I don't know about that, Victoria," Madrid answered, suddenly uncomfortable. "I'm not a religious man."

She contorted her mouth to something that might pass as for a sad smile. "It doesn't matter. God has a plan for you. You are a good man, Alex. I prayed—and you came."

The argument was pointless—but more importantly, wasting time. "So you will come with me now?"

"I can't," she said again.

"Why not?"

"My daughter was born on the last day of September." Victoria Jamerson said through her tears and motherly pride. "That is three days from now. September will be home for her birthday, Mr. Madrid. You will bring her to me. I know you will. And I have to be here when she arrives."

Madrid wanted to argue, but snatching the woman's last fiber of hope, delusional as it was, seemed inordinately cruel. He looked at his watch, rose from the sofa. Victoria Jamerson struggled from the chair and followed him to the kitchen. When he had one hand on the door knob, he turned and asked, "How many sets of underwear does your daughter own?"

Victoria Jamerson stared at Madrid. "What sort of a question *is that*?"

"A pertinent one, Victoria. Does September do her own laundry?"

"September had enough to do with her schoolwork. She helps me in other ways."

"I'm sure she does," Madrid replied diplomatically, "but you do the laundry."

"I do the laundry," she replied, as if it were an admission.

"So you would know—how many sets of underwear your daughter has. Maybe not the exact number—but a close guess."

Victoria shifted her gaze to the tiny flowered wallpaper.

"Ten sets?" Madrid asked. "Two sets? Six sets?"

"Seven bottoms. Four brassieres," she confessed to the wall. From the corner of her eye, she watched Madrid process the information, still unsure why he'd asked.

It was not the number he'd wanted to hear. *September had taken only what she was wearing—which probably meant she hadn't planned to leave—which probably meant this would not end well.* Madrid nodded, moved towards the door. On the porch, he heard the dead bolt slide in place behind him.

The rain had almost stopped. The big orange cat was back—on top of a pile of neatly stacked wood, still wary. Madrid reached out slowly, stroked its head. The feline stretched lazily, purred loudly. Madrid walked to the Blazer. He could feel Victoria's eyes on him.

She watched him from the window. She wanted him gone, but the sense of urgency was fading. At least he was out of the house. Even if Lyle returned early, she had a modicum of deniability. She knew Alex Madrid would never contradict her. She watched the big mixed breed dog stand up in the back seat as Madrid approached the vehicle. Alex Madrid took his jacket from the front seat. The front door was open. The dog jumped from the vehicle and lumbered towards the house. She saw Madrid turn and begin to chase him.

Toto had watched Madrid step from the house—had watched him with the cat. Now it was only about the cat. Madrid reached inside the vehicle—placed his hand an inch from the dog's muzzle.

Toto reacted to the scent, his muscles bunching and twitching. "Go get him, Toto," Madrid growled in a low voice.

Toto bounded from the car. It was like a Clydesdale chasing an Arabian. Madrid followed the pair around the house, his coat in one hand, Toto's leash in the other. Fuzzed up and wild eyed, the cat had taken refuge in crook of a small cherry tree. Toto stood on his back legs at the base, head raised. He barked viciously, drool slinging from his jowls. Madrid continued past them to the back of the house. From the patch of grass under September's bedroom window, he scooped the metal box, tucked it under his jacket. Back at the cherry tree, he snapped the leash onto Toto's collar.

"Sorry, pal," he said to the big orange cat—and meant it.

Chapter 23

September 26th—12:11 p.m.

Madrid drove the Blazer onto the Black Creek College campus. There was a break in the rain, but the sky remained dark and unpleasant. A few students, the brave and the broke, were headed for lunch at the cafeteria near the center of campus. Aside from that small group, the campus seemed quiet, mostly deserted. The metal box Madrid had taken from September Jamerson's closet was still under the front seat. Still unopened. He was curious, but other matters were more pressing.

Madrid parked outside the security building—commanded Toto to stay. The big mutt was stretched out across the back seat again. With an impressive display of black muzzle and white teeth, he yawned—resumed his nap.

Angie was again behind the front desk of the security office. She ate popcorn from a grease-stained, brown paper bag. A copy of *The Great Gatsby* was propped in front of her. She was about halfway through it. Angie offered Madrid an uninterested glance, used her index finger to push her glasses back up her nose, and continued to read.

"Did Andy Frazier come in?" Madrid's asked, directing his question to the top of her light-brown head.

"No," she replied without looking up.

"He's scheduled for today."

"Yeah, I know." Her hand disappears into the bag of popcorn. "Called in. Said he was still too broke up about the Toliver thing."

Madrid noted the chill in her tone. "Is Pete around?" he asked.

"The chief doesn't work on Sundays," Angie replied flatly.

"Pete a religious fellow?" Madrid asked.

"Don't know," Angie shot back. "I know he doesn't work on Sundays—you'd have to ask him about the religious stuff."

"Maybe I will. You got his home number?"

"Yeah." It came out more a question than an answer. "You're going to call him at home? On Sunday morning?"

Madrid glanced at his watch. "It's past noon. Give me the number."

Angie referred to an index card that was taped to the corner of her desktop. Madrid used Wilson's office to make the call. Pete Wilson picked up after the fourth ring.

"Hello," he said in a heavy voice.

"This is Madrid. I need to talk with you."

"About the Toliver murder?" Wilson asked.

"More about September Jamerson."

There was a long pause, as if Pete Wilson was trying to place the name. "The girl that took off."

"Yeah."

"Did you find her?"

"No."

"You gotta an idea on where she is?"

"Not really. But I've had a couple of conversations with her mother, Victoria."

"Oh, yeah?" Wilson asked.

Madrid could hear the surprise and skepticism in Wilson's voice. "Yeah," Madrid replied firmly. "There's stuff going on out there. Stuff we need to talk about."

"We're not social workers, Madrid."

"Lyle Holiday beat the crap out of her last night, Pete."

"Beat the mother?"

"Yeah."

The line went quiet. Finally, Wilson said, "I don't take to men beatin' on women, Madrid. But even so, I don't see what that's got to do with Black Creek College."

"September Jamerson's a student at Black Creek, Pete. If Holiday is abusing his wife, it's better than even money he's abusing the stepdaughter, too. You know these over-the-top-religious-assholes are all about control. Control is about fear. Fear is about pain."

There was another long pause. "You've been thinking on this, haven't you?"

"Yeah."

"You know, this girl's only my responsibility when she's on college property," Pete Wilson countered.

"You're right, Pete," Madrid conceded. "There's no reason for the college to get involved. I probably need to be talking to Josh Galloway. With the election coming up, he'll be looking to get his picture in the paper again."

"Don't try to play me, Madrid," Pete Wilson snapped. "You know I ain't going to be a part of anything that helps Galloway become sheriff of this county." Another pause. "Might as well come on out here. You know where I am?"

"No."

Wilson gave Madrid directions. He jotted them on a piece of scrap paper he pulled from Wilson's wastepaper basket.

The directions took Madrid about fifteen miles west of Black Creek. He followed a two-lane blacktop that wound to the top of a ridge line. Locusts and sourwoods were transitioning from green to red. *High Vista Ski Slope and Resort* was painted on a large wooden sign to the right of the road. The lettering was badly faded—barely legible—like a distant memory. Madrid turned right, nosed the Blazer off the blacktop and onto a narrow gravel road. He drove a few hundred yards before coming to the gate house. It was tiny structure with broken windows and a half-finished stone facade. Past the gate house, the road got worse. The gravel gave way to deep ruts—wound its way through a canopy of white pine, oak, and maple. After almost a mile, the road opened into a large flat area that Madrid surmised was to have been a parking lot. Further up the mountain, chair lift towers sprouted like giant mutant trees. A sprawling log building with large chimneys at each end stretched across the far side of the parking lot. A deep porch extended across the front of the building. Not far from the front door, Pete Wilson sat in a big rocking chair.

Madrid climbed out of the Blazer. Wilson offered a nod.

"Do you mind if I let the dog stretch his legs?"

Pete Wilson extended his arms, palms to the sky. "There's over two hundred acres here. He can stretch all he wants."

Toto bounded from of the truck, began working the parking lot in ever-widening circles. Madrid climbed the five steps to the wide porch. From the table next to the rocker, Wilson picked up a sizable red mug. He extended it to Madrid, as if making a toast. "Want one?"

"Coffee?" Madrid asked.

"Irish coffee," Wilson replied with a grin.

It was one of Madrid's five rules of negotiation. *If they drink, you drink.* "Sure," he replied, "thanks."

With an audible grunt, Pete Wilson pushed himself from the rocker. He went inside—took his mug with him. Madrid pulled up another rocking chair. It was heavy and solid with comfortable contours in the seat and back.

Madrid could hear the arrhythmic drip of the last rain sliding from leaves and hemlock boughs. A sense of calm followed him into the chair. He watched Toto sniff intently at the edge of the woods. This was a hell of a lot better than The Paradise Court.

Wilson was back in a couple of minutes. He handed Madrid a steaming mug. The coffee was hot and strong—the whiskey was stronger.

"This is good," Madrid said.

"Jameson's. Best Irish whiskey there is."

Madrid nodded, changed the subject. "Nice place to live."

"Yeah, it's a sweet deal," Wilson replied with self-satisfaction. "I'll enjoy it for as long as I can. I keep an eye on the place, and they let me stay here rent-free. It will last until the lawyers decide they've had enough of suing each other. Which I hope is never."

"Bankruptcy court?" Madrid asked.

Wilson worked his heavy shoulders up and down. "Something like that, I guess. Bunch of high rollers got in bed with one of those S & Ls that didn't have their feet on solid ground. I don't understand all the high-falutin' financial mumbo-jumbo, but the bottom line was that some shmo bought something he couldn't pay for."

Madrid nodded. "When you boil it down, that's usually what's left."

"Didn't help the bastards when we got two back-to-back winters with almost no snow."

"I guess it's tough to sell real estate on a half-finished ski slope with no snow," Madrid said.

"Guess so," Wilson replied, working not to slur his words.

Madrid gulped another tenth of an ounce. "Two hundred acres?"

"More like two-sixty. They were planning on four slopes, maybe a pond for ice skating—crap like that. I got a plat and I tell them I walk the property every week. It's really more like every couple of months. Nothin' much ever happens up here. I figure in another year or so it'll get sold off to another developer. Or maybe somebody lookin' to get into the ski business. When that happens, I'll be looking for another place to live. But until then, I plan to enjoy the hell out of it."

The two men rocked in the chairs—sipped Irish coffee. Finally Pete Wilson said, "You wanted to talk about September Jamerson."

"Yeah."

"Okay. I'm listenin'."

"I met her mother yesterday afternoon. She told me a little about her daughter. Asked me to help find her. Then I got another call this morning. She asked me to come to the house," Madrid continued, leaving out the part about searching the girl's room. "It was obvious Victoria had taken a beating."

Pete Wilson took a healthy pull from his mug, stared at the porch floor. Then he looked at Madrid and asked, "Did she say it was Lyle?"

"No."

Wilson nodded. "Don't matter—it was Lyle. I'd bet my left nut on it. I should have done more when I was out there. But she didn't want to talk to me. I guess she was more afraid of him than I figured."

Toto wandered to the edge of the porch, spotted Madrid, went back to smelling things.

"There's a lot going on in that house, Pete," Madrid said. "If September Jamerson threatened to talk, Lyle Holiday had motive to shut her up."

"Jesus, Madrid. You saying he killed her?"

"I'm saying he might have. But it could be what you said in the first place—Lyle Holiday gave her plenty of reason to run."

"I guess it could be either one," Wilson said quietly. He stared past the parking lot, into the woods. Somewhere, not far away, a woodpecker went to work on a tree trunk—the sound like a burst from a muffled machine gun.

"I still think we need to make sure September Jamerson and Miranda Toliver aren't connected." Madrid said.

Wilson contorted his face into a grimace, and asked skeptically, "You trying to pin the Toliver girl on Holiday, too."

"No. I'm just thinking maybe they knew each other—they took a class together. Something."

Wilson shook his head heavily. "I'm with you up to there, Madrid. But that's where you lose me. Hell, as small as Black Creek College is, everybody's going to have a class or two with everybody else before they get out of there. You keep wantin' to believe this Padrick kid was just wanderin' by and got caught in Galloway's headlights—like some Bambi deer. But that's just somethin' Julie Kingston stuck in your head. What did you find out at Jamerson's house that makes you believe Padrick didn't kill that girl?"

"Nothing," Madrid admitted.

"Nothin'," Wilson repeated. "That's what you got. It was Padrick. And that lucky son-of-a-bitch Galloway fell all over him. You'd think the man's luck would change in eleven years, but his ain't."

"I'm not following you," Madrid said.

"You don't need to," Pete Wilson said in a soft, terse voice. "It was a long time ago."

Before Madrid could respond, Wilson rose abruptly from the rocker—steadied himself on the door casing as he went inside the house. Madrid used the opportunity to pour half his coffee over the porch railing.

A couple minutes later Wilson was back on the porch with a fresh mug.

"What were we talking about?" Wilson asked, then answered his own question. "Oh, yeah, Dicky Padrick. But I'm talked out on him. *Lyle Holiday*. That's who we need to talk to. You and me. What-da-ya think?" The last part came out slurred—sounded a little like a bad John Wayne impersonation.

"When?" Madrid asked.

"Tomorrow," Wilson answered firmly. "Tomorrow morning. First thing. Don't know if it'll do us any good, though."

"Might be fun even if it doesn't," Madrid said as the rain started again.

Wilson took another sip of Irish coffee. "Wouldn't bet against it."

Chapter 24

Black Creek Jail
September 26th—2:58 p.m.

It had been going on for nearly half an hour.

"Bet you seen your sister naked," Junior Jenkins said in a wolfish tone. He needed to make someone's life miserable. Misery was what Junior knew. *Want to be the happiest guy in the room? Simple. No problem. Make everyone else more miserable than yourself.*

"She's a hot piece of ass, Dicky."

Dicky Padrick moved to the far side of his cell—as if it might help.

"Your sister looks like the kind that likes it. But she don't want you to *know* she likes it."

"Stop talking about my sister," he mumbled, his words dying before they reached the bars that surrounded him.

"She ever rub those little titties up against you, Dicky Boy? You know, let her pervert retard brother get a little feel?"

Dicky's large pear-shaped body was perched on the edge of the bunk. He stared at the gray painted concrete of his cell floor, pressed the palms of his plump hands against his ears. But Junior's words filtered through—a harsh light on his darkest thoughts.

"I bet she doesn't even bother to close the door when she's getting' dressed. Probably walks around in her little panties pretendin' not to notice you? You're just her retarded brother. You ain't suppose to care about stuff like that, are you Dicky Boy?"

Dicky turned, stared at Junior, his jaw slack. His mouth hung open, his expression a mask of bewilderment.

Junior Jenkins recognized it instantly. "Fuck yeah, she does." He nodded encouragement from across the room, brushed his long greasy hair from his eyes. "And you just sit there like the dumb fuck you are, tryin' to hide your boner."

Dicky continued to stare.

"That's fucked up, Dicky."

Dicky Padrick's blonde head nodded.

"But that ain't all your fault," Junior said A hint of empathy crept into his tone. "If I had me a sister that looked like yours," Junior said. "Whew—damn. I'd be doin' anything it took to get in her pants."

Dicky was rattled by Junior's sudden insightfulness. He stared back at Junior—tried to make sense of it.

Junior's grin stretched further. "Bet you was thinkin' about your sister when you was tryin' to screw that chick in the parkin' lot. You were feelin' up that dead girl—thinkin' about your sister, weren't you, Dicky Boy?"

Dicky continued to stare—slack jawed—bleary eyed. Junior Jenkins knew things. He knew things that were in Dicky's head. Things that were bad.

* * * *

Madrid sat in his regular booth at Marcy's Holistic Café and Country Fried Grill. Toto was under the table. Madrid sipped a glass of iced Lemon Zinger tea. The waitress arrived with his order—a large bowl of curried white bean soup and a small loaf of freshly-baked whole wheat bread.

On the table, next to the soup and bread, September Jamerson's journal rested face down. It was bound in imitation red leather. There were thirty-eight entries each penned in a loopy feminine hand. They spanned a period of just over a year. Madrid had already read through it twice.

He spooned his soup, drank some herb tea, looked out the window of the old depot, watched the rain wash over River Street, occasionally pinched off some bread and fed the troll under the table. He thought about Victoria and September Jamerson. And he thought about Lyle Holiday—dark thoughts tinged in blood. He moved the half-eaten bowl of soup aside, picked up the red journal, opened it to a random page.

> *December 25, 1975 – I don't really remember how Christmas was before Daddy died. But I know it couldn't have been like this. This was awful. Lyle says Christmas trees are pagan symbols. No tree, no presents, no nothing. Well that's not exactly right. Momma gave me a necklace. It's real pretty. It's got silver and three white*

little balls on the end. There pretty. Momma says there pearls. She says they come from the ocean. I haven't seen the ocean yet. Momma says there are seven of them. The atlantic one is the closest, so I guess that's the one I will go to. I gave Momma a card I made her. It had a poem I made up about her and me and Christmas. I started to make it about Daddy too, but that would be too sad. Momma cried when I gave it to her. She said she was happy. I don't know about that. I don't know if I should have made up the poem and put it on the card. We had beans and cornbread and canned tomatoes from the garden for dinner. I'm sick of beans. Just another Thursday. But Momma made a pie for dessert. It was good. She used the blue berries she and me picked last summer. I can't wait to go to college. I don't know where Momma is going to get the money. She told me not to worry about it but I can't stop. I want to go to college, but I wish we could run away. Me and Momma. But that isn't right. This farm is ours—not Lyle's. It belongs to Momma. At least I hope it still belongs to Momma. Lyle came into my bedroom last night. He took down the picture of Jesus. He cut it right out of the frame. He said I didn't understand Jesus. I didn't argue with him. I didn't want the dam picture anyway. Momma went to sleep early. She could barely hold her head up after dinner. She gets like that sometimes after dinner. I worry about her. Lyle came back into my bedroom. He had his Bible and a flashlight. He read stuff from the Bible. I pretended to listen but not really. I don't remember what he read. He made me take off all my clothes. He told me to lay there and not to move. He shined that light on me for a long time. He said the light would cleanse my soul.

January 8, 1976 - I need to tell somebody. I can't tell Momma. She is already so sad. Momma sleeps a lot. All times of the day. Even when she is awake she seems real tired. I try to talk with her about my schooling, but it's like she can't focus on my words. Lyle is coming into my room most every night. He's still got his Bible and his flashlight, but he don't bother to read no more. He touches me. God. I can't believe I actually wrote that down. Lyle is like one of those serpents he's always talking about from the Bible. I told him to keep his hands off of me. Lyle got real mad. He put my pillow over my face. God, I thought for sure I was going to die. I was trying to kick him. My chest felt like it was on fire. He said if I mouthed off again, they'd never find my body. If I tell anyone, he said he'd kill Momma and they'd never find her body either. I believe him. He's crazy. There is something in his brain that isn't right. He is an evil man, but maybe that's just the craziness. I don't know why my Momma would take up with a crazy man. But she did. I need to tell somebody, but there is no body I can tell.

Madrid glanced up, saw the waitress approaching the booth. He laid the journal on the seat next to him. The waitress was short and slightly plump, with blonde Shirley Temple curls and an impish smile. In one hand she carried small pitcher of tea, in the other was a plate with a cooked hamburger patty cut into bite-sized portions.

"The tea is for you," she said lightly. "This is for your friend. It's meat."

"I can see it's meat," Madrid said.

"You can?" she asked. Her eyes grew wide with mock surprise. She bent at the waist, looked under the table, popped back up, looked at Madrid. "Marcy said he is a seeing-eye dog. You don't look blind to me."

"Sometimes I have to squint when the letters are small."

More smiling.

Madrid smiled back. "Is this meat holistic or country fried?"

The waitress giggled. "I don't really know."

"That's okay, because it doesn't really matter. Toto is completely opened minded on the subject of meat."

The waitress giggle again and left. Madrid surreptitiously served the improbable holistic carnivorous treat. He wiped his hands on the napkin, picked the journal back again.

April 1, 1976 – They say this is April Fools Day. That's what I feel like. A dam fool. They said because I don't go to regular school, I had to take a test so that I could get signed up to Black Creek College. Momma said I did fine. I don't think I did too good. They said they would let me know in two weeks. I wish I was smarter. I wish I could figure out a way to get me and Momma away from here. Maybe I will. Maybe if they let me get into Black Creek College I can learn something to help me figure this out. Maybe. God, I hope I passed that test. Momma told me to pray. I did pray on it a little, but I'm not too convinced on praying. Nothing

I ever pray for ever happens. I guess there's a God, but he don't listen to me. If he did, Lyle wouldn't be in my bedroom almost every night. If God listened to me, Lyle would be dead.

Someone switched on the television set mounted to the wall in the diner. A man was talking about the weather. He spoke in a serious tone, moved his arms with sweeping gestures in front of a map of the southeastern United Sates. A hurricane was expected to make landfall off the coast of South Carolina—probably between Charleston and Myrtle Beach. Another one was in the Gulf of Mexico. He predicted it would move across the panhandle of Florida.

Madrid looked out the window at the rain. Went back to the journal.

May 1, 1976 - I can't believe it. I'm in!!!! They are going to let me into the college. They said I qualified for some special exception, but I don't care. I'm going. I'm going to study harder than anyone else in that whole dam school. I'll show those people. I'll make Momma proud. She says she is already proud. But I'm going to make her really, really, really proud. Lyle is not happy about me going. He's been even meaner than usual. Last night he threw his dinner plate against the wall. He told Momma her cooking wasn't fit for a dog. That's just not right. Momma is a good cook. She tries really hard. It's just that she's so tired. I told her she needed to go to the doctor. She won't go. She says she is fine. I know she says that so I won't worry. But I worry anyway. I heard that cancer can make you tired. I pray that Momma doesn't have cancer. I pray that God will listen to me. Maybe he's starting to listen. I'm going to Black Creek College.

July 4th, 1976 – They say this is the biggest forth of July ever. It's like a big birthday and a forth of July all rolled into one day. I don't know. It didn't seem that different to me. But we went into town. That was different. We didn't go all the way into town. Lyle drove us in his truck. He made me sit in the middle. Momma didn't say much. He drove us up on a hill that was over the river and the railroad tracks. We sat on a blanket. Lyle made me sit next to him. I was hoping to see a train, but I didn't. Lyle said the trains don't run at night. Some people in town shot off some fireworks. They went up really high. At first I thought they were going to land right on us. Like a bomb or something. The colors were kind of pretty, but I didn't like it much. They were loud and they reminded me of guns and killing. Killing always makes me think of Lyle. Lyle told me he had killed people before. I don't know if he was telling me that so I would be scared of him or if he really had killed people. I wouldn't put it past him to kill someone. He said if I told anyone that he would take his ax to my cat Poncho and that I would have to watch. Lyle don't like that cat but Poncho has never done anything to Lyle. Lyle made me move my bed away from the wall so it won't make noise when he is on top of me.

August 31, 1976 – The college is not like what I was thinking it was going to be. The other students don't really talk to me much. They mostly look right past me like I wasn't even there. Sometimes I think they are laughing at me. This one girl told me I had nice shoes but I don't think she really meant it. There the same shoes I wear everyday. I might start wearing my Sunday shoes. They are better looking but there a little small and kind of hurt my feet if I wear them too long. I wonder if I should even be at the college. I keep remembering what they told me about being a special exception. But if I quit the college where would I be? Here. I'd be here all the time. I couldn't take that. I don't know how Momma stands it. Maybe that's why she sleeps so much. Lyle's been giving her some sort of special drink at dinner time that's suppose to perk her up. It don't seem to be working. Momma is sleeping more than ever. I'm doing more work around here now. I don't mind helping Momma. I just wish she was feeling better. She went to sleep in her chair. Lyle made me go out to the barn with him. He made me do things. It's the first time he made me do it in the daytime. I closed my eyes, but he told me I had to look at him. Looking made it ten times worse. I don't know how much longer I can stand this. Momma got me an old car so I could get to school. I think about driving away and never coming back.

Madrid read the last entry one more time. It was dated one day before September Jamerson went missing. It was rambling—and poignant.

> *September 9 – Sometimes I think it is getting better and sometimes I'm sure it is getting worse. I shouldn't say this, but sometimes I think I live in hell. But there is a boy in my English class. His hair is longer than mine, but he ~~his~~ is really cute. I've seen him looking a me a couple of times. I don't know what to make of that. Sometimes I think people look at me and can see that I've been with Lyle. That's why they don't talk to me. I know that's crazy, but sometimes that's how I feel. Maybe Lyle has passed on some of his craziness to me. But there is one girl who does talk to me. She is really friendly and really pretty. She said my name was pretty. I never thought of it like that. I always just thought it was kind of stupid, but she said it was pretty. Then she said September like three or four times in a row and it did sound kind of nice. But it might be just because she was the one saying it and she is nice and pretty. I told her that I liked her name better. Miranda is a pretty name. I actually like going to history class now. I've been thinking about telling her about Lyle, but I don't know. I need to talk to somebody. But if I tell Miranda and she tells other people. Well, I would just die. If Lyle didn't kill me, I would probably kill myself. I've been thinking about that some. I probably shouldn't say that. But it is the truth. When he is on top of me I think about it and right after he leaves I think about it a lot. It takes me a long time to go to sleep. Some days I feel as tired as Momma. I'd probably do it if it weren't for Momma. But then momma would be all by herself. I just couldn't do that to her. I might tell Miranda. Maybe. Maybe not. Maybe. Maybe not. Maybe.*

Madrid closed the journal, slid it into the pocket of his jacket. *And maybe September did tell Miranda,* he thought . Maybe that's why Miranda Toliver is dead and September Jamerson is nowhere to be found. But if that's what happened, it would be hard to plug Dicky Padrick into the equation. September might have been talking about a different Miranda. Those were long odds—it would be easy enough to check.

Madrid left the half-eaten food on the table, slipped the cherubic waitress a healthy tip. He gathered the dog and they walked outside into the rain.

Chapter 25

Gatlinburg, Tennessee
September 26th—5:32 p.m.

During the steep climb to the ridge that overlooked the small tourist town, The Wizard had wiped the lipstick from his mouth—had traded the woman's wig for his wide-brimmed straw hat. Earlier, he had explained to the other three what they should do—and, equally important, what they shouldn't. Flex had offered the only comment.

"I ain't worried about Charlie Blades," his bravado had assured them. "Charlie Blades should be worried about me."

"'Fools rush in...'", the Wizard had replied softly.

"You're an idiot," Rex Thompson had added.

Standing back from the window, Charlie watched them slowly roll into the driveway—first a wood-paneled station wagon, then a black van with curtained windows. It was late afternoon and getting dark. Headlights struggled against the rain that poured steadily from the black clouds that enveloped the mountain top. It droned loudly on the metal roof of the cottage, cascaded over the windshields of the approaching vehicles. Charlie could make out the shape of two people in the lead car. He had no idea about the van. The stainless steel .357 was in his right hand. Charlie's thumb caressed the hammer, the six-inch barrel tapped nervously against his thigh. *Six shots,* he thought. *Another six rounds in the moon clip, but after that, it was loose shells. That would be a slow reload. Didn't matter though,* he told himself. *Twelve rounds. One way or the other—it would be over by then.*

The station wagon stopped halfway down the driveway. The passenger door eased open—a familiar figure in a floppy hat stepped out. He stood for a moment in the downpour, letting Charlie Blades get a good look. Then the little man strolled unhurriedly towards the cottage. By the time he reached the stone steps of the covered porch his clothing was soaked through.

Just as he raised his gnarled fist to knock, Charlie opened the door—stayed out of sight to those in the driveway. The Wizard stepped inside, gently closed the door behind him. Leisurely, he gazed around the room.

"I was hoping for something a little nicer," he said wistfully. "But it's better than what I've become accustomed to."

"Yeah," Charlie replied—felt a pang of guilt. "I guess it is."

The smaller man stepped back, looked Charlie up and down. It had been two years since the two men had stood in the same room. Communications had been passed by go-betweens, often in code that meant nothing except to Blades and the little man behind bars.

"You look the same."

"You too," Charlie said.

"Maybe," The Wizard said with a forced, gap-toothed smile. "But looks can be deceiving."

Charlie Blades found nothing to add. His eyes moved back and forth between The Wizard and the driveway.

The smaller man nodded at the big revolver. "You seem a tad nervous, Charles."

Charlie Blades jerked his trollish head to the parking lot. "Wasn't expecting all this company," he lied.

The smaller man nodded. "For now, they each serve a purpose, but that won't last much longer. After Madrid, we're going to need to thin the herd."

Charlie looked out the window. The two vehicles retreated slowly back up driveway. Their headlights burned like the angry eyes in the fading light.

"I told them to come back in a couple of hours. You and I need some time to talk."

"Okay," Charlie replied. He watched until the station wagon's lights were lost in the tree line. The barrel of the magnum was still tapping his right thigh.

"We've got two years to catch up on," The Wizard said. "But more importantly, we have plans to make."

Charlie tore his eyes from the window. The house was almost dark. He flipped a switch by the door. A single lamp by the sofa offered a weak, yellowish light. "And I'm guessin' you want to see the girl."

"That would indeed be lovely," The Wizard replied.

* * * *

Madrid rolled the Blazer through the standing water in the parking lot of The Paradise Court. He opened the door, coaxed the dog from the back seat. He stood impatiently while the dog stretched, then leisurely strolled under the metal porch roof. From the far side of his motel door, Madrid could hear the muffled ring of the phone. He used the key, pushed the door open, the ringing grew immediately loud and shrill. He moved to the scarred table that separated the two beds, picked up the heavy black receiver. "Yeah," he said, without warmth.

There was a pause, then a female voice said, "You could stand a little work—charm wise."

"Charm is overrated," Madrid replied. "Read that in *Cosmo*."

"Don't believe everything you read," Julie Kingston retorted.

"Sage advice."

There was a pause, then Julie spoke in measured words. "I understand you've had a busy day."

"Oh yeah?" Madrid asked. "Where did you hear that?"

"I'm in the news business."

"I don't see how my day was really news worthy."

"I didn't say it was. But I'd still like to talk with you about it. Victoria Jamerson...."

Madrid cut her off. "This line runs through a switchboard in the office. You shouldn't assume this is a private conversation."

Another pause. Julie said, "I see."

"Maybe I'll run into you tomorrow," Madrid said. "There are a couple of things I'd like to talk with you about."

Another pause. "So why does it have to wait until tomorrow? Are you busy this evening?"

Another pause. "Sort of busy," Madrid replied unconvincingly.

"Sort of busy doing what?" she challenged.

"I'm down to the last two chapters of a Nancy Drew mystery. I was kinda hoping to finish it up."

"Nancy's got a pretty tough case, huh?"

"Suspenseful," Madrid answered.

"Well, I don't want to keep you from that," she said in a dismissive tone.

Another pause. This one a little longer.

"What?" Julie asked finally. "Are you waiting for me to ask again?"

"I was just curious if you would," Madrid answered.

"God," she replied, exasperated. "You're just like a damn girl."

"I should probably take offense at that," Madrid replied casually.

"Yeah, I think you probably should."

Another pause.

"Sooo.... Do you like Chinese food?"

"Yes, I do," Madrid answered. "Is there a good place around here?"

"What do you think?" she asked incredulously.

"I'm guessing no."

"And you'd be right. I learned to make it myself."

"I'm impressed," Madrid replied.

"Don't be. A half a billion Chinese people do it every day."

"Still impressed," Madrid said.

"Save your opinion until you've tasted it. That's my offer. Chinese food—and some conversation."

Madrid sat on the edge of the bed, looked around the dismal motel room. The door was still open. The fading light spilled in like a depressive fog. Rain continued pelting the overgrown parking lot. It washed over the sad little fountain, eroded Madrid's psyche. He thought about Charlie Blades and The Wizard, about Dicky Padrick and Miranda Toliver, about Victoria and September Jamerson. They tumbled in his mind like jagged stones. He wanted to get the hell out of Black Creek, but for now, getting away from The Paradise Court would have to do.

"That would be nice," Madrid heard himself say. "What can I bring?"

"Bring your dog," Julie replied lightly. "I'll make something for him, too."

Chapter 26

Gatlinburg, Tennessee
September 26th—7:00 p.m.

The stage had been set.

Under The Wizard's careful guidance, the furniture in the living room had been strategically arranged—then rearranged—then adjusted again. They had commandeered lamps from other rooms—had adjusted the lighting as best they could.

"Not perfect," The Wizard had said fussily, "but better."

Charlie Blades built a fire in the stone fireplace. Some of the wood was wet and hissed angrily as it heated up. They waited for the flames to reach the proper height. When the backdrop had been deemed acceptable, Charlie disappeared into the basement. He unlocked the heavy door. The naked bulb cast a weak glow over the hard surfaces of the room. Anna Marie sat on the edge of the bed, her left wrist handcuffed to the bed rail. Charlie used the key. The cuff fell away, clanged noisily against the iron railing.

Anna Marie rubbed her arm, looked up at Charlie expectantly. She spoke in a halting whisper, as if sharing a secret. "I heard people upstairs."

"Yeah," Charlie Blades nodded dismissively. "Just one guy. I'm taking you to see him now."

She waited a moment, asked in the same whisper. "Is he going to rape me?"

Fair question, Charlie thought. *The guy's been in prison for two years. Probably hasn't been near a woman in a long time. Hasn't been near a woman like you for even longer. But first-hand experience had taught Charlie that The Wizard wasn't a rapist—at least not in the typical sense. He was a voyeur.* "No," he replied in a tone that relayed little comfort. "He just wants to look at you—maybe talk some."

"Talk about what?" she asked.

"You need to stop asking all these fucking questions. You need to start listening." He leaned forward, his face only inches from hers, his voice an angry hiss—like the fire upstairs. "Listening and doing what the fuck I tell you is how you're going to get through this. It's how you're going to survive. Do you understand?"

Anna Marie stopped talking. She stared back at the freakish, hairy man. Her green eyes were glazed with fear. She nodded absently. The word "*survive*" reverberated in her head like a slowly-pounded drum.

Charlie began his instruction. He was not unlike a stage mother before an important audition. He went over the big things and then the little things. Sit like this, comb your hair like that—do this—make *damn sure* you don't do that. Smile—not too much—make sure it looks real. *Natural.* When the preparation was complete, Charlie Blades took his prodigy by the hand. He led her from the dank basement, up the wobbly steps. At the top of the stairs he waited—listened. The magnum was tucked into his belt. He wrapped his hand lightly on the butt of the weapon. Paranoid was better than careless. Charlie Blades eased the door open.

* * * *

Warmth and a soft light washed over Anna Marie as she stepped into the room. She barely noticed either. Her eyes darted anxiously. The room was different, but she was too nervous to focus on what had changed. There was a fire—and a chair sitting a few feet in front of the hearth. She felt the big man place his hand on her back, spread his long fingers between her shoulder blades. With a gentle shove, he guided her toward the seat. She fixated on the fire, walked towards it like a doomed moth. Her legs felt heavy and tired. When she reached the chair, Anna Marie turned, smoothed the front of her white dress. She sat—knees together, hands folded neatly on her lap. Sat just like Charlie had coached her. Vaguely, she was aware the heat from the fire felt good on her back.

A man sat on the couch directly in front of her, a small man not much larger than herself. He was no more than six feet away. He sat perfectly erect--motionless. Around his small bald head a piece of red cloth, maybe a woman's silk scarf, blindfolded his eyes. The big man stepped behind the couch. He paused for a moment, his large hands suspended on either side of the smaller man's head. He stared at her, as if contemplating, or trying to remember. A moment later, he untied the scarf. It fell away from the small man's face, cascaded softly onto his lap. The small man blinked as if awakening from a nap, reached for the round-lensed glasses laying next to him. He carefully placed them on his face. He tilted his head to the right, then back to the left. After a moment, he smiled. Anna Marie could see the gap between his front teeth.

* * * *

The Wizard heard them as they approached the top of the stairs. They stopped. Charlie would be careful—wondering if the others had slipped back in. He was such a predictable bastard. The blindfold was a last-minute decision. It added a layer of drama—heightened his remaining senses. The door opened, he heard them moving towards him—caught a whiff of the girl as she passed. *Lilac soap*, he thought. He listened to the creaking floor, tracked Charlie as he moved around behind the sofa. And then there was nothing—silence—a moment for rebuilding trust. Blades could snap his neck like a dried chicken bone. He could claim the girl for his own—the two of them could fade into the night. The Wizard sat calmly. Waited. Charlie wouldn't do that—he was such a predictable bastard. The scarf slipped away. The Wizard placed the glasses on his face. The girl became a mirage suddenly in focus.

Silhouetted by the fire, the light danced around her, played in her long red curls. It hinted at the curves of her body—cast the angles of her face in seductive shadows. He studied her as he would an artistic masterpiece. Like a connoisseur with a rare bottle of wine, he consumed her in small, measured sips. She wore white sandals with enough heel to accentuate the shape of her calves. The white dress started just below her knees, ended with a soft lacy collar that encircled her supple neck. She sat perfectly still, posed like a virginal temptress. This one was perfect. Better than any of the others—maybe even better than the first one. *Better than mother*, he thought with a smile.

Chapter 27

September 26th—7:06 p.m.

There were two stone pillars—maybe ten feet tall, tapered and pointed at the top. *Phallic,* Madrid thought. The heavy wrought-iron gate was open. Madrid rolled past it onto the cobblestone driveway. On either side of the drive, a carefully manicured band of grass mirrored the serpentine path. He followed it through a stand of hardwoods and balsam. A quarter of a mile later, the driveway ended in a large oval parking area that served the massive three-story English Tudor. Next to the mansion was a detached three-car garage built to look like a carriage house.

Madrid rolled slowly to a stop—let out a low whistle of admiration. Toto, stretched out across the back seat, tilted his head twenty degrees. "You can look," Madrid told the dog, "but don't touch. There's nothing here I can afford to replace."

Stone steps led to the impressive porch. Two solid chestnut doors formed an eight-foot arch. Recessed into the stone wall, the doorbell button glowed. Madrid stabbed it with his index finger. From deep inside the mansion, he could hear the rich peal of a chime.

"Ask not for whom the bell tolls," Madrid muttered to the himself. He was freshly showered and shaven—clean blue jeans—his best, and only, button-down shirt. He waited empty-handed—felt slightly self-conscious and definitely out-of-place.

The door swung open—like a curtain on the opening act of a play. Madrid caught a glimpse of the backdrop, but his focus was on Julie Kingston. She wore white corduroy bell bottoms slung low across her hips. The material of her black turtle neck was thin and clung to her body—accented the curve of her waist, the swell of her small breasts. Madrid was fairly certain her shoes matched her belt—more certain she wasn't wearing a bra.

Julie smiled at Madrid, but saved most of it for Toto. "You brought him," she said, sounding pleasantly surprised.

"You told me to bring him," Madrid reminded her.

"I know."

"He can stay on the porch if you've changed your mind."

"Of course not." She opened the door wider.

Madrid and the mutt stepped inside.

To the left of the foyer, a staircase ascended to a large balcony with a heavy oak balustrade. To the right, a massive carved-stone fireplace dominated the wall. The room was furnished in oversized leather upholstery accented with brass nail-head trim. Mission-style oak tables and lamps had been professionally arranged . Overhead, darkly-stained exposed timbers braced the roof system. Heavy wrought-iron chandeliers hung from the ceiling. Through glass eyes, animal heads stared down from high on the walls. The house was dark and masculine—and on a stormy night—probably borderline creepy.

As if reading his thoughts, Julie said, almost apologetically, "The house belongs to my father."

"It's nice," Madrid replied. "Roomy."

"Like the Astrodome," she replied.

He followed her through the house, past the empty living room. The walnut dining table had been built to seat twelve—or to land a small aircraft. The chairs surrounding it could best be described as small, ornate thrones.

"This was going to be his get-away-hunting-lodge-poker-with-the-boys house," she explained as they continued to walk, "but he's only been here a couple of times." Madrid waited for Julie to elaborate.

"He's tried to get me to change it—make it more like I would like it. I don't think I will, though. It's his house," she said. Then added vaguely, "Or somebody's house. Not mine, anyway. I'm just keeping an eye on it for a while. Camping, so to speak."

"Not a bad place to camp."

"I suppose," she replied without much conviction.

They were in the kitchen. Like the rest of the rooms Madrid had seen, it was large—ten foot ceilings—walls of smooth dry-stacked stone. The floor was covered with large squares of tile. They were about the same color of the stone, laid in a diamond pattern. Most everything else was stainless steel—cabinets, countertops, the over-sized commercial-grade appliances. The cook top was set into a stone island near the center of the room. It had eight gas burners. A large stainless steel hood was suspended from the ceiling with thick stainless steel chains. Resting on three of the burners were cast-iron woks. In the far corner of the room, next to a large window, a small table was set for two. There was a pair of candles and a yellow flower in a narrow crystal vase.

"You hungry?" she asked.

"Sure," Madrid answered, watching the dog. The big mutt had gone straight for the rug by the back door. He fluffed it with a big paw, circled it twice, laid down—claimed it as his own.

"You sure you don't want me to put him back outside—or in the car?" Madrid asked his hostess.

Julie looked over at the dog, pursed her lips, tilted her head and shrugged. "I don't see why. He looks pretty comfortable to me."

"He's good at getting comfortable."

"It's a nice quality to have," she said enviously.

"Yeah," Madrid agreed. "I guess it is."

"Dinner's going to be a few minutes," she said matter-of-factly, " but I've got cheese and crackers—and some smoked almonds, if you want to nibble."

"That sounds good," Madrid said, "but I'll wait. I like to be hungry when I eat."

"Is that some sort of vague double entendre?"

"I'm not that clever," Madrid replied.

"Really?" Julie countered with an amused expression.

"Actually, fairly obtuse." Madrid answered.

"Then I'll try not to use too many big words tonight."

"I'd appreciate that," he said.

"I have beer and wine," she said hesitantly. The beer's out in the guest house. The wine's down in the cellar."

"Would you like something?" Madrid asked.

"No," she answered immediately.

"Then I'm good," Madrid replied.

Julie went to the refrigerator, took out three metal bowls sealed with plastic wrap. She dumped the contents of the first bowl. A colorful collage of peppers, snow peas, carrots, and onions spilled onto the maple cutting board. She selected a large knife from the rack. It looked sharp, and like everything else in the room, expensive. She focused on the vegetables and began to chop and slice.

"Anything I can do to help," Madrid asked.

"No. Make yourself at home."

Madrid thought about home—The Paradise Court—a hotplate and a fridge with a bad compressor. Madrid spotted an upholstered bar stool in the corner of the room. He pulled it a few inches away from the wall—sat down—leaned back—watched her work.

A few moments passed. Without looking up, she said, "This is a little awkward, isn't it."

"Not for me," Madrid answered.

Neither one spoke for a while. The sound of the blade against the wood divided the time into unequal portions.

"Why? Is it awkward for you?" Madrid asked.

Julie looked up, but not directly at Madrid. "I'm not sure." She returned her focus to the cutting board, sliced the last pepper and raked all the vegetables back into the bowl. She lined up the oil and seasonings next to the stove. They were all in neatly-labeled brown-glass bottles. Julie turned a knob on the cook top. Blue flame burst forth, began to lick at the base of the first wok.

"I could leave," Madrid said half-heartedly.

"That would be rude," she replied without looking at him.

"I would take some smoked almonds with me," Madrid replied.

Julie smiled, glanced at Madrid from the corner of her eye. "That would somehow make it *less* rude?"

"Couldn't say. Etiquette isn't really my forte. But if I take the crackers and cheese, then the dog is going to want to share."

"Good reasoning skills for one so obtuse."

"More selfishness than anything else."

She raised her eyebrows, "Umm." Julie took the next bowl, dumped it onto the cutting board. I think he'll prefer this," she said, pointing the tip of the big knife at a small mound of beef. "Unless he's a vegetarian, too?"

"No," Madrid answered. " But we *do* have similar taste in music and art."

"And that would be?" she asked skeptically.

"Well," Madrid replied thoughtfully. "We both like *Alvin and the Chipmunks*—their early work—before they sold out to the man. And as far as art—you really can't go wrong with anything painted on velvet."

"I suspected you were the worldly type."

"Try not to flaunt it," Madrid said from his stool, "but it's hard."

Julie cut the beef into uniform cubes—raked it back into the bowl. She necklaced oil into the first wok. As she waited for it to heat, she lit the burner under the other two. She dumped the cubes into the oil—the wok sprang to life with smoke and sizzle. Toto raised his head, sniffed the air with a circuitous motion. Julie reached up, pushed a button on the hood. The motor was almost silent. She added oil to the other two woks, dumped vegetables in one, brown rice in the other. She went to the refrigerator, removed a smaller bowl, dumped marinated tofu into the wok with the vegetables—splashed a dark liquid onto the rice. With spatula in hand, she moved purposefully between the three vessels.

"Are you going to tell me about seeing Victoria Jamerson this morning?" she asked, without looking up.

"Depends," Madrid answered amicably.

"On what?" There was a note of challenge in her tone.

"I don't want to read this conversation in the newspaper. "

She stopped stirring, looked directly at Madrid. "I wouldn't do that."

She sounded genuine, Madrid thought—even a little hurt.

"I didn't ask you here to get a story," she said firmly. "I'm concerned about Victoria—and her daughter."

The aromas from the woks filled the kitchen. It was almost dark outside and the lights in the room radiated softly off of the stone walls. The cavernous space had taken on a warm, intimate quality. Julie was standing directly in front of him, one hand on her hip, the other wrapped around the spatula. Her expression was somewhere between defiant and pouty. *Damn*, she was easy to look at. "Fair enough," he heard himself reply.

Julie turned—adjusted the burners under the vegetables and rice until the blue flame was little more than a flicker.

"Victoria called me this morning," Madrid began.

He recounted the visit, described Victoria Jamerson after her night in the woods—the bruises and scrapes. He detailed September's room—the locks on the door, the books—and the room arrangement. He left out the part about finding the journal.

"Lyle Holiday is having sex with the girl," Julie said bluntly.

"Yeah, you're probably right," Madrid replied.

"Do you think Victoria knew?" Before he could answer, she answered her own question. "She knew. At least on some level, she would have to know."

He thought back to the journal. "Yeah, probably on some level, she knew. But given everything else—I'm not sure it even matters."

"I think it matters." Anger simmered in her tone. "Maybe not...I don't know. But Lyle Holiday shouldn't be allowed to get away with this—what he's doing to both of those women."

"I agree," Madrid answered.

Julie went back to stirring the woks, her moves agitated, the tension in her body evident. Madrid watched her jaw muscles clench and define. "Before I left," he said, "I asked Victoria how many sets of underwear September owned."

Julie looked at him, but kept stirring. "That's an odd—and personal question."

"Personal—I guess. Odd, no. If the number Victoria gave me was right, then September left with only what she was wearing. She didn't pack—which probably means she didn't plan to leave."

Julie processed the information. "So you don't think she ran away."

"I think she had plenty of reasons to run—but if she did run, she made the decision in a hurry."

Julie turned off the burners under each wok, pushed the button to switch off the blower in the hood. The kitchen fell suddenly silent. His thick forearms folded in front of him, Alex Madrid sat motionless on the bar stool. She studied his face, futilely tried to read his eyes. After a moment she spoke in a voice barely loud enough for Madrid to hear. "Do you think September's dead?"

"I don't know," Madrid answered. "I hope not—but I don't know."

* * * *

The "date" had taken just under an hour. A voyeur in the shadows, Charlie had watched from the darkened corner of the room. He had placed himself strategically so that he could see the driveway, the front door—and the girl. Anna Marie had followed Charlie's directions. She was both obedient and seductive—and it appeared effortless. Charlie had been forced to share her, and she didn't seem to mind.

The Wizard hadn't touched her—had never even left the couch. But still, Charlie had been reminded of his place. The little gap-toothed bastard had spoken just ten words: "stand up", "turn around", "stop", "sit", "turn left", "turn right". She had advanced through the sequence like a well-trained show dog. *We're both just well-trained dogs,* Charlie thought to himself. And then it occurred to him—it had always been that way.

Looking back, he now realized it had all been staged. Part of him knew it even back then. Staged much like the scene he had just witnessed. But that night, it had been strictly a one-act play. Charlie Blades had been the novice performer—skillfully coached—masterfully manipulated. Hormones and booze had been cast in supporting roles. It had been Charlie's first drink. That night had been his first for a lot things.

The pair had stood outside her bedroom door—in the dark narrow hallway—had spoken in whispers, like schoolboys about to play some grand prank. One had wide shoulders, massive hands and a broad, acne-ravaged face. The other was slightly built, pale skin, a high forehead, and wisps of adolescent beard on his narrow chin.

"She's waiting for you," the smaller one had said with an excited grin.

"Yeah, right," the soon-to-be eighteen-year old Charlie Blades had replied. Skeptical. Self-conscious.

"I'm telling you the truth," the small, gap-toothed boy had replied in an encouraged whisper.

"I go in there and she'll start screamin'," Charlie had said. " Then the cops'll come. Then I'll get my ass thrown in jail. And when I get out, I'll kill your scrawny ass."

"You got it all wrong, Charles. I'm telling you she wants you. Who do you think told me to get you over here tonight?"

"She wanted me to come over?" Charlie had so wanted to believe.

"She talks about you all the time, Charles."

"Oh, yeah?"

"Yeah. She's heard about your "talent"."

Vodka had dulled his reasoning. "What talent are you talking about?"

The smaller man had rolled his eyes. "The talent hanging between your legs, Dumb Ass. Momma knows about it—wants to see it for herself."

"Oh," Charlie had said, is if it were suddenly clear.

"You'd be doin' me a favor, Charlie Boy. I big one."

"Yeah?"

"Yeah. Open the door, Charlie."

His hand had moved towards the glass door knob. Had inexplicably stopped. "I don't think so."

"You gotta trust me. Go on inside," the smaller young man urged. "Just spend a few minutes with her. I promise you, Charles, your life will never be the same."

And it never was.

For twenty years, Charlie Blades had played it over in his head a hundred times. Hell, closer to a thousand—maybe two thousand. But parts of that night would always remain a blur. He was inside the room, the door closed behind him. But he never remembered touching the knob. There was a lamp, draped with a thin purplish cloth. The light spread across the big bed, left the rest of the room shadowy and undefined.

Lilly was on the bed—on top of the flower-print spread. She was lying on her side, her head propped on one elbow. Her long red hair had been swept to one side, had cascaded over her neck and left shoulder. Her legs, white and flawless, were bent slightly at the knee. She was wearing something—some sort of nightgown, or negligee. There were small ribbons in the front that she hadn't bothered to tie. Charlie could never remember what color it had been. Black? Red? The color hadn't mattered—it was see-through. She was posed like a well-aged, practiced centerfold. She had watched him, motionless. Her face was like that of a fine China doll—cool, smooth and emotionless. Part of him wanted to run away, another part wanted to never leave.

Then Lilly had adjusted her position. Much, much later Charlie had realized it was a calculated movement. Most of the nightgown had fallen away. She acted as if she hadn't noticed.

"I heard you two outside my door." Her voice had been soft, husky whisper. "I was wondering," she continued, her tone mocking, "if you had chickened out, Charlie. Maybe you're afraid to be with a woman."

His mouth had been dry. "No," he croaked.

She shifted on the bed, more of the nightgown had fallen away. Her large red nipples had stared back at him. "Are you afraid of me, Charlie?"

Again, "No." This time stronger.

"Then get over here," she had commanded. Later Charlie would recall the hint of distain in her voice.

Charlie stood next to the bed. He remembered being naked, but never sure how he got that way. She had guided his hands over her body. Softness, firmness, and heat. They had circled her breasts. She had demanded he pinch her nipples—hard.

Then harder. Her head had rolled back on her shoulders. Harder still, until she could stand it no longer. "Stop!" she had told him sharply. And Charlie had stopped. He had wondered if it was over, if she were about to send him away if he'd managed to screw it up. But the pause was short. Lilly had opened her eyes, had looked at him and smiled. It was the most perfect smile he'd ever seen.

Lilly had moved to the edge of the bed, guided Charlie's large, rough hands up and down her back, over her round bottom and all the way down her legs. Then they had started up slowly, over her calves, and past her knees. She had allowed his hands to inch up the inside of her thighs, she had stopped them just short of their destination. Charlie still remembered the soft wisp of red public hair that had brushed his fingers.

Lilly had pulled away from him—had told him to close his eyes. Reluctantly, he had obeyed. He remembered her beautiful face fading to black. Even back then, a well-trained dog. She had told him to lie on his back, to be completely still, and not to open his eyes. Charlie had complied. And then Lilly had started.. She had known more of what he wanted than he knew himself—and she had taught him to want more. She had teased him with her fingertips, had tantalized him with her hot, wet mouth. Then she would bite, or claw, or slap him with an open palm. He had laid still, except for the involuntary convulsions of pleasure or pain. His eyes had stayed closed. Occasionally, he had heard himself whimper—like a distant child.

Then she had stopped. Charlie felt her lie on the bed next to him—close, but not touching. Lilly had placed a sharp-tipped fingernail on the end of his hard penis. Charlie had laid perfectly still—had waited. It had seemed like a long time. Finally, Charlie felt her shift in the bed. Her body was against his. Lilly whispered to him, her breath hot in his ear.

"Are you going to do what I tell you, Charlie?"

"Yes."

"You're going to stop when I tell you to stop?"

"Yes."

Then Lilly had run the tip of her tongue along the edge of his ear. She had asked him in a low, tortured voice, "You'll stop no matter how much you want to keep fucking me?"

Her words had exploded in his head. He had replied like a man pleading for his life. "Yes."

"I'm just not convinced, Charlie," she had taunted.

Charlie's breathing had become ragged. He had continued to plea. "I'll stop when you me tell to. I swear."

She had let out a soft contemptuous laugh. "They all swear, Charlie." Then after a moment had said, "Open your eyes."

She had guided him on top of her, then had made him wait. Finally, she had reached down between his legs, had slowly eased him inside. Lilly had laid beneath him, her eyes closed, her breathing shallow and rapid. Her mouth was open slightly and the tip of her pink tongue played on her full lips. Charlie had wanted to kiss her. He had pressed his face against her, for a fleeting instant had experienced her mouth and tongue. Then she had turned her head violently.

"No!" she had told him, like a scolded puppy. "Don't do that again." Without moving the rest of her body, Lilly had stretched her arm, found the switch for the lamp.

Charlie Blades still remembered that sound—a metallic click. The room went dark, Lilly's beautiful face had disappeared beneath him. And that had been the last time he had seen her alive.

Charlie held Anna Marie firmly by the wrist, led her back down the dark, murky staircase. When they were inside the room, she asked, "Is that all? It was a sliver of hope slathered with desperation. "Is that all he's going to do—just look at me sometimes?"

"No," he replied brusquely, without elaboration. "That's not all." He took the handcuffs, snapped one side to her wrist, the other to the rail on the bed. "That's just all for now."

Anna Marie sat on the edge of the bed. Charlie towered above her. She stared up at him, sensed his displeasure, but didn't understand it. "I tried to do what you told me," she said, bewildered.

Charlie didn't reply. At the door, he turned to face her. He stood there for a moment—thought about Lilly. With three quick, long strides, he was back to the bed. Charlie Blades sandwiched Anna Marie's face in his meaty hands. He kissed her—just the way he had wanted to kiss Lilly nearly twenty years ago. Hard and long. He moved across the room, turned off the light in the make-shift jail cell, turned the key, listened to the deadbolt slide into place.

"Please don't turn out the light," Charlie heard her plead through the thick wooden door. "I don't want to be in the dark. "Please! Please just leave the light on!"

Charlie heard the panic in her voice. He ascended the steps, his feet purposely heavy and loud on the treads. He could still taste her lip gloss when he reached the top of the stairs. Before he closed the door, he heard her begin to cry. Small consolation, but it helped.

Chapter 28

September 26th—8:26 p.m.

"This is really good," Madrid said, using a fork to gather a piece of tofu with some rice and vegetables. He had given up on the chop sticks. They were sitting at the table by the window in the kitchen. The candles had been lit. The dog had already scarfed down the beef and rice, had looked at Madrid as if to ask, "Why don't we eat like this more often?"

Deflecting the compliment, Julie replied, "It's a little spicy for most people."

"I can't speak for most people," Madrid said, glancing at the dog who was asleep on the rug by the door. "But it's the best meal either of us has enjoyed for quite a while. Thanks for the invitation."

Julie looked at Madrid's half-eaten plate. "You're not finished are you?" In the next breath added with an embarrassed tone, "Jeez, I sound like somebody's mother."

Madrid laughed.

"It's not funny," she said, but she was smiling.

"It's *sort of* funny."

Madrid ate, Julie worked her chopsticks. Neither spoke, but the tension had evaporated. Finally, Madrid said, "I went out to see Pete Wilson after I left Victoria Jamerson's."

"At his place at the ski lodge?"

"You sound surprised."

"Pete Wilson isn't the most sociable person I've ever known. I'm a little surprised he asked you to come out."

"It was strictly business. I think he only asked me out because he didn't want to drive in."

She paused, dabbed the corner of her mouth with the linen table cloth. Then asked carefully, "Was he drinking?"

"Feeling no pain." He watched his reply register in her expression—wasn't sure how to read it.

"Interesting choice of words," she said vaguely.

"How so?" Madrid asked.

Julie turned, looked pensively towards the window. The dinner scene reflected back to her in the glass. "This is a bad time of year for Pete," she said, still staring out into the darkness beyond the glass. "Fall is bad, I'd guess October is the worst. I'm sure Miranda Toliver's death doesn't make it any easier for him."

The candlelight played on of her long elegant neck, reflected in her silky black hair. Madrid said, "I'm not following you."

"I'm guessing Pete didn't tell you about his wife?"

"No," Madrid replied. Pieces of carrot and bamboo shoot were skewered on his fork, temporarily suspended between the plate and his mouth. "I didn't know he was married."

"Widowed," Julie corrected.

"A recent thing?"

"No." Julie shook her head. "Mary Alice died.... ." She paused, counted in her head. "It must have been eleven years ago, nineteen sixty-five—it will be eleven years at the end of next month."

"You were in Black Creek eleven years ago?" Madrid asked.

"No, but my father's company owned the newspaper. But that's not how I know. Pete told me about it."

Madrid said nothing. He stabbed another piece of tofu, chewed—waited for her to continue.

"Mary Alice worked in a little 'mom and pop' grocery. It was called McCarson's. There was a diner attached to it—I think Pete said Mary Alice mostly waitressed. McCarson was also Black Creek's local bookie. He took bets—mostly on college and professional football, from what I've been told. The building is still out on Old Highway 64. But it's been closed for a long time."

"How did she die?"

Julie pushed her plate to one side and folded her arms on the edge of the table. "McCarson had a heart attack," she began. "A pretty big one, but he managed to survive. Mary Alice had been closing the place at night. Somebody came in near closing time and robbed the place. Pete told me that most of the folks around here thought it had to do with the gambling money. Whoever it was, they tied Mary Alice to a chair and cleaned out the place."

"People don't die from being tied to a chair," Madrid said.

"*Most* people don't, but Mary Alice was asthmatic. The thief, or thieves, covered her mouth with duct tape. Doc Wallaby was the county coroner back then. He said the excitement probably triggered an attack. She suffocated to death."

Madrid pictured Dicky Padrick scrambling and wheezing in the parking lot.

"She was only twenty-three years old, Alex. She and Pete had just celebrated their first anniversary." Julie shook her head. "It had to be a terrible way to die."

At twenty-three, Madrid couldn't think of many ways that weren't terrible. " No arrests?"

"No. Sheriff Boyd got hold of McCarson's client list. The old man wasn't happy about giving it up, but Boyd didn't give him a lot of choice. Some of Black Creek's more prominent citizens got called in for questioning. Even the mayor. Turns out he was a big Baltimore Colts fan."

John Mackey, Lenny Moore, Raymond Berry, and Johnnie U. Madrid recalled them like old friends he'd never really met.

"It was embarrassing for a lot of people," Julie said, "but no one ever solved the case. A few months later a truck driver was arrested in Abington, Virginia for raping a waitress at a late-night diner. Sheriff Boyd and Josh Galloway went up to interview him, but the guy had an alibi for Mary Alice's death."

"What kind of alibi?" Madrid asked.

"He was on the west coast."

Madrid offered a conciliatory nod—stabbed another piece of tofu and some broccoli.

"Mary Alice's death is Boyd's only unsolved murder. In fact, it's the only unsolved murder in this county since 1912."

Madrid thought back to his meeting with the dying sheriff. Not much chance he would clear the case before leaving office. "Any theories?"

Julie drank some tea, dabbed the corner of her mouth again. "Lots of theories—according to Pete. It happened on a Saturday night. The night before Halloween. Black Creek is in the heart of the Bible belt....well, you know?"

"Devil worshippers?" Madrid asked cynically.

"You asked for theories," she replied with an apologetic smile.

"Maybe a devil worshipper who didn't cover the spread," Madrid countered.

Julie's tone turned serious. "Pete has another theory. There's nothing much to support it—but that hasn't stopped him from holding on to it for all these years."

"Does Josh Galloway play into this theory?"

Julie stared at Madrid without attempting to mask her surprise. "Why would you ask that?"

"Pete said something about Josh Galloway being lucky for eleven years," Madrid answered. "But he didn't want to elaborate."

"Josh Galloway became Pete's number one suspect," Julie said flatly.

"Why?"

"Well.... ." Julie's reluctance was palpable.

"Pete thought Galloway had a thing for his wife," Madrid replied, answering his own question.

"He told you?" she asked in an astonished tone.

"No."

"So how did you know?"

"I didn't, but most murder falls under either money, lust, anger, or stupidity. I just picked the one I thought would fit best."

"I see."

"Anything to it?" Madrid asked.

Julie offered a slight shrug, tilted her head to one side. "Before my time here. But I doubt it. Mary Alice and Galloway had dated a couple of times before she and Pete got together. Pete didn't like that much. But that's the way men are."

"How men are?" Madrid asked—an amused challenge.

"How men are," Julie repeated. "Rack up as many babes as you can. But the one you settle down with is suppose to be some vestal virgin."

"Vestal virgins are overrated," Madrid said evenly.

Julie let the comment pass. "Personally, I think Pete just needed something to cling to. When all the other suspects had faded away, Pete was alone in Black Creek. About all he was left with was his distain for Josh Galloway."

"When Mary Alice died," Madrid asked, "who was the first one on the scene?"

"Not Galloway," Julie answered, like she'd been asked the question before. "Actually, Sheriff Boyd was the first one there. Pete was right behind him. Josh Galloway was on the other side of the county."

"How much money was taken?"

"That's hard to say," a cynical smile playing on her lips. "McCarson said there was probably a couple of hundred in the cash register. Pete said he was pretty vague about how much was in the safe. Mary Alice's purse was still on a shelf under the cash register. She had about thirty dollars. It was still there."

"So tell me again," Madrid asked, still not following the logic. "Why does Pete Wilson think Josh Galloway is so lucky?"

"Maybe because Galloway only lost an ex-girlfriend. Pete Wilson lost the love of his life."

* * * *

Bill o' fare at the Black Creek Jail: Macaroni and cheese, a naked hot dog on a crusty piece of bread, a carton of milk, an apple sliced into four pieces, and two Oreo cookies. The meal, as it were, had been sitting on the metal tray on the floor of the cell for over two hours. The edges of the apple had begun to turn brown.

Junior Jenkins looked over the offering with disgust—wondered if this, or something very much like this, was all he had to look forward to for the next twelve to fifteen. If he ended up doing the max, he'd be closer to forty than thirty—just a few years younger than his old man was now. He'd been here nearly a week and the bastard hadn't even stopped by to say hello. God, he needed to figure a way out of here. But all of Junior's hours of strategizing had produced only one plan. It was a plan of desperation—nothing original about it. But it was tried and true.

The cell door would open silently. Junior would move down the stairs, almost as if floating. He would slip out the back door, move into the parking lot. He would be outside these walls, surrounded by fresh air. The sun would be burning through the morning mist. Birds would be singing in the trees. Then the men carrying his body would load him into an ambulance, or maybe a hearse—and they would drive him away to freedom.

On the other side of the room, Dicky Padrick had viewed his offering with more optimism. He had eaten one of the Oreos immediately, had saved the other two for dessert. His tray had included a cup of fruit cocktail instead of a mealy apple and his hot dog had been dressed with mustard, ketchup, and sweet pickle relish.

"Hey, Padrick," Junior Jenkins had called to him in a loud whisper.

When Junior wanted to talk, it was usually about Dicky's sister—about her doing things when she was naked. It was never about what Dicky wanted to talk about. He had tried to ignore Junior, picked up the cup of fruit cocktail. A suspiciously-bright-red piece of cherry had floated in the heavy syrup. Dicky had selected it as his first target.

"I know how to get out of here," Junior had said, matter-of-factly. "How to get both of us out of here. But it takes two people and we have to do it at the same time."

Dicky had put the cherry in his mouth, chewed it twice—swallowed.

An hour later, Junior was still talking—and Dicky Padrick was beginning to listen.

* * * *

The meal was over and the conversation had dwindled. Alex Madrid and Julie Kingston were standing under the cover of her front porch. She hadn't bothered with the porch lights, which was fine with Madrid. Toto had faded into the night, exploring the well-maintained grounds. A thick fog had settled in, had blended with the darkness, and enveloped them. "Do you think your dog is back?" Julie asked, a hint of concern.

"Hard to say." Julie was standing close, her arms wrapped across her body. Awkwardness and intimacy competed for the space between them. "This was nice," he said. "I appreciate you asking me—asking us. I haven't ....it's been... ." Madrid gathered his thoughts. "It's been awhile since I've had good company and a home-cooked meal." Madrid grimaced. "Geez—that sounded like the tag line from a restaurant ad." He could see Julie smile in the darkness.

"Yeah, a little," she admitted. "But If it makes you feel any better, I felt the same way. I haven't been on a date in nearly a year."

Madrid turned, looked her up and down in the murky light, as if seeing her for the first time. "Really?" he said, his tone laced with disbelief.

"Really."

"So this was a date?" he asked.

"It's right on the line," she answered. "It could still go either way."

"So what would push it over the line?" Madrid asked.

"Less talking," she said.

Later that night, Madrid would recall the kiss like a well-written piece of music. It had started slowly, had become more complex and intense towards the middle, then had gracefully wound itself down and softly concluded. Maybe the best kiss he'd ever experienced? Hard to say. Definitely in the top three.

Chapter 29

September 26th—9:45 p.m.

Drive around Black Creek until you spot Alex Madrid. Get him out of his car. Bust him up a little. If he fights back—bust him up a lot. It was a simple plan. They were simple guys.

The pair had traded the Camaro with the flames, the skull, and the loud muffler for a black Plymouth Duster. The smaller one drove—the bigger one was folded into the passenger seat. On the edge of town, from the shadows of a service station parking lot, they had waited for Alex Madrid. When he finally rolled by them, they eased out of the lot, and followed him down River Street. He drove past Marcy's Holistic Café & Country Fried Grill, made a left turn. The pair watched him cross the bridge that led to the Black Creek College campus. The rains had made the river swollen and fast.

"Not too close," the bigger one cautioned.

"Fuck you," the smaller one replied.

They had watched Madrid pull into a poorly-lit parking lot behind one of the dormitories.

"What do ya' think he's doin' here?" the bigger one asked.

"Don't know, don't care," the smaller one replied.

"It ain't going to get much better than this," the bigger one said.

"You're right about that," the smaller one had replied with nervous agitation. "We'll take him when he comes out."

* * * *

In the lobby of Newhouse Dormitory, a color television was bolted to a bracket mounted high on wall. It stared down at the three coeds who were sprawled among the mismatched collection of vinyl-clad upholstery. The girls stared back at the movie of the week. A handsome Richard Chamberlain was desperately trying to explain something to somebody less handsome.

Madrid had driven through the campus on his way back to The Paradise Court. His decision to visit the dorm had been impromptu.

It was a brick building, three stories with a flat roof. It appeared sturdy and timeless—like the woman now planted in front of him. She had wide hips and gray hair that curled tightly against her head. Her small dark eyes projected her intensity. The name tag on her blouse read simply, "Miss Prescott".

"It's late," Miss Prescott told Madrid curtly.

"I know," Madrid replied, not quite apologetic. "This won't take long. I just want to ask Miranda Toliver's roommate a few questions."

"About what?" the woman challenged.

"The Beatles," Madrid replied without mirth. "Which Beatle is her favorite. Maybe get her thoughts on when she thinks the group is getting back together."

"Is that supposed to be funny?"

"More clever than funny."

"You want to ask her about Miranda," the stout woman said in an accusatory voice.

"That's right."

The woman's dark eyes narrowed, her round face contorted into a scowl. "That's going to upset her."

"I'll be tactful," Madrid replied with the slightest hint of diplomacy.

The woman turned abruptly, walked to a corner of the lobby, squeezed herself behind the counter. Madrid followed. She opened a log with hand-written pages—silently read a recent entry. Then she stabbed the paper with a short thick finger. "She's not here." There was a lilt of triumph in her voice. "Allison's taking a few days at home. You can't blame her," the woman told Madrid as if he were about to do just that. "The poor dear has been through a lot. She's a sensitive girl."

"So she'll be back when?" Madrid asked.

"I don't know," Miss Prescott answered irritably.

"Do you have a home number where I can reach her?"

"I don't know," the woman said protectively. "Allison's a sensitive girl."

Madrid nodded. "You've already mentioned that. I have no desire to upset her. I just want to ask her a couple of questions. I'm sure Miranda's death has been tough on her."

"On all of us," she said.

Madrid nodded again.

The woman wrote the number on a slip of paper. "You're not going to call her *tonight*, are you?"

"No," Madrid answered. "It's late and she's sensitive."

She handed Madrid the paper.

"Has anyone come for Miranda's belongings?"

"Not yet."

"Has anyone from the Sheriff's department been up to her room?"

"No."

"I'll be back tomorrow to take a look."

"I don't know why you'd need to do that," the woman said. "They already got the boy that killed Miranda."

"That's what everyone says." Madrid headed for the rear exit of the lobby. Richard Chamberlain was still staring down at the girls on the couch.

* * * *

A white globe hung above the back entrance to Newhouse Dormitory. It cast an anemic yellowish glow. The bigger man flattened himself against the building just beyond the arc of light. He was dressed in black—the pants the bottom half of a karate gi. The long-sleeved shirt clung to his muscular torso. His shoulder-length hair was captured by a wide black headband cinched across his forehead. His feet were bare. A set of nun chucks were tucked into his waist band. He waited, took shallow breaths, worked to control his nerves.

The Plymouth Duster was strategically positioned on the far side of the small parking lot, directly across from the back door of the dormitory. The parking lights had been left on. The smaller man stood in the middle of the lot, backlit in amber. A grease-stained ball cap was pulled low over his eyes. His purpose was to distract first—join the fracas second. With a series of quick jerky motions, he surveyed the lot. There was no one. It was Sunday night and the Black Creek campus was dead. This had worked out better than he had hoped for. When they were finished, they would leave this guy curled on the asphalt--whimpering and crying like a little bitch. The smaller man shifted his weight from one foot to the other, then back again—an excited little victory jig.

Madrid stopped two feet short of the door. Through the small rectangular glass, he could see the parking lights and the silhouette of the hairy little man dancing around like some demented elf. He had figured they would show up eventually, but hadn't figured it for now. The .45s were in the Blazer—with the dog. "Damn it," Madrid whispered to himself. The big one would be hiding somewhere—maybe between cars, but he would have to expose himself before closing. *No*, Madrid concluded. He wouldn't be between the cars. Keebler was out there for a reason—to hold Madrid's attention. The big one would come from behind—which meant he was probably just outside the door. The door swung to the right, which would block Madrid's view in that direction. So the big one would be to his right, Madrid told himself. And that was good.

* * * *

The smaller man halted his jig, watched the door swing open, saw the light from inside the building spill onto the walkway. The blonde man strolled out, his head down. He was unhurried—maybe preoccupied. The smaller man watched the bigger man come off of the wall—slip out of the shadows like the proverbial Ninja. He wondered if the blonde man would crumple under the first massive blow. He'd seen plenty of others who had. He fretted that there would be nothing for him. The blonde man would be finished, unconscious—unable to detect further pain. That was often the problem when the bigger man took the first shot. With two long, silent strides he was directly behind their target, poised like an oversized shadow. The smaller man was never clear about what happened next.

* * * *

The Okinawans called it ushiro-geri. Like most devastating techniques, it was fast and basic.

Madrid opened the door, stepped into the night. Right foot, left, then right again. The whole thing took less than two seconds. At the last instant Madrid planted his body, dropped his center of gravity, and stole a glance over his right shoulder. The gorilla was on top of him. Madrid exploded the back kick; his heel landed solidly just above the big guy's knee. Madrid felt the leg collapse—an instant later heard the scream. He spun to his right. The big man had already begun to topple. Madrid timed the fall—stepped towards him. With a tight arc, Madrid swung his left elbow. He planted it on the soft underside of the big man's chin. The recoil sent the black head band sailing. The big man fell to the concrete—didn't move.

The smaller man ran towards them—his head down. He screamed shrilly—manically—like a television Indian on the warpath. Madrid picked up the nun chucks from the pavement—timed his swing. Nothing fancy—no blurring-fast figure-eight nonsense. Just one shot straight over the top. It connected an inch above the smaller guy's left ear. He stumbled, fell over his partner on the sidewalk. The smaller man landed face down, struggled to get up. Madrid swung the weapon hard, landed it across the smaller man's left hamstring. The smaller man yelped. Madrid repeated the action, hit him in exactly the same spot—got exactly the same reaction.

"Stop screaming or you'll wake up the other girls," Madrid told him in a conversational tone.

"Fuck you," the smaller man managed. The words came out in an angry, high-pitched whimper.

He looped the weapon around the man's throat, tightened it until it produced the leverage he needed. Madrid could hear the smaller man begin to wheeze. Madrid jerked him to his feet. Then he released the weapon and watched him teeter on his one good leg.

Madrid stepped back and said, "You guys really aren't very good at this, are you?" The smaller man continued to struggle for balance, standing on one foot—testing the damaged leg. The ball cap was gone and a wall of hair had fallen over his face.

After a moment, Madrid said, "You're right. There's no need to answer that question—it was clearly rhetorical."

The smaller man wobbled back and forth—to and fro. He pushed the hair away from his face—stared at Madrid, said nothing.

"You need to tell me who sent you."

The little man looked at his partner crumpled on the sidewalk, the big man's right leg protruding at an odd angle. He summoned up his final ration of bravado—spoke in a voice that was stretched and cracked with pain. "I ain't telling you shit."

Madrid smiled. "Oh, you're going to tell me," he replied in an amused tone.

And the smaller man did tell him.

And it didn't take very long.

And it wasn't a name Alex Madrid had expected to hear.

Chapter 30

September 27th—6:23 a.m.

"*Thirty days hath September, April, June, and November.*" It was night—it felt late, but the group of small girls were skipping rope in front of a large stone church. "*Thirty days hath September, April, June, and November.*" Colors from the back-lit stained glass pierced the darkness. High-pitched and melodic, the voices rang like pleasant-sounding chimes. "*Thirty days hath September, April, June, and November.*" Without changing cadence, the first jumper skipped out from under the rope. Another girl, exactly like the first, hopped in—took her place. The group of girls seemed to be growing. "*Thirty days hath September, April, June, and November.*"

The voices continued the singsong chant, but the melodic quality of their tone began to erode. It was now harsh and shrill. Dicky Padrick was standing at the edge of the darkness. One of the chanting little girls spotted him—pointed him out to the others. They rushed to him as a group—surrounded him. Padrick stood lump-like—his flaccid arms dangled by his sides. The girls dragged him back into the light. It had grown stronger from behind the stained-glass of the church—bright enough to reveal their faces. They were all the same—slightly-altered versions of Miranda Toliver—in miniature. One of the girls grabbed the jump rope—tossed one end high into the air. It disappeared into the darkness. When it fell back into the light, it remained suspended in air. At the end of the rope was a hangman's noose, expertly tied. "*Thirty days hath September, April, June, and November.*" Two of the small blonde girls lifted a third. She placed the noose around Dicky Padrick's soft, thick neck. Dicky Padrick appeared confused, barely aware of his situation. He didn't resist, but managed a weak, unconvincing protest.

"It wasn't me," he said pitifully, looking down on the growing sea of blonde curls. "I didn't hurt you. It was a big man in a black suit. I tried to stop him, but ...."

His words were lost in the incessant chant. "*Thirty days hath September, April, June, and November. Thirty days hath September, April, June, and November.*"

With a violent jerk, the noose tightened. Panic registered in Dicky's eyes. His arms flailed uselessly. More little girls appear from the darkness. Their faces were no longer childlike. The rope grew thick and heavy. In unison, they began to pull. The images in the stained-glass morphed into something ominous, but undefined. The ever-growing mob continue their maniacal chant, "*Thirty days hath September, April, June, and November. Thirty days hath September, April, June, and November.*" Dicky Padrick's tennis shoes—a pair of worn high-topped Keds—came onto focus. They were red—the shoestrings removed. The heels lifted from the painted gray concrete—maybe an inch—and then a moment later—another inch. Dicky was on the balls of his feet. Another pull—the tips of his toes struggled to maintain contact. *"Thirty days hath September, April, June, and November."* Another pull. The chanting stopped—the church's stained glass went black.

A spasmodic jerk and Alex Madrid was awake. He could hear the rain on the metal breezeway outside his room. Through the dim light, the dreariness of his surroundings came slowly into focus. The room was cool, but he was sweating heavily. He threw off the blanket—sat up in the bed, tried to clear Dicky Padrick from his head. Toto, his chin on his paws, watched his roommate impassively. Madrid stared back. The phone rang. The shrill sound surged through his head like an electric shock, left behind the residue of dread. He picked it up in the middle of the second ring.

"Yeah," he said without enthusiasm.

"At least your not one of those cheerful morning people." It was Julie Kingston. She sounded like she'd been up for awhile

"What time is it?" Madrid asked as he fumbled in the murkiness for his wrist watch.

"Six thirty or so," Julie answered.

Madrid looked at the luminous hands on the Timex. "Yeah," he said groggily, "that's about right."

"I've got some news," Julie said. "And none of it's good."

Madrid turned on the lamp between the beds, swung his feet onto the cold floor. "Okay," he replied in a resigned tone.

"I just got a call from Victoria Jamerson. Lyle Holiday is dead."

"No kidding," Madrid said.

"No kidding."

"Any chance it was natural causes?"

"Not hardly," Julie answered. "Kitchen knife in the chest."

"Damn," Madrid mumbled.

"Yeah," Julie replied.

"Any details?"

"Victoria said she woke up and found him that way."

"Do you believe her?"

Julie Kingston sidestepped the question. "She was really upset."

"Not exactly a *yes* or a *no*."

"Like you said," Julie reminded him, "you never know who might be listening."

"Good point."

"I told her not to talk to anyone until she gets a lawyer."

"You think Victoria Jamerson has a lawyer? Or even knows one?" Madrid asked skeptically.

"I'll talk care of that," Julie replied. "But it's going to take awhile. There's a woman in Asheville. I'll try her first, but it will probably be this afternoon before I can get anyone face to face with her."

"Has anyone called the law?"

"Victoria should be calling now. She wanted me to do it, but I told her it would look better if she made the call."

"That was lawyerly of you."

"I gave her another piece of advice, too."

"Yeah?"

"Yeah. I told her not to talk to anyone until you got there. My guess is that you'll be getting a call in a few minutes. Somebody from the Sheriff's Department. They probably won't be too happy."

"Why did you tell her that?"

"I asked Victoria to give me the name of someone she trusted. It was a real short list—September, me, and you. September's out. With the paper, I have a real conflict of interest. I've probably already overstepped my bounds. So that leaves you—which was probably the best choice anyway. I get a sense you're familiar with both sides of the law. I'm just about dressed and then I'm on my way out to the Jamerson place. So am I going to see you there?"

"If they call," Madrid answered.

"They'll call," she replied confidently.

"Then I guess I'll see you."

"There's something else I need to tell you," Julie said somberly.

"About Victoria?"

"No. About Dicky Padrick. He's in the hospital. His skull is cracked and they're not sure he's going to live."

"What happened?"

"They think he tried to hang himself with a bed sheet. The knot slipped and he landed head first on the floor of the cell."

Their pale faces came back into focus. Madrid could see their blue eyes and blonde curls—could hear their mantra growing louder. *Thirty days hath September, April, June, and November.* In his dream, the boy had been lifted slowly from the concrete. In reality, Dicky Padrick had come crashing back down.

Chapter 31

September 27th—7:48 a.m.

The call had come just as she'd predicted. "We're out here at the Jamerson house," Josh Galloway had growled. "The crazy old bitch just killed her husband with a butcher knife. But maybe you already know that."

"News to me," Madrid lied.

"Boyd said to give you a call. The old woman wants to talk to you."

There were four cars in the Jamerson's driveway. Julie Kingston's Mercedes was the last in line. Julie stood next to it, under a large red umbrella. As he approached, Madrid noted how her long black hair fell onto the shoulders of her yellow turtle-necked sweater—how her black boots hugged her calves and disappeared under the hem of her long denim skirt. Julie raised the umbrella a few inches. Madrid stepped beneath the nylon dome remembering the kiss they had shared just a few hours earlier.

"I talked with the lawyer," Julie said, all business. "She can't get here until about noon."

"Okay," Madrid said.

Julie handed a lidded Styrofoam cup to Madrid. "They're waiting for you."

Madrid took the cup. "Thanks," he said, getting a whiff of the coffee.

"It's for Victoria," she said.

"Oh," Madrid replied. "She likes it with milk and honey."

"I know," Julie said with a hint of smile. "Me too."

"I'll remember that," Madrid said.

"See that you do."

On the front porch, the tall, thin deputy leaned against the support post, watched Madrid cross the soggy lawn. His narrow face hadn't seen a razor in two days—his uniform might have doubled for pajamas the night before. The metal name tag on the pocket of his shirt said "Hodges". He reminded Madrid a little of Barney Fife—only with bad teeth and probably a fucked-up childhood. The deputy took the last deep drag from his cigarette—flipped it at Madrid's feet.

"Been waitin' on you," Hodges said, showing some yellow fang.

Madrid opened the screen door, the skinny deputy followed him inside. Again, the kitchen held the fading smell of breakfast. A black iron skillet with half-cooked eggs had been abandoned on the cold stove, the yellow yokes stared up at the ceiling. Next to the skillet, congealed grease coated a plate of link sausages. Another deputy, with short blonde hair and a square jaw, leaned against the kitchen counter his arms folded across his chest. He nodded as Madrid entered. Slumped, his weight on his elbows, Sheriff Avery Boyd sat behind the kitchen table. Clear tubing ran from his nose to a small canister of oxygen. His skin was the color of ash. He studied Madrid through dark, recessed eyes.

"Most unusual, Madrid," the dying man said in a tired voice.

"Yeah," Madrid responded, "I suppose it is. I appreciate your flexibility on the matter, Sheriff."

Conserving his breath, Boyd nodded.

The deputy leaning on the counter asked, "You know Mrs. Jamerson well, Madrid?"

"I've talked to her a couple of times."

The deputy continued in the role as surrogate interrogator. "About the disappearance of her daughter?"

"Yes."

"Anything else?"

"Like what?" Madrid asked.

"I don't know—maybe problems with her husband?"

Madrid looked directly at Sheriff Boyd, answered the deputy's question. "No. She didn't mention anything about that."

"Funny she wants to talk with *you* in her darkest hour," the deputy said.

Madrid continued to address the sheriff. "This is a funny town with lots of funny people. Not many are funny *ha-ha*, though."

The sheriff shook his head slowly, replied in a labored voice. "No, not many."

After another moment he said, "You got ten minutes."

Madrid walked past the deputy into the parlor. To his right was the doorway that led to the hallway, Madrid paused. From the back bedroom, male voices conversed in low somber tones. A reflective burst of light exploded into the dark hallway. Madrid heard the high-pitched whine of a Polaroid camera—tried to imagine the images taking shape.

"Can't go in there," the deputy said.

Madrid turned his attention to the parlor. It was pretty much as he'd left it less than twenty-four hours earlier. Victoria Jamerson was back in her chair by the window. She wore the same dress—the same worried look. The exception was Josh Galloway. He was sitting a few feet from her, straddling a straight-backed chair—watching the beleaguered woman as if she might suddenly evaporate. The deputy who had been leaning on the counter followed Madrid into the room, said to Galloway, "The Sheriff wants to see you in the kitchen, Sergeant."

Galloway reluctantly pulled his eyes away from Victoria Jamerson, looked at Madrid. "Guess you heard about Padrick." There was the unmistakable note of triumph in his voice.

"I heard," Madrid admitted.

"Still think he's innocent?" A smile tugged at the corner of his mouth.

"If he wakes up, I'll ask him," Madrid replied.

"Good luck with that," Galloway half chuckled as he followed the other deputy to the kitchen.

When he was gone, Victoria Jamerson turned from the window. "Thank you for coming, Mr. Madrid," she said, her voice quiet and sad.

"You're welcome, Victoria," Madrid said, handing her the cup of coffee. "Julie Kingston sent you this."

She took the cup, looked out the window, then back at Madrid. "She's a very nice young woman," she said in a far-away voice.

"We don't have a lot of time, Victoria," Madrid said firmly. "There are some things I need to tell you—things you need to understand."

Victoria bowed her head, wrung her hands, as if launching into an anguished prayer. "I'm sorry I dragged you into this—you and Miss Kingston." Tears were building behind her tired hazel eyes. "I just didn't know anyone else to call."

"You did the right thing, Victoria," Madrid told her with more confidence than he felt. "I'm glad you called."

"Thank you," she whispered. A pair of tears escaped from the corners of her eyes, raced slowly down her face.

"Julie Kingston has arranged for a lawyer," Madrid began. "It's a woman. I get the sense she'd good at what she does. She's coming from Asheville, but she won't be here until mid day. My advice to you is not to talk to anyone until you meet with her."

"I can talk to you, Mr. Madrid," she said stubbornly. "And Miss Kingston."

Madrid moved to the edge of the couch, leaned in, spoke in a instructive whisper. "Listen to me, Victoria." There was a hard urgency in his tone. "You need to be extremely careful what you say."

Her reply was an equal mix of desperation and confusion. "I don't know what you mean."

"It's like this, Victoria. If you killed Lyle Holiday, I *don't* want to know. I have no right of confidentiality. You can tell me if you *didn't* kill him, but *do not* tell me if you did. If you tell me you killed him, I might have to repeat it in court. The same goes for Julie."

Victoria Jamerson smiled sadly as another pair of tears formed. "Miss Kingston was right. You know what to do."

"I know more about what *not* to do," Madrid confessed.

"Do you think I killed Lyle, Mr. Madrid?"

Madrid sat back on the couch. He studied the woman in the chair by the window—wondered if she still expected September to come walking up the driveway on her birthday. Victoria Jamerson had endured a lot. It was hard to guess how or what she was thinking. "I hope you didn't, Victoria," Madrid replied quietly, with measured words, "but I could understand if you did."

"You're not sure, though?" Her voice was calm.

"No," Madrid confessed.

Victoria Jamerson nodded knowingly. For the next several moments she divided her time between staring out the window and sipping her coffee. Occasionally, she would close her eyes as if about to fall asleep. Madrid watched her, occasionally glanced at his watch—calculated how much time they had left.

Finally, when Victoria spoke, her eyes were fixed on a blank section of wall. Her voice had a peaceful, dreamy quality. "I start every morning the exact same way, Mr. Madrid," she began. "It's been this way for—I don't know—at least two or three years. I can't say exactly when it started. But I can't remember it being any other way. When Lyle and me were sharing the same bed, I would look over at him—first thing in the morning. I'd watch his chest—hoping to see he had stopped breathing. Sometimes it was before sun up—when it was still dark. I'd just lay there and listen. When he moved into the back room, I'd tiptoe down the hallway. I'd stand in the doorway and watch and listen. Every day was the same, Alex. I'd start every day disappointed that God hadn't taken that evil man from this earth. And every day that disappointment would pile up on me just little bit more. It kept getting heavier and heavier on my spirit."

Part of Madrid wanted her to stop talking, and for a moment, he thought she might.

Victoria closed her eyes tightly, scrunched her face in a painful expression. When her eyes snapped back open, she was again staring at the spot on the wall. "But this morning was different," she continued. "This morning I didn't check on Lyle. I didn't check on him 'cause I knew I couldn't stand any more disappointment. This one morning I just got up and started makin' his breakfast. The same breakfast I make for him every Monday morning. Eggs, sausage, and a pan of biscuits. I almost had it ready before I realized it—the quiet in the house. I must have stood there for five minutes—listenin'. I turned off the eggs so I could hear better. There was nothing. This house was dead quiet—like I was the last person left on earth, Alex. That's when I started to pray. It shames me to say it, but I was prayin'. I tiptoed back into the hall. Lyle's door was closed. He usually don't close it, but this mornin' it was closed. I opened it real quiet. I saw him layin' there. His eyes were open and his mouth was open—like he was surprised—starin' up at God for an answer. My daddy's knife was stickin' into Lyle's chest. There was blood everywhere on the bed. But I was still half expectin' him to be breathin'. I stood there watching him for a long time, I guess." Victoria tore her eyes from the wall, looked at Madrid. "I wasn't disappointed anymore."

The blonde deputy walked into the room. "Sheriff says time's up, Madrid," he announced, almost apologetic.

Madrid looked at his watch. It had been ten minutes—just what Avery Boyd had promised. "Remember what I told you," Madrid said, so the deputy could hear. "Your lawyer will be here in a few hours. Don't talk to anyone about this until you talk with her first."

Victoria Jamerson had gone back to staring out of the window.

"Tell me you will do what I said, Victoria," Madrid pressed.

Without changing her focus, she nodded. "Thank you for coming, Alex. Thank you for listening to me."

"You're welcome," Madrid said.

"Gotta go," the deputy said.

The deputy stayed with Victoria in the parlor. Madrid moved to the kitchen. Josh Galloway was leaning against the counter where the other deputy had stood. He'd crammed some sausage links into a biscuit he had taken from the pan—was munching happily.

"Help yourself," Madrid told him.

Galloway replied around a mouthful of food, "Lyle's not going to be needing his biscuits. Hated to see 'um go to waste." Galloway chewed twice, swallowed, then asked, "So what did you two talk about?"

"The weather mostly—a little baseball. Turns out she's a big Pittsburg Pirates fan. Loves Willie Stargell. But hey, who doesn't?"

Galloway eyed the pan of biscuits. "You ain't nearly as funny as you think you are, Madrid."

"Probably not."

Sheriff Boyd took a deep draw of oxygen, spoke in a thin, raspy voice. "Is Victoria ready to talk with us?"

"She's going to wait for her lawyer, Sheriff."

Boyd nodded as if he already knew the answer.

The skinny deputy with the wrinkled uniform was standing next to the door. "That's when you know they done it—when they start calling for their friggin' lawyer."

Galloway selected another biscuit from the pan. "What Hodges says is true."

Madrid turned to Avery Boyd. "I appreciate you letting me talk to her, Sheriff."

Boyd nodded slowly.

"There's no blood on her or her clothes," Madrid said to the sheriff.

"She could have taken a shower and changed clothes," Galloway countered.

"Could have," Madrid countered, "but I'm betting she didn't. You might want to check the shower and the laundry hamper."

Boyd nodded.

When Madrid was almost to the screened door, Galloway said, "Heard about that trouble on campus last night."

Madrid turned, waited. "What trouble was that?"

"Two of our local bad asses took a beatin' behind Newhouse Dorm."

"Some of those Newhouse girls can get pretty rough," Madrid replied.

"Prescott is a nosy old bitch," Galloway continued. "She watched you leave, Madrid. Said you got into it with those boys behind the dorm."

The deputy from the parlor had walked back into the kitchen. "I took the call," he said looking at the sheriff. "Actually, what she said was those two guys jumped you."

Josh Galloway didn't conceal his irritation. "Yeah," he grunted, "it was something like that."

"Oh, yeah." Madrid worked up an un-amused smile that come off more as a sneer. "You're talking about that little thing in the parking lot with Lurch and Cousin It."

"Yeah, funny man," Galloway growled "Those boys ended up in the hospital."

"*Those boys,*" Madrid countered, "need to be more careful."

"The little one's got a broken collar bone," Galloway retorted, anger building. "You broke the big one's leg and you might have give him brain damage."

"Brain damage?" Madrid asked skeptically.

"Yeah, fuckin' brain damage," Galloway repeated.

Madrid paused, as if pondering the possibility. "How would you be able to tell?"

Chapter 32

Gatlinburg, Tennessee
September 27th—10:48 a.m.

"Tonight," The Wizard replied in response to Charlie Blades' question.

A blanket of gray fog wrapped the A-framed chalet—rain drummed steadily on the roof. The yellow blaze from the stone fireplace pierced the gloom. The two men sat at the kitchen table. Strewn before them were grease-stained wrappers recently peeled from pieces of fried chicken and biscuits.

"We go tonight, Charles," the small, gap-toothed man reiterated. "This is Alex Madrid's final day."

Charlie swallowed a mouthful of scalding hot coffee—watched the smaller man pick through the biscuit crumbles. The plan was complete—as usual, each detail intricately choreographed. The Wizard had walked Blades through the sequence—right up to the part where Charlie placed Alex Madrid's gun to the back of Rex's head. "You and I will simply slip into the night like we were never there."

"Then we come back here," Blades said, "for the girl."

The Wizard nodded. "One last dance, so to speak," The Wizard replied nostalgically, "for old time's sake."

"We leave her here?"

"She'll be fine," The Wizard replied calmly. "A couple of Phenobarbs and a glass of wine—the princess will never know we left the castle."

"After that?"

"You and I need to go our separate ways. At least for a while."

Charlie gauged the reply—nodded.

"Take the girl with you, Charles. Enjoy her for a while. When we get our money back from Madrid, you will have enough to live nicely for a long time."

Charlie Blades played it over in his mind. He could see it unfolding just as the little man had described. They had talked for a long time. Charlie had pled his case. The Wizard had seemed convinced. Charlie wasn't a thief. A killer, a rapist, and psychopath—yes. But he hadn't taken the money.

And with Charlie eliminated, that only left one person.

The same person who'd taken The Wizard's last redheaded girlfriend.

And his dog.

Charlie thought some more. It was a good plan.

* * * *

In the cramped, poorly-lit office, Alex Madrid sat across the battered metal desk from Pete Wilson. Both men held large Styrofoam cups of coffee. A box of blueberry muffins from the local bakery sat unopened in the middle of the desk. Wilson was eyeing it as if it might grow wings and take flight.

"Guess we won't be going out to talk with Lyle Holiday this morning," Wilson said in a reflective tone.

"No," Madrid replied. He was slumped in the chair, his legs extending in front of him.

"Who all was out there?" Pete asked.

Madrid listed the names, described the blonde deputy. "There was at least one or two in the back bedroom," he added.

"Did you see him, Lyle—the body?"

Madrid. "No."

"But they're sure he's dead?"

Madrid took a sip from the cup, fought back a yawn. "Yeah," he said sleepily, "they seemed real sure about that."

"I'm surprised Boyd let you talk to Victoria."

Madrid tilted his head, tried to get the muscles in his thick neck to relax. "Yeah, me too."

"You think she did it?" Pete asked.

"Victoria?"

"Yeah."

"No," Madrid answered. Took another sip of coffee, then added, "I think part of her wanted to kill him—but I don't think she did it."

Pete Wilson breached his threshold of self control. He reached over the desk, opened the box—after careful scrutiny, selected a muffin. "You never know about people," Wilson said around a happy mouthful of muffin.

"You never know," Madrid agreed. "Don't get me wrong— she's not sad that he's dead."

"Sarah Prescott called me this morning," Wilson said.

"The dorm mother at Newhouse?" Madrid asked.

"They don't call 'em that anymore—it's residential manager—or something. But yeah. She told me all about your little adventure. I should' a gotten that call from you."

"Not really that much to tell."

"Sarah had a little different take on it—but then she was the one cleaning blood off the sidewalk at dawn."

"I'm sorry about that," Madrid said.

"Um huh," Wilson replied, "tell that to her," he said, finishing off the muffin with a second bite. "What do those guys have against you?"

"Don't know exactly. I'm working on it."

Angie from the front desk stuck her head in the door. "President Chalmers is on the phone, Boss," she said to Wilson.

Pete Wilson pulled himself erect in the chair, brushed something invisible from the front of his uniform. "He is?"

"Yes, sir," Angie confirmed in an official tone. Then she jerked her head in Madrid's direction, added with a note of disdain, "Wants to talk with him."

Twenty minutes later, Madrid was comparing the differences in the President's office to the one he'd just left. The carpet was thick— the furniture reproduction Chippendale. One wall was covered with leather-bound books. Another wall was glass that looked out over the small campus. A green rectangle of soccer field was visible in the distance, beyond that, the Pisgah River. Madrid had been waiting for ten minutes—scanning the numerous awards and credentials that took up most of the remaining wall space.

"'Educated men are as much superior to uneducated men as the living are to the dead.'" Chalmers was posed in the doorway—a dapper little man in an expensive gray suit—crisp white shirt and red necktie. He added with unabashed arrogance. "Aristotle."

Madrid replied, "'Twenty years of schoolin' and they put you on the day shift." He paused. "Bobby Zimmerman." Madrid paused again, then added, "Witty repartee. Shall we continue?"

"No," the college president replied curtly. He strode purposefully across the office—positioned the ox blood leather chair just so. Sat.

Madrid took one of the smaller matching chairs on the other side of the massive mahogany desk.

When President Chalmers finally spoke, his tone was authoritative. "You are continuing to investigate the death of Miranda Toliver?"

Madrid nodded. "Yes."

"Even though Richard Padrick is clearly guilty?" Chalmers retorted.

"Define 'clearly'," Madrid countered.

"I don't have to define anything to you, Mr. Madrid. I want you to conclude the investigation immediately."

Madrid studied Chalmers . He was one of those guys who spent a lot of time on his look. His face was taut and tanned, his eyes the same shade of gray as his suit. His salt-and-pepper hair had been meticulously combed and sprayed into place. "Why would you want me to do that?"

"No, no," Chalmers said with a dismissive wave of his hand. "*I* don't provide *you* with the reasons for the decisions *I* make."

"Maybe not," Madrid replied. He uncrossed his legs, settled back into the chair. "But it would be better for *you* if you did."

Chalmers shot back, anger sharpened his tone. "You are an employee of Black Creek College, Mr. Madrid." He raised his chin slightly—added, "Ergo, you work for me."

Madrid's smile spread slowly. It was the one that made him look more canine than happy. "You're hoping Dicky Padrick dies," Madrid said with sardonic amusement.

The arrogance drained from Chalmer's expression. "I would never... ."

"Sure you would," Madrid interrupted. "Because you're convinced that's the way to play it. Damage control—plain and simple. Miranda Toliver's dead—nothing's going to change that. Dicky Padrick, the brother of one of your teachers... ."

It was Chalmers' turn to interrupt. "Miles Padrick is a full professor."

Madrid raised his shoulders an inch and left them drop. "Doesn't matter. As bad as this is, if Dicky Padrick dies, it's all in the rearview mirror. The boy went crazy, killed the girl, hung himself in remorse." Madrid worked in a little Curtis Mayfield. " '...a terrible blow, but that's how it goes... '"

"You're wrong, Madrid."

Madrid shook his head dismissively, "Don't think so, Dr. Chalmers. I'm guessing it will go something like this. Miles Padrick, your full professor, takes a leave of absence—which turns into a sabbatical—which turns into a teaching position a couple of thousand miles from here. TV people stop coming around, papers stop writing about Miranda's death. Pick up the pieces and move on. But for that to work, two things have to happen. Dicky Padrick has to stop breathing. That's number one. Number two is everyone has to accept that Padrick was the guy who killed Miranda Toliver. If number two doesn't happen, number one doesn't help you."

Chalmers sat back in his chair—gave Madrid a fresh look. "I'm not saying that you're right, Madrid. But you seem like a man who can see the big picture. So you will stop the investigation?" Chalmers asked. This time it was more of a plea.

"Not until I'm convinced Padrick killed her."

"Then you're fired," Chalmers said in a quiet defeated voice.

Madrid nodded. "You probably should have opened with that. Would have saved us some time—and all this drama."

Chalmers sat motionless in his big chair. "I usually don't enjoy the termination of employees," he stated in an acrid tone. "Your case is the exception, Mr. Madrid."

"I try to make it fun for everybody."

"You have an hour to collect your things and leave the campus," Chalmers said to the desktop. "If you come back, I'll have you arrested for trespassing."

Madrid stared out the wall of windows. At some point during the course of their short conversation, the campus had disappeared behind a wall of fog and rain.

* * * *

Madrid spotted Julie Kingston's Mercedes parked outside the administration building. She stood under the same red umbrella she had used at Victoria Jamersons' house. This time she didn't offer to share. She gave Madrid a look even colder than the rain. "What did you tell her?" she asked anger seething in her tone.

Madrid hunched the collar of his jacket closer to his face. "Tell who?"

"Damn it, you know what I'm talking about," she replied sharply. "What did you tell Victoria this morning?"

Madrid paused, collected his thoughts. "I told her that if she killed Lyle, I didn't want to know about it. And I told her to stay mum until she talked to your lawyer."

"That's what you told her?" Julie asked with disbelief.

"That's what I told her."

Madrid watched Julie Kingston's anger dissolve to confusion. "Well," Julie said with an emotional gulp. "That's not what she did."

Rain was washing down Madrid's face. He closed his eyes—swiped the water away with the palm of his hand—asked, "What did she do?"

"She made a full confession."

Madrid stood motionless—could see the battered woman with her grateful cup of coffee sitting next to the window. Could still hear the inexplicable thread of hope in her voice.

"And then she, she… " Emotion overwhelmed her. Julie stared at the wet asphalt, clenched her fist—tapped it lightly on her thigh. When she looked up, her eyes locked on Madrid's. Her voice was steady and controlled. "After she confessed, Victoria took a bottle of sleeping pills."

"Goddamn it," Madrid said loudly, to no one. Then added, "Is she dead?"

"No. They got her to the emergency room and pumped her stomach. They're pretty sure she will be all right."

Madrid said, more a statement than a question. "She told Boyd she put the knife in Lyle?"

Julie nodded. "I'm sorry I blew up at you, Alex."

Madrid could feel the darkness growing inside of him.

"I have to go back to work," Julie said, her voice just loud enough to reach Madrid through the downpour.

Madrid nodded without looking in her direction, shoved his hands into the pockets of his jacket. Walked away.

Chapter 33

Gatlinburg, Tennessee
September 27th—4:30 p.m.

The only window in the basement dungeon was too high to reach—too small to crawl through. It had been covered with cardboard, held in place with duct tape. A few hours earlier, the big, hairy man had come down the stairs with lunch—or maybe breakfast—or possibly dinner. With no sunlight and no watch, Anna Marie had lost all track of time and date. At the foot of her cot was a half-eaten roast beef sandwich, some corn chips, and the wrapper from the Hershey bar. The big man had removed her handcuffs, but had taken her shoes. The concrete was cold on her feet.

Anna Marie heard them moving on the floor above her—heavy footfalls blended with the muffled voices. They had been up there for a while. She moved around the dingy, claustrophobic room—tried to count. She thought maybe five or six, but they were on the other end of the house. Mostly a guess, but the nightmare was now locked in her head—a half dozen men marching down the dark, narrow staircase. They would come for her—like a pack of wild dogs. When they were finished—if she survived—there would be nothing left of her life worth salvaging.

The cold concrete made her feet ache. Anna Marie laid back onto the cot, pulled the blanket over her, curled into a fetal position. She waited, listened—stared at the naked light bulb protruding from the wall above the door. Until now, the light had always buoyed her spirit. Like fleeing cockroaches, the light had scattered her terror into darkened corners just out of sight. But most importantly, the light had provided her sanity just enough warmth to survive. Until now.

* * * *

Gray light filtered in through the filmy barred windows— negated any trace of color on the third floor of the county jail.

Bernie, the old black jailer, opened the cell door. Without taking his eyes off of Junior Jenkins, he set the food tray on the floor. With the tip of his polished boot he nudged it in Junior's direction. The screech of metal on concrete forced Junior to wince, raised chill bumps along his tattooed arms.

He started to curse the old man, but the look in Bernie's eyes made the words stick in his throat. Junior had seen the look plenty of times in his short life—a toxic mix of loathing and disgust.

But that wasn't the only thing different about Bernie, today. On his left hip was a revolver, the butt of the gun facing forward ready for a cross draw. The brown, oil-rubbed holster was molded around the weapon like a second skin. Junior could see the barrel peeking through the end. Maybe an old .38 special, Junior thought. The jailer's right arm was across his thin body, his caramel-colored hand rested lightly on the handle of the weapon. The old man looked calm—comfortable. It produced the opposite effect in Junior.

Bernie spoke. There was a hardness in his voice. "Pick it up," he said, nodding to the tray.

Junior looked at the tray—hot dogs, beans, and an apple—pretty much the same crap they served him every day. He reached over, picked up the tray, sat back on the bunk—waited.

"I know what you did to that boy, Junior." Bernie's words came forth like air from a leaking tire. "You messed around with his head—made him do somethin' that boy would never think up on his own."

The jailer had spoken as if it were fact, but Junior countered. "I didn't do nothing."

Junior was sure Bernie's hand twitched on the handle of the gun, then wondered if he had only imagined it.

"When you been around a long time—like me," Bernie said in an unhurried, dead even tone, "you get to where you can read things about people." He paused. "I can read you, Junior. And I could read that Padrick boy." He paused again. "He wasn't the suicidin' kind."

"But I was.... ."

"Shut up, Junior," Bernie snapped. Anger had boiled to the surface of his tone. "This ain't no discussion. This is *me* tellin' *you* how it is—and how it's goin' to be."

Junior was sure the gun hand twitched again. Still balancing the tray on his lap, he slid further back onto the bunk.

Bernie lowered his voice, told Junior in a harsh whisper, " "If that boy dies, I'll make sure it comes back to you." He waited for Junior to digest the threat, then added, "If the Padrick boy dies and it turns out he didn't kill that Toliver girl...well... ."

Junior tried to work up a wiseass grin that never materialized. He replied weakly, "You can't prove anything."

In disbelief, Bernie slowly shook his copper-colored head. "You still don't get it, Junior," he said, almost empathetically. "This ain't about provin'."

* * * *

From the window of the A-frame, The Wizard watched them—the two monstrous Rottweilers milling about the front yard of the cottage—oblivious to the rain—lifting their hind legs—pissing wherever it suited them. Johnny Lorenz, the last of the group, stood motionless by his van. He was hunched under a black poncho, his face hidden beneath the hood—like the Grim Reaper minus the skeletal hand and the scythe.

The image, along with the dogs, made the Wizard's chest tighten. He wondered if Charlie might be right—there were too many cast members for this production. In unison, both dogs turned towards the house. They seemed to be staring through the glass—straight into his soul.

He was five years old—maybe six. He remembered it being in the fall and he had just started school. As he did every day, he had walked home—alone. The old lady had been on her porch waiting for him—as she was most everyday. He had forgotten her real name, but always thought of her as "Miss Thelma". It seemed she always wore some shade of blue dress and a white apron. That day was no different. She watched him approach, then gingerly descended the porch steps—arthritically made her way up the walkway to the gate which separated her yard from the sidewalk. Miss Thelma asked him about his school. She told him things would get better. She patted his small head, made a sympathetic clucking sound in the back of her throat. She told him that is wasn't right for a small boy to be walking home by himself. He had listened patiently, appreciative of the attention—

waiting for the reward. Miss Thelma never let him down. She reached into the pocket of her apron—handed him two cookies wrapped in wax paper. They weren't just cookies. They were homemade. Sometimes they were still warm. Some days they were peanut butter, some days oatmeal and raisin, and other days chocolate chip. They were big and weighty and felt solid in his small hand. They were all delicious, but chocolate chip was his favorite. That day it had been chocolate chip. He had followed his ritual—took one cookie for then—buried the other deep in his book satchel for later.

Their road was really more of a rutted dirt lane, their house really more a shack. When he got there, a pickup truck was in the driveway. He remember it was red and shiny—like a fire engine, but only a lot smaller. Mostly he remembered what was in the bed of the truck—two large cages. Inside each, was a large black dog. As he entered the shabby, overgrown yard, they erupted into a hellish wall of noise. The effect was like the blow back from an explosion. The boy was sent stumbling to the ground. He could still hear the barking and snarling—still see flashing white teeth. The cages seemed to bounce in the bed of the truck, barely able to contain their lethal cargo. Though only a few feet away, the front stoop seemed hopelessly beyond his reach. Petrified, he had laid in the yard—had waited to die. It went on that way for a while, fear torturously stretching each moment He had no idea of how long he laid there, but remembered the noise ceasing with a single command.

A man was standing on the boy's front porch. He was short—powerful, with thick, curly black hair and a thin black mustache. Just past the man, through the screened door, the boy could see the faded silhouette of his mother. She wore only her brassier and her underpants. She had one hand on her hip. She looked angry.

"Get in here," the man had commanded with the same voice he had used on the dogs.

And like the dogs, the boy had obeyed.

The screen door had slammed behind him. More softly, the heavy outer door had followed. He remembered his sense of relief. The dogs were outside—he was safe—with his mother.

Her hand still on her hip, she'd asked, "Why were you laying in the dirt?"

He remembered staring up at her—remembered his confusion. Had she not seen the dogs?

"I'm going to have to wash those clothes, now," she had informed him in an irritated voice.

The black-haired man said to the boy's mother, "Why didn't you tell me you had a kid? What the hell are you gonna do with him, now?"

The boy's mother had smiled. Without seeming to move, the distance between the boy's mother and the man evaporated. She had one hand on the man's chest. Her other hand began to work beneath his undershirt. He could still remembered the man's belt—thin and black, tipped in silver to match the buckle. It was unclasped and dangled loosely from the loops of his gray trousers. The boy's mother moved closer, her breasts changing shape as they pressed against him. "He won't be a problem," she said in a whisper, just loud enough for the boy to hear. "Will you, Weems?"

The boy had shaken his head obediently, but his mother never saw him. She stared intensely at the curly-haired man—pressed closer. They had momentarily dismissed his presence.

"Why do you call him Weems?" the man had asked without looking at the boy.

"It's his name," she had said in an amused voice.

"Odd name," the man grunted.

In a voice laced with shame, his mother had confessed, "He's an odd little boy."

"You gonna' put him in his room?" the man had asked. "I ain't doing this in front of no kid."

"What room?" *the boy had thought. "This* is *the room."*

"He can go outside," his mother had replied. "He can sit on the porch. It's not cold—he'll be fine for a couple of hours."

He could still remember his disbelief—and the panic that had washed over him. Salvation had ridden in on an unlikely horse.

"Dogs 'll go nuts," the mustached man had told her. "Bark their fucking heads off. I won't be able to concentrate."

"I need you to concentrate," his mother had told the man. Her green eyes had darted around the room, as if seeing the space for the first time. They came to rest on him. She grabbed his arm, held it firmly as if afraid he might escape, led him to the bathroom.

Given the option of the front porch, this wouldn't be bad at all, he'd thought. Then she had opened the door to the tiny linen closet. "Sit in here for a little while, Weems," she had told him. "There's plenty of room for you. Mommy won't be long." Years later it would occur to him she only called herself "Mommy" when something bad was about to happen.

The boy was able to sit on the floor, his knees bent, but not quite tucked under his chin. Awkwardly, he tried to position the satchel at his feet. His mother reached for it. "You don't need that, in here," she had said.

Remembering his freshly-baked treasure, the boy had spoken for the first time since entering the house. "I want to keep it," he'd said meekly.

She hadn't argued. "Then keep it," she'd replied with irritation, "but don't open the door until I come for you. Do you understand, Weems?"

"Yes," he had managed.

A suggestion of smile had crossed her beautiful face. "Try to take a nap. Mommy won't be long."

His world went dark except for a sliver of light that leaked in under the bottom of the door. He thought about his cookie, but wanted to save it for a better moment, so he sat and listened. At first there was only an occasional murmuring voice. After a little while he could hear the bed rhythmically creaking and squeaking. Then it would stop. Then it would start again. It went on like that for a while. The boy heard his mother call out—as if in pain. But he knew she was all right. He'd heard her call out like that before.

The door to the bathroom had opened. He'd heard the toilet seat lift and the sound of water hitting more water. In the middle of the stream, the man had called to his mother, "Let's go get a beer."

"I really don't like beer," his mother had replied. The boy had taken her reply as rejection until she added, "I like gin and tonic."

"Then you drink your gin and tonic—I'll drink my beer. Give me a little while—I'll be ready to go again" The man flushed—said something about the dogs, but his words were trapped in the swirling rush of water. They had disappeared before the boy could understand.

The bathroom door closed. The boy waited for his mother to come for him. She had promised she would—and because he was only five—maybe six, he had believed her. Crouched in the darkness, he heard the front door open, then the screened door slam closed. A minute later the screened door slammed again. The boy had waited, his small legs were beginning to ache from the cramped position. Except for the dripping tub faucet, the house was quiet. His legs were feeling worse. Back and forth he debated, but as it always does in the end—pain won out.. He reached up through the darkness, fumbled for the shape of the door knob. The latch released. He spilled sideways onto the bathroom floor. Like pricks from a thousand small needles, feeling began returning to his legs.

Then he heard it—a sound, at first confusing, then undeniable. Toenails clicking on the wooden floor. The dogs were in the house. The boy had scrambled from the dirty tile floor—had thrown his small body against the already-closed door. From the other side, the big dogs heard the noise—rushed the door. The boy slid the flimsy barrel lock into place just as the first dog hit the door. The force splintered the door trim. The lock twisted but remained tenuously in place. The second attack opened a crack between the frame and the door. The boy could see a terrifying slice of black fur and white teeth. He dove back into the closet as the bathroom door burst open.

Looking back, he was sure he was screaming, but the only sound he remembered was the dogs. They were tearing at something—something in the bathroom—the boy's book satchel. Suddenly, there was a violent eruption. He could hear the two going after each other, growling—slamming into the walls, snarling—crashing into the tub. The boy heard the yelps, then the piteous scream of submission. Again the house was quiet. The light no longer visible under the door, the boy waited in his pitch-black lair. Before long his legs began to ache again, but moving outside the closet was no longer an option. Minutes stretched into hours. The boy had lost all track of time. He was five—maybe six years old.

When he woke up, the light was in his eyes, his mother was leaning over him. He remembered the smell, would figure out years later it was gin. The mustached man was in the room just out of sight. "My dog is dead," the boy heard the man say."

"Those fuckers could have killed my boy," she had yelled back at him in slurred angry words.

The boy's mother had pulled him from the closet—held him until his legs began to regain function. The boy's eyes had darted around the bathroom, bewildered, still terrified. There was blood everywhere, even splatters on the ceiling. Half in and half out, the losing dog's mangled body lay draped over the edge of the bathtub. Its dead eyes stared back at the boy as he clung to his gin-soaked mother. His book satchel had been ripped apart. Torn fragments of blood-covered wax paper littered the floor.

The next Monday afternoon, the boy had walked home from school. He had looked for the woman on her porch, but she wasn't there. Tuesday was the same. On Wednesday, the boy had waited at the gate, stared at the house—had willed her to come foreword. From next door, a younger woman had come to the sidewalk. The boy remembered she'd had a baby on her hip.

"I'm afraid your friend is gone, young man," she had told him in a sweet, sad voice.

"Gone where?" the boy had asked.

The younger woman had hesitated, had looked at her baby, then back at the boy. "She's gone to heaven."

Weems, The Wizard, Grabowski stared back at the two Rottweilers in the front yard of the A-framed cottage. He muttered to himself, "Those motherfuckers took the last cookie Miss Thelma ever made for me." He considered it a moment longer, then added, "The last cookie *anybody* ever made for me."

Chapter 34

Black Creek, North Carolina
September 25th—8:03 p.m.

By the time Andy Frazier saw Alex Madrid, it was too late. Andy was outside of the hospital, leaning against the hood of his father's Chevy Impala—thinking about the conversation he'd just had with two guys inside. The sun had been down for a couple of hours—the vapor lights cast the parking lot in an orange-yellowish glow. Madrid had pulled in quickly, had tucked the Blazer in tight against the bumper of his dad's car, then had gotten out unhurriedly. He walked up to the younger man and said, "Andy Frazier," as if greeting a long-lost friend.

"Hey, Alex." Andy could hear the nerves vibrating in his tone. "I heard about you getting' fired this mornin'." Andy dropped his eyes to the asphalt, stared at the toes of his shoes. "That wasn't right, man." He realized the last statement had come out weak and unconvincing. When he looked up, Madrid was standing directly in front of him, not quite an arm's distance away.

"Haven't seen you around for awhile, Andy." Madrid said, his voice still friendly.

He knows, Andy thought.

"I um....I um." Andy remembered the pair he'd just left—the bruises, the plaster, and the counterweight at the end of the traction device. He thought about the nurse dispensing pain medication in tiny paper cups. "I was meaning to call you," Andy said finally.

"I'm sure you've been busy."

Andy nodded.

"How are your little friends, Andy?" Madrid asked, not as friendly as before. "They show you their 'boo-boos' they got last night?"

Andy felt his chest tighten, his lungs working for air. "They're not my friends, Alex," he said in a rush of words. "I don't even like those guys."

"No kidding?" Madrid asked, as if genuinely confused.

"No." He said in a pant.

"You see, they spoke highly of you," Madrid said easily. "Well...not so much highly, but by the time it was all over, your name was mentioned. Several times, in fact."

Andy Frazier's' reply verged on a whimper. "I screwed up, Alex. It was a really big mistake."

As if seeking a fresh perspective, Madrid tilted his head, looked at the boy from a slightly different angle. "Yeah, Andy," he said in a hard resolved tone. "Big mistake for them—big mistake for you."

Madrid's words hit him like a sledgehammer to the gut. Andy felt the moisture soaking into his pants, the remainder streamed down his leg—a warm mixture of fear and humiliation. In the small space between them, the odor of urine filled the night air. The excess puddled at his feet, then following he contours of the parking lot, slowly crawling into the shadows under his father's car.

Madrid's eyes never left the younger man's. In a matter-of-fact whisper, he said, "You got thirty seconds to convince me I shouldn't put you in there with your buddies, Andy."

In a panic, Andy clawed at his thoughts, frantically grasped for words. His legs began to quiver. Like an impressionist painting, the hard angles of Madrid's face became blurred. Andy blinked away his tears—Madrid came back into focus. "Tic tock," he heard Madrid say.

The story came out in bits and fragments—a jumbled stream of words. When Madrid pieced it back together, it went something like this. Andy had been at a party. Everyone had been drinking. Frick and Frack had shown up uninvited, but nobody was going to run them off. More drinking. Andy had complained about Madrid siding with Dicky Padrick. Frick and Frack had bragged that for a hundred dollars, they'd change Madrid's mind. "Okay," Andy had said. Then soon afterwards had added, "I'll think about it." But that wasn't the way it worked, the little one had informed him. The deal had been offered and he had accepted. They were going to get their hundred and somebody was going to get a beating. Andy could decide if it was Madrid or himself. He had chosen Madrid—and had paid up front.

"I thought if I gave them the hundred," Andy pled, "it would be over. They'd just go away and buy more beer—or whatever."

"The night Miranda Toliver was killed," Madrid said. "Tell me what you saw—don't skip anything—don't make up anything."

Andy Frazier's humiliation continued to unfurl. He told Madrid about watching Miranda from the shadows in the student center, seeing her leave through the rear door—about his masturbation.

"That's it?" Madrid asked when he was through. "You didn't see anyone outside the Student Center?"

"No."

"What about Dicky Padrick?"

"No," Andy relied adamantly. "Never saw him until I got to the parking lot—after he got shot."

"So that's it?" Madrid repeated. Disappointment rang in his voice.

"That's it, Alex," Andy Frazier pled. "I swear...swear to God."

Madrid replied, "Like God really gives a damn about any of this."

Chapter 35

The Paradise Court
September 27th—9:06 p.m.

On the office porch, Joy Springtime pointed her rocking chair towards Black Creek. From inside, her bottle of vodka whispered to her in seductive tones. But for the moment, the call of cash spoke louder. She rocked back and forth—marked time like a bloated metronome. She waited for headlights to slice through the night—waited for Alex Madrid.

Madrid rounded the sweeping curve that followed the river. She was under a squared-off halo of red neon that wrapped the edge of the porch. He pulled off the asphalt, eased the Blazer across the parking lot. Before the tires had stopped crunching on the gravel, she was out of the chair, moving towards him in a hurried rolling gait.

Madrid rolled his window down.

"Got some information that you might be interested in," she said, her breathing heavy. "You said to keep my eye out," she reminded him.

"It's been a long day," Madrid told her.

The woman leaned against the Blazer, lowered her blonde head so that she and Madrid were almost eye to eye. "Man came by today lookin' for a room."

The smell from the woman was strong. Madrid recognized *Charlie* perfume, with undertones of perspiration and alcohol. "This is a motel," he replied wearily, "of sorts."

"Yeah," she continued, ignoring the barb. "But I had the 'no vacancy' sign on."

Madrid looked up at the sign. The only letters still working were the "o", the "v", the "c", and the "y".

"The guy was real stubborn about it," she said, leaning a little closer.

From the shadows of the back seat, Toto shifted his mass. The movement made the woman back up a step. Madrid was grateful for the distance.

"Said that he didn't see any cars parked anywhere," she went on. "First I told him that we were closed for repairs. I don't think he believed me. Said he wasn't too particular. Would take whatever we had—and that he was a cash-paying customer."

"Okay," Madrid said encouragingly.

"Yeah. That's when I start to get suspicious. I finally told him that all the rooms was rented. He wanted to know who had rented them." She stepped away from the Blazer, checked the road in both directions, then leaned back towards Madrid. That's when I started gettin' a little scared."

"Did you tell him who was renting the rooms?" Madrid asked.

Joy Springtime weighed her answer against the possible payoff. "Well..." she said vaguely, "Not really."

Madrid almost chuckled. "What does *not really* mean?"

She shifted her weight uncomfortably, replied defensively "You didn't say not to tell anyone."

"Describe him," Madrid said.

"Tall. Like a basketball player. Kind of good looking."

Good looking ruled out Charlie Blades. "What else?"

"I don't know," the woman said. "Dark hair—no wedding ring."

"Did you see what he was driving?"

"No. He parked where I couldn't see. I wasn't about to follow him outside."

"Probably smart," Madrid mumbled, as he reached for his wallet.

"There's more," Joy Springtime said nervously, glancing over her shoulder. "After he left, another guy came by. Asked for you by name. I told him that I didn't know anybody named Alex Madrid. He just smiled and said he'd wait. That's what he's doing now. He's parked outside your room. I didn't tell him which one; he just seemed to know."

"What did this guy look like?"

"Black man. 'Bout your height, but kind of wiry. Seemed like he was always moving—not exactly fidgety—or nervous. Just always moving."

Madrid handed her six bills that totaled a hundred and fifty dollars. She took the money—counted it, then folded it into a tight stack. Even in the murkiness of the parking lot, Madrid could read her disappointment.

"Might be a good idea to go somewhere else for the evening."

"You said there wouldn't be any trouble," she replied disapprovingly.

"No," Madrid said evenly, "I never said that."

Joy Springtime waddled across the parking lot, locked the office door, then wedged herself behind the wheel of a red Datsun. She put the car on the highway, gunned it down the long straight stretch out of Black Creek. Madrid watched her taillights until they melted into the night.

* * * *

Victoria Jamerson's hospital room was supposed to have been guarded. But the attending nurse was the ex-fiancé of the deputy assigned to Victoria's room. She had broken it off three months earlier. He was still hopeful. She had suggested they walk down the hall for coffee and leave Julie Kingston with Victoria Jamerson.

"What if she tries to kill herself again?" he'd asked in a hospital voice.

"She won't," the nurse assured him.

The deputy hadn't argued.

Julie had pulled a chair up close to the bed. She had a Thermos of hot tea, a pair of white porcelain mugs, and a plate of lemon cookies. Victoria was twenty one years older. Julie had degrees from two universities. Victoria, many years ago, had aspirations of becoming a singer. Julie had interned at *The Washington Post,* Victoria had waitressed at Carl's Diner where she had met the love of her life. Julie had taken a job with *The Miami Herald* , Victoria had given birth to a beautiful daughter.

And so it went. Outside, fog rolled in—crowded against the window. In their softly-lit cocoon, the two women sat close—sipped tea and nibbled cookies. They talked about their lives, carefully skirting around any sorrow they might have encountered along the way. Occasionally Victoria would smile and pat the back of Julie's hand.

Two old friends that had never met.

* * * *

At the back of the darkened courtyard, directly in front of Madrid's room, a black '74 Jaguar XKE was parked nose facing out. The windows were down—Madrid caught a few notes of Miles Davis blowing *Bitches' Brew*. He walked to the center of the courtyard, paused by the sad little fountain. Waited. This wasn't the kind of guy you snuck up on. Like robotic eyes, headlights blazed to life, momentarily washed over Madrid and the dog, then blinked back to darkness.

Madrid approached the car. The driver's door opened without triggering the interior lights. The man who emerged was Madrid's height, but twenty pounds lighter. He looked—and moved—like a middleweight boxer. He wore black pants and a black crew-neck sweater.

"Arthur." Madrid said.

"Alex," Arthur replied.

"Nice car."

"It'll do," the man replied easily.

"Still listening to Miles," Madrid said.

"Yeah."

"Old school."

"Been thinkin' about switching to K.C. and the Sunshine Band."

"Probably thinking about swapping the Jag for a nice Buick sedan, too," Madrid said.

"Thinkin' about it." Arthur glanced casually at the Mastiff-Shepard mix. "You still got The Wizard's dog, huh?" Arthur let the mongrel sniff the back of his hand. "Diablo seems to have mellowed out a touch."

"Not as much as you'd think. I changed his name to Toto."

Arthur offered a relaxed chuckle. "No shit?"

"No shit," Madrid replied.

Arthur held the smile, his white teeth radiant in the scant light. "You think Weems goin' to appreciate your cavalier sense of humor?."

"I got my fingers crossed."

Another chuckle. "So how's life here in Black Creek, North Carolina."

"About what you'd expect."

"I would expect it to suck," Arthur replied.

"Then you probably wouldn't be disappointed."

"They got any brothers in this town?"

"Haven't seen any," Madrid replied.

"So what the hell do you do all day?"

"Well," Madrid answered, "this morning I got up early to see a woman who might—or might not—have buried a knife in her husband's chest last night. Then I got called up to the office of the president of the college. We had a big important meeting—then he fired me. Then tonight, I cornered a teenager in a parking lot and talked *real* mean to him."

Arthur nodded his head as if impressed. "How mean?"

"He peed in his pants and then he cried."

"Damn," Arthur said with mock admiration. "*Had* to make you proud."

"You know," Madrid replied, "you'd *think* so."

As they were talking, the fog rolled in. It crept silently over the flat roof of the building, slithered over the breezeway and down the walls—mixed with the darkness inside the horseshoe shaped courtyard.

"They're coming," Arthur said in a conversational tone.

"Coming tonight?"

"Be my guess."

Almost relieved, Madrid nodded. "How many?"

"Five—unless they pick up more on the way. But I'd count on five."

Madrid's relief was short lived. "Five," Madrid repeated.

"A few more than you counted on, huh?"

"Maybe."

"It was just like you said. I stayed on Vorcheck. In a couple of days he took me right to Weems. They met up at some lame-ass carnival up in Tennessee. Weems is hooked up with a couple of new guys."

"I thought he might stay away from Blades for a while. Once he broke out, the cops will be looking to put the two of them together."

"Yeah," Arthur agreed. "Makes sense. I gotta' give him his due—not many people walk out of max security. He *is* a clever son-of-bitch."

"That's why they call him The Wizard."

"You ever heard of a guy named Rex Thompson?" Arthur asked.

"No."

"He's one of the guys with Weems."

"What's he look like?"

"Tall—dark hair."

"Hmmm," Madrid said. "The woman in the office said a guy like that came by earlier."

"Don't take him lightly, Alex . Boy's got some talent. Not in the same class as Charlie Blades—but he's fairly dangerous."

"What about the other guy?"

"Don't know him," Arthur shrugged. "Blonde muscle-head. Either Rex or The Wizard had him out on lookout duty."

Apprehensive, Madrid asked, "Where's Vorcheck?"

Arthur paused for half a beat. "Great beyond, man. Nicky's dead."

It wasn't the answer Madrid had hoped for—but it was the one he expected. "How?"

Arthur raised his shoulders, then let them drop, the gesture lost in the darkness and fog. "Couldn't say. They didn't shoot him, didn't knife him, and didn't beat him. Wasn't a mark on the little bastard."

"O.D.?" Madrid asked, looking to cushion his guilt.

"Maybe." Arthur answered indifferently. "Maybe they just scared his ass to death." He paused, added. "You know that girl Nick used to hang with sometimes? Little skinny thing with those big baby doll eyes."

"Yeah," Madrid answered. Inside him, dread began to flow like thick, syrupy bile.

"Mousy blonde. Her name is Rhonda something."

"Right. Nicky used Rhonda Something for taxi service—left her out in the parking lot when he went in to meet with Rex and Weems. While she was waitin' around, somebody broke her neck."

Madrid felt himself wince. "Goddamn it," Madrid said angrily.

Addiction, greed—and being an asshole had made Nick Vorcheck perfect for his part. Madrid had cast him as the sacrificial goat. He hadn't figured for the girl. "You think it was the blonde muscle guy?"

"Probably so."

"Goddamn it," Madrid repeated.

"She didn't have to be there, Alex," Arthur replied. "She knew Nick. Probably knew him as good as anybody. Damn sure knew how he was—and *what* he was. Everybody got choices. You make 'em, then you live with 'em."

The statement applied equally to Madrid.

"They're all holed up over in Tennessee, little place on top of a mountain."

"Is Blades there?"

"Affirmative. I got close enough to see him through the window a couple of times."

"Anybody else?

Arthur glanced down at the giant mongrel sitting next to Madrid. "Johnny Lorenz showed up this afternoon. Came in a van. Probably got a dog or two with him. He usually works them in pairs."

"Wonderful."

"Yeah. Figured you'd be all excited about that."

The two men stood silently in the darkness—Madrid digesting the information, Arthur waiting.

Arthur spoke first. "So, what you gonna do?"

"Stick with the plan."

"Your plan that good?"

"Not really, but it's the one I got."

Arthur waited, then said, "I got some time. Five on two's a lot better than five on one. If I was in one of those old cabins across the lot, we'd put them in a cross fire. I'm guessin' that's a better plan than the one you got."

Madrid considered it—it *was* a better plan. Arthur Johnson was a shooter. But in Madrid's psyche, Rhonda's face was still clearly in focus—her head at a peculiar angle—bewildered blue eyes staring up at him.

"Thanks," he said. "But this is my doing—my fight."

"Could be your last one."

"Could be," Madrid agreed.

"How you fixed for firepower?"

"Two .45s," Madrid answered. "Six clips."

Arthur did the math quickly. "Forty-four rounds."

"I can shoot each one eight times," Madrid said optimistically. "Still have four bullets left over."

"Gotta admit—that's a hell of a plan."

"Thought you'd like it."

Arthur walked to the back of the Jaguar and popped the trunk. From somewhere he pulled a flashlight, clicked it to the on position. "Hold this," he said, handing Madrid the cylinder. Inside the trunk were two burlap-looking blankets and a smallish wooded box. Arthur unwrapped the first blanket. "Twelve gauge," he said, as if describing a beautiful woman. "Twenty-inch barrel—pistol grip—triple-ought buck. Five rounds loaded. Got five more, but... ."

"Yeah," Madrid said, finishing the thought.

Arthur unwrapped the second blanket, spoke in the same tone. "AR-15—modified. Semi-auto, or three-round burst, or full auto. Thirty round mag."

"Yeah," Madrid said again. He moved the beam to the back corner of the trunk. "What's in the box?"

"Eggs." Arthur worked the top off the box as Madrid held the light. Inside, packed in molded foam, were two olive-drab orbs. "M-61 fragmentation hand grenades," he said proudly.

"Jesus," Madrid said. "Where did you get these?"

"Fell off the back of a truck. Caught them before they hit the pavement."

Madrid played the light over each weapon.

"Take what you want, Alex," Arthur said. "I'm having a sale."

"What kind of sale?"

"It's like one of them Midnight Madness sales. Nothin' down—pay me next time you see me."

"That could be a long time from now."

"Could be," Arthur said. "The offer to hang around is still good, too."

"I know," Madrid answered.

"Your answer still the same?"

"Yeah."

"You gonna kill them or they gonna kill you," Arthur said in a calm, philosophical voice. "Either way, it ain't goin' to bring your niece back, Alex."

"I know that, too."

"'Long as you know."

They unloaded the trunk. Arthur slid behind the wheel of the Jaguar. He turned the switch and the twelve valves erupted in a deep purr.

"I owe you," Madrid said.

The sleek black car began to roll. "See you around, Alex," Arthur Johnson said over his shoulder.

Madrid watched the car slide away into the fog.

* * * *

She dreamed she was back home. Anna Marie tried to tell her mother where she had been, about the basement and the awful men living above. She was sitting on the sofa with their beagle, Lucky. Part of her knew Lucky had died when she was twelve, but he seemed healthy—and happy she was back. Lucky nudged her shoulder with his nose, wanting to be petted. Anna Marie rubbed the slick fur behind the dog's soft floppy ears. Lucky nudged her harder.

Anna Marie's eye lids opened slowly—languidly slid shut—then snapped open again. Charlie Blades towered over her, his face in shadow. His long arms protruded from the sleeveless blue jeans jacket. His simian-like hand was on her shoulder, nudging her.

"Wake up," he said.

Anna Marie twisted awkwardly to a sitting position. He was standing close, his heavy brass belt buckle, just below her eye level. His rough hand moved to the side of her face—back and forth, his thumb traced her jaw line. Anna Marie sat motionless, stared at the floor. Waited.

"We're getting' out of here soon," Charlie Blades said. Anna Marie heard the finality in his voice—didn't know how to interpret it.

Without taking her eyes from the concrete floor, she asked, "Where are we going?"

"Not you," she heard him say.

Panic squeezed her. "You're leaving me here?" she said, struggling to get the words from her throat.

"I'll come back for you in the morning." There was uncertainty in his tone—subtle but undeniable.

For a brief moment, despair trumped fear. She raised her chin, stared directly into the eyes of her nightmare, asked defiantly. "What's going to happen to me then?"

"I brought you some food," Blades said, tilting his massive skull towards the paper plate on the cot next to her.

Anna glanced at the plate—a thick slice of bologna peeked out from between two slices of white bread. Next to it was a mound of orange-colored potato chips.

Earlier, Charlie Blades had poured cola in a paper cup, then crushed three sleeping pills, dumped them into the dark, bubbly liquid and stirred the mixture with his index finger. Now he handed it to Anna Marie.

"Drink this."

Anna saw the residue of the white powder still floating on the surface. She took a small sip.

"Drink it all," Blades said menacingly.

She drank, then asked, "Are the other men coming down here?"

"Why?" he answered with a sinister grin. "You want me to call them? Maybe have a little goin'-away party?"

Any remnant of defiance evaporated. Anna Marie replied in a soft, submissive voice, "No, please don't do that."

Charlie Blade's grin stayed fix. He looked at her the way an alley cat looks at an exotic bird. Her hair had fallen over her right side of her face. She peered up at him from behind the red veil. Fingers laced together on her lap, the muscles in girl's slim forearms pulsed nervously. Through the thin material of her dress, he could easily trace the contours of her thighs. Her nipples strained forward in clear detail, beckoning him. He pictured her in the shower, the warms suds sliding over the curves of her body. His perfect woman—lots of red hair—naked—scared—compliant.

"If I'm not back in the morning, you'll know what to do," he said.

Anna Marie continued to stare, not sure of what she had just heard. "What did you say?" she asked in a meek, confused tone.

"You'll know what to do."

Like Lucky the dog, desperation nudged her along. "How will I know?" She watched the giant troll of a man moved closer. She felt his hand on the side of her face, the palm calloused and rough as it slid across her cheek and down her neck. He continued downward, cupped each of her breasts. Anna fought the reflexive urge to pull away. Her quest for the answer was stronger than her repulsion. He pinched each of her nipples until a painful whimper escaped past her pink lips.

"You'll know," he replied in a deep, lustful voice. He turned, and with three strides covered the distance between the cot and the door. Once outside the room, he worked the door lock—flicked off the light switch.

As her eyes began to grow heavy, Anna Marie was left with only darkness, fear, and slightest glimmer of undefined hope. She prayed—for her sister, and for herself. Had she known his pivotal role in her fate, she would have prayed for a man she'd never met. A man named Alex Madrid.

Chapter 36

September 28th—12:01 a.m.

Off the shoulder of Highway 64, just across the county line, Rex Thompson had parked the wood-paneled station wagon under a canopy of sourwood and maple trees. The front seat was back as far as it would go. He was slumped there, shrouded in a veil of darkness and fog. He played over the conversation with the fat, blonde woman at The Paradise Court. At first, she had been tight lipped, but two hundred dollar bills had stripped away all traces of reluctance. Once the Franklins hit the light, she told him Alex Madrid had rented the entire motel. She told him she didn't know why he wanted the whole place to himself and his big, ugly dog. But Rex knew. She had offered up the room number where Madrid slept. He had peeled off another hundred to keep the conversation quiet. He had issued an obscure, but undeniable warning of what would happen if she got chatty. Then he had driven away.

Two hundred yards down the road, he had eased the wagon off the pavement. Staying tucked into the shadow of the tree line, he had walked back to The Paradise Court. Then he had sketched the layout of the motel—had cut the telephone lines—made sure there were no back doors. He had found the room number the fat woman had given him. At the back of the horseshoe-shaped courtyard, he had located Madrid's room. A logical choice—it offered the best field of fire. But it wouldn't be enough, Rex had thought. The Wizard was bringing too much firepower, too much talent, and the element of surprise. At this point, killing Alex Madrid was academic—killing Charlie Blades remained a challenge.

* * * *

Disoriented, Julie Kingston struggled to awaken. She was slumped in the chair next to Victoria Jamerson's hospital bed, her long legs were stretched in front of her, crossed at the ankles. The nurse was gently patting her shoulder.

"Wake up, Honey," she told Julie in a late-night-hospital whisper. "It's way past visiting hours and I've gotta get you out of here."

Julie's eyes worked back into focus. Victoria was asleep on her back, her mouth slightly open, her dark gray hair strewn in sharp contrast with the crisp, white pillow case. The single fluorescent tube above the bed bathed the room in a cold, subdued light. It washed the darkness from under her eyes and most of the bruise on her cheek. Her face had the pallor of death.

As if reading her mind, the nurse said, "She's going to be fine, Honey. She's just in a deep sleep. The doctor gave her something to help her rest. You know, take the edge off."

Julie felt the stiffness in her neck. She sat up in the chair, slowly rotated her head from side to side, rubbed her eyes. She looked around the room for a clock. "What time is it?" she asked sleepily.

"Just after midnight, Honey," the nurse replied, without looking at her watch. "I should have come to get you sooner." The nurse paused. "I guess I just lost track of time."

Julie stood up—looked at the nurse. Her lipstick had been freshened, her hair combed slightly different than the last time Julie had seen her.

"You missed a button," Julie whispered.

* * * *

The pistol-gripped shotgun was loaded, lying across the bed next to the two hand grenades. The percolator gurgled insistently, masked the other odors in the dingy room with the smell of coffee. Madrid slathered a copious serving of organic peanut butter on two pieces of whole wheat bread, then topped each with another slice. He tore the first sandwich into four reasonably-equal pieces. He fed the first quarter to the dog.

"Five," Madrid said, in a heavy voice. "And two dogs." Oddly, the two dogs weighed heavier on him than the five men. They revealed Weems "The Wizard" Grabowski's intent—his version of lions in the coliseum. He was bringing them along for blood sport. A spectacle. If Madrid went down, he'd let the dogs finish the job—then he'd turn them on the mongrel. Madrid fed the dog another quarter of a sandwich as the bloody scene played out in his head. He could hear his dog's screaming yelps, could see him fighting vainly.

The big mutt stared at Madrid, waited for the next offering. Madrid considered opening the door and sending him on his way—but he knew Toto wouldn't go far. Certainly not far enough. He considered putting the .45 to the dog's head. There would be blood everywhere. Gruesome, but a thousand times more merciful than the other possibility.

Madrid handed over another piece of sandwich. The big dog inhaled it. Beaten badly, and nearly starved, Madrid had rescued the dog from the brink of death. He sat on the edge of the bed, continued to think about the five men—the dogs. "Maybe I didn't do you any favors after all," he said quietly.

He fed Toto the last quarter of sandwich—had one of those *"Of Mice and Men"* moments.

* * * *

In the VW microbus, Charlie Blades and The Wizard felt their way along through the fog. The route they had mapped, a series of winding back roads, was designed to keep them off of I-40—away from the cops. Behind them, Johnny Lorenz strained to keep their tail lights in sight. Flex was sitting next to him, still pissed off about having to ride in the van with the dogs.

"You think there'll be a bonus for the one that plugs this guy?" Flex asked.

Lorenz shifted the butt of his unlit cigar to the other side of his mouth, rubbed his hand over his graying crew cut. He replied in a gravelly voice, "Did he say anything about a bonus?"

"No."

"Then why you fuckin' askin' me about a fuckin' bonus?" From behind the seats, one of the Rottweilers growled.

Flex glanced over his shoulder. "Just making conversation."

"A little free advice, Junior. Don't spend this time counting your money. Spend it thinking about Madrid. Your bonus will be not getting' your dumb ass killed."

"There's five of us," Flex countered with dismissive confidence. "How hard you think it's going to be?"

Lorenz shifted the cigar butt back to the other side of his mouth, grinned around it, and replied, "Don't know. Think it's going to be harder than *you think* it's going to be."

"You know this guy?"

Using the yellow center line as a guide, Lorenz guided the van through a series of deep curves "Madrid?" he responded when they were back on a straight stretch of road.

"Yeah," Flex said.

"Know him some. He's got one of my best dogs—one of my meanest ones, anyway."

"So what do you know?"

Johnny Lorenz shifted the cigar again. "I know this," he said thoughtfully. "If Alex Madrid was easy to kill, he'd been dead a long time ago."

Chapter 37

September 28th—12:47 a.m.

In Black Creek, if you needed gas after midnight, you had two options. You could steal it, or you could go to Tommy's Gas and Beer. The place sat back from the road, a low brick building with dirty concrete floors, and metal bars over unwashed windows. Besides what was on the sign, Tommy sold cigarettes, rolling papers, *Penthouse* magazines, a selection of fine wine for less than three dollars a bottle, and not much else.

Julie Kingston had left Victoria Jamerson asleep in her room. She had checked with the nurse about Dicky Padrick. He was no better—no worse. Back at her office, she had picked up notes for a story that was due later that morning. Pulling out of the newspaper's parking lot, she had noticed the fuel gauge. Maybe enough in the tank to get home, she'd thought, but not enough to get home and back to the office in the morning.

The two vans had reached the county line. Rex was waiting there for them. He, Flex, and Johnny Lorenz had joined The Wizard and Charlie Blades in the microbus. Rex had detailed the layout of The Paradise Court. There had been a half dozen questions. Rex had answered them as best he could. The Wizard had withheld comment until the end.

"An extra three thousand for the man who stops Madrid without killing him. Fifteen hundred for my dog. I want both of those bastards to be looking into my lovely brown eyes when they die."

When the meeting was over, Flex climbed into the passenger seat of the station wagon—started working on what he would do with the extra forty-five hundred . Rex Thompson navigated through the thick fog. The other two vehicles stayed close enough to keep tail lights in sight. Rex made a series of turns, strained his eyes through the darkness and the mist—looked for anything vaguely familiar. After five minutes he erupted in an angry, resigned voice, "Somewhere in this goddamn fog, I've missed a fucking turn."

"You're lost?" Flex asked.

"What the fuck did I just say?"

"Hey," Flex replied defensively. "Don't take it out on me. We just find a house, wake up one of these hillbillies and ask 'em where the hell we are."

Rex eased his way around the curve. Ahead, like an oasis in a white misty desert, the neon of Tommy's Gas and Beer presented itself on the obscured horizon.

"This will do," Rex said. He slowed down, pointed the nose of the big station wagon towards the parking lot. Neither man paid any attention to the Mercedes 450 parked in front of the gas pumps.

The inside of Tommy's Gas and Beer smelled like something between an ashtray and a fart. Tommy Jr. was behind the counter—pimply faced—bleary-eyed, with that creepy/horny expression that teenage boys sometimes get at that time of night. Like a heat-seeking missile, he was locked onto Julie Kingston. Neither of them noticed the station wagon pull up in front of the store.

Julie told him she needed gas.

"I can pump it," he told Julie with a suggestive stupid grin. "You know, if that's the way you want it. I'm good at pumping."

Julie reply was a withering stare.

The bell attached to the front door tinkled. A tall man eclipsed the doorway then proceeded inside. He wore a black motorcycle jacket and black driving gloves. A Baltimore Orioles ball cap was pulled low on his forehead. He looked past Julie, addressed the kid in a no-nonsense voice.

"Looking for a place to stay tonight."

Tommy Jr. reluctantly tore his eyes from Julie, replied in a mildly stoned voice. "Slim pickin's around here, mister."

"Somethin' just outside of town," Rex Thompson, he said hurried persistent tone. "Lookin' for a little privacy."

"There's The Paradise Court," the kid said, rubbing the scant strands of wispy beard on his chin. "But I think it's closed down."

"Sounds good. How do you get there?"

"I think it's closed," the kid repeated.

"Not what I asked you," the man said in a hard voice.

Julie pulled a five dollar bill from the pocket of her jeans, slid it across the counter. "High test," she mumbled and moved towards the door.

When she was halfway out the door, she heard Tommy Jr. ask, "Want a receipt?"

Julie filled her lungs with the cool night air. A blonde man in the front seat of the station wagon looked her up and down. In the far corner of the parking lot, two vans were parked with lights out and engines running. Julie walked to her car—fought the urge to run. At the pumps, she hesitated for a moment—slid behind the wheel. She eased the Mercedes out of the parking lot, into the fog. Back on the pavement, her foot fell heavy on the accelerator. She glanced down at the gas gauge, wondered if she made the right decision.

Just over a minute later, Rex Thompson folded himself behind the wheel of the wagon.

"You see that chick just came out of there?" Flex asked.

"Yeah," Rex said, though he'd hardly noticed her at all.

"You think all the pussy in this town looks that good?"

Rex turned over the engine, slipped the car into reverse. "Couldn't say."

"If it does," Flex said dreamily, I ain't leavin' town. I mean ever."

"You don't get focused," Rex replied, checking the rearview mirror, "you ain't leavin' anyway." As they eased forward, the headlights from the microbus and the van erupted—blazed white against the fog. "Madrid will make sure of that."

"I'll worry about Madrid when we get there," Flex replied indifferently. "What about that kid inside?"

"What about him?" Rex pulled onto the pavement, pointed the convoy towards The Paradise Court.

"He can identify you," Flex said.

"Not any more," Rex replied with finality.

The man had parked in the driveway of an abandoned mobile home nearly a half mile away—then worked his way back through the woods. He stared across the foggy patch of highway at the red neon of The Paradise Court. The lights were on, but no one appeared to be in the office. In his pocket was a .38 special—snub-nosed with a walnut grip. In his hands was a double-barreled sawed-off twelve gauge. He cradled it across his chest, like a protective mother with her baby. His fingers drummed on the stock of the weapon—he could feel his heart thumping inside his chest. He told himself to calm down. This wasn't anything new—he'd killed before. He moved to the edge of the woods and was about to ease across the highway when he heard the approaching car.

There were headlights, low to the ground. They swung into the courtyard, struggled against the fog. From inside his darkened room, Madrid heard an engine sputter and cough. He heard the tires moving slowly over the fine, dirty, white gravel. The engine fell quiet—the car continued to roll until it was only a few feet from the Madrid's door. He stepped back into the room, picked up the AR-15, leveled it at the driver's side of the windshield—waited.

The headlights continued to blaze. The driver's door swung open. Beyond the glare, a trim figure rose and took shape in the vaporous night. It was a shape Madrid recognized. He lowered the weapon, stepped outside the motel room and snapped, "Turn off the lights."

"They're coming," Julie Kingston said, her voice light—a half an octave high.

"Who's coming?" Madrid asked, but he already knew the answer.

"They're in three cars," she answered frantically. "I couldn't tell how many. They were asking about this place at Tommy's. I think they're right behind me."

Like icy water through a burst dam, Madrid felt the panic fill his being. He tried to force it back, but there was too much. He could feel himself beginning to drown beneath it. He looked at Julie Kingston. "You've got to get out of here—now!"

"I can't." She waved her arms frantically at the Mercedes. "I'm out of gas, Alex!" Her tone brimmed with panic and incredulousness. "I am out of gas."

Madrid heard the sound of engines on the highway. They slowed. He could hear one of the tires ease off the asphalt shoulder and onto the gravel parking lot. He grabbed Julie Kingston firmly by the arm. When he spoke, his voice was firm and calm. "Do exactly what I tell you and you might just get through this."

Inside the motel room, Madrid asked, "Do you know how to use a shot gun?"

"My father used to take me to shoot skeet and trap," Julie answered.

"Well, this is exactly the same thing," Madrid told her, "only they'll be shooting back." He shoved the weapon in her hands and spoke hurriedly. "Take this and go into the bathroom. Toto is in there. If the shooting stops, let the dog out first. Lock the door. Stay in there. If anyone tries to come in, empty the shotgun. He grabbed the AR-15 and moved the selector to full auto. "After that," he told her, "aim this at anything that moves and pull the trigger."

"After that?" she asked.

Madrid shook his head. "There is no *after that*, Julie. Make sure you hit something."

Chapter 38

September 28th—1:00 a.m.

Except for the fog, The Paradise Court was exactly as Rex Thompson had described it. Per The Wizard's choreography, the three vehicles rolled slowly into the parking lot—lights out. The VW micro bus, then Johnny Lorenz's van, followed by the wood-paneled station wagon. The Wizard had gone back and forth on whether to use two vehicles or three. He considered stashing the station wagon somewhere close—just in case things didn't go as planned. But finally, he decided the two vans weren't enough. Just beyond the fountain, the vehicles stretched across the mouth of the horse shoe—sealed off any escape. The north-facing cherub watched them with sad, concrete eyes.

Flex was out of the station wagon before it stopped rolling. He crouched low, moved through the fog to the left side of the horseshoe. Under the metal porch roof, he pressed himself against the building. His left hand was wrapped around a .44 magnum, the same Smith and Wesson Model 29 Clint Eastwood had used in *Dirty Harry*. Clipped to his belt were two canisters, one was smoke, and other was teargas. The Wizard wanted Madrid outside—in the open. Flex planned to serve him up. He eased down the line of empty rooms, picked his way around the tangle of discarded porch furniture.

Ignorance, arrogance, and the promise of an extra three grand had squelched his fear. As the Mercedes took shape in the fog, some of that changed. He recognized the car, recalled the black-haired vision who had floated past him just minutes before. He halted his advance—struggled to process the information. Was she warning him? Couldn't be—no way she could know. Maybe she was Madrid's girlfriend. He could picture her inside the motel room—already half naked—maybe on her knees. "Focus," he whispered angrily to himself, remembering Rex Thompson's warning. He pushed the image of Julie Kingston from his head. Had he known what was about to happen, he might have savored it a moment longer.

Alex Madrid moved across the dark motel room. Like a blind piano player, his left hand played across the top of the bed until he located the two M-61 grenades. He dropped one into each side pocket of his field jacket, kept moving to the door.

Julie Kingston's arrival had changed everything. Whatever plan he'd conceived was gone. Like a child's balloon, it had floated away into the foggy night sky. Julie Kingston had risked her life trying to save his. If she was to have any chance to survive, Madrid would have to take the fight outside. By the door, suspended from an exposed wire, an electrical switchbox was duct-taped to the wall. The wire ran through the ceiling, onto the roof of the building, connected a series of high-intensity lights. With the muzzle of the .45, Madrid toggled the switch to the "on" position. The courtyard exploded into white glare. It reflected off the fog, and for a small measure of time, a white wall separated Madrid from the five men at the other end of the courtyard. He opened the door—slipped from the motel room—took cover behind the low-slung Mercedes.

Eyes darting madly, his head never moving, The Wizard crouched in a tight wad between the front bumper of the station wagon and the rear bumper of Johnny Lorenz's dog van. The fog wrapped and concealed him like a soft, fluffy blanket. Through the gap between his two front teeth, he softly whistled an unintelligible series of notes—repeated it—happily repeated it again. He closed his eyes tightly, pictured his plan unfolding.

Flex, his sacrificial lamb, was on point, working his way along the left side of the horseshoe. Rex was spaced a few yards behind him, with instructions to take care of anything Madrid didn't. Johnny Lorenz was perched in the doorway of the van, smack in the middle of the courtyard. On The Wizard's command, preferably when Madrid was outside the room, he was to release the dogs. Then he was to follow them, pull them off of Madrid while he was still breathing.

Charlie Blades, was held in reserve, only a dozen or so yards from where The Wizard crouched. Charlie's mission was three-fold: (1) remove from Alex Madrid any avenue of escape; (2) mop up anything—or anybody, left standing; (3) make sure nothing happened to Weems "The Wizard" Grabowski.

The Wizard continued to whistle through his teeth. The sudden, blinding surge of light provided the crescendo for his non-descript tune.

Like a nightmare floating through the fog, Charlie Blades inched his way along the wall opposite Flex and Rex. The .357 was strapped under his left shoulder. In his massive right hand, the Browning twelve gauge automatic looked almost like a kid's toy. His focus was primarily on the room at the center of the horseshoe-shaped courtyard, but he knew Alex Madrid could be anywhere.

Charlie peered through the foggy murk. Ahead of him, to his left, he watched the outline of the Mercedes take shape. Like Flex, he immediately recognized it from the gas station. "Luckiest son of bitch on the planet," Blades mumbled. An instant later, the courtyard burst into light—played off the fog—created a visual white mass. Now it would be neither quick nor clean—which was just fine with Charlie Blades.

He stepped out from under the breezeway. The shotgun blast ripped through the fog; the first of the roof-mounted lights disintegrated into darkness.

The light and the first blast came only seconds apart. Rex Thompson could see the muzzle flash from Charlie Blades shotgun—could hear glass shatter. Blades was further up the opposite wall than Rex Thompson had figured—everyone trying to cash in for the extra three grand. He crouched low, fired the AK-47 at the three lights mounted on the roof above Charlie Blades. They were harder to hit than he'd imagined, but near the end of the first clip, all the lights were gone and the courtyard had reverted to blackness. Rex dropped the first clip, heard it clang on the concrete pad below his feet. From behind him, The Wizard was screaming something about dogs in a high-pitched voice. Rex jammed the clip into the belly of the weapon, strafed it across the rooms at the end of the courtyard. Windows exploded. Then Rex Thompson pivoted thirty degrees, fired a burst in Flex's direction. The blast caught his partner just below his right shoulder. One of the bullets shattered a rib, two more passed through his heart and out the other side. Flex fell to a crumpled heap and died with his nose on the concrete.

"One down," Rex Thompson thought to himself—a moment later wondered if he'd acted too soon.

Julie Kingston choked back another wave of panic. "Open this door for no one," he had told her. "No matter what they say—or what they promise."

Madrid had instructed her to keep the lights off, but the pitch-black bathroom was squeezing down around her—tiny—claustrophobic—like an upright coffin with plumbing. The dog was panting heavily—sucking the air from the room with shallow, steady rhythm. Though muffled through the walls, the first shotgun blast was loud enough to make her jump. Toto lurched forward, toppled her back over the rim of the tub. Julie reached blindly into the darkness, pulled the shower curtain and rod down on top of her as she fell into the cast-iron vessel.

Then more gunfire. The big mongrel barked savagely, thrashed around the room, threw himself against the door. Julie struggled to sitting position, then rose unsteadily to her feet. The shotgun was no longer in her hands. Toto bounded into the tub, knocked her against the back wall, then he was out again. Julie reached across the short expanse until her hand found the doorknob. She twisted and pulled—and like water rushing through the spillway of a dam, the big mongrel was gone.

The courtyard had been lit for less than ten seconds, which was more than Madrid had figured—the good news. He now knew the approximate location of two shooters, less than half—the bad news. In front of the sleek Mercedes, his crouched body had been peppered with flying glass from the car's windshield. Somewhere in front of him, Madrid heard The Wizard screech, "Turn them loose!" From behind him, almost at the same instant, Madrid sensed movement. He turned just in time to see Toto hurl himself through the hole in the wall that had, a moment ago, been a window. The dog landed awkwardly, his front legs buckled, his barrel-shaped body crashed to the concrete—face first.

Pain and agony. Pain was five pounds heavier—Agony was ten pounds meaner. Johnny Lorenz had the two massive Rottweilers poised for attack. The gunfire had agitated them to the point of frenzy. "Turn them loose," the little bastard had commanded from somewhere in the fog. Lorenz knew it was too early, but The Wizard was picking up the tab for this party. Besides, nothing had gone as planned, anyway. Lorenz released the collars. The two sleek monsters launched themselves from the van, ran blindly into the fog.

Madrid rolled from behind the car. He was flat on his stomach, back arched, a .45 in each hand. He could feel their heavy bodies galloping towards him. The dark rushing figures took shape, the one on the right a half a step behind the one on the left. Madrid pulled the triggers—the pistols jumped in his hands. The sound of the shots were simultaneous—like a small bomb—followed by a single, unified yelp Madrid ducked his head as the lead dog tumbled over him.

Toto was back on his feet. He surged past Madrid and the two downed canines as if none of the three even existed. Madrid popped up to his knees, began to fire with controlled blindness—fourteen shots into the darkness and fog. He aimed into the middle of the courtyard and fanned his arms outward until both chambers were empty.

Madrid scrambled back behind the Mercedes, deftly loaded two more clips, released the bolts, slammed the rounds into the chambers. Took a breath.

The motel window behind Rex Thompson shattered as two of Madrid's rounds zipped past him. He'd heard The Wizard's order to Lorenz to release the four-legged killers followed by Madrid's first two shots. He sprawled onto the concrete porch, flattened himself behind Flex's freshly-slain body. Rex kept his head down—waited. Madrid had stopped shooting. Rex belly-crawled forward through the pool of blood leaking from his former companion. The cement pad tore at his knees and elbows. Not important. He was nearly even with the Mercedes. Another three or four feet, and Rex would have a shot.

Johnny Lorenz watched his two best dogs disappear into the foggy murk—a second later heard the shot. Or was it two shots? There was a single yelp. His dogs went silent. There had been two shots. Like lambs to the goddamn slaughter, he'd sent them too soon. The little motherfucker had panicked—Johnny had gone stupid with greed. Now his two best dogs were gone—wasted. Two of Madrid's rounds ripped through the sheet metal of the van. Lorenz scrambled to the floor—cursed Alex Madrid, cursed The Wizard—mostly cursed himself.

Julie Kingston stood just inside the open doorway of the bathroom—her mind attempting to process a quickly-moving slurry of thoughts and emotions. She'd felt around in the darkness long enough to find the pistol-gripped shotgun. She held it on her hip, the muscles in her slender forearms flexed and defined. The bedroom window was gone. Like curious little ghosts, wisps of fog floated into the room. Bullets from somewhere across the courtyard had slapped into the wall above the bed—buried themselves in the knotty-pine paneling. Julie wondered if Madrid was still alive. She didn't see how he could be—but somebody was still shooting at something.

Outside the window, on the other side of the courtyard, she could see the hazy form of a dark figure. Like a huge angular snake, it methodically slithered along the concrete pad. The big snake stopped, rose a foot or so above the slab, as if about to strike. By only a fraction, Julie Kingston adjusted her aim—pulled the trigger. She pumped the weapon—jacked the empty cartridge—squeezed off another round.

The first round had slammed into his left shoulder—shattered his collar bone. The muzzle of the Browning shotgun dropped onto the gravel by his feet. The second round went through his right leg, just above the knee. Charlie Blades heard a savage, painful roar erupt from inside him. He stumbled sideways into the center of the courtyard, struggling to stay upright, working with his right hand to free the magnum from the shoulder holster. His momentum sent him tumbling into the fountain. Above his head, the cherubs stared disinterestedly into the darkness. Charlie struggled back up to his good knee. His right hand on the butt of the pistol, he sensed a force bearing down on him. Like a sledge hammer through the fog, the dog rocked him back against the fountain. Charlie's head snapped back against the limestone. He was only barely aware that the dog he had tortured for nearly three weeks now had him by the throat.

Madrid could hear the dog. Just below the surface of the frenzied snarls, the undertone of human pain was barely audible . A shot gun blasted from the room behind him—a second later, it blasted again. Automatic gun fire ripped into the backside of the Mercedes. Madrid could picture the gas tank exploding—tossing the car skyward—landing on him, like the Coyote in a Roadrunner cartoon. From his pocket, he took one of the M-61 grenades, pulled the pin. Staying low behind the nose of the Mercedes, he extended his right arm, arced the green orb towards the mouth of the horseshoe. A fraction of a second before the explosion, Madrid heard The Wizard scream something to Charlie Blades.

Crouched against the wall of the van, Johnny Lorenz worked the math as he slid his last clip into the belly of the AK-47. Firefights always seemed longer than they actually were. Even so, even in a hick town like Black Creek, pretty soon, somebody would be calling somebody. Then, not long after that, whatever was left of the army, would be fighting their way through the local cops. Not that it would be such a challenge, but dead cops brought other cops. Lots of angry, gun-totting cops happy to shoot first and make up the story later.

Lorenz made a quick decision, half the clip for Madrid—the other half would be his exit strategy. He duck-walked to the open side doors of the van, raised the weapon to his shoulder. The small metal canister fell from the sky, tracked only inches from the muzzle of his rifle. It landed with a slight metallic thud on the fine stone, rolled under the van below his feet. Johnny Lorenz recognized the sound. He was out of the van, feet on the ground—running blindly.

The Wizard was frozen. Fear halted his mind, locked down his body. He was still crouched between the back of Johnny's van and the nose of the wood-paneled station wagon. Still crouched there when the knee slammed into his face. The impact ignited a painful explosion of white light in his head—sent him sprawling face up on the far side of the wagon.

Lorenz was airborne, then went down face first, slid for a foot or two in the gravel. He popped back up onto his feet just as the grenade exploded under the van. The concussive force knocked him back to the ground. Slower this time, he struggled back up to his feet.

He turned back to the courtyard. The outline of his van came and went behind the wall of flame.

"....live to fight another day," he thought to himself.

Johnny Lorenz turned back to the highway. Someone was standing there—blocking his path—a dark shape in the fog. The AK-47 was somewhere behind him—in the darkness, on the ground. Johnny Lorenz never had time to process the blast from the double-barreled shotgun. And like Flex and Rex Thompson, Johnny Lorenz never knew who pulled the trigger that ended his life.

Chapter 39

September 28th—1:03 a.m.

The gunfire stopped. The shabby courtyard was bathed in yellow light, mirrored in the few remaining pieces of glass, broken by jerky shadows that played in rhythm with the flames. Madrid waited—listened. The burning van popped and crackled, and from somewhere in the inferno, twisting metal moaned mournfully. He eased his head around the grill of the car, came face to face with the dog.

Toto was panting heavily, drool hung from his jowls. The fire reflected in his eyes—made him look like some mythical hellish creature. Madrid touched the side of the dog's face. Blood transferred onto his hand.

"You okay, big guy?" he asked.

The dog continued to pant and stare. Madrid wanted to check on Julie, but wasn't ready to turn his back on what was in front of him. He stood slowly, a .45 in each hand. From the direction of Black Creek, he could hear a siren—thin, shrill and still far away. The van continued to churn fire. The heat made the fog swirl madly and disappear into the black September sky. He wondered if the two vehicles on either side would get hot enough to explode—wondered if anyone had called for a fire truck.

Madrid methodically checked each victim. The first two he recognized them from Arthur Johnson's description. They were at the side of the courtyard, just under the breezeway. The tall one had caught the brunt of a shotgun—maybe twice. His body was draped over the shorter one, a guy with shoulder-length blonde hair, as if trying to protect him. He took the remaining grenade from his jacket, placed it in the right hand of the tall one, then moved to the center of the courtyard.

The explosion had dislodged one of the cherubs. It laid on the ground, at the base of the fountain—next to Charlie Blades. It stared up at Madrid with concrete, "*why me*?" eyes. Blades was slumped against the fountain, his legs extended in front of him, the toes of his huge black boots pointing skyward. There was a hole in his left shoulder, another one in his right leg. The fountain shadowed the most of his face, but Madrid got a sense of the damage. He trained one of the .45s on Blades—leaned closer. The smell of blood mixed with the odor from the stagnant water in the fountain. Charlie Blades opened one eye. From somewhere deep inside fallen monster, a low groan worked its way to the surface. Madrid stepped back, cocked the .45. The eye slid slowly back to the closed position. Madrid recalled his reoccurring Charlie Blades nightmare. Even near death and unarmed, Charlie Blades was still scary as hell. Toto wandered over, stood with his muzzle just inches from Charlie's face. Growled. It was deep and controlled, as if Toto was informing Charlie about the recent change in pack status.

"Easy," Madrid told the dog in a quiet, but stern tone. He picked up the .357 from the gravel, tucked it into his belt. Arthur Johnson had said there would be five. If he was right—and he usually was about matters such as this—there were still two unaccounted for. The distant siren had been joined by others, and they were getting closer. Madrid backed his way towards the motel room, kept his eyes on the courtyard. He stumbled over one of the dogs. He was on his side, his eyes half closed, the light from the fire reflecting off his shiny black coat. And he was still breathing—short shallow breaths dying breaths. Madrid watched him for a moment. "You deserved a better fate," he muttered to the dog. He pulled the trigger of the .45, watched the dog's body relax.

Just in time to see the execution, Julie Kingston opened the door to the motel room. Madrid looked up, read her shocked, sickened expression.

"It was the humane thing to do," he said.

"I suppose," she replied numbly.

"Are you all right?" Madrid asked.

Like a scratched record, her answer was exactly the same.

Madrid placed his hands gently on her shoulders—looked her up and down. She wasn't bleeding. The sirens continued their advance.

"I need you to do something, Julie," Madrid told her, still lightly gripping her shoulders.

"Okay," she replied in a disconnected voice. "I can do something."

Madrid told her what he needed. He and the dog followed her into the motel room. He collected the pistol-gripped shotgun, the

AR-15, and the box that had contained the grenades. The sirens were getting closer, a chorus of highs and lows, urgent and growing deafeningly loud. Madrid stashed Charlie Blade's .357, unloaded the AR-15. He tossed the rifle into the burning van with the grenade box as the first vehicle pulled into the parking lot of The Paradise Court.

What happened over the next fifteen minutes could be described as loosely-organized chaos. There were guys with guns, and guys with fire hoses, and guys with gurneys and medical bags. And like the ocean at high tide, a wave of county vehicles was followed by an even larger wave of pickup trucks. Each vehicle sported some version of red flashing lights. In concert, they transformed The Paradise Court into a pulsing inferno. From the parking lot, scanners and CB radios chirped back and forth like raspy crickets. Volunteers, mostly young men in their late teens and early twenties, excitedly milled about—waiting for someone to give them direction—wanting to help—trying to stay out of the way.

The wood-paneled station wagon and the VW van had been hosed down. The fire was out and the courtyard smelled like burnt rubber. Lights had been spread out over the courtyard. They were on tall stands, and were running off of a generator on one of the rescue vehicles. The two guys from the ambulance were huddled over Charlie Blades. Madrid recognized them from the night Dicky Padrick had been shot.

"I think this one might still be alive," one of them said.

Josh Galloway looked directly at Madrid, said, "That would be different."

One of the deputies wandered by, got a good look at the damage the dog had done to Charlie Blades face and neck. "Gawddamn," he said in disbelief. "Something ate his Gawddamn face off."

Madrid told Galloway in a subdued voice, "Probably not as bad as it looks."

Galloway's crew-cut head recoiled. He replied sharply. "I got four men dead." He nodded over to Charlie Blades, "Or damn near dead. You better start explainin' what the hell happened here."

"Four." Madrid said.

"Yeah, fuckin' four," Galloway answered. "Three here, and one out in the parking lot. That one has most of his fuckin' face blown off."

Galloway looked over at the bullet-riddled carcass of the Mercedes—did double take, asked Madrid in an anxiety-strained voice, "Is that Julie Kingston's car?"

Madrid nodded, "Yeah."

"Is she here?"

Madrid offered the same answer.

Galloway snapped at one of the EMT guys, "Go see if she's hurt."

"She's not hurt," Madrid said quickly. "I think she's in the bathroom—throwing up. I don't think she wants company right now."

"So what the hell was she doing here?" Galloway asked.

The question remained suspended in the foggy night air. The EMT looked at Galloway, then at Madrid, then back to Galloway. "You want me to check her over?"

Galloway aimed an accusatory stare at Madrid. "No," he said slowly. "Give her a couple of minutes."

"You said you've got one down in the parking lot," Madrid said.

Galloway responded with a surly, "Yeah."

"Mind if I take a look?"

They looked. In the parking lot, almost halfway between the van and the road, the dead man was on his back, his left leg folded back under him. One of the deputies shone a high-powered flashlight. Galloway had been right—there wasn't much left of his face—but enough for Madrid to know it wasn't Weems Grabowski.

"You know him?" Galloway asked.

"Hard to say," Madrid answered.

"How 'bout a guess?"

Madrid figured they would know soon enough. "I'd guess it was a guy named John Lorenz," Madrid answered. "Lives in Georgia. Ex-military. He's a dog trainer—if that's what you want to call it. I'd guess the two animals outside my room are his."

"So what's he got against you?" Galloway demanded.

"Don't know," Madrid answered. "I'm actually quite delightful—once you get to know me."

The deputy moved the flashlight to Madrid, shone it in his eyes.

"Get that damn thing out of my face," Madrid snapped.

The deputy looked at the Sergeant, moved the light back to the body on the ground.

"That big mutt that runs around with you—that one of this Lorenz fellow's?"

"Used to be," Madrid admitted.

"So," Galloway said, "you steal it from him or something?"

"*Or something.*"

"So where is he?"

"Who?

"The dog, Asshole."

"I guess he's inside the room with Julie Kingston," Madrid replied calmly.

"Please don't tell me all these dead bodies are about some dog?" Galloway asked incredulously.

"No," Madrid replied flatly.

Another deputy walked up. His hands were cupped in front of him, as if he were carrying a baby bird. "You ought a see this, Chief."

The flashlight deputy shone his light. "It's a grenade, Chief," he said excitedly.

"I can see it's a grenade, Russell," Galloway said. "Where'd you get it?"

"Off one of those big guys. Not the one by the fountain—the other one that was piled up on the blonde-haired guy."

Galloway turned back to Madrid, "You know anything about this?"

Madrid eased towards the deputy. The pin was still in place. He turned to Galloway. "I think you're both right—it's a grenade. If it were me, I'd put it down—leave it the hell alone. I wouldn't be carrying it around for show-and-tell."

Galloway told the deputy. "Put it down somewhere. Somewhere safe," he added without being specific. "Then have somebody call ATF. Don't need to be in any big hurry. Them sons of bitches don't go to work 'till noon."

"Anybody check the van?" Madrid asked Galloway.

"Check it for what?"

"Bodies."

The hand-grenade deputy said, "We didn't see anything, Chief. But it's still pretty hot."

"You expectin' somebody else, Madrid?" Galloway asked.

"I wasn't even expecting these guy," Madrid lied. "Just curious."

"Yeah, well we're all a bit curious, Madrid. You're going to need to come with us and answer a shit load of questions."

* * * *

There were voices in the dark.

The second voice had just arrived.

The first voice, in an excited whisper, "Is he dead?"

"Yes."

"You killed him?"

A pause. "No" the second voice admitted. "There was other folks there. A lot of them. They wanted him dead, too."

The first voice, seeking one more layer of assurance, "You're positive he's dead?"

"There were five—maybe six men. I killed one of them myself," the second voice confessed. "It was me or him."

The first voice, suddenly concerned, "Are you hurt?"

The second voice, "No."

A third pause, the longest yet. The first voice spoke in a carefully measured tone. "You told me that he might be hard to kill."

The second voice, confident—resolute, "No one is that hard to kill."

Chapter 40

September 28th—8:12 a.m.

Something in the room was different—there was the light. Natural light—it filtered through gray clouds and heavy rain—struggled through the filmy window where the cardboard had been. It cast the basement cell in weak, ashen hues.

Anna Marie blinked twice, tried to shake off the heavy feeling in her head. Slowly, little bits of information began to process. Across the small room, against the unpainted cinder-block wall, her shoes were paired together next to the door. Anna Marie realized she was cold, sat up in the cot, pulled the blanket around her. She squirmed around until the bottom edge of the blanket was between her feet and the cold concrete.

"If I'm not back in the morning, you'll know what to do," the giant troll-like man had said. Fragments from their last conversation worked their way back to her. *A going-away party.* She remembered Charlie Blades hands on her body—wondered what he might have done to her while she slept. Wondered who else might have joined him. She listened. Occasionally the house would creak, then there was silence. Were they back? Was everyone asleep? *"You'll know what to do,"* he'd said.

But she didn't know what to do—didn't have a clue. What if he didn't come back—*never came back?* What if he'd lied to her and left her to die in this hell hole of a basement in this house that was god-knows where? Panic breathed energy into Anna Marie's thoughts. She looked at the plate of food by her feet—wondered if it was to be her last meal. The bread was crusty. From the wrapper, Little Debbie stared back at her with dead, cartoon eyes and a frozen, knowing smile. Anna Marie wanted to scream. But what if she wasn't alone after all?

Then she looked up.

It was the proverbial brass ring—but in the shape of a key. A mirage she told herself—an illusion—the by-product of failed hope and renewed desperation. It hung in the air, about seven feet or so from the floor, suspended from a thin, almost invisible, strand of fishing line. Anna Marie sat on the edge of the cot, perfectly still, watched it, as if were a tiny bird about to take flight. She eased herself from the bed, the blanket slid from her shoulders, down her legs, crumpled into a pile around her feet. She stood directly below the key—it seemed to disappear into the underside of flooring above her. Anna Marie backed away, looked at it from another angle—reassured herself the key really existed. She moved back under it, raised herself on her tip toes, reached as far as she could. She jumped once, then again—this time higher. Her breasts flailed up and down, a half beat behind the rest of her body. The key hung undisturbed. Anna looked around the room, found the chair. She positioned the chair—wrapped her fingers around the cool jagged teeth. She jerked hard—the line snapped. She slipped the key into the lock—tried to turn the deadbolt. It slid into place with a definitive click. She turned the knob—with the slightest creak from the hinges, the door swung open.

Anna Marie listened. The house was still quiet.

* * * *

Alex Madrid walked out of the Sheriff's office—stood under the rusty breezeway—rubbed his eyes against the gray morning light. The fog was gone. His Blazer was in the parking lot, getting battered with hard rain that periodically changed direction in the gusting wind. "Remnants of a hurricane that hit the Gulf coast," he'd heard someone say.

Madrid had spent the past six hours with Josh Galloway and the Barney Fife-looking deputy. They had used an empty office for the interrogation. Galloway had done most of the talking—had mostly asked the same four or five questions over and over again. To appear cunning, he would occasionally mix up the order. No one had mentioned Julie Kingston.

At three o'clock a deputy stuck his head in the door and announced that Charlie Blades had died on his way to the hospital. Around four o'clock, the small office had started getting crowded. Two state cops had shown up. An ATF agent had wandered in a few minutes after that. The ATF guy was small and wiry. He wore gold-rimmed, aviator-style eyeglasses that rested on a prominent nose. He had wanted to know about the hardware that was found at The Paradise Court. Madrid had sipped coffee from a Styrofoam cup—had said very little. Around 6:00 a.m. the sky had begun to lighten and a middle-aged guy in an expensive suit had knocked on the office door. He had longish salt and pepper hair, stylishly cut, and a black Burt Reynolds style mustache. In his left hand he held a briefcase covered in what appeared to be alligator skin. When he had spoken, he had sounded bored—and more than a little sanctimonious.

"My name is Trevor Williams," he'd told the group. "I'm representing Alex Madrid. I understand you have him in custody."

Madrid had raised the coffee cup, as if to offer a toast.

Galloway had looked to Madrid, back to Trevor, then back to Madrid—as if the two had conspired some prank at his expense. "This your lawyer?" he'd asked Madrid.

"Apparently," Madrid had replied.

Trevor had looked at Madrid, as if noticing him for the first time. Something between disappointment and distain had registered on his smugly-handsome face. "Have you been treated well, Mr. Madrid?"

"A damn sight better than he treated those four guys back at the motel," Barney Fife had replied.

Trevor ignored the deputy, asked again, "You have been treated well?"

"They talked kind of mean to me—scared me real bad a time or two, Trev."

Trevor Williams had simply replied, "I see." Then he added, "Miss Kingston said I probably wouldn't like you much."

"Did she mention how easily my feelings get hurt?"

"No," Trevor Williams had replied. "She didn't."

* * * *

It took most of an hour to locate Julie Kingston. From the pay phone by the park, Madrid called her house. A female voice with a French accent informed him Julie wasn't home. The accent intrigued him—made his mind go places it didn't need to be. Madrid dropped another dime—called the *Black Creek Herald.* A male voice with no French accent reported that Julie had gone home to change clothes, but would be back soon.

Twenty minutes later, in the parking lot of the *Black Creek Herald*, Madrid sipped fresh coffee and peeled the pleated paper cup away from his second blueberry muffin. Rain drummed on the top of the Blazer, cascaded over the windshield and made it hard to see. Julie pulled into the lot three minutes later. The last time Madrid had seen her, a deputy and another woman had been loading her and the dog into the back of a white panel truck with Rescue Squad printed across the sides in bold red letters. This morning, she was driving a Ford Country Squire station wagon, white—a luggage rack on top . The wipers furiously battled the rain. She docked the cruiser barge next to his Blazer. Coffee in one hand and the bag of muffins in his teeth, Madrid hopped out and slid into the passenger seat. It took maybe four seconds, but by the time he got the door to the wagon closed, he was fairly wet.

Madrid took the bag from his mouth, glanced into the back seat at the dog. Toto seemed no worse for wear, content to have good upholstery to lay on and a beautiful woman to chauffer him around. Madrid took a long look at Julie. Her hair was in a pony tail, tied with a green ribbon that matched her eyes. She was wearing one of those thick cable-knit sweaters that usually made Madrid think of New England fishing captains—but this morning, not so much.

"How are you?" Madrid said.

"Okay," she answered.

She was alert, probably running on adrenaline, but Madrid detected the edge of fatigue in her voice. "You get any sleep?"

"A little," she answered vaguely. "I dozed off and on—maybe an hour. What about you?"

"Not yet."

"I appreciate what you did last night," Madrid said.

"I'm not so sure it would have ended much differently either way."

"Don't kid yourself," Madrid replied.

"You knew they were coming, didn't you?"

"Thank you for looking out for my dog."

"That's your answer?'

"For now—that's my answer."

"Deniability?" she asked.

"Deniability *is* everything it's cracked up to be."

They sat in the front seat of the wagon, watching the rain pound the windshield. Madrid handed her a cup. "I brought coffee—with milk and a little honey."

"You remembered," she said, a hint of surprise.

Madrid nodded. "Want a muffin? They're blueberry."

Without taking her eyes off Madrid, Julie reached into the bag.

"Where'd you get this car?" Madrid asked.

"It was my mother's."

Madrid nodded. "Big," he said.

"Mine got all shot up," she replied evenly.

Madrid nodded again.

"I noticed that piece of junk you drive didn't get a scratch."

"Lucky I parked in the back," Madrid answered.

Julie took another bite of muffin. "Yeah. You're a fairly lucky guy, Alex Madrid."

"Sometimes."

"Where are you going to stay?" she asked. "The Paradise Court is shot—no pun intended," she added with a hint of tired smile.

"I don't know yet," he answered. "I still have a couple of things to do."

"Like what?" she asked.

Madrid wasn't clear if the woman or the reporter had posed the question. "Better if you don't know," he replied, addressing both possibilities.

"So even after last night, I'm not entitled to a few answers?" There was irritation in her tone.

"Back to deniability," Madrid countered.

"Yes, I keep forgetting." The irritation was still present.

"Thanks for sending Trevor."

"My father has him on retainer," she replied dismissively.

"Since I've never met your father, I'm guessing it's still *you* I should be thanking."

"How did you like him?" she asked. "Trevor."

Madrid sipped his coffee. "Oh, he's great. We're meeting at the club later today. Maybe play eighteen—talk about the market."

Julie smiled. "He's a good lawyer." Half-turned behind the steering wheel, her body contorted into a feline stretch as she fought off a yawn. After it passed, she said, "He's asked me to marry him."

Madrid was without a witty retort. "No kidding," he said.

"Twice," Julie said. "No kidding."

"Quite a catch," Madrid said.

"Trevor would be pleased to hear you say that, Alex."

"I wasn't talking about Trevor,"

She drew back slightly, cocked her head in mock surprise. "Oh."

"When I got in this car," Madrid confessed, "my first inclination was to kiss you until we were both gasping for air."

"So why didn't you?"

"I didn't know where your head would be after last night."

Julie Kingston took another sip of coffee, dabbed the corner of her mouth with a paper napkin. "Coffee and muffins are nice," she said finally, "but you should have trusted your instincts, Madrid."

* * * *

Next to the empty highway, The Paradise Court stood like a deserted movie set. Driving rain washed the last layer of color from the already-bleak surroundings. The VW and the station wagon had been towed away, but the blackened carcass of the van remained at the mouth of the courtyard. At each corner of the vehicle hardened puddles of blackish-gray rubber were formed on the white gravel. A residual stench filled the air. Oblivious to the rain, Toto padded over the courtyard, back and forth, nose to the ground. He stopped at the fountain. There were still traces of blood clinging to the wet limestone.

Madrid walked past the fountain, unlocked the door to one of the side rooms. From beneath the mattress, where he'd hidden it the night before, he extracted Charlie Blades' stainless steel .357. Madrid pressed the release, flipped the cylinder into view. Six rounds—Charlie hadn't gotten off a shot.

It took fifteen minutes to find the first track. It was near one of the broken down cabins, at the edge of the woods—a small footprint struggling to survive in the rain. Fifty feet or so from the parking lot, through a tangle of underbrush, Toto found the second track a few minutes later. There was a path of sorts. It led away from the motel, deeper into the woods, and eventually down the side of a steep hill. Madrid struggled with the footing—slick, wet leaves broken up with even slicker moss-covered rocks. The rain continued to pelt the brim of his Asheville Tourists ball cap and soak through his nylon jacket. Madrid blocked out the fatigue and the chill, but knew that couldn't last forever.

A few feet ahead of him, Toto seemed happy to be sloshing through the woods. He would stop—sniff the air, look back at Madrid—like he was on the trail of something important. And he was able to find something important about every ten feet. A pair of gray squirrels chased each other in the canopy overhead. Toto watched them—sniffed the air—looked back at Madrid. The dog added them to his list of things that were important.

At the bottom of the hill, the trail leveled off and gently meandered over the forest floor. Eventually it bisected a small, but swollen stream. Usually not much more than a trickle, it was now almost a yard wide. On the other side, the ground was a muddy quagmire. In the middle of the black goo, filled two-thirds with water, was a shoe. Madrid hopped the moving water, pulled it from the muck—a Hush Puppy–size six and a half.

"Stylish, yet comfortable" Madrid told the dog.

Toto plowed through the water, sniffed the shoe. Looked at Madrid. Moved up the trail.

Past the stream, for the next half mile or so, a thick, claustrophobic stand of hemlock and rhododendron crowded the path. On the other side of the lush greenery, the vegetation was smaller—thinner—like there had been logging or a fire a decade before. And then there were no more tracks.

Toto stopped—strolled past Madrid—backtracked up the trail. He stopped, sniffed the soggy ground—looked back at Madrid—like it was something important

Chapter 41

September 28th—9:02 a.m.

Lilly Grabowsiki speaks softly to her son. Concern registers in her voice, a slightly-pinched expression forms on her beautiful face. "My darling boy," she says, almost a plea, "you must be more careful. Mommy doesn't like it when you get hurt." She leans closer, watches the blood seep through his shredded pants leg. "What have you done to yourself?"

Lying on the ground, propped against a maple tree, the boy looks up at her. Her presence is an anesthetic to his throbbing pain. "He hurt me, Mommy," he replies in a piteous tone.

"Who hurt you, my darling boy?" she asks, leaning closer. Her hair brushes his cheek. He catches a hint of her perfume—it reminds him of lilacs.

"That man," the boy replies as another wave of pain washes over his small, frail body.

"What man, my darling boy? Tell Mommy who he is."

The boy thinks hard, struggles to summon the name. "Alex Madrid," he says finally—tears streaming down his cheeks. "He hurt me, Mommy."

"Don't you worry, my darling boy," she whispers. "It will all be over soon."

The boy struggles to understand. The boy watches helplessly as his mother fades into nothingness. He wants to call out to her—but realizes the futility. She is gone—never coming back. The boy made sure of that a long time ago. His pain surges to the surface and he begins to scream.

Lily had been just a dream, but the agony was real. Somewhere, just before dawn, he had managed to get himself off of the trail—prop himself against a small boulder. A few feet away, a rain-swollen creek raced by him. The Wizard endured another wave of pain, slowly opened his eyes. What he saw made him forget about his mother. His view was eclipsed by a wall of fur, broken by two yellow eyes, black gums, and white teeth. Noses only inches apart, the hellish beast released a low rumbling, growl. Panic forced air from his lungs—something between a moan and a shriek. His damaged body convulsed.

Alex Madrid stood just behind the dog, the fingers of his left hand curled around the dog's thick leather collar. He stared down at the top of the man's pale, bald head. The little man's glasses were gone—he squinted up into the rain—reminded Madrid of a turtle who had ventured into a bad place with no shell. The right side of his body was burned. It started at his cheek, just below his right eye, continued down to just above his knee. Madrid's right foot was firmly planted on The Wizard's left hand. His weight pressed the 9mm he held into the soft, rain-drenched earth. Secretly, he marveled how the little turtle man had been able to make it this far.

"Get back, Toto," he said, like a parody of a Beatles lyric.

The Wizard watched the dog move away. Madrid towered over him, his face expressionless under the brim of the hat.

"Weems, Weems, Weems," Madrid said in a "tisk-tisk" tone. "You never seemed the woodsy type to me, but hey—look at you now.....who knew?"

"I'm hurt," the little man said in a forced tone, as if negotiating.

"I can see that," Madrid replied, no trace of compassion. "Rub some dirt on it—walk it off—you'll be fine."

The Wizard closed his eyes—opened them slowly, unable to blink away the nightmare.

"Almost had you, Madrid," he said, forcing the words past his swollen lips. "Charlie says you're the luckiest son of a bitch he's ever seen."

"Lucky," Madrid repeated, as if tasting something bitter. "Luck is like hope, Weems. Just two different words for something that doesn't exist." He paused, then added, "At least not for you."

"It was a good plan," the little man mumbled from his damaged face.

Madrid squatted, like a catcher, their eyes nearly on the same level. "You think so, Weems?" he asked with sudden sincerity.

"I walked out of a maximum security prison." The last three words came out thickly. Blood tinged saliva appeared at the corner of his mouth.

Madrid reached under his right foot, took the Browning from the little man's boney fingers. The gun left a well-defined imprint in the soft earth. He stood up, said, "That's what you think, Weems? You were just sitting around in the prison yard one day, and this brilliant plan shimmied down to you on a ray of sunshine?"

Weems *The Wizard* Grabowski squinted at Madrid with his remaining good eye, struggled to put his words into context. "I'm here," he countered in an uncertain voice.

"Yeah, you're fucking here, all right" Madrid said, his voice callous and tired, "what's left of you."

"It was a good plan," he repeated, but there was an emptiness in his tone .

"And it went pretty much like this," Madrid said, as if reading from a script. "A guard came to you one day. His name was George. He was an older guy—a little stooped—a little beaten down by life—not far from retirement. He'd sent a couple of kids to college, and there wasn't much left for him and the wife. George mentioned he could get you the kitchen detail. Two hundred up front and twenty a month after that. You hesitated, because you're careful, Weems—a fool and his money kind of thing. A couple of days later, George sweetened the deal—told you there wouldn't be much work and you'd get fed like the guards—not like the other inmates. You said okay. Charlie took care of the money. Even after the half a million that went missing, I figure you still had three times that squirreled away here and there. Things went like George has said—you didn't work much—and you ate good. After a couple weeks you heard George's wife was sick—cancer—terminal. Not something *he'd* tell you—but you knew. You overheard it—or someone else found out—passed it along. Got you to thinking, Weems—made you start looking for an angle. So when the old guy came to you with this idea—it kind of made sense. A desperate logic on both sides of the ledger. George needed cash—you needed to get the hell out of prison." Madrid paused, a cruel smile tugged at the corner of his mouth. "How am I doing so far, Weems?" he said over the rain.

The little man said nothing. His back was against the wet, moss-covered rock, he struggled to sit up just a little straighter. Alex Madrid stood again, his eyes hooded beneath the bill of his cap. The rain had plastered his jacket to his broad shoulders. The muscles in his chest and arms looked like hard knots under the wet cloth. The Wizard wondered if Charlie Blades would be able to take him. It really didn't matter now. Charlie Blades was gone—had to be—or he would be the one standing there. Not Madrid. The Wizard calculated his next move—and the one after that. The way he figured it, he still had one last chance to kill Alex Madrid.

"George told you it would be expensive" Madrid continued. "Ten grand—half up front and the rest when you were on the other side of the wall. Probably sounded cheap to you, Weems—but a lot of money to him. Economy of scale. Some friend of a friend of a cousin of a brother drove one of the food trucks to the prison every couple of weeks. No real connection back to the guard. But they had to work together—maybe a fifty-fifty cut, but I'm guessing no better than sixty-forty. George was pretty good at negotiating. It was a box truck—not huge, but not too small. George told you to be there to help unload. He put you inside the back of the truck. You moved the goods to the edge, the others carried it inside the building. At the back of the bed, there was a damaged crate. Powdered milk, powdered eggs or some other exotic prison delicacy. The guard refused delivery. Not George, but someone else. The crate stayed on the truck. A little guy like you might fit in that crate—if you folded yourself tightly enough. But it might also be the first place someone might check. Hell, it *would be* the first place someone would check. Because it was obvious—and easy. We all like the easy stuff, Weems."

Weems, The Wizard, forced the pain back inside, listened to Madrid's version of the escape. The son of a bitch had obviously talked with people—talked with the *right* people. Maybe he had even figured out bits and pieces on his own. Maybe Charlie Blades had been wrong—maybe this wasn't all about luck.

"And that's kinda what happened, Weems," Madrid continued in a conversational voice. "That broken crate at the back of that box truck got a lot of attention. Got checked four times, from what I hear. The two guards at the kitchen and two more guards at the gate. And George and three other guards swore you weren't inside it. And they were right, Weems.

"Misdirection. Like a half-assed magician at a kiddies show. Get all the little scamps looking at your left hand—and all the while—the shiny bauble is in your right. It was kind of like that, wasn't it?" Madrid added with a dramatic mock, "*The Wizard.*"

Weems Grabowski looked up at Madrid, "It worked," he said.

"Oh yeah, it worked," Madrid replied, nodding approval. "Worked like a charm. While the guards took turns looking in the crate, you were just a couple of feet away. The truck had a false back—sixteen inches to be exact. You'd needed George to move the wall to get you in, but that only took a few seconds. It was well engineered, and after you were snugged in, you didn't need anyone to get you out. I'm guessing the hardest part was the claustrophobia. The space was tight, dark—probably hot. Sixteen inches isn't a hell of a lot of room—and the guards were only a few inches beyond that on the other side of that plywood wall. But what the hell," Madrid added with a casual shrug, "It was worth it, huh? You rolled out the gate—no one the wiser—and here you are." Madrid spread his arms, palm up in a welcoming gesture. "Just you, me—and our dog, of course, enjoying this lovely morning in the woods. Yeah, it was a good plan, Weems. A real good plan."

"I should have killed that fucking dog," he said with an agonizing series of grunts.

"You should have done a lot things, Weems."

"Maybe old George and I will share a cell."

"George the guard?" Madrid asked, amused.

Weems Grabowski stared back at Madrid.

"No," Madrid replied with an exasperated tone. "You still don't get it, Weems. George took your money, *and then he took the money I gave him.* Of course—I guess technically—it was still *your* money. This was a big risk for him, so he needed a big reward. George and the wife are going to wait a couple of years, then buy a fishing cabin on the Gulf of Mexico. Wouldn't have been my first choice, but hey—to each his own. An interesting aside, though—turns out his wife doesn't have cancer. She was born under the *sign* Cancer. Easy mistake. I can see how a moron like you might have been confused."

The rain had let up, only a fine mist filtered down through the foliage. Madrid took in a deep breath, blew it out, said in a fatigued tone, "Bottom line, Weems. Good news—bad news. *Good news*: George isn't going to jail. He's going to retire in a couple of months—his conscience, and his pockets, a little heavier. *Bad news*:

You're not going to jail, either. See...that was the back half of the deal. Before he'd agree to let you escape...I had to make George a promise. I promised him you wouldn't survive."

Choices get easier when you know you're going to die. *Maybe* and *what if* slip below the horizon; they no longer cloud your view—your path becomes clear. At least that's the way it was for Weems Grabowski. Until that moment—somewhere in the deep recesses of his psyche—he had convinced himself there was still hope. Charlie Blades would find him—get him something for the pain—get him the hell out of here.

But it wasn't Charlie who'd shown up. Madrid stood over him with barely a scratch. There wouldn't be any deals. Madrid still blamed him for his niece's death. *And that was totally unfair! Madrid was the one who shot her, for Christ's sake!* The whole thing was totally unfair, but it didn't matter now. The only thing certain was that Weems *The Wizard* Grabowski was about to die. Maybe it would be in the next few minutes, or maybe, Madrid would make the agony would stretch out for hours. Weems had one more chance to kill Alex Madrid—and he could see no reason not to take it. Choices get easier when you know you're going to die.

"So do it, motherfucker," The Wizard said. Below the pain, an angry, and calculated defiance was audible.

"There's no need for name calling, Weems," Madrid replied. "Who knows, if you can hang on for a couple of weeks, it will be squirrel season. Maybe you'll get lucky and some hunter will wander by."

"I know about hunting," the little man said, the words tumbling from his swollen face. "My favorite prey is pretty little red-headed girls." He took a deep breath that rattled in his bird-like chest. "Your niece was a fighter," he continued, forcing the words past his swollen lips. "I used to fuck her—three times a day." He paused, contorted his face into what he thought was a smile, then added, "Until you killed her."

The hallway had been dark, just enough light bleeding in from the main room for Madrid to make his way along. The guy had come out of a bedroom—second-rate talent, but big as hell. Later, the coroner's report would read he had been six-feet seven, and nearly three hundred and fifty pounds. At that critical moment, his mass had filled the doorway. On his hip, he'd held the rifle—a lever action—better suited for deer hunting than close-quarter combat. The giant man had hesitated. It was only a second, maybe waiting for his eyes to adjust to the gloom—maybe an instant of panic. No one would ever know. Madrid had fired the .357 twice from a six feet away. The revolver had spit fire—the sound of the explosions had rolled down the narrow hallway. The first shot had hit him just below the sternum, the second ripped through his heart. He had toppled like a fallen tree into the hallway. A half a beat after that, a similar sound—softer from inside the bedroom. Alex Madrid had stepped over the man's body—found his niece on the floor behind him. One of the slugs from the .357 had torn through her neck. She had stared up at him with a mixture of bewilderment and fear. He'd tried to stop the bleeding, but less than a minute later, he'd watched her die.

Weems waited for Madrid's reaction, but it never came. His face was like stone, his blue eyes like cold, polished glass.

"Old news, Weems," he said after a moment. "Even if it were true—which it isn't. That's why you had Charlie. He did most of your killing and all of your fucking. Notice I said *did*—past tense." Madrid rose, stared down on the burned, crumpled little man. "My dog ripped his throat out." Madrid could hear the anger edging into his voice.

The little man fixed his good eye on Toto. The dog was sitting maybe five feet away, just behind Madrid. The little man made another calculation, then played his last card. "Me and Charlie got another girl," he said triumphantly.

The words hit Madrid like cold steel. The knot in his stomach tightened, contorted his body. He could almost swear, for an instant, his knees buckled. White noise filled his head, suppressed any attempt at reason. After what seemed like a long time, Madrid said, "You're full of shit, Weems."

"In my pocket," he said, motioning with his head to the damaged side of his body. "I got a picture. See for yourself."

Madrid knelt. The muzzle of Charlie Blades' stainless .357 pressed against Weems Grabowski's nose. The fabric around the front pocket of Weems' jeans was wet, bunched, and dirty. Madrid worked the first two fingers of his left hand inside until he felt the hard edge of something—maybe a Polaroid picture. With the tips of his first two fingers, he pinched the corner—wiggled it back and forth—slowly extracted it from the confines of the fabric.

The Wizard looked on like some comic-book villain, one half of his face grotesque, the other half, cruel and smug. Madrid stood up, the barrel of the .357 remained pointed at the little man who remained canted back against the rock. Madrid forced himself to look at the photo. The white edge had been scorched by the fire, but the picture itself was undamaged. Like Polaroids often were, the colors were harsh, but the image was clear. The girl was on a cot, lying on her back. It wasn't Sarah, but she had red hair, like his niece—only curly. It splayed out over her pillow. Her eyes were closed—asleep or maybe dead, Madrid thought. The camera's flash made her skin...well...a whiter shade of pale. The girl had been posed. Her legs were spread, the right one dangled lifelessly from the edge of the cot. Her white dress had been wadded under her arms. Beneath it, she was naked except for a pair of small, white panties—pushed to one side.

Madrid found himself unable to look away from the photo—which was precisely what The Wizard had figured.

The snub-nosed .32 revolver was on the ground, tucked between his back and the boulder. Weems' left hand was behind him, his thin, boney fingers wrapped around the handle. He was better from his right side, but the fire had made his right side no longer an option. The pistol held six rounds. He would need them all—three for Madrid, three for the dog. Madrid towered above him, stared hypnotically at the image of Anna Marie. That wouldn't last—Weems had to move now. He pulled the revolver from beneath him—squeezed off the first round.

Madrid stared at the girl in the Polaroid, but saw Sarah, his niece. He wondered how many pictures of her, pictures like this, The Wizard and Charlie Blades had passed back and forth. Late at night, the mystery of his niece's last thoughts often haunted him.

He tore his eyes from the picture, looked at Weems, propped against the boulder, lying in the mud. There was a small pistol in his left hand. *Fuck*, he thought—then everything went black.

Chapter 42

September 28th—10:16 a.m.

Behind the eight-foot mahogany desk that had once belonged to her father, Julie Kingston sat—tried to write. She had an exclusive, and before that, she'd had a front-row seat to Alex Madrid's private war. It was the kind of story, reported just so, that could make a career. But fatigue, anxiety, and a steady stream of mostly-well-meaning visitors had ground the process nearly to a halt. Their shadows had taken shape in the translucent glass door that separated her office from the rest of the building.

Clarence Johnson had been in three times. A tall, slender man in his late sixties, Clarence was dressed in black trousers, a carefully ironed white shirt, and a small black bow tie. He had a shock of silvery-white hair, combed back from his face, that stopped just above the collar of that white shirt. People said he looked a little like Einstein. Maybe not as sharp as Albert, but forty years in the newspaper business had taught him to watch and to listen. Clarence knew things about people—knew things about Julie Kingston. So when he asked how she was doing, it meant something slightly different than when other people in the office asked the same question.

It had started with white wine spritzers. Just a couple of times a week after work—then every day after work—then most of the weekends. Then she had moved up the ladder to Crown Royal. It wasn't that bad—she could stop whenever she wanted, she'd told herself. The rationalization had held until the day she'd picked her mother up at the airport. She wasn't drunk, but she'd had a couple—just a little buzz—enough to take the edge off. Her mother would ask her all the usual questions—the same questions she asked Julie every time they were together. But that day her mother had said very little. She had found a station that still played Sinatra. The normal tension between them had evaporated, but that might have been simply the Crown Royal. Her mother was humming along with Frank, her eyes forward, her large pocketbook resting on her lap. Julie had noticed that she wasn't wearing her lap belt, but the moment had been too tranquil to ruin.

The pickup truck had come from a side street, right through the stop sign. Julie had barely touched the brake before they slammed into the side of the Chevy. In the next instant, her mother was gone, the passenger seat empty, her shattered body halfway through the windshield.

The police had come. Julie had left in the first ambulance, her mother in the second. The order of their departure had doused any remaining hope. The police had found open beer in the cab of the truck—a couple more empties on the floorboard. The pickup guy had been charged. No one had said anything to Julie—but she was sure they knew. The look from the doctors and nurses, from the Highway Patrol officer who interviewed her in the hospital, from her father who now rarely called and never visited. And Julie knew. With the same set of circumstances, stone-cold sober, things might have been different. That's what she told herself, anyway. She told herself that every day.

Clarence walked into her office—didn't bother to knock. He placed a white paper bag on her desk, opened it. He peeled the lid from a Styrofoam cup—hot tea with lemon and honey—just the way she liked it. Next to the tea he placed a scone on a paper napkin.

"From Marcy's?" Julie asked.

Clarence nodded.

Emotion crept into her voice. "Thank you, Clarence."

Another nod. "You don't need anything more to deal with right now," he began, carefully selecting each word. "But sometimes, that's not how it works out. We don't get to choose, Julie ," he added apologetically.

Julie felt a fresh wave of anxiety wash over her. "Tell me, Clarence."

"Dicky Padrick just died," he said quietly. "They think maybe it was a blood clot in his brain."

She placed her hand over mouth, as if about to be sick. "Oh, god," she said around it. Oddly, her first thought was of Alex Madrid. If he knew. And where he was.

"I'm thinking we should run it front page," Clarence said. "Below the fold."

"Whatever you think," she answered, just above a whisper.

* * * *

It had been hell. The climb out of the valley, up the trail that traversed the muddy hillside. At first Madrid was confused—disoriented. His head throbbed, even blinking his eyes was painful. And his legs were weak. After the first two steps he'd wanted to sit. And there was blood—a lot of blood. Like a macabre mask, it painted the right side of his face.

Madrid had managed to stumble through the bramble of rhododendron. When the trail emerged, he had been unsure which way to turn. He had stood there, looking one way, then the next—trying to sort it out. In the end, he had followed the dog. Toto seemed to know where they needed to go. The climb out had been a torturous, monotonous, a seemingly-never-ending series of one foot in front of the other. His lungs seemed to bang against his ribs, struggling for air. Madrid stopped often, but was afraid to sit down—afraid he wouldn't get back up. The dog would stop, too—turn his massive head, and wait. The rain pounded them both, transformed Madrid's bloody mask to a pink stream that ran down his neck and under his shirt. And it went on like that—a few steps—then rest—an occasional stumble—a few steps—a look from the dog—and more rain.

The trail ended at the far side of the parking lot of The Paradise Court. Next to the burned out van, three teenagers, two girls and a boy, stood huddled under a massive umbrella. The boy and one of the girls were blonde and slender—looked enough alike to be related. The other one was shorter, with long brown hair, parted in the middle. With wary expressions, they watched Madrid and the dog wander out of the woods. The boy repositioned himself in front of the girls—the protector. Madrid moved past them, towards the damaged fountain in the middle of the courtyard. His gait was stiff and awkward.

"Good morning," he mumbled as he passed.

"Good morning," they all replied, the irony unrealized, and therefore, unappreciated.

Under the breezeway, Madrid found one of the porch chairs laying on its side. He turned it upright, sat heavily and heard himself groan.

"What happened to you?" the blonde boy asked.

Madrid looked at the boy, as if seeing him for the first time. "Fell in the woods," he replied. "Hit my head on a rock."

Like a quasi-choreographed six-legged turtle, the trio moved closer under the umbrella. The dog tilted his head, watched them curiously.

"My name's James," the boy said in a serious voice. "People call me Jimmy."

"Hello, Jimmy."

"What's yours?" the boy asked with a mixture of suspicion and respect.

Madrid adjusted himself in the metal chair. "Herman," Madrid said. "Herman Melville. My friends call me Mel."

"Jesus, Mel," the blonde girl said, leaning closer. "You look like you're hurt pretty bad." The last word came out as *ba-yad*. She had one of those soft syrupy accents that was easy on the ears.

"Probably not as bad as it looks," Madrid said, not having any idea of how bad it actually looked.

"You might ought 'a go see a doctor, Mel," the blonde girl said.

"I'll be all right," Madrid replied without much conviction.

"I'm studying to be a nurses' aid," the brown haired girl said proudly.

Madrid looked at her. She smiled, revealed a set of braces, then closed her mouth self-consciously.

"How many classes so far?" Madrid asked.

"Two, Mr. Mel."

"Perfect," Herman Melville declared.

It was coming back to him—slowly—random fragments—mostly out of sequence. He didn't know how long he had lain there—face down on the wet forest floor. He remembered the dog, nudging him at first, then using his head to root and bull him over onto his back. The cool rain had done nothing to sooth the fire in his head. Toto was standing over him, making sounds that were between a grunt and a whine. The dog's breath had been warm on his face, and had smelled...well...not minty-fresh.

Weems was still leaned back against the rock. The little man stared at them with dead eyes. There was a hole in his chest where his heart should have been. Madrid didn't remember pulling the trigger of Charlie's .357—figured it had been a reflex action. Madrid had forced himself to his knees, had waited for his equilibrium, then stood. Instinct took over. He wiped Charlie's .357 down and placed it on Weems' lap. It might not fool an expert, but the odds of an expert ever examining Weems' body were long. The .32 was on the ground next to Weems' left knee. Madrid left it there. He took the Browning 9mm and checked the clip. It was full, another round in the chamber. Madrid slid it under his belt at the small of his back.

The Polaroid was face down on the ground. Madrid had flipped it over; the redheaded girl was still waiting for him on the other side—now lost and hopeless. Madrid moved his eyes to Weems "The Wizard", then back to the photo.

In a voice that brimmed with fatigue and pain, Madrid mumbled to the dog, "I won the battle and lost the war." He had slid the Polaroid into his pocket and started the trek out.

The five of them paraded back into the motel room, the three kids, Madrid, and the dog. There was glass everywhere and bullet holes had splintered the pine paneling above the two beds. The blonde girl found a broom and started sweeping glass.

"Your dog's gonna get his paw cut up, Mel."

"There's a first aid kit in the Blazer," Madrid told the boy. "Could you get it?"

The boy hesitated, not sure about leaving the two girls.

"Gawd, almighty, Jimmy," the blonde girl told him. "Just go get it. He's not goin' to rape us while you're gone." She grinned, added, "Are you, Mel?"

Before Madrid could reply, Jimmy offered Madrid a hard, squinty look—spoke in a voice that probably scared the hell out of seventh graders. "You mess with these girls, Herman, and I'll kick your ass." He added for emphasis, "I kin do it, too."

"Good to know," Madrid replied.

The brown-haired girl rolled her eyes, then demanded in an exasperated voice, "Go get the damn kit, Jimmy. I need medical supplies if I'm going to tend to Mr. Mel." She turned to the blonde girl who had stopped sweeping glass. "I'm dating an idiot."

The blonde girl didn't argue.

Thirty minutes later, Madrid had packed what he needed from The Paradise Court. He was in dry clothes—the gash on his head had been cleaned and closed with a butterfly bandage. The brown-haired girl had been thorough—if not gentle. She had offered stern warnings about keeping the wound clean and changing the dressing—topics they'd apparently covered in her first two classes. Madrid had given each, including Jimmy, a hundred dollars of Weems' money—had suggested they keep the encounter to themselves.

Chapter 43

September 28th—12:20 p.m.

Julie Kingston was gone for the day. That's what the tall older guy with the long white hair had told Madrid when he stopped by the office of the *Black Creek Herald.*

"You're Alex Madrid?" More as a statement than a question.

Madrid confirmed it with a nod and a tired, "Yeah."

"I'm Clarence," he said, extending his hand. "Julie was hope...said you might come by this morning." He glanced at his watch, raised his bushy white eyebrows in mild surprise. "Morning's gone," he said, almost nostalgically. He looked back at Madrid. "Come with me."

Madrid followed him a few steps down a narrow hallway. Clarence stepped into a small office, motioned with his head for Madrid to follow. When they were both inside, Clarence closed the door quietly. He reached into his black trousers, handed Madrid a silver-colored key.

"You've been to the Kingston home," Clarence stated.

"Yes."

"Just before you get to the main house," Clarence explained, "there is a smaller drive that leads to a guest cottage. I imagine you will find it quite comfortable. You can get some rest."

"Thanks," Madrid said.

Out in the hallway, through the translucent glass, a female form took shape. There was a gentle knock. Clarence opened the door halfway and a young woman with curly black hair and large eyeglasses filled the void. "Sorry to bother you, Mr. Wilkes. But we just got a story off the wire—about a girl in Gatlinburg, Tennessee."

Fatigue and raw nerves coaxed a reflex response. "What kind of story?" Madrid asked.

Clarence and the girl looked at Madrid, then at each other. "Go ahead, Cindy," Clarence said.

"Well," she began uncertainly. "A young woman," Cindy referred to the piece of paper she was holding, "Anna Marie Coles, walked into the Police Department in Gatlinburg this morning. She claimed she'd been kidnapped and held captive in a house up on the side of mountain. She thinks it was two or three days, but isn't really sure because they mostly kept her in a room with no windows. Said she was drugged most of the time."

"Interesting," Clarence said, still watching Madrid.

"There's more, Mr. Wilkes," Cindy added—a hint of drama, "The girl says she might have witnessed the murder of the Park Ranger in Tennessee. One of the men she described" she glanced furtively at Madrid, "sounds a lot like one of the men—one of the dead men—at The Paradise."

"Let me take a look at it," Clarence said, extending his hand—eyes still on Madrid.

"Yes, sir." She closed the door quietly, her shaped faded away behind the glass.

"Did you find that interesting, Mr. Madrid?" Clarence asked.

"I'm not going to waste your time, Clarence." Madrid pulled the Polaroid from his hip pocket. "I need to know if the girl in Gatlinburg is the same girl in this photograph."

The older man's face remained composed.

"Did you pull this off of one of the dead men at The Paradise Court?" The question was broad enough for interpretation. "Yeah," Madrid answered.

Clarence was still staring at the photo. "I will find out and let you know." He added,

"These were bad men, weren't they, Mr. Madrid?"

"They were," Madrid added.

"Before you go, Mr. Madrid, there's something I should tell you."

Madrid detected the change in his tone. He'd heard it before—too many times—from too many people. He braced himself for bad news.

"It's about Dicky Padrick," Clarence said.

* * * *

Madrid hadn't noticed the narrow drive on his first visit to Julie Kingston's home. Like Clarence had said, it peeled off from the larger one in a deep curve. The guest house was about a hundred yards northwest from the main house, nearly invisible, tucked into a grove of hardwoods, and nestled up to a small pond with a proportionally small dock. The cottage had the organic feel of something that had sprung from the earth and taken shape slowly over time. It was a mixture of English Tudor and whatever architecture was favored by gnomes. It was small, well-thought-out—looked expensive.

The wormy chestnut door was unlocked.

The two stood in the doorway. "Not half bad," Madrid said to the dog.

The interior was dominated by a squatty stone fireplace and naturally-finished quarter-sawn oak woodwork. The walls had been painted a light shade of green. Toto padded across the floor, onto the Oriental rug, and stopped in front of the big leather sofa. He placed one hefty paw on the cushion, looked back at Madrid. "Don't even think about it, pal."

Madrid shaved, showered—did his best to keep the bandage above his right eye dry. He dressed in a pair of gray gym shorts and set the dog's food and water bowls on the bathroom's ceramic tile floor. He had burned through all of his adrenaline, and the pain in his head throbbed a steady beat. Madrid found aspirin in the medicine cabinet and Andeker beer in the fridge. He combined three of the first and two of the second.

Something poked him on the shoulder—gentle, but steady. Like a submerged diver, his consciousness struggled back up from the murky depths—to the light at the surface. He was stretched out on the sofa, his head laid back against the arm. The television playing low.

Julie stood over him, the dog sitting next to her, his tail slowly thumping against the Oriental rug. She was in a silky white sleeveless t-shirt and black running shorts—equally silky. Madrid was eye level with her long tanned legs and the dog. He focused on her legs and said, "Stop poking me."

"What happened to you?" she asked, touching Madrid lightly on the forehead. She had an empty beer bottle in her left hand.

Madrid sat up. His head wasn't quite as bad as it had been. He looked at his wrist, remembered he'd left his watch in the bathroom. "How long have I been asleep?" he asked drowsily.

"I don't know exactly when you got here," Julie said. "But I'd guess about an hour. It's about two thirty."

Madrid swung his legs to the floor, thought for a moment. "Yeah, that would be about right."

"You haven't answered my question. What happened to you?

"Fell on a rock."

"You don't seem like a 'fell on a rock' kind of guy, Madrid."

"Been awkward since I was a child," Madrid explained. "Probably should have taken those ballet lessons my mom was always pushing for. She said I'd be sorry."

"That's a perfectly darling story, Madrid." Julie perched on the edge of the coffee table, leaned forward and gave the wound a closer look. "What really happened?" Madrid shifted on the sofa. In an exhausted voice, he confessed . "I got shot...I think...don't remember much except waking up."

"Unbelievable," Julie said, shaking her head slightly. "All the shooting last night and you don't get even a scratch. But you managed to nearly get your head blown off before lunch today—*in Black Creek, for God's sake!* "

Madrid leaned back on the sofa, studied her. Julie wasn't wearing a bra. He was about to run with that thought when she said, "Stop staring at my boobs and focus, Madrid. What about the guy who shot you?"

"Apparently he got shot, too," Madrid answered. "Only he's not going to be waking up."

"Weems Grabowski?"

Madrid offered a blank stare.

Julie rolled her eyes. "Off the record."

"Off the record—yeah."

"Clarence called," Julie said quietly. "He talked with someone in Gatlinburg. The woman in your picture is the same one who walked into the police station this morning."

"He's sure?" Madrid asked, wanting it to be true.

"If Clarence Wilkes says it's so, you should believe him."

"Is the girl all right?" Madrid asked.

"All things considered."

Madrid searched for a tactful approach, but fatigue, and getting shot in the head, made that difficult. Finally, he simply asked, "Did they rape her?"

"I don't think so," Julie said. Then added, "Not in the physical sense, anyway."

The heavy drapes had been pulled and the bedroom was nearly dark. They were in the king-sized bed, Madrid on his back, Julie on his left, curled against him. There had been no offer, or even suggestion, of sex—just two people seeking rest and refuge from waking up alone.

Julie's arm was flung over his chest, her head resting on his shoulder. It wasn't particularly comfortable, but Madrid didn't care. He could hear her steady breathing, smell her freshly-shampooed hair. Madrid laid there, soaked in her warmth, savored the curves of her body. He wanted to burn the moment into his memory—to have something to take with him.

In the dim light, he stared at the ceiling, his eyes heavy, as his mind doggedly trudged through his thoughts and his fears. Charlie Blades and the girl in the Polaroid. Julie said she hadn't been raped, but there was no telling what she had endured with Blades and Weems. *She was never part of the plan, but I should have seen that coming a mile away,* Madrid told himself. *Should have known they would grab another one. It was simple and predictable—that's what they did.*

Three minutes later he was asleep.

Chapter 44

September 28th—8:15 p.m.

The room was dark—that no-street light, no-moonlight kind of dark. Thick, like a heavy black blanket—the same kind of darkness that was in his head. Madrid listened to the rain. It worked its way along the copper gutters of the cottage, dove noisily into the downspouts. Madrid wanted to go back to sleep, but knew it wouldn't happen. His demons had been roused.

Dicky Padrick meandered into his still-groggy sub-conscious. Dicky Padrick was dead. *Or had he dreamed that?* Madrid fought through his sleepiness. No. Madrid remembered now—that wasn't part of a dream. Dicky's sister, with her blonde cheerleader face had asked Madrid to help. But in the end, he hadn't helped at all. Her brother was dead.

From somewhere in the cottage, Madrid heard the dog stir. It brought him back to the present. He realized Julie was no longer next to him. He felt for her, but the sheets were cool, the bed empty. She too seemed like a dream.

Madrid fumbled at the edge of the bed until he found a table, and then a lamp. He switched it on—checked his watch. He'd been asleep about six hours.

He wondered where Julie had gone In the tangle of sheets, she'd had left a fading imprint. And a note.

> *Alex,*
>
> *Had to go back to work. Get some rest. There's plenty of food at the main house. You and Toto make yourselves at home.*
>
> *See you later,*
> *Julie*

Madrid wandered about the cottage for a few minutes, then gathered his clothes, his wallet, and his car keys. "Load up," he told the dog,

Toto was already at the door.

Outside the Paradise Court, lightning danced across the night sky. Tree tops were bent first in one direction, then violently whipped in another. Gusts of wind drove the heavy rain sideways. It made a rat-a-tat sound against the plate-glass windows of the motel office. A weather alert crawled along the bottom of the small TV screen. *The remnants of two hurricanes are expected to converge over western North Carolina and eastern Tennessee sometime between 10pm and 2am tonight. Residents of these areas should expect heavy rains, high winds, and severe flooding. Anyone living in low-lying areas should evacuate. Downed trees and power outages are likely.*

Seeking solace from the ice and vodka, Joy Springtime tipped the blue tumbler. It was her second refill and she was beginning to feel pleasantly numb. Draped in a black and orange muumuu, perched precariously on a white camel saddle, she took inventory of her life. Literally. She surveyed the items strewn about the room—the sum of what she'd gathered along her journey. They were treasures, trinkets, memories, and junk. Most of it fell into the last two categories. But it was hers. And now she had to figure out what to do with it—what to take—what to leave behind.

The creditors would arrive soon. They would gather at her door, wear disappointed expressions and speak to her in low, calculating voices. *Let the motherfuckers come,* she thought. Thanks to Alex Madrid, the motel was unusable. The bloodless vultures might carry away the crumbs, but they would not pick at her bones. Joy Springtime would be long gone.

Joy didn't notice the headlights sweep across the parking lot, didn't hear the front door open. Lightning flashed, hit something nearby. There was an immediate explosion—like a slightly-off-target artillery round. It rattled the windows—shook the wooden floor beneath her. The television cut off—the weather girl disappeared into a rapidly-decreasing white vortex. The lights went black, then, a moment later, struggled back to life. Fear, and an unexplained sense of intrusion made her scan the room. The dark figures stood motionless in the doorway, dripped rain on her floor.

From the doorway, Madrid watched her. Joy Springtime teetered like a giant black and orange Weeble—without guarantee of not falling down.

"Goddamn it, Madrid!" she said angrily, nearly toppling off the camel saddle.

"Sorry," he replied contritely, "but it's pouring, and that last round of lightning was close."

Joy struggled to her feet, felt the vodka rush to her head. "What do you want?" she asked irritably. "I might have one or two rooms fit to stay in, but I doubt it."

Without moving, Madrid continued to survey her living quarters. The room had a vandalized feel—everything tossed haphazardly about. The sleeper sofa was pulled out. Yellowed sheets were plastered to the large sag in the middle of the mattress. The knotty pine walls were covered with unframed movie posters that ranged from *Blazing Saddles* to *Chinatown* to *Harry and Tonto*. The room reeked of cigarettes, booze, and air freshener. "I got a place to stay," he replied.

Joy looked at him suspiciously. "Remember, we got a deal." She waved a finger in his general direction. "You better not be backin' out on me."

"I didn't forget."

She nodded her frizzy blonde head emphatically. "Good. 'Cause I didn't want to have to sue your ass." The letter "s" was beginning to be a challenge. She abruptly changed subjects. "Did you see the six o'clock news?"

"No," Madrid answered.

Joy made a pecking motion towards the floor with her index finger. "They was here," she said. "Looking for you, too."

"Who was here?"

"Television people." Joy took a drink from the blue tumbler, then swirled the ice cubes in the bottom of the glass. "They asked me where you were." She moved to a cabinet in the corner of the room, refilled the glass, added two more ice cubes. "I didn't know what to tell 'em. That little faggot kept asking me. Over and over. Finally, I just told him to piss off."

"Okay," Madrid replied.

"Remember. We got a deal," she repeated.

"I'm here to settle up," Madrid said.

"I'm ruined," she told Madrid, feeling suddenly fortified. "Insurance company said it was an "act of war" or some bullshit thing like that. I'm fucking out of business. This place has been in my family..... " She stopped and tried to count in her head. "Twenty four—or maybe twenty-nine years."

"You're not out of business," Madrid told her. "Get three estimates on what it will take to get this place back to where it was before I showed up. If they're reasonable, you pick one and I'll pay. I'll also pay you something for the time the rooms are out of commission—but don't go greedy on me."

She squinted her eyes, stared at him with a mixture of amazement and suspicion. "You're screwin' with me."

"No, I'm not, " Madrid replied—quiet, but emphatic.

"You got that kind of money?"

"Yeah."

"You don't look it," she challenged.

"I'm what they call 'elegantly understated'."

Joy thought moment. "What if I don't want to fix this place up? Can I just keep the money?"

"And lose all that family tradition?" Madrid asked sardonically.

The sarcasm was lost on her. "What about it?"

"It doesn't make any difference to me," Madrid told her. "This is my mess. I'll pay for it—within reason. But don't come back to me with ridiculous numbers thinking I won't know the difference."

"I wouldn't do that," Joy said, though the thought had already crossed her mind.

Madrid nodded. "You think you can get this together by the end of the week? I don't know how much longer I'm going to be around."

"Don't you worry," she assured him.

"Good."

"Good, hell," she replied, misinterpreting the context. "This is fuckin' great." A smile stretched across her broad face. She spoke as if they were old friends. "You know, the first time I laid eyes on you....and that crazy-ass dog of yours...I knew you two was trouble. Just had that look about you."

"And now?" Madrid asked.

She laughed too loudly. "The look ain't changed none," she said. "But this might work out good."

"Three estimates," Madrid repeated, turned to leave.

Joy followed him out to the outer office. "So where you stayin'?" she asked when Madrid and Toto were on the far side of the counter, halfway to the door.

Madrid thought for a moment, finally said, "Around."

"Julie Kingston," Joy said.

Madrid offered no reply.

"Good lookin' woman," Joy continued, as if he had. "I used to be good lookin', too."

Madrid nodded.

"You don't believe me."

"I believe you."

"Wait," she commanded. "Don't fuckin' move. I'll prove it."

"You don't... " Madrid started, but she was gone. He waited, watched the rain splatter against the plate-glass, wished he were somewhere else. Joy was back in less than a minute. She dropped a high school year book heavily on the scarred countertop. It was bound in black. The red lettering spelled out *Black Creek Warriors—Class of 1960.* Joy Springtime cracked open the volume. The book fell open to the page she wanted and the smell of old paper joined the other odors in the room. In the crease was a wad of yellowed newspaper articles that she set to one side.

Joy Springtime stabbed the page with a pudgy finger whose nail had been painted fire-engine red. "There," she said with a mixture of triumph and sadness.

The picture was black and white and took up most of the page. It was of two girls in profile, facing each other, pompoms extended, faces turned toward the camera—smiles frozen in time. They were dressed in cheerleader sweaters and matching skirts—short enough to reveal nicely-shaped legs. The pair looked enough alike to be sisters. The caption below made vague reference to the fact. It read, "Myrtle and Mary Alice—The trouble twins".

"You're Myrtle?" Madrid asked, as he studied the old photo.

"That's was me," Joy answered in a quiet, nostalgic voice, "Sixteen years and a hundred and fifty pounds ago."

"You changed your name," Madrid said.

"Wouldn't you? What kind of fuckin' people name their kid 'Myrtle'?" She stopped, shook her head violently. "Guess they did their best," she said, her words becoming slow and thick. "My grandmother was named Myrtle."

"So how did you end up with 'Joy Springtime'?" Madrid asked.

"Almost as bad as 'Myrtle', huh?" she answered.

"No," Madrid said truthfully. "I kind of like it."

She took a greedy pull from the blue tumbler until the ice cubes sounded a lonely rattle in the bottom of the glass. "I got the hell out of this crappy town," she declared. "Took the tuition money my folks gave me and went out west. God they were pissed!" she added with a lop-sided grin. "Joined a commune."

Another bolt of lightning flashed across the tiny drab lobby followed by another explosion. Joy Springtime didn't seem to notice. She was on a roll. Madrid let her talk. It beat going back out in the storm—if only slightly.

"...I guess I was a hippy—whatever that is, really." She steadied herself on the counter with one hand, made a waving gesture Madrid didn't understand with the other. "I got me a hippy name and got into hippy stuff." She raised her eyebrows to make a point. "Hippy stuff is fuckin' good—but it don't pay shit."

Madrid smiled and looked at the yearbook some more.

"We did drugs and stayed naked a lot. Lots of sex," she said with drunken wistfulness. "That part was great. Every night, when we weren't too stoned. Got into girls, too. Sometimes they're better than boys—'cause they know exactly what you want...you know?" She raised her eyebrows again.

Madrid nodded uncomfortably.

"That's why I was sayin' Julie Kingston is good lookin'," Joy said.

Madrid raised his hand. "Let's save that for another time." If he ever did see Julie naked, he didn't want that image playing in his head—but now it probably would.

"The girl standing next to you," he said, turning the yearbook in Joy's direction. "Is she the same Mary Alice that married Pete Wilson?"

Joy eyed Madrid suspiciously. "Yeah," she said after a moment.

"A friend of yours?" Madrid asked.

"Why you askin' me?"

"Just curious."

"Bes' friend I ever had," she answered, as if Madrid had challenged her—then added a melancholy footnote. "Maybe the only real friend I ever had."

"Sorry to hear that," Madrid said.

"You had buddies in high school, didn't you?" she asked.

"Yeah."

"I bet you're still close with them."

"Not really," Madrid replied.

"That's 'cause you're an asshole," she declared. "Nobody would want to be fuckin' friends with you. 'Cause you're an asshole."

Madrid offered a canine smile and no denial.

"Me and Mary Alice were tight—like sisters," Joy continued. Emotion flowed into her tone.

Madrid kept looking at the picture of the two of them. "Must have been tough when she got killed," he said.

With fumbling fingers, Joy unfolded the yellowed newspaper clippings, slid them across the counter towards Madrid. She wiped her eyes, then her nose with the sleeve of the muumuu.

Madrid sifted through the clippings—awards for this, a picture for that. In most of them, the two were mentioned together—as if one didn't exist without the other. To reinforce the thought, Joy said, "That's why I left Black Creek. I couldn't stay here without Mary Alice."

"Tell me about her," Madrid prompted.

Suspicion crept back into her tone. "Why d'you want to know?"

"Nobody was ever arrested for her murder." Madrid continued, his tone like a sharpened prod. "You ever wonder who killed her, Joy? Ever wonder who killed your best friend?"

She nodded her head in a bobbing motion that made her entire body shake. "Every goddamn day I wonder." More nodding and shaking. "You think I know sompthin' 'bout Mary's murder and I ain't telling nobody all this time?" she sputtered defensively.

"I didn't say that."

"That's not what you said," she countered, her tone venomous, "but it's what you fuckin' meant." She turned precariously, left Madrid and Toto standing at the counter.

Chapter 45

September 28th—9:48 p.m.

Victoria Jamerson had never grasped her arrest until a handsome man in an expensive suit told her she could go home as soon as her doctors agreed to release her. Trevor had informed her that bail had been posted, but refused to mention any names. He had also instructed her not to talk about her case—had warned her not to leave the county.

Victoria had assured him she wouldn't be leaving—that she was waiting for her daughter to return. Trevor hadn't seemed interested.

Now, back at home, in her chair, by the window—she waited in the dark. The storm had knocked out the power—an unlit lantern sat on the table. She wasn't sure how much fuel was in the canister—didn't want to waste any. Poncho, the cat, was curled in her lap—nervous, but happy to be out of the storm. Victoria ran her fingers through his thick fur and continued to stare out the window. The ground was saturated, and when lightning flashed, it reflected white off the water—made her yard look like the surface of a lake. The wind made the house creak and moan. Victoria didn't believe in ghosts, but felt herself shiver just the same. Lightning flashed—the yard lit up—the driveway was empty.

Any trace of pretense was gone. Joy Springtime gripped the neck of the Smirnoff bottle as if she were trying to choke it to death. The blue tumbler had been replenished with ice cubes. She divided what was left of her focus between Alex Madrid and the rim of the glass as she poured.

"You're talkin' 'bout my bes' friend, Mister," she said, picking up the conversation as if she had never left the room. From beneath the counter she located a fresh pack of Newports. With ritualistic order, she tapped one out, guided it between her lips, and used a yellow Bic lighter.

Madrid waited until she'd taken the first couple of drags before he spoke. He was still looking at the picture of the two cheerleaders. "Tell me about your best friend—after she married Pete."

"Mary Alice was a year out of high school," she answered, pointing the cigarette at Madrid. "Tired of this fuckin' dump of a town. She liked the boys and the boys liked her," she said in a rush of air and smoke."

"So why did she marry Pete?"

"Lots o' reasons," she answered, tossed her head loosely. "Pete was good-looking back then. Ain't bad-lookin' now, but *good*-lookin' then. And Pete was crazy about her." Joy leaned over the counter, said in a low voice, "Pete waddn't the first to ask her."

"Josh Galloway?"

Joy rocked back from the counter, as if she'd been slapped. "How'du know that?"

"I didn't," Madrid said, "until now."

Joy took another healthy drink from the tumbler. "Tricky son of bitch," she mumbled into the bottom of the glass.

Madrid wondered how she was still standing.

Joy Springtime raised her head. "Three musketeers. That's what she called 'um. Poor 'ole Pete never stood a chance with that girl. She wanted too much. Wanted it quick. Pete was just a comfortable place to park."

Madrid was still looking at the photo. Something had been trying to click from the moment he'd first seen it, but he couldn't get it to come. "Have you got another picture of Mary Alice—a better one?"

"Got lots of 'em."

She steadied herself on the counter, precariously navigated back to her living quarters. Madrid heard things being moved around. Then cursing. More things being moved. Joy came back with three photos—color—eight by tens. She held them delicately between the tips of her thumb and index finger. Madrid looked at the first photo.

"That was only a couple of weeks 'fore Mary Alice died." Joy took in a massive quantity of air—released it in a sigh. "Before she was killed."

They were on the shore of a lake, four of them. Myrtle, before she became Joy Springtime, Mary Alice, Pete Wilson, and Josh Galloway. The men were tall and thin back then. They wore the self-assured mask of youth, held beer cans, and had cigars clamped in the corner of their mouths.

"You and Galloway dated?" Madrid asked.

Joy took another drink. "I guess," she answered cryptically in slurred whisper. "Think he hung around me 'cause I was close with Mary Alice. Fuckin' Three Musketeers."

"You think Galloway had anything to do with Mary Alice's death?" Madrid asked.

She shook her head. "Know for a fact he didn't."

"For a fact?" Madrid said.

"The night Mary Alice was killed, Josh was parked outside my momma's house—way up to the other end of the county. He was doin' me on the hood of the patrol car," she answered, looking directly at Madrid. "Josh is a som' bitch, but he didn't kill Mary Alice." A moment later, she added, "I was pretty back then."

The second shot was pretty much the same as the newspaper picture. Cheerleaders—skirts with rolled up waistbands and sweaters a size too small. The last one had been taken when they were younger. Madrid gave it only a cursory glance, placed it on the stack with the other two.

Then he took another look.

The two girls were in some sort of park—ten, maybe twelve years old. They were dressed in colorful print dresses. Small white handbags with long straps hung from their shoulders. The pair stared back at him with toothy, girlish smiles.

He stared some more—and finally it clicked. "Damn," he heard himself say. He told the dog to stay put, opened the office door, darted back through the driving rain to the Blazer. He found what he was looking for in the back seat, covered it with his jacket, and ran back into the motel office.

Joy was on a stool behind the counter, steadying herself with both hands. "Where'd you go," she asked, as if just realizing he'd left.

Madrid laid the photo from the Blazer next to the one of Myrtle and Mary Alice with their colorful dresses.

Joy shifted her bulk over the counter, squinted her eyes, tried to focus. In a suspicious, confused tone she declared, "That woman ain't Mary Alice's mother."

Madrid tore his eyes from the photos, looked directly at Joy Springtime, and said evenly. "I know. That's not Mary Alice."

Joy Springtime had watched them leave. Madrid and the dog had disappeared into the storm. She was alone again with her blue tumbler. She slid it away—not too far, tried to think. Madrid had taken her photographs with him. The bastard hadn't even asked. Just took them with a vague promise of return. The lights in the office flickered, but held. Joy fumbled under the counter, came up the Black Creek phone book and a pair of reading glasses. She found a number and dialed.

"Gimme Josh Galloway," she said.

A female voice from the other end asked who was calling.

"Tell'em it's Myrtle," she barked. "I need to tell him sompthin' 'bout Mary Alice Wilson."

Joy didn't have to wait long. "Alex Madrid was here," she told Galloway without preamble. "He's either figured it out—or he's about to."

"Figured what out?"

"I don't know for exact. But I'm pretty sure it's got something to do with you and Pete and Mary Alice."

"All that liquor's made you crazy, Myrtle," Galloway growled in a low tone that Myrtle could barely hear over the static on the line. "Half this county's gonna be under water by day break. I ain't got time to waste with *you*."

"You do what you want, Josh," Joy said quietly.

Galloway picked up the veiled threat in her tone. "Tomorrow," he said, diplomatically. "This storm'll be outta' here. You and me will sit down with a pot of coffee and talk this out. Let me call you. It'll kind of be like old times, Myrtle."

"Old times," Joy parroted in a heavy, tired voice.

"I'll call," Galloway repeated in a voice meant to convey assurance. "But we need to keep this between you and me."

"Sure. It'd be better that way, I guess."

"I think it would," Galloway said. "Try to get some sleep Myrtle. I'll see you tomorrow—first thing."

"Like old times," Joy repeated with an inebriated lilt.

"Yeah," Galloway repeated. "Like old times."

"Don't kill him, Josh," she said in a slushy tone. "Fucker owes me money."

Joy wasn't sure he'd heard the last part. There was a click on the other end of the line. Josh Galloway had either hung up, or they'd been cut off by the storm. It didn't matter—she'd said all she had to say. Lightning flashed over the empty parking lot.

"Like old times," she said cynically.

The blue tumbler had nothing to add.

She picked up the phone—dialed a number from memory. After six rings, Pete Wilson picked up on the other end.

In a sad, nostalgic voice, Joy Springtime said, "It's time you and me had a talk, Pete."

Chapter 46

September 29th—12:03 a.m.

A lamp with a stained-glass shade burned on the coffee table next to the sofa. Julie Kingston stepped onto the covered porch of the cottage—laid her umbrella on the stone floor. He'd left the door unlocked. And when she stepped inside, the quiet confirmed what she already sensed—Madrid and the dog were gone. The bed was made, the towels hung neatly.

Julie's note was precisely where she'd left it. At the bottom Madrid had added,

> *Thanks for the beer and the bed. But mostly, thanks for the company.*
> *Alex*

"Almost like they were never here at all," she said quietly to herself.

The interior of the Blazer smelled of wet dog. Madrid switched the wipers onto high—tried to make sense of what he'd just seen. At the edge of Black Creek, Madrid took the low road that paralleled the river and the railroad tracks. On the bridge that separated the town from the college, emergency vehicles were positioned on either side. Their pulsing red lights struggled against the rain—cast eerie shadows across the buildings on River Street.

* * * *

At dinner, the old black man had brought Junior Jenkins a tray with a generous mound of cooked apples. They had tasted a little funny, but what the hell—everything in here tasted a little funny. Junior like cooked apples—with cinnamon. These apples had been sprinkled with lots of cinnamon—which made them taste a little less funny. Junior had eaten them all, and would have eaten more—but no one had offered.

Now, open mouthed and drooling, he was asleep on his bunk—a hard sleep—deep—dreamless. Junior Jenkins didn't hear the rain—was unaware the lighting that crashed outside the archaic jail . Junior didn't hear the door open at the top of the stairs, certainly didn't hear the key slide quietly into the door of his cell. When the hinges on the iron door had protested mournfully, Junior's senses were blissfully enveloped in a thick, black fog.

Junior's visitor stood over him—poked him in the ribs with the key. Junior was too deep in the black fog to respond. The visitor nodded his head approvingly. Then, taking his time, the visitor meticulously fashioned Junior's top sheet into a noose.

Bursts of static-filled communication crackled over the hand-held two-way radio, filled the cab of the cruiser. Voice calm, the female dispatcher spoke in an efficient, but feverish pace. The Rescue Squad was sent to pull a man from a pickup truck who had tried to forge a swollen stream. Lightning had exploded a cabin in the northern end of the county. It was on fire. The Northern County Volunteer Fire Department were notified and sent on their way. Another haggard voice, gravelly and male, responded that it would take a while to get there. At the western tip of the county, back in a hollow, a tree had fallen into a house. The woman inside had gone into labor. An ambulance was on the way, but someone would have to get her to a paved road. And so it went—one crisis flowed into the next.

The dispatcher requested Josh Galloway's location. "Sergeant, what's your twenty?" she asked in a flat authoritative tone—waited a moment—repeated her request. Galloway shifted his bulk behind the wheel, reached for the radio. He adjusted the volume until the woman's voice became a whisper. The storm grew louder outside the car.

Josh Galloway was more concerned with another storm—one that had been brewing for more than a decade—one that seemed determine to destroy him. Fragments of his conversation with Myrtle rattled in his head. *Had she just figured it out, or had she known all along? What had she told Madrid? What had Madrid told her? Why was that nosy bastard asking questions about Mary Alice in the first place? Pete Wilson had put him up to it. There was no other explanation.*

Josh used the tip of his left boot, pressed the metal button on floorboard, switched the headlights onto high. He used his right foot, pressed the accelerator. The big cruiser lurched through the rain. Up ahead, on one of the few straight stretches of pavement, red tail lights came into view through the downpour. Galloway closed quickly. For a brief instant, he wondered who would be out on such a hellish night—but the thought was fragmented—fleeting. His focus was divided between Mary Alice—The Three Musketeers—and the mistake that continued to haunt him. He flipped the switch for the blue light—powered around the slower vehicle. Standing water sprayed from both sides of the cruiser. The back end of the car wiggled, tried to break loose. Galloway let off the gas, worked to keep it on the pavement. By the time he regained control, the other vehicle was behind him.

Josh Galloway didn't notice the driver he'd just passed, or the big dog in the back seat.

Lightning flashed. The unfinished gate house was revealed like an incomplete ghost, it's broken window like a jagged, knowing smile. Overhead, thunder boomed. The dog shifted his weight uneasily in the back seat. Madrid killed the lights—waited for his eyes to adjust.

Like the thunder, the conversation with Joy Springtime reverberated in Madrid's head. He was still trying to piece it together, but he was beginning to believe, it had gone something like this. Mary Alice had been the small-town high-school queen. Not beautiful, but small-town pretty. Not brilliant, but smart enough to play the people she needed to play. Madrid figured Mary Alice had probably been long on ambition—short on planning. Now she was nearly fifteen years gone. It happens that way sometimes—when you're young and naïve—playing both ends against the middle. You end up pissing somebody off. Somebody bigger and stronger than you. Then comes that hard reality—*Pretty only gets you so far.*

Then there was Pete Wilson. Madrid hadn't wanted it to be so—but it always came back to Pete. The guy who'd been unconcerned about September Jamerson's disappearance—the guy who'd shown up right after Madrid had found Dicky Padrick with Miranda Toliver. Padrick's nearly-hysterical jail-cell performance floated back to Madrid. *What if it had happened pretty much like the kid had said—a big man dressed in black had smashed her to the ground?* Pete

Wilson was a big man with a lot to lose if Miranda Toliver connected him to September.

Madrid wondered how many days September Jamerson had moved about the Black Creek College campus before Pete Wilson had spotted her—realized the girl's uncanny resemblance to his dead wife. *What had gone through his mind? What fairy-tale scenario had begun to take shape in his head?*

Madrid knew it was all just theory—another fairy-tale scenario of sorts. His hypothesis was simple—and thin—based on nothing but a couple of old photos, circumstance, and a one-sided conversation with a depressed, nostalgic drunk. He had nearly talked himself out of the idea—until Galloway had passed him a few miles back. The roaring engine and the flashing blue light made his hypothesis suddenly plausible.

Madrid opened the door of the Blazer, was immediately greeted with cold, heavy rain and a roar that sounded like a train in the tree tops. He locked the hubs—shifted into four-wheel drive. The road was more mud than gravel. Tree branches, heavy with rain, crowded in from either side. Madrid's idea had been to ease up to the entrance of the lodge without any lights. After a few yards of driving blind, he was forced to change the plan. The low beams glistened off the thin torrents of water streaming down the ruts in the road. About three-quarters of a mile up, was a stand of large hemlock and white pine. There was a flat area that Madrid had remembered from his first visit. He maneuvered the Blazer through the trees until he was far enough off of the road not to be seen—killed the lights. From the floor board he took a flashlight and a black vinyl hooded poncho. Madrid slipped the barrel of the 9mm he'd taken off Weems Grabowski into his belt. Toto bounded over the front seat and onto the thick wet mat that covered the ground below the evergreens. Madrid called the dog over to him, removed the collar with the jingly tags, tossed them into the back seat. Toto's gray and black brindle coat blended into the wooded back drop—made him nearly invisible.

Madrid reasoned that if Pete Wilson had taken September Jamerson, he would keep her nearby. Maybe in the lodge, but there were probably better options. Maybe there were other buildings, up the slope, tucked into the woods—far enough away to muffle any call for help. Madrid kept the flashlight in his pocket, felt his way along through the darkened woods. A quarter of a mile later, Madrid's course led him just beyond the base of the unfinished ski slope. Silhouetted against the dark sky, Madrid could barely make out the shape of the first two lift towers. Wind slapped against the chairs—propelled them in arrhythmic pendulous motions. The rusting metal sang out in a screechy, mournful chorus.

In the shadow of the tree line, Madrid and the dog picked their way up the slope in the darkness and the rain. It was a slow, steady climb. Madrid could feel it in his calves and thighs. When they were near the top, he stopped. Under the poncho, he felt sweat soaking through his shirt. At the bottom of the hill, he could see lights at the lodge. The long front porch was lit—like Pete Wilson might be expecting company. Madrid remembered the flashing blue light—wondered where Josh Galloway had ended up. *Had to be somewhere on the property,* he thought. Maybe inside with Pete. Maybe there was another connection Madrid hadn't figured—a side deal between two of the Musketeers. It seemed unlikely, but hell, it *all* seemed unlikely.

Overhead, one of the chairs from the lift squeaked urgently. Madrid and Toto passed under it on their way to the other side of the slope.

Along with the destruction, the storms brought opportunity. A cleansing of sorts—the restructuring of natural order. Swirled into the darkness and the windswept panic, heroes emerged and villains were revealed. Josh Galloway didn't really see himself as either—just a guy with an opportunity to clean up his past—reset the course for his future

He pressed the gas pedal—jammed the gearshift into reverse. The big cruiser lurched. The deep voice of the engine was joined by the high-pitched whine of the spinning tires. It was a frustrating chorus Galloway hoped was being swept away by the wind that howled outside the car. He let off, shifted into drive, pressed the gas again. The car nudged forward a couple of inches, then floundered like a whale on a remote, muddy beach. Riding a wave of anger and frustration, Galloway slammed his hand against the steering wheel.

He needed a new plan—something simple, brilliant, and plausible. *Deniability.* Tough to claim when your cruiser is stuck in the middle of a soon-to-be victim's driveway. He pushed the door open—wedged himself out of the car. An instant later, muddy water rushed in over the tops of his boots, drenched the cuffs of his trousers. Josh Galloway pushed the button of the high-powered flashlight, followed the beam with his eyes. The car was high-centered between two deep ruts. He held onto the car, slipped and slid along as he made his way back to the trunk. He popped the lid, took out a 12-guage automatic shotgun and a Smith and Wesson .38 special. The serial number on the pistol had been destroyed—first with a file and then with acid. Out of habit, Galloway checked the load, then snapped the cylinder back into place. He shoved the weapon under his belt. The handle pressed uncomfortably into his bloated stomach. The deputy sheriff worked his way back to the front of the vehicle. A few yards up the driveway, he found firmer ground. He turned off the flashlight and started towards Pete Wilson's home.

At the edge of the parking lot, a few feet into the woods, Pete Wilson stood motionless. From beneath the wide-brimmed hat, his focus was on the well-lit lodge porch. He replayed the call from Myrtle. She'd been drunk, but Pete could relate—he'd spent a lot of the last dozen years in the same condition. And that had made it easer to translate her babble. Myrtle missed Mary Alice—had loved her like a sister—had loved Pete, even though she knew it was wrong. She had confessed to loving Josh Galloway as well—but that was a different kind of love—whatever the hell that meant. And she was sorry for telling Alex Madrid.

But what had she really told him? Pete wondered. *What did she really know?* But then there was the part about the pictures—the newspaper clipping of Mary Alice and the picture of September and her mother. If Alex Madrid hadn't already put it together, it wouldn't be long.

Now Madrid would be coming, or maybe Josh Galloway—or maybe both. But they wouldn't be coming together—that was nearly certain. Pete Wilson figured one at a time would probably be manageable. But Alex Madrid was a hard guy to kill. He'd squandered his opportunity at The Paradise Court. Should have used the double barrel on Madrid—instead of the other guy.

Madrid worked his way to the far side of the slope. Like he'd figured, there were buildings tucked into the tree line—most half finished, with unused lumber and pallets of shingles left stacked in the over-grown yards. But the buildings were dark—void of life—like log-cabin crypts. It had been over a half hour since he'd left the Blazer at the bottom of the slope. The rain had stopped briefly, then started again. It came in angry, wind-driven spurts that stung his face. The dog seemed oblivious to the weather, just happy to be outside, unconcerned that Madrid's theory might be proven absurd.

Madrid checked his watch, used his flashlight just long enough to get his bearings. The faint remnant of road bed led him further down the slope—closer to the lodge. The next building he came to was a cabin tucked into the mountain, maybe twenty yards off his path. It was shielded by a stand of rhododendrons, and on a warmer night he would have probably missed it completely. Toto reacted first. A few paces ahead, through the gloom, Madrid saw the mutt stop dead on the trail, lift his massive head. A moment later, Madrid smelled it, too. Wood smoke.

Madrid sniffed the air for direction, but the wind continued to swirl. There were strong whiffs followed by nothing. After a moment, he saw it—a thin strip of light from a heavily-curtained window. The cabin was a small A-frame with a covered stoop. Madrid stood by the window and listened. There was music—Elton John—*"Goodbye Yellow Brick Road."* Madrid glanced down at Toto—offered a hint of ironic smile. The pair worked their way to the back of the cabin. The windows in the back were shuttered, but on one, a vane was missing and band of light spilled onto the wet ground. The opening was too high up to see anything. Madrid clicked on the flashlight and scoured the area around him. Under a pile of brush, the beam revealed a hefty piece of wood. It was round, maybe two feet and a half feet long. Madrid killed the light, rolled it under the window and stood it on end. He placed his feet on the mostly-flat surface, wiggled and gyrated for a moment until he found his balance. The missing slat was eye level. He could see part of the stone fireplace. At the edge of the raised hearth an old braided rug lay on the pine floor. There was a pair of cane-backed rocking chairs and a metal bucket with pieces of split firewood peeking over the rim.

Madrid stood on the end of the log—waited. Toto wandered off, seamless with the night. Five minutes passed. Madrid thought about Miranda Toliver, about Dicky Padrick, about Victoria Jamerson, and about her daughter—who might, or might not be, inside the cabin. Eventually, someone would have to come and stoke the fire, but

Madrid knew he didn't have until *eventually* to wait for that to happen. He stepped down from his perch, walked back to the front of the house. Madrid wasn't sure from which direction he'd come, but the dog was back at his side.

He rested his right hand on the butt of the 9mm, knocked lightly on the heavy door with his left. From inside there was the sound of foot falls—soft and light. The music died—Elton was cut off in the middle of *Funeral for a Friend.* Beyond the door—silence. Behind Madrid, the rain droned steadily, cascaded off the steep roof of the porch. He knocked again, this time a little harder.

More silence. Finally, a female voice, barely strong enough to penetrate the heavy wooden door, asked, "Who is it?"

Madrid could tell from her tone—she really didn't want to know.

From his position among the trees, Pete Wilson watched Josh Galloway trudge awkwardly up the driveway—his Tony Llamas ill-matched for the muddy terrain. Galloway was past the steepest section of the climb, but Pete could still hear him breathing hard. A shotgun was cradled in his right arm. The big deputy passed within fifteen feet of where Pete stood—never looked back—his focus locked on the brightly-lit lodge.

It was funny how little events could change big decisions. A rainy night, a high spot in a neglected driveway, a stranded cruiser. Josh Galloway had come to The High Vista Ski Resort to kill Pete Wilson. And it still might come to that—but this killing would be harder to explain than his last. This time there were no allies—no time for carefully-crafted alibis. As he began to cross the parking lot, the idea of diplomacy bored its way further into his thoughts. If what Myrtle/Joy Springtime had said was true, Pete might have the Jamerson girl. That was a big *if.* But *if* it were true—that would change everything. Maybe they could make a deal—one that would last until after the election. Pete could keep the girl, continue with his fantasy. Josh allowed Mary Alice into his head for the first time in many years. She was on top of him—naked—wild. He could see her blue eyes, that far-off, half-possessed look she got. Josh Galloway understood why Pete Wilson missed his wife. Josh Galloway missed her, too. He forced this thoughts back to the present. He needed to convince Pete Wilson that Alex Madrid was the common enemy.

Somebody was going to have to kill him. It would be easier with two of them. Josh was beginning to see the situation through the eyes of a politician. Yeah, he thought—that might work. Everybody gets something. After all, wasn't that the definition of negotiation?

Josh Galloway felt a sudden surge of optimism.

Pete Wilson waited until Josh Galloway was silhouetted in the light of the lodge. Silently he stepped out of the woods—began to close the distance.

* * * *

"Who is it?" September Jamerson asked again.

"My name is Alex Madrid."

Silence, then, "Go away." The voice was a mix of fear and steadfastness.

"I'm working for your mother, September." Madrid told her—a shade of the truth. "She hired me to find you—she's been very worried."

"You're lying," the girlish voice challenged from the other side of the door. "My mother doesn't have money to pay you."

"I didn't say she was paying me," Madrid countered.

The door knob was black wrought iron, orb-shaped, pitted from the weather, with a keyed deadbolt above. Madrid turned the knob. The door moved a fraction—the metal tongue allowed it no further.

The girlish voice spoke again, contrite and a little scared. "Tell her I'm just fine." She had moved closer to the other side of the door. "Just go away and leave me alone."

A contingency for which Madrid hadn't planned. Madrid looked down at the dog. Toto was sitting a few feet away. The dog looked at Madrid, looked at the door, looked back to Madrid—as if the answer were that simple. Maybe it was.

"I'll go away," Madrid said, "but only after we talk. I need to see you. I need to be able to tell Victoria that I've actually laid eyes on you and that you're all right. Then I'll tell her you left on your own and that you're not hurt."

"Tell Momma I'm not hurt," the voice said, emotion infusing her tone.

"I can't do that until I see it for myself, September."

The lock was substantial. Madrid had picked a few in his time. It wasn't slick and easy, like on TV. Even if he had the tools, it would take him several minutes. Maybe longer. He could shoot the lock, or try to bust down the door, or he could try plan "C". Madrid worked the flashlight beam over the porch. There was no furniture, no flower pots, no door mat. He ran his fingers over the top ledge of the door trim. The exposed ceiling joists offered possibilities, but except at their lowest point, they were too high for Pete Wilson to reach without standing on something. If Pete bothered to hide a key, Madrid figured it was somewhere with easy accessibility.

As if reading his thoughts, September Jamerson's voice floated through the thick slab of wood. "I think there's a key at the end of the railing—near where it meets the house."

Madrid moved to his left.

"Other side," the voice from inside the cabin guided.

Madrid ran his fingers along the outside of the porch railing, stopped when he felt the protruding nail. He followed the nail until he touched the cool metal key. He slid the Browning 9mm out of his belt with his right hand, worked the key with his left. Pete Wilson was still unaccounted for. Madrid didn't ruled out the possibility he was standing next to the girl, whispering instructions to her—waiting for him to step inside.

The bolt retracted—like a turtle head into a shell. A thin, vertical strip of light appeared on the darkened porch. It grew wider as Madrid eased the door open. The smell from the fireplace rushed through the crack to greet him. Madrid stayed planted on the porch, let the door swing open past ninety degrees. September was standing in the middle of the room. Behind her, a queen-sized white metal bed with brass accents dominated the wall. It was unmade, strewn with stuffed animals—bunnies, kitties, and a big English bulldog.

September Jamerson was tallish—slender—bizarrely nostalgic. Madrid caught himself in the middle of a double take. He thought back to the two pictures, the one of September with her mother, the other of Mary Alice and Myrtle posing in the high school yearbook. This girl looked strikingly like the latter.

Her hair fell just above her shoulders. It was thick and curly and someone had dyed it blonde. Her jeans stretched snugly across her girlish hips. On her feet were heavy woolen socks. Above her jeans,

September wore a vintage blue and white cheerleader sweater. The letters "B C" were prominently displayed.

Go team, Madrid thought to himself.

The sleeves were pushed up past her elbows. Twin bands of gauze bandages wrapped her wrists—strips of white athletic tape held the bandages in place.

In September's right hand, she held a knife best described as a small sword. The handle was made from something that looked like pearl. September glanced down at the weapon—like she wasn't sure how it had gotten there.

Madrid remained in the shadows of the porch—like a secret not anxious to be revealed. He was encouraged by the knife. If September was ready to fight, it meant Pete Wilson wasn't there to fight for her. He waited, watched her—listened. Madrid was in no hurry. There was no back door. September Jamerson wasn't going anywhere.

* * * *

September Jamerson waited for the man on the porch. When Madrid stepped out of the shadows—into the soft light of the cabin—he was not what she had expected. He was shorter—meaner looking. The rain had matted his blondish hair to his skull. The wet black poncho disguised the contours of his body, but she could see the thick muscles in his neck, the heavy veins that mapped across his forearms and hands. His blue eyes were a paradox—cold and friendly at the same time. They moved around the room like a high-speed camera—seemed to record it all in just a matter of seconds. He offered her a reassuring smile. The smile reminded her of a shark.

There was a gun in his right hand. It was scary, but nothing compared to what stood next to him. It was the biggest dog she'd ever seen—or maybe a wolf. September had never seen a wolf, but they couldn't be any scarier than this. The animal stared back at her with wild yellow eyes. It's black gums curled back to reveal the kind of long white teeth usually reserved for children's nightmares. It growled—a deep rumble. September Jamerson was certain the floor shook beneath her.

"Quiet, Toto," she heard the man say in a no-nonsense tone.

Toto. She tried to place the name, but it was too far out of context.

"He doesn't like your knife," the man said. His voice was calm, but there was an edge to it.

September's gaze pivoted back and forth between the pistol and the dog. Finally she said, "What should I do?"

"It would be better if you laid the knife on the floor," the man told her, his tone a little softer. "You won't need it, anyway. Nobody's going to hurt you."

Without taking her eyes off the dog, she lowered the knife by her side—bent her knees until the tip of the blade was touching the floor, then released the handle. The weapon made a thunking sound on the wood. Toto walked over to her, sniffed the knife. Then he went over to the bed, got eye to eye with the Bulldog—looked back at the man by the door.

"My name is Alex Madrid," the man repeated. "I'm here to take you home."

Chapter 46

September 29th—1:37 a.m.

At nearly the same moment Madrid stepped into September Jamerson's refuge, Josh Galloway stepped onto the porch of the lodge. His cowboy boots nearly silent on the wide planking, he eased up next to one of the front windows, pressed himself against the building, strained his neck and peeked inside. Suspended from the high ceiling, the sprawling antler chandelier cast a soft light over the cavernous front room. Inside the big stone fireplace, flames glowed yellow and red, in need of another log. A big leather chair and small table had been pulled close to the dying fire. On the table was a lamp with a shade that looked like animal hide. Next to it, a tall glass, and a paperback.

Displayed on the heavy slab of wooden mantle was a softball trophy. Josh recognized it immediately. He had one just like it—on his fireplace mantle. It was from a county invitational tournament they'd won nearly twenty-five years earlier. Next to the trophy was a picture of Mary Alice. She was wearing that smile that could mean anything and tell you nothing.

For a moment Josh Galloway was back at McCarson's store, just him and Mary Alice—late at night—closing time. They were arguing. She'd told him she wouldn't leave Pete—actually, she told him she wouldn't leave Pete for *him*.

The wind gusted hard—snapped off a tree top in the woods behind him. It cracked like a rifle. Josh Galloway spun on his heels, strained his eyes against the darkness. The overgrown parking lot was empty. Reluctantly, he turned back to the lodge—wondered about Pete—wondered if he'd really snatched the girl. The drunken raving of an ex-lover? Maybe not. He moved quietly to the door, turned the knob. It was unlocked.

* * * *

Pete Wilson watched Josh Galloway from the shadows, his fingers resting lightly on the triggers of the double-barreled sawed off twelve gauge.

* * * *

Madrid stepped further into the cabin. September stepped back, maintained her distance, like dance partners with no music. Madrid picked up the knife.

"I'm not here to hurt you," Madrid repeated.

September looked unconvinced. "Then just leave," she said in a tight voice that teetered on panic. "I don't want you here."

"I need to take you home," Madrid said. *Or somewhere.*

"I don't want to go back there." Her voice was steadfast, gaining resolve. This is my home now."

Madrid looked around the room—assessed—compared the cabin to the house she'd shared with her mother and Lyle Holiday. Passages from her journal flashed back to him like scenes from a pornographic horror movie.

"Lyle Holiday is dead," he told her.

September hesitated a moment. Said finally, "He is?"

Madrid studied her reaction. Her tone was no more convincing than her expression. He'd told September Jamerson what she already knew.

"What happened to him?" she asked, almost conversationally.

"To your step-father?" Madrid asked.

"To Lyle," she replied with firm distinction.

Madrid hefted the heavy knife, looked at it, then looked at her. "Stabbed in the chest."

After a moment, September shook her head, just enough motion to move her blonde curls. She stared at the floor, replied in a voice just above a whisper, "I didn't stab him."

"Never said you did."

September looked up, an expression of relief spread across her face.

"Your mother," Madrid continued in the same casual tone, "confessed to the whole thing."

"But... ." The thought died in her throat."

"But what?" Madrid said. "She killed him. End of story. She wouldn't say she killed him, if she didn't."

Silence.

"Would she, September? Would your mother admit to murder if she weren't a murderer?"

More silence.

September's gaze went back to the floor, her painted pink lips formed words with no sound.

"Are you saying she didn't kill him?" Madrid asked without accusation.

More silence.

The clock inside Madrid's head was ticking. Pete would be coming for her. It would be better if they were gone. But it might be his last shot at questioning her—and there were things Madrid wanted to know.

* * * *

The breaking tree had nearly ruined everything. Josh had turned quickly, but hadn't seen Pete at the edge of the parking lot. Pete could have killed him right there, but he wanted Josh inside the lodge. *A deputy mistaken as an intruder.* It was plausible, if only barely. He waited until Josh was through the door, swallowed up inside the massive structure. *Patience. This will take a few minutes. Don't make a mistake by rushing.* They had trained together. Pete knew the routine. Josh would check each room on the main floor—probably start in the front and work his way to the back. But whatever the order, he would clear the main floor first. That would leave the loft. And the loft is where Pete wanted him. Josh would be trapped upstairs—only one narrow set of stairs leading down. No where to run—no where to hide.

Pete worked his way along the darkened perimeter of the parking lot until he reached the side of the lodge. He parted the wet, waist-high weeds that had grown in front of the electrical box. It was mounted on a salt-treated four by four post that had been placed a few feet from the building. The service was supposed to have been temporary—just for the construction phase. But since the lodge was never "officially finished", the service had never been switched inside.

Pete opened the gray metal cover. In the blackness, Pete's fingers played over the circuit breakers until he found the one he wanted.

Then he waited.

He closed his eyes—visualized Josh Galloway moving through the lodge—room by room. Then he flipped the main breaker. Almost before the lodge went black, Pete Wilson was around the corner, at the back of the building and through the utility room door. The utility room was a short hallway that opened into another hallway that ran between the kitchen and the main room. Pete stopped when he reached the edge of the back hallway.

He could hear Josh Galloway above him. As Pete had figured, killing the lights had temporarily frozen him in place. Pete had to make a decision; Josh was starting to move again. Something crashed to the floor one floor above.

Pete Wilson felt his way along. The hallway ended at the main room of the lodge, between the fireplace and the staircase that led up to the loft. Pete held his position in the mouth of the hallway—back just far enough to stay out of the sight line from the staircase. Above him, was a reflective glow from a flashlight. The knotty-pine ceiling was revealed—four, maybe five seconds—then back to darkness.

* * * *

"What happened to your head?" she asked, nodding to Madrid's bandage.

"Fell on a rock," he explained.

"Did it hurt?"

"Yeah."

"A lot?"

"Enough."

"You should be more careful."

"People keep telling me that."

"He loves me," September said. "Pete loves me."

"We were talking about your mother," Madrid replied impatiently. "And about Lyle Holiday."

A defiant, child-like quality entered her voice. "I don't want to talk about Lyle," she said. "I'm glad he's dead. I want to stay here with Pete. He loves me. He makes me happy. I make *him* happy."

September added a forced sultriness to the last statement that left Madrid unconvinced.

"*If* he loves you," Madrid said, "it's because you look like his dead wife, September. The blonde curls, the cheerleader sweater. You're the replacement."

"I know all about Mary Alice," September replied stubbornly. "I don't care. Pete loves *me*." She looked down at her bandaged wrists, back to Madrid. "He saved ~~by~~ my life."

Pieces of the puzzle began falling into place. "Pete might have saved your life, but he took others trying to keep his secret safe."

"I don't care about Lyle."

"I'm not talking about Lyle," Madrid said in a hard voice. "I'm talking about Miranda Toliver."

"Mir... ." September stopped, looked around the room—finally back at Madrid. She replied in an emotionless tone. "I don't know Miranda Toliver."

"Really?" Madrid shot back.

"Really," she replied in a small voice.

"You mentioned her in your journal."

A grim pallor washed over the young woman's face. Her eyes grew hard and cold, her posture slumped beneath the weight of humiliation and defeat. Her voice came low, from the back of her throat. "You read my journal."

"Yeah," Madrid admitted. "I read it."

"Get you all hot and bothered?"

"No," Madrid said, his voice flat. "It made me sad for you, September. Sad you had to go through those things with Lyle. Nobody should have to endure that. I can see why you needed to reach out to someone—someone like Miranda."

The iciness in her stare melted. She blinked back tears—asked, "Did Momma read it?"

"No," Madrid answered. "I'm sure she doesn't know it even exists."

"Swear?" A tear escaped from the corner of her eye.

"Yeah."

She shook her blonde curls again. "No," she demanded. "You gotta say it. You gotta say *swear*."

The clock continued to tick inside Madrid's head. "I swear."

She looked past Madrid to some point on the wall. Stared at it—said quietly, "Momma would die if she read my journal."

"Did you talk to Miranda Toliver about Lyle, September?"

She nodded poignantly—as if confessing.

"What about after you got here?" Madrid asked "Did you contact Miranda?"

"When I was staying at the lodge," she said. "Pete told me not to use the phone. He said it would just be for a while. Until we got away from Black Creek."

"But you called," Madrid said, not a question.

Another nod.

"Pete found out that you called."

Nod.

"And then he moved you up here."

"He wasn't mad," she answered defensively. "Pete said it was for my own good. He was right—I shouldn't have called her. I could have ruined everything."

"Okay."

"Pete comes to me every night." She turned, gazed at the bed with the stuffed animals. "He holds me until I fall asleep." She turned back, looked directly at Madrid. "Pete loves me."

"I guess he does," Madrid answered. "But we've got to go, September. We need to get you to a doctor—then we can sort the rest of this out."

"Tomorrow's my birthday," she replied. "It was going to be special."

Still is, Madrid thought. *Just not candles and balloons.*

"We have to go," Madrid said again.

September looked at Toto. "Does he bite?"

"Sometimes."

"He killed the man at The Paradise Court?" she said.

"Yes," Madrid said, not taking the time to ask how she knew that detail.

"Will he stop biting if you tell him?"

"Yes."

"But you didn't tell him to stop with the man at The Paradise Court?"

Madrid thought back to what had been left of Charlie Blades' throat. "No," Madrid answered. "That man deserved what he got."

The sound of distant gunshots traveled up the empty ski slope—entered through the open door of the cabin. The fur on Toto's back bristled, a low rumbling growl escaped through clenched teeth.

"What was that?" she asked.

"We've got to go," Madrid told September Jamerson for the final time.

Chapter 47

September 29th—2:08 a.m.

Pete Wilson stepped from darkness of the back hallway—to the slightly-less darkness in the main room. He anchored the stock of the twelve gauge against his hip—adjusted the sawed-off barrels to match the angle of the staircase—pulled both triggers at once. The weapon bucked against him. Twin bursts of fire exploded, like from the mouth of a small, two-headed dragon.

Pete ducked back to the cover of the hallway. Josh Galloway had been exactly where he'd wanted him. And that should have been it—the battle should have been over. Pete waited—listened. The echo from the blast finished it's journey around the cavernous room. *No agonizing screams. No pleas for mercy. No sound of a body tumbling down the staircase.* Except for a drip of a stopped-up rain gutter and a gust of wind that tickled a white pine branch against an upstairs window, the lodge was silent.

Pete snapped the barrels open, jacked the two shells. Invisible in the gloom, they rattled noisily across the floor. The clatter was followed instantly by a loud thud. The floor shook beneath Pete Wilson's feet—like a small earthquake, the epicenter only a few feet away. Mentally flatfooted, it took Pete Wilson a moment to process the sound—a moment he didn't have to waste. Finally it hit him—a sickening realization. Josh Galloway was no longer in the loft.

Pete backed down the hallway, fumbling the reload. Panic made his fingers thick and awkward. He plucked a pair of double 00 shells from his vest pocket. One shell found the open mouth of the barrel, the other the floor. He could see Josh Galloway's bulky mass step into the mouth of the hallway, his form vaguely silhouetted against the glass windows at the front of the lodge. Pete snapped the barrel closed.

* * * *

Josh Galloway had been two stair treads from the top, on his way down the staircase from the loft. Then the lights had died.

Instinctively, he'd stopped. *The storm? Probably.* All over the county trees would be toppling, taking power lines down with them. *Probably—but maybe not.* He had listened. Heard a sound from the rear of the house—muffled. Maybe a door opening—maybe his imagination. He had needed a quick decision—rush down a dozen stairs into an open room, or retreat two steps and cover?

Back up in the loft, he'd been crouched behind the wall when the first shots exploded, one indistinguishable from the other. They had sounded like a cannon, the sound reverberating off the hard surfaces of the pine lodge. Like a fast-moving glacier, fear had encased him—frozen him in place. A moment later Josh Galloway had heard the spent shells skittering across the floor. He had recognized the sound—understood the opportunity presented. In that instant, his fear had melted. Adrenalin had jolted him into motion. Blindly, he had bounded halfway down the stairs, the shotgun in his left hand. His right hand had found the railing. He had launched himself over, had landed hard and awkwardly on the floor below. A searing pain had stabbed into his left leg, just above the ankle. Josh was pretty sure it had broken—was completely sure it didn't matter. The shotgun was still in his left hand.

He moved to the mouth of the hallway, made a quick guess where Pete Wilson might be. He pulled the trigger—again, again, and again.

* * * *

The first blast hit Pete Wilson in the left shoulder, the second just above the left knee. The combination spun his body—an ugly spiral that left him crumpled on the floor. Two more shots followed in quick succession. The pellets flew over him, rattled around in the stainless-steel kitchen, blew out a window on the back side of the lodge. From the floor, Pete rolled onto his side, fired the single round he'd been able to chamber back down the hallway. On one leg and one arm, he staggered—somewhere between a hop and a crawl—back into the kitchen. A long commercial island—stainless steel sides, with a thick maple butcher block top, bisected the room. Pete Wilson hobbled to the far end, positioned himself behind it. He needed to reload He jammed his right hand inside the vest pockets for more shells. Nothing. Maybe they'd fallen out, or maybe they were never there at all. Pete couldn't remember how many he'd had. Certainly not enough. He had planned for an ambush, not a gun fight.

The pain was beginning to register. At the end of the island, Pete shifted his weight, seeking relief. The tile floor beneath him was becoming slick with blood. His shirt clung to his chest and he could hear himself breathing—ragged and uneven. Pete Wilson sank to the floor—struggled for self-control. The edge of panic, mixed with humiliation, left a bitter taste in the back of this throat. A montage of images flickered across his mind, mostly Mary Alice—and then September. He considered the irony of the same man taking both women from him. Rage forced him back up to his knees. Something fell to the floor. It sounded vaguely like a shotgun shell. Pete reached down, groped through the darkness—found it in the growing puddle of blood. Slimy and wet—cut glass, cylindrical—a salt shaker. Pete gripped it in his right hand. He was now armed with an empty shotgun and salt. Pete rested the gun on the butcher block, waited for Josh Galloway—not knowing one of them was only seconds from drawing their last breath.

Like a finger on a switch, September Jamerson had started jabbering—staccato and relentless. Her transformation had been sudden—an unsettling series of transitions—back and forth between September-the-child and September-the-woman. At first, Madrid had thought it an act—a stalling tactic. But now, he was wondered if she'd managed a clean break from reality. Again, he thought back to her journal. *Reality then.* Madrid glanced around the room—her log-cabin prison. His gaze settled back to her bandaged wrists. *Reality now.*

Nestled amid a family of dust bunnies, Madrid had found the pair of moccasins under her bed. They were cheap imitations of the real thing, the kind tourists bought on the Cherokee reservation a couple of hours up the road. September had sat in one of the rocking chairs by the fireplace. She had waited for Madrid to slip the shoes onto her feet—like a child on her first day to school. When he looked up, she had the cheerleader sweater bunched under her chin. Her small breasts were stretched almost flat against her arched torso. Her pink nipples were small and taut.

"You can touch them," she said, her voice shifting freely between the woman and the child.

Madrid reached up, grabbed a handful of sweater, jerked it roughly back down to her waist. He leaned in closer, whispered in her ear, a cold edge to his voice. "I *do not* have time for this." He took her by the hand, tried to be careful of the bandages, and pulled her out the cabin door. Somewhere between the cabin's porch and the edge of the slope, her stream-of-consciousness soliloquy had begun. Madrid's terse requests for quiet had done nothing to quell her torrent of words.

"Pete doesn't make love to me," September Jamerson said. "You know—like screw me or anything. He can't get it hard since Mary Alice got killed. Do you say *screw* or *fuck*?"

"Fuck," Madrid answered over his shoulder. "As in *shut the fuck up*."

"I should be dead now," she continued. "I would have bled to death in my car. But Pete saved me. He saved my life. He's going to take care of me. Where are you taking me?"

"To see your mother." It was the most benign answer he could come up with.

"I miss her."

"She misses you, September," Madrid said. "But you need to be quiet now."

"Did I tell you Pete can't get it hard?" They had crossed the slope—had started down the other side. Her voice went loud then soft, modulating with the wind.

"You told me," Madrid said. "Be quiet."

"It's not rape if he doesn't get hard," she explained.

* * * *

Pete Wilson had waited in the dark, behind the island in the kitchen, for as long as he could stand it. Fear had cycled down to uneasiness, then spiraled further—almost to apathy. The imaginary footsteps in the hallway had grown silent—the ominous shadows had melted into the gloom. Pain had sped the process along.

On the front porch of the lodge, standing at the top of stairs, Pete propped himself on the rail and post. Pain burned along the left side of his body. He was sweating profusely. It soaked through his clothes—mixed with the blood. The night air blew cool against his face. His body was starting to chill—his thought process beginning to slow.

Pete turned, looked back into the lodge. Though the open front door, he could see Josh Galloway. He was sprawled, face up, in the middle of the room. *Lucky shot*, Pete thought. *About time that bastard's luck ran out*, he thought some more. But now he'd probably never know—never *really know* if Josh had killed Mary Alice. He forced his worries back to the present—back to September. She was up there—waiting in the cabin for him. *What if he couldn't make it?* Getting from the kitchen to the porch had been a struggle. Walking up the trail to the cabin seemed next to impossible. Pete could see himself collapsing, maybe somewhere not far from where he stood now. He would tell himself he was only going to rest for a few minutes, but then he would lose consciousness. Bleed out—then die. September would be trapped, a prisoner of the refuge he'd created for her. *She might figure a way out. It wasn't Alcatraz.* But what if she didn't bother to try. Pete remembered the look in her eyes when he'd found her on the edge of campus, sitting in her Ford Pinto, alone in the dark. At first he'd thought she was with a guy, or maybe smoking a joint. Then he'd seen the blood, and that "*What have I done?*" look in her eyes. Pete still wasn't sure why he hadn't rushed her straight to the emergency room, or at least to the college infirmary. It was that look. And that face. Almost the same face as Mary Alice's, but without the mischievous, conniving glint in her eyes. *September was perfect*, he thought. And he had to get her out—she was counting on him—and he was counting on her.

The truck was an option. It was parked around back, but he could make it. The slope was wet, steep, and overgrown. But he could drive the truck as far as it would go. If he got lucky, it might make it most of the way. Then maybe he could walk the rest. Take his time. He could make it.

Pete closed his eye, pictured September holding him, reassuring him. Dressing his wounds and telling him that everything was going to be all right. He could hear her voice. He opened her eyes. For a moment the wind and rain relented.

And he could still hear her voice.

She spoke to him from above—not in the spiritual sense. And in truth, she wasn't speaking to Pete at all. Fragments of speech, rode wisps of air current down the slope. He heard the words "Momma" and "dog". Then something else about "'lions and tigers and bears'". He shifted his weight, struggled with his balance. September had managed to free herself from the cabin. Pete's thoughts traveled a circuitous route. Confusion, despair, hope. And when he finally put it together—anger. It was Madrid. Had to be. *Alex Madrid.* There was no other explanation. Joy Springtime had been right after all. Madrid had figured it out—at least made the connection. Then, somehow, he'd found September. Pete wondered what Madrid had told her—how much she'd told Madrid. *Had he tricked her into leaving? Maybe he had forced her—or maybe he didn't force her at all.* However it happened, Alex Madrid was taking September away—taking her away from him.

Pete Wilson hobbled back into the lodge. Pete found Josh's .38 caliber service revolver—checked the load—slid it into his belt. In Josh's coat pocket he found more twelve gauge shells. He slid two into the empty barrels of the sawed off, put two more in his vest pocket. There was a walking stick next to the fireplace, a gift from one of the teachers at the college. It was a piece of twisted laurel, tapered at the bottom, the face of a bearded mountain spirit carved into the top. Pete picked up the stick, leaned on it heavily—started for the door. A trail of blood followed him out.

Chapter 48

September 29th—2:32 a.m.

September was getting crazier as she walked down the slope—a psychotic snowball gathering mass and momentum. The dog was up ahead, invisible in the shadows. Madrid had given up trying to keep her quiet. His only option would be to knock her unconscious—an option he couldn't bring himself to exercise.

September stopped dead in her tracks, stared up at one of the chairs on the lift, like it were a hovering spaceship. "Look," she said to Madrid in an excited whisper.

"It's a chair," Madrid said impatiently.

"Pete said he would let me ride it." Back to her child voice. "He said I could ride it all day, if I wanted."

"Yeah...well...maybe someday you can," Madrid said, "but not tonight."

September looked down the slope, then back up at the chair. Then her head snapped in Madrid's direction. "I'm not stupid."

"I never thought you were," Madrid negotiated.

She shook her head again—almost violently. "They'll never let me come back here," she said in sudden realization.

"Who won't let you?"

"You know," she replied accusingly.

Madrid knew.

"I'll be in jail—or some loony hospital—if I'm lucky."

"Why would you go to jail?" Madrid asked.

"Because I've been bad," she confessed. "I've done bad things."

"What sort of things?" Madrid asked.

"None of your goddamn business," she spat angrily. She jerked her arm free and started to run. She took two steps back up the hill, in the general direction of the cabin, then she cut quickly, like a half-decent high-school running back, and started down the slope towards the lodge. Madrid caught September between her ninth and tenth stride. Their momentum carried them to the ground. They slid along the wet grass, ended up in a tangle of briars. September leapt to her feet. Madrid reached up, grabbed a handful of wet sweater and yanked her back to the ground. She screamed—a high-pitched primal sound that emanated from deep inside her.

Madrid clamped his hand over her mouth. He was on top of her, his face inches from hers. "Don't do that again," he said in a low, angry voice.

"Or what?" she demanded in a voiced muffled against his palm.

"Or I'm going to shut you up," he told her in a harsh whisper, "by whatever means it takes. Do you understand?"

She nodded, her face pressing back and forth against his hand.

"Are you going to scream again?"

Her face moved back and forth. Madrid slowly released his hand—waited. Toto was standing above them—curious—unexcited. Madrid could feel the dog's warm breath on the side of his face.

"Is he going to bite me?" The little girl voice again.

"Let's go," he said, picking her off of the wet ground. He looked down the slope. The lodge had been well lit on his trek up the hill, now it was completely dark. Madrid wondered what to make of it.

The beam from the flashlight washed over them as they entered the clearing. Pete Wilson was leaning against the hood of the Blazer. Madrid could make out something in his right hand.

"Move away from him, September," Madrid heard him say. His voice was weak and strained. September pulled away. Madrid let her go. She ran towards Pete Wilson, disappeared behind the glare of the light. "Put the gun down, Madrid."

Toto growled.

"Don't want to have to waste a barrel on that dog."

"Quiet," Madrid told the mutt.

"The gun," Wilson said. "Not goin' to tell you again."

Madrid pinched the handle of 9mm between his thumb and forefinger, slid it from his belt, tossed it onto the floor of wet pine needles.

"Are you all right, Mary Alice?" Madrid heard him ask.

"Yes," September answered, "but you're not. Oh god, Pete! You're bleeding!" September's tone took on a note of hysteria. "You're bleeding all over!"

"I'm okay," he said, the words barely clearing his lips.

The flashlight was trained on Madrid's eyes. It slipped to his neck, and then his chest. The beam continued downward—like a slow nod. The last leg of the descent was sudden. The beam bounced on the spongy ground, pointed back towards Wilson and September. Madrid moved to his right, a forty-five degree angle, then closed on Pete Wilson. Pete was on the ground, slumped against the front tire of the Blazer. Madrid took the shotgun, placed it on the roof of the truck, picked up the light, shown it on Pete Wilson. September had been right. Pete's clothes were soaked with blood. Madrid felt for a pulse.

"He's going to be all right," September said. She was on her knees, holding his head between the "B" and the "C" of her cheerleader sweater. "He just needs to rest for a little while."

It took a few minutes for Madrid to convince September that Pete wasn't going to be all right. That there was nothing either of them could do to change that. There were hysterics, followed by short intervals of calm—then more hysterics. September vacillated between acceptance and denial—until acceptance finally won out and denial limped away into the darkness. It took Madrid more time to convince her that there was no purpose in taking Pete's body with them. Somebody would need to investigate, he explained. Based on the exchange of gunfire, Madrid had a suspicion that someone wouldn't be Josh Galloway.

Madrid grabbed Pete Wilson under each arm. He dragged his slumped-over body away from the Blazer. September wrapped her arms around Pete's ankles—did her best to help. The rain started up again, found its way through the tree limbs, pelted their backs.

"You're not going to leave him out here all night, are you?"

Madrid wasn't sure, but said, "No."

"That wouldn't be right," she said, mostly to herself.

They propped him against a nearby tree, left him sitting nearly the same as when he died. Madrid retrieved the 9mm and slid it back into his belt. September dropped to her knees, placed her head at an awkward angle, then kissed Pete Wilson on the lips. The kiss lasted for several seconds, then she said in an emotionally-choked voice, "I love you, Pete."

Madrid placed his hand gently on her shoulder. "We need to go, September."

Madrid opened the passenger door. Without taking her eyes off of Pete, she climbed in. When she was seated, Madrid closed the door. Toto followed him around the truck, bounded onto the driver's seat, then over the center console. Like a king reclaiming a throne, the big mutt arranged himself across the back seat. Madrid slid the key into the ignition, adjusted the rearview mirror. The big engine turned over. The low beams spot-lighted the macabre figure they just positioned. Madrid was about to shift into reverse—stopped when he felt the gun muzzle press against his temple. At the same time he heard the hammer lock back into place.

"You killed him," September said, her voice calm, matter-of-fact. "If you'd just left us alone, Pete would still be alive."

In the rearview mirror Madrid could see the snub nose pressed against the side of his head. It looked like a .38. There was no reason to think it wasn't loaded. September's hand was steady, her long delicate forefinger wrapped around the trigger.

"All he wanted was to be happy," September said accusingly. "That's all either one of us wanted." Composure leaked out of her tone "Why couldn't you just leave us the hell alone and let us be happy?"

Madrid kept his head perfectly still, his eyes focused on the mirror. Both of Madrid's hands were on the steering wheel. He needed her to relax, to lose focus—only for a second. "You were locked up like a prisoner, September," Madrid replied, his lips barely moving. "Your mother was worried about you. Lyle roughed her up pretty good while you were gone."

"Good!" September yelled into his ear. "Lyle roughed me up plenty, too. That son of a bitch was all over me," she continued, a venomous quality building in her voice. "On top of me, under me, behind me, and always inside of me. Where was my *mother* then, Madrid?"

Madrid said nothing.

"Not protecting me!" she continued, answering her own question. "Pete Wilson was the only person who ever protected me—and you got him killed, Alex Madrid! So don't talk to me about my mother. Talk about Pete. He *really* loved me."

It happened in an instant. Madrid watched him shift on the back seat. From the gloom there was a flash of white teeth, then his massive head was between them. Most of September's thin forearm disappeared into his mouth. The dog was frozen, statue still—his low growl eclipsed the sound of the engine. Madrid heard September exhale sharply, as if she'd been punched in the stomach. The muzzle of the snub nose hadn't moved.

"He's biting me," September said—incredulous, her voice barely audible.

"No, he isn't," Madrid answered softly. "Not yet."

"Make him stop," she said in a tense whisper.

"Can't," Madrid replied, working to keep any emotion out of his tone. "Toto tends to do whatever Toto wants. But I *will* promise you one thing, September. If that gun goes off, he's going to go crazy. Crazy all over you. First thing he's going to do is rip your arm right off your body—you can count on that. Then he's going for your throat. At that point—for you—it will pretty much be over. But if he can't figure a way out of this truck, eventually, he's going to eat you."

"Oh, god." The words rushed out of her mouth.

"Yeah," Madrid said encouragingly. "Might want to take a moment and think about it."

"You're lying," she whispered with little conviction.

"Yeah, I'm lying," Madrid shot back. "Pull the trigger and see how long it takes before you hear your bones start breaking. Two nights ago this dog killed a man almost three times your size."

"Get him off me," she hissed, approaching the edge of hysteria.

"Let go of the gun."

"No," she answered defiantly, some of the little girl working back into her tone. "You make him stop."

"Not how it works." Madrid answered.

"I can kill you," she threatened.

"Then we die together," Madrid countered. "I go quick and painless. You—not so much."

"So what do I do?"

"Take your finger off the trigger and just relax."

In the rearview mirror, Madrid watched the digit retract. He moved his left hand slowly upward until it was next to his right ear. He palmed the gun, rotated the barrel away from his head. He eased the hammer back down—released the cylinder. The .38 had a full load.

"Make him stop," September said.

Madrid looked at the dog. "Let her go, Toto."

The dog didn't move.

"I'm serious, damn it. Let her go."

The dog released her arm. Madrid reached into the back seat, rubbed the side of the dog's head. "Good boy," he said.

"You lied. You said you couldn't make him stop. You're just a lying bastard."

"It's a character flaw," Madrid replied. "I'm working on it."

September rubbed her arm, tried to examine the teeth marks in the scarce light.

"I didn't mean for Pete to die," Madrid told her.

"That's just another lie," she replied accusingly.

It would be thirty-nine days before anyone heard September Jamerson speak again.

Chapter 50

September 29th—6:06 a.m.

Madrid had lost count of how much coffee he'd drunk—but it was a lot—maybe a personal record. He had taken September to the hospital. The E.R. doc had examined her wrists, applied fresh bandages. He had shined a light in her eyes—had asked her a dozen questions she hadn't answered. He'd asked Madrid if she had taken any illegal drugs. Madrid had sipped coffee—offered no comment.

Out in the hallway, another doctor, this one older, had addressed Madrid in his best professional voice. "It seems she's been through some type of emotional trauma."

"Never rule out the obvious," Madrid had replied.

Occasionally September cried. Then laughed. Then cried some more. But mostly she just sat silently—the classic thousand yard stare. Just as she'd predicted, the decision was made to transfer her to a psyche ward in Asheville.

Tomorrow would be her birthday, so maybe a handsome doctor would sing "Happy Birthday" to her. But Madrid figured it was more likely some nurse would give her a fistful of drugs—sit her in the corner of a room whose walls were painted institutional green, or maybe gray. Maybe somebody would stop by, tell September Jamerson, "Everything is going to be all right." But even if they did, they wouldn't really believe it.

It was still dark when the two deputies had rolled up outside the emergency room. Madrid had never seen either of them. Both were young, blonde hair cut military style, one about a head shorter than the other. The taller one had done most of the talking. He'd asked a lot of questions, with no idea of where he was going with them. Madrid had provided him with selective answers. He told them about finding September in the cabin, but not about his visit with Joy Springtime. Told them about Pete Wilson dying next to the car, but not about September Jamerson threatening to blow his head off.

"You didn't go see who Pete was shooting at?" Tall Deputy had asked, when Madrid had finished the tale.

"No."

"How come?"

"Because I needed to get medical attention for the girl. And I figured whoever Pete was shooting at was dead. It would wait."

"We gotta go out there," Tall Deputy had said to the shorter one.

"Yeah," Short Deputy had replied through a clenched jaw. He had looked at Madrid, added, "You need to go, too."

"Wouldn't miss it," Madrid had replied.

They rode in the cruiser, the deputies up front, Madrid and the dog in the back. An ambulance with two attendants followed them out. They arrived at the failed ski slope right about dawn, when the sky was just beginning to transition from gray to pink. The rain stopped, but the wind continued to gust through the tops of the evergreens. The deputies found Pete Wilson just as Madrid and September had left him—propped against the tree. Except for the blood, he looked like he might be sleeping.

Further up the road, it took all five of them to rock the stranded cruiser from the deep rut. One of the ambulance attendants, a guy who only weighed about a buck and a quarter, worked the gas. Madrid and the other three pushed. Once it was clear, the three vehicles rolled into the overgrown parking lot of the lodge.

The front door was standing open and there was dried blood on the steps and porch. The five men backtracked the trail into the main room. Josh Galloway was on the floor. No one mistook his condition for slumber. His remaining eye was fixed toward ~~to~~ the ceiling. Half of his face had been destroyed by the blast. Short Deputy muttered something, turned and walked back outside. One of the ambulance attendants, a guy who looked about fourteen years old, went with him.

Madrid and the remaining deputy followed the trail down the hallway and into the kitchen. Buckshot had splintered the pine-paneled walls.

"What the hell you think happened here?" the taller deputy had asked. He was visibly shaken, but hanging in.

"What usually happens when people start shooting at each other," Madrid answered.

"Why would they want to shoot each other up like this?"

"History," Madrid answered. "And September Jamerson." But Madrid knew there was more to it. There were pieces of the puzzle no one had yet been willing to reveal. Now, maybe no one would ever have to.

"You guys missing anyone?" Madrid asked.

Tall Deputy jerked his head back over his shoulder, towards the open door. "You talkin about Rodney?"

"No," Madrid answered. "I'm talking about somebody who didn't show up for work this morning—somebody unaccounted for."

"I don't think so."

"You mind checking?"

Tall deputy walked out to car, used the radio. Madrid waited on the porch.

"We got everybody—except for Sergeant Galloway."

Madrid nodded. "Okay," he said. "Thanks."

"Why did you ask?"

"Just curious," Madrid answered. "I'm a curious guy."

* * * *

From the other end of the phone line, a female voice at the *Black Creek Herald* informed Madrid that Julie Kingston had gone home. So at ten minutes before noon, Madrid and Toto were standing on Julie Kingston's front stoop. It had stopped raining and the sun was threatening to burn through the thinning gray cloud cover. Julie answered the door in her pajamas. They were the color of ivory—silky—shimmery. She wore a pair of reading glasses. They were big, with black frames—the kind Clark Kent would have worn—if he'd been a girl. In her left hand was a large steaming mug. Her long black hair had fallen over one eye. She brushed it back, tucked it behind her ear.

"Leisurely morning?" Madrid asked.

"I've been up all night," she'd replied, not as friendly as Madrid had hoped. "I was just getting ready to get in bed."

Madrid started to speak, but Julie pointed a painted fingernail skyward, moved her head slowly from side to side. "Don't say a word, Alex."

"Okay," Madrid said. "But I need to ask you a favor."

She raised her eye brows above the frame of the glasses. "Do tell."

Madrid nodded.

"What sort of favor?"

"I need a dog sitter—just for a while."

"A while? That's a non-defined measure of time."

"Few hours. Tops."

She opened the door wider. "Come on in, Toto," she'd said without taking her eyes off of Madrid. Toto brushed past her and through the door—like he owned the place.

"Thanks," Madrid had said.

"I like your dog."

"And me?"

"See you in a few hours."

"I didn't know you wore glasses," Madrid said.

"A hell of a lot you don't know, Madrid."

Madrid stopped by Marcy's. The rain had stopped and the lunch crowd had taken most of the best seats. Gordon Lightfoot was playing on the jukebox. Madrid found an empty stool at the counter—ordered some tofu with vegetables and two large coffees to go.

"Where's your dog?" Marcy asked.

"Staying with a friend," Madrid answered.

"Hmm," she said. "Surprised to see you out and about."

"Why is that?"

"Everyone is talking about Josh Galloway and Pete Wilson," Marcy said in a somber tone.

"That was unfortunate," Madrid replied, "but I didn't have anything to do with it."

"Wrong place—wrong time?" Marcy asked, not bothering to mask her cynicism.

"Something like that."

"Seems to happen with you a lot, Alex Madrid."

"I've noticed that, too."

The sun had begun to break through the clouds and there were patches of blue sky. The river hadn't crested, its waters, long over the banks, continued to creep towards the Black Creek College campus.

Emergency vehicles were still posted on either side of the bridge to prevent anyone from trying to cross. Madrid pointed the Blazer in the other direction and ten minutes later rolled into the parking lot of The Paradise Court. It looked no less dismal under clearing skies. The carcass of the burned out van was still in the courtyard. The air outside the office still stank of burnt rubber.

The "No Vacancy" sign was lit, the office door locked. Madrid knocked. The metal storm door rattled angrily under his assault. Joy's car was in the far corner of the lot. He knocked again. Louder. Somebody stirred from somewhere inside. After a moment of two, the sound came closer. Joy Springtime answered the door. Her blonde hair was matted on one side—mascara smeared around her eyes.

She peered at Madrid through the dirty glass. After a moment, recognition registered in her bloated expression. "Waddah ya' want?" she asked in a rush of words.

"We need to talk," Madrid said.

She wiped her mouth with the back of her hand. Red lipstick spread across her face, like a gaping wound. "We already talked—last night." From the other side of the glass, her words came out thick and hard to understand. "I'm talked out."

"You need to rethink that, Joy," Madrid said.

"Or what?" she challenged.

"Or I'll rethink payment on the damages."

She moved her face closer to the glass. "You're a bastard, Madrid."

"When I need to be."

The lock clicked, the door opened. Madrid followed her back to the counter. Joy wedged herself behind the barrier, plopped heavily on the upholstered stool. Madrid set the Styrofoam cup in front of her, peeled back the lid. Steam rolled off the top and the smell of coffee filled the drab little foyer.

"Didn't know how you took it," Madrid said.

"With a little sugar and a lot of whiskey," she answered. To make the point, she reached under the counter, came back with a single serving bottle of Jameson's—like the kind you get on an airplane.

Madrid placed his hand over the cup. "After we talk," he'd said—no nonsense. "I need some straight answers."

She placed the tiny bottle on the counter. Gave it one last look, then turned to Madrid. "'Bout what?"

"The Three Musketeers," Madrid said.

"Already told you 'bout that."

"Tell me again," Madrid said. "But this time tell me the truth."

An hour and a half later, Joy Springtime's coffee was cold—untouched. An iridescent film floated on top of the inky black liquid. Her story had been told—retold—edited—and retold a third time. Madrid still wasn't sure it was the truth. But at least it made sense.

Joy sat slumped on the stool—her expression a lugubrious mask as Madrid dialed numbers from the phone book. The first number didn't pick up, the second gave him the information he was looking for.

"Out of town," Madrid said. "Back tonight."

Morosely, she asked, "So when do I get my money?"

"Tomorrow—afternoon," Madrid answered.

She nodded. "Good. I'm getting' the hell of this shit-hole town."

"Do what you want," Madrid said. "But until tomorrow, stay sober—or at least stay off the goddamn phone."

"Your sayin' what happened last night—Josh and Pete getting' killed—was my fault." It came out sounding like a confession.

Without much tact Madrid replied, "There's plenty of fault to go around."

Déjà vu. Madrid had rung the doorbell of the main house. From inside the mansion, he'd heard the deep note of the chime bouncing around in the emptiness. He left the Blazer parked out front, followed the path back to the guest house. It was unlocked. He sat on the leather sofa, stared out at a pair of Canada geese floating on the pond. That lasted maybe ten minutes, until sleep claimed him.

Sometime after that, Julie stepped onto the porch. She was wearing a black skirt, a black v-neck sweater, and shiny black boots with three-inch heels.

Toto was on her left hip. He was wearing a wide, black leather collar, and they were connected by a thick, black leather leash. *Jesus,*

Madrid thought, *they match*. To the big mutt he said, sarcastically, "Don't *you* look fancy?"

"He looks handsome," Julie countered.

Toto tilted his head—left then right.

"Hmm," Madrid replied.

Julie unsnapped the leash and Toto wandered over to the unlit fireplace, ruffled the rug, and laid down.

"Made yourself at home, I see."

Madrid stood up. He'd left his shoes out on the porch. With the heels, Julie was about an inch taller than him. So when he spoke, they were not quite eye-to-eye. "I was waiting for you."

"So you could get your dog back?" she asked, a hint of smile played on her lips.

"No," Madrid answered. He reached toward her with his left hand, gently stroked a strand of her hair. Julie stood perfectly still. Her smile had vanished, replaced by an unmistakable intensity in her green eyes. Madrid's fingers followed the path of her raven-black hair past her shoulders, to the middle of her back. His hand traveled downward, to where the bottom of the black sweater met the top of the black skirt. He slipped his hand underneath the sweater, slowly followed the curve of her spine back up. She was against him now, their bodies pressed tightly together. Her long fingers were spread across Madrid's shoulders. Julie tugged at the tail of his shirt. Madrid could feel her fingernails lightly raking across his back.

They kissed—a mixture of mouths and tongues, of gentleness and desperation. Madrid stepped back, bunched the hem of her sweater in each hand. Julie raised her arms above her head. She was wearing a tiny bra, black and lacy. Her small breasts curved deliciously above the lace, her dark nipples strained against the thin fabric.

Madrid leaned back without taking his hands from her waist. For a long moment, he studied her—appreciatively. "Wow," he said finally, his voice a ragged whisper.

Julie unbuttoned his shirt, ran her hands over the hard contours of Madrid's chest. They kissed again—no less desperate. Madrid managed the first button of her skirt between his thumb and forefinger. He was about to start on the second, when he felt her hand on his. Julie broke the kiss, stepped away.

"I need to tell you something." There was seriousness in her tone.

"Okay," Madrid said.

"They don't match."

"They don't match?" Madrid repeated.

"The bra and panties—they don't match. I got dressed in a hurry this morning."

Madrid nodded. "Not a deal breaker," he assured her.

Chapter 51

September 30th—10:16 a.m.

Madrid hadn't called ahead. He knew the man he needed to see would be there. A gravel driveway, with a uniform strip of grass that bisected its center, led Madrid off the main road. The man lived on a small farm, a lot like the one where September Jamerson had lived, but this one was well kept. The house was two stories, white, with a green metal roof and green shutters. A covered porch wrapped three sides. Beyond the house a gray barn set on a stone foundation. A pair of palomino-colored draught horses offered Madrid disinterested glances—went back to eating grass.

Madrid stepped onto the wide porch. Before he knocked, he could hear a woman's voice inside. She was singing—maybe in Italian—maybe opera. Madrid opened the screen door and rapped lightly. Both doors had been painted green to match the shutters. The song ended. The woman answered the door. She was short—no more than five feet, slight—fit. Her hair, mostly gray, was pulled back from her narrow face. She had high, prominent cheekbones. Fine lines bracketed her eyes and at the corner of her mouth. They suited her. She focused an unflinching gaze on Madrid.

She said, "Good morning."

Madrid doubted it actually was. He introduced himself—watched his identity register in her expression. Some of the brightness left her eyes.

"I've heard your name recently," she said, not quite an accusation.

Madrid nodded.

"Wait here, please."

Through the screen, he watched her fade into the center of the house. She was back in a couple of minutes. "Come in," she said, forcing a smile. "Would you like something? I have some iced tea, or I could make some coffee."

"Thank you," Madrid said, "but no."

She looked at Madrid—like she wanted to say something, forced another smile instead.

Madrid finished her thought. "I'll try not to be long, ma'am."

The diminutive woman's gaze stopped at Madrid's chest. "Thank you," she replied, not much more than a whisper.

Madrid followed her down a wide hallway, worn oak floors beneath their feet, matching wainscoting on either side. The man he'd come to see was in one of the back rooms of the farmhouse. There was a brick fireplace at one end of the room, at the other end, a bank of windows overlooked the pasture and barn. Until recently, it had been a den—now converted to a sick room. A hospital bed with wheels, side rails, and a control pad dominated one wall. A round end table with a small forest of orange pill bottles, and a plastic pitcher of water, stood next to the bed. The woman stopped in the hall. Madrid continued inside. She quietly closed the door behind him.

Next to the pill table, Sheriff Avery Boyd sat in an over-stuffed recliner. The chair seemed to swallow him in brown leather. He wore bedroom slippers and light-blue flannel pajamas. Something yellow had spilled on the shirt—crusted above the breast pocket. Clear tubes ran from his nose to the oxygen canister next to the chair. Morning sun streamed in through the windows, filled the room with light—did little to change the effect.

His gold-rimmed eyeglasses had grown disproportionately large on his thinning face. The sheriff used his boney index finger to push them up his nose, said in a raspy voice, "Better be important, Madrid. You've upset my wife."

Madrid moved directly across from the sheriff—stood next to the fireplace—crossed his arms in front of him. "Couldn't be helped," he replied without apology.

Boyd offered a slow, wary nod—adjusted his glasses again. "This about Josh and Pete Wilson?"

"That's part of it."

Another slow, thoughtful nod. "Josh shouldn't have tried to arrest Pete like that," Boyd said in a far away voice. "Josh gets reckless sometimes. Caught up with him."

"Most everybody gets reckless," Madrid said stonily. "At one time or another."

The sheriff fixed a pale, watery gaze on Madrid, said nothing.

"And let's don't have any confusion about what happened last night, Sheriff. Galloway didn't go out there to arrest Pete. If he had, he'd have brought plenty of help. He went by himself—because he didn't want any witnesses. Galloway was there for an execution."

Boyd sat stone-faced.

Madrid continued. "But ol' Josh hadn't figured on Pete getting the same phone call he'd gotten. Unlike yourself, Joy Springtime doesn't play favorites. So the odds got evened up. And Pete Wilson got harder to kill."

Body stared out the window. "That's a fancy story, Madrid," he said.

"It gets a lot fancier, Sheriff—when I get to the part about Mary Alice Wilson."

The sheriff's drawn, ashen face never changed expression. "What about Mary Alice?" he asked in a strained whisper.

"You could have stopped this, Boyd, " Madrid said. "A lot of people would still be alive. Maybe not Miranda Toliver, but Dicky Padrick, Galloway, and Pete Wilson. Maybe even that asshole you had in the jail with Padrick."

"Hung himself," Boyd said, as if recalling a lost fact.

"That's what they say," Madrid countered. "But there's a lot of things that aren't exactly what they seem—here in Black Creek."

"It's that way in a lot of places," the sheriff said—as if it were an explanation.

"Yeah," Madrid agreed. "It is. But I'm not talking about a lot of places. You could have stopped this," he repeated.

The sheriff moved his head an inch or two from side to side. Then he turned away from Madrid, a series of small, painful-looking adjustments. He stared in the direction of the pasture. Maybe at the horses—maybe at nothing. "Got back from the hospital last night," Boyd said, still staring out the window. "Got maybe a week or two. They said maybe a month—but I know better."

Madrid didn't speak—didn't move.

"Knowin' when you're going to die got some advantages, Madrid," he said slowly, his voice barely strong enough to carry across the small room. "Gives you some time to make peace—ask the Lord to forgive you." He pulled his eyes from the window, fixed them back on Madrid. "But there's some things you don't talk about. Not to God or to anybody—sure as hell not to you."

"It's about your wife, isn't it," Madrid asked, arms still folded.

"Leave Gabriella out of this." His frail body exploded into a series of racking coughs. A few seconds later, the door opened. The small woman took two steps into the room, offered Madrid an accusatory stare.

* * * *

Boyd covered his mouth with his right hand, held the left one up in a "*wait, I'm going to be all right*" gesture. Madrid and Gabriella Boyd waited. The sheriff wiped his mouth with a handkerchief, stuffed it into the breast pocket of his pajamas.

"You need to leave now," she told Madrid.

Avery Boyd shook his head. "I need to talk to him, Gabriella."

"You're too weak, Avery." Her words hung in the stale air of the room, then settled on her husband like a stain. "I...I...I just meant.... ."

"We won't be long, Gabriella," Boyd said, a tenderness below his rasp. "I promise."

She took one last look at Madrid.

After the door had closed, Madrid said again, "It's about your wife."

Boyd nodded. "I got no problem with dyin'. Nobody gets out alive. But it's going to be hard on her. I don't want her saddled with the guilt of my sins after I'm gone."

"I don't care what you want," Madrid answered, hardness in his tone. "I just care about what I want."

"Which is what, exactly?" Boyd asked, a mixture of wariness and distain.

Madrid was ready for the question. "A get-out-of-jail-free card for Victoria Jamerson—for starters."

"Huh. You don't ask for much, do you? The woman confessed to murder," Boyd said.

"Pete Wilson confessed to the same murder—just before he died," Madrid countered. "The way I look at it, that trumps Victoria's confession."

"Is that the truth?" Boyd asked.

Madrid offered half a smile that was neither happy nor friendly. "You're way too far into this to start worrying too much about truth, Sheriff."

"What if I *can't* make it go away," Boyd said. Almost belligerent. "That's more the D.A. than me."

"I don't award points for trying," Madrid answered. "Either it happens or it doesn't. Make it happen."

"And if it doesn't?"

Madrid looked at the closed door, then back at the withered man. "Then people are going to know. Going to know about Mary Alice, about Pete Wilson, about Josh Galloway. But most of all Boyd—they're going to know about you."

"Gabriella didn't have anything to do with this." It came out as a raspy plea.

"Tell that to Miranda Toliver's mother—or Dicky Padrick's sister. There's a lot of people that didn't have anything to do with this. And they're dead now. So don't give me a fucking sad story about whose fault it is and whose fault it isn't. You made this mess. I'm giving you a chance—a last chance—to clean it up."

Avery Boyd seemed to shrink further into the chair. "You said *for starters*. What else do you want?"

"I want to know *exactly* what happened to Mary Alice Wilson. No half-truths, no bullshit."

"What does it matter now?" Boyd asked in a disgusted tone.

"It matters," Madrid said. "This train wreck started with Mary Alice Wilson, and it's been collecting victims all along the track for nearly fifteen years. Right now—in this room—is where it stops."

"That's two. What else?" Boyd asked.

"Free pizza for life," Madrid said. "My life—not yours. But make good on the first two, I'll be willing to negotiate the last one."

* * * *

The story came out in bits and pieces, not always in the right order. Like dusty shards of broken memories, Avery Boyd examined each piece, explained it to Madrid, then tossed it aside for the last time.

"......You had to know her—be around her," he said of Mary Alice. "It wasn't like she was that beautiful. She was good lookin'—sure. But beautiful—no. But she knew how to get what she wanted. And she knew more about sex than any five women in this town."

Madrid could hear a remnant of lust in the dying man's voice.

"Should have stayed the hell away from her." He looked at the floor. Lust morphed to shame. "Gabriella had just lost the baby," he said, his voice sad and small. "It was a boy." He looked out the window again. "Did I tell you my daddy was sheriff of this county, Madrid?"

Madrid was leaned against the wall, his arms still folded across his chest—didn't respond.

Avery Boyd continued his story. "Doctors said she couldn't have any more kids. I thought that boy was going to be the next Sheriff of this county. I should have stayed away from Mary Alice, but..... ."

Madrid listened. The dying man's story was basically consistent—dovetailed almost perfectly with the tale Joy Springtime had recounted. Until he got to the end.

"Josh Galloway, the tough guy," Boyd said in a tired mocking tone. "He was just a big pussy—especially when it counted. He called me that night. I was on my way home. The sniveling idiot actually called me on the radio—told me Mary Alice was dead. I used a pay phone and called him at McCarson's. Josh sounded like he was about to cry—like a little girl. I told him to get away from McCarson's. I told him to go see Myrtle—make sure she would alibi him.

"I must've got there five minutes after Josh was gone. And there was Mary Alice, laying on the floor. Had her panties down around her ankles." Boyd paused, looked directly at Madrid. "And there was one big problem."

Madrid shifted his weight fractionally. "Just one?"

"One big one," Boyd answered. "The crazy little bitch wasn't dead."

"Galloway hadn't killed her?" Madrid asked.

Slowly, Avery Boyd's head swiveled back and forth on his withered neck. "Josh had wanted to marry her. Said she wouldn't leave Pete to marry him. That pissed him off some. Josh lost his temper—which he was prone to do—especially back then. He choked the hell out of her. Mary Alice passed out. Hit her head. There was some blood. Galloway panicked. Then he called me."

"That should have been a problem for Galloway," Madrid said. "Not for you."

"Maybe," Avery replied. "Maybe I panicked a little, too. Mary Alice was mad—real goddamned mad and real goddamned scared. She started making threats. Said she was going to tell Pete—and Gabriella."

"And you already had Galloway's confession," Madrid said.

"Yeah," Boyd replied, a trace of humor buried deep in his rasping voice. "I did."

"Josh Galloway died thinking he'd killed Mary Alice?"

Sheriff Avery Boyd stared at Madrid, his pale blue eyes like icy blue stones. "What do you think?"

"I think you left your two deputies, Pete Wilson and Galloway, twisting in the wind for fifteen years, Sheriff."

"Felt kind of bad about Pete from time to time," Boyd said, no remorse in his tone. "But he should have known what he got when he married that whore."

"Then September Jamerson showed up," Madrid said. "Kind of like Mary Alice rising from the grave. She screwed the whole thing up for you."

Avery Boyd shook his head. "The Jamerson kid didn't screw it up, Madrid. *You* did."

"I guess that's one way to look at it."

"First time I saw her picture, I figured Pete had something to do with it."

"And you were willing to let that go?" Madrid asked.

"Figured maybe I owed him," Boyd said, staring at a spot on the floor. "You said no bullshit."

"Yeah," Madrid nodded. "That's what I said."

"Now there's three of us who know the whole story, Madrid. You, me, and God."

"You left out Mary Alice," Madrid said.

"I'll worry about her in the next life." His words sounded as if they were clawed from the back of his throat. "We got a deal?"

Madrid stood on the steps of the farmhouse. The sun was high in the sky, brilliant after almost a week of rain. A sprinkling of poplar leaves dotted the manicured lawn, yellow, orange, and brown. Early fall, the subtle smell of decay in the air. The draught horses had moved to the other side of the pasture. He followed the neatly trimmed path back to the Blazer. Alex Madrid turned the vehicle around, followed the driveway out to the road—turned right—back towards Black Creek. The ghosts of Miranda Toliver and Dicky Padrick rode along with him.

About The Author

Frank B. Robinson II grew up in Western North Carolina, where he resides with his wife, Nancy, and their four dogs. Frank is an independent businessman, a student of the acoustic guitar, and holds a black belt in Shorinryu- Shorinkan karate. *Thirty Days Hath September* is his first novel. A second novel, *The Circle: A Moses Wolf Novel*, is scheduled for release sometime in 2013. Readers interested in contacting the author with comments or questions may reach him via email at: booksbyfrank@comporium.net.

Thirty Days Hath September is available (as all future books by Frank will be) in a Kindle edition on Amazon.com and in other ebook formats through various retailers, including but not limited to Smashwords.com and Barnesandnoble.com.

Midwest Gem Trails

A Field Guide for the Gem Hunter, the Mineral Collector and the Tourist

includes

**SOUTH DAKOTA • MICHIGAN • ILLINOIS • IOWA
WISCONSIN • OHIO • KANSAS • NORTH DAKOTA
NEBRASKA • INDIANA • MISSOURI • MINNESOTA**

By JUNE CULP ZEITNER

THIRD EDITION

Completely Revised

a GEMBOOK

Price $2.00

Published by

GEMBOOKS

MENTONE, CALIFORNIA

CONTENTS

Foreword

How To Use This Book 4

SOUTH DAKOTA 6

New Finds 6
Fairburn Type Agate 6
Blue Chalcedony 6
Tourmaline 8
Selenite 8
New Discoveries 8

HOT SPRINGS AREA 8
Cycad 9
Sand Barite 11

ARDMORE AGATE BEDS 11

OELRICHS AGATE BED 12

THE CUSTER AREA 13
Tepee Canyon Agate 14
Garnets 15
Fairburn Agates 16
Pegmatite Minerals 19

RAPID CITY AREA 21
Jasper Conglomerate 22
Golden Barite 23
Black Agates 24
Chalcedony 24

THE BADLANDS 25

PIERRE SHALE FOSSILS 27

THE MISSION AREA 27
Sand Calcite Crystals 28

NORTH DAKOTA 30

WESTERN NORTH DAKOTA 30
Badlands and Buttes 30
Gems and Fossils 30
Crystals and Specimens 31

THE CENTRAL PLATEAU 31

THE DRIFT PRAIRIE 32

THE RED RIVER VALLEY 32

NEBRASKA 33

NORTHERN NEBRASKA 33
Fossils 34

NORTH CENTRAL NEBRASKA 35

WESTERN & CENTRAL NEBRASKA 36

EASTERN NEBRASKA 37

KANSAS 38

THE HIGH PLAINS 38
Moss Opal 38
Fossils 38
Concretions 38

THE SMOKY HILLS 38
Gem Material 38
Barite Roses 38
Concretions 39
Fossils 39
Other Collectors' Items 39

THE RED HILLS-WELLINGTON AREA 39
Gems 39

THE FLINT HILLS 39
Gems 39
Geodes 39
Fossils 42

INDEX MAP 40

THE GLACIATED REGION 42
Gems 42
Celestite 42

THE OSAGE CUESTAS 42
Gems 42
Fossils 42

THE CHEROKEE PLAIN 42
Crystals 42
Meteorites 42

MISSOURI 44

NORTHWESTERN MISSOURI 44
Gems 44
Fossils 44

NORTHEAST MISSOURI 44
Gems 44
Geodes 44
Fossils 44

CENTRAL MISSOURI 44
Gems 44
Fossils 45

THE OZARKS 45
Gems 45
Crystals and Specimen Minerals 46
Fossils 46
The Elephant Rocks 46
Missouri Caves 46

IOWA 47
WESTERN IOWA 47
NORTHERN IOWA 47
Gems 47
"Coldwater" Agate 47
Fossils and Specimens 48
Geodes 48
Gem Grotto of the Redemption 48
CENTRAL IOWA 48
Crystals and Fossils 48
SOUTHERN IOWA 50
Crystals 50
Keokuk Geodes 50
MISSISSIPPI RIVER BORDER 52
Gems 52
Iowa Pearls 53

MINNESOTA 54
Lake Superior Agate 54
THE NORTH SHORE 55
Thomsonite 55
Special Note 55
THE MESABI RANGE 56
THE CUYUNA RANGE 57
CENTRAL & WESTERN MINNESOTA 57
Fossils 58

WISCONSIN 59
LAKE SUPERIOR-GOGEBIC DISTRICT 59
Gems and Specimens 59
CENTRAL WISCONSIN 59
Gems 59
Crystals and Specimens 60
Fossils 60
SOUTHERN WISCONSIN 61
Gems 61
Crystals 61
Fossils 61

MICHIGAN 63
THE KEWEENAW PENINSULA 63
Beaches 63
Mine Dumps 63
UPPER PENINSULA IRON RANGE 63
ISLE ROYALE 66
LOWER MICHIGAN 68
Crystals and Specimens 68
Fossils 68

ILLINOIS 69
Gems 69
NORTHERN ILLINOIS 69
Minerals 69
Fossils 69
CENTRAL ILLINOIS 70
SOUTHERN ILLINOIS 72
Crystals 72
Fossils 73

INDIANA 74
Gems 74
CENTRAL INDIANA 74
Fossils 74
SOUTHERN INDIANA 75
Fossils 76

OHIO 77
Gems 77
Fossils 77
Fossil Collecting 77
NORTHWESTERN OHIO 78
NORTHEASTERN OHIO 79
SOUTHWESTERN OHIO 79
SOUTHEASTERN OHIO 79

FOREWORD

When **Midwest Gem Trails** was first published in 1956, there was a shout of fear from old-time collectors.

"You've ruined our collecting! Now, every place will be swarming with people looking for rocks and nobody will have a chance to find anything!"

These fears were unfounded. Oh, yes, there are more collectors here, all right, but far outweighing that is the fact that in the last few years there have been more amazing gem, mineral, and fossil discoveries than at any time since the early exploration of the Midwest. At present, there are not only more places for collectors to go, but there are also more things to hunt for.

Take Kona dolomite, Mary Ellen jasper, pyritized snails, or blue chalcedony. Why weren't they in the first edition? Simply because only in the past few years have they been brought to light or have collectors been alert enough to appreciate them.

The gold rush lured settlers to the far West. Those people were mineral-conscious. By and large the Midwest was settled by farmers to whom rocks were merely obstacles to be dragged from the fields. Until recent years, most midwesterners were too busy fighting a hostile climate, grasshoppers, droughts, dust storms, and blizzards to go around picking up rocks for the fun of it.

One reason for the phenomenal growth of the rock hobby in the Midwest is the infinite variety offered by the large area. The Great Lakes, the Mississippi, Missouri, and Ohio Rivers, the moraines of the great glaciers, the Black Hills — all are part of the great Midwest. Collectors may search the mine dumps, stream beds, quarries, hillsides, caves, alluvial deposits, and pegmatite outcrops. There are still many places in the Midwest entirely untouched by rock collectors. Just as an example, in the last few years scuba divers have recovered large colorful thomsonites and datolites from beneath the cold waters of Lake Michigan.

After a book such as this is published, it is true that a certain number of old areas may be closed. It is my hope that collectors using this book as a guide will be guided also by the Golden Rule so that the words, "rock collector," will stand for the highest human values, and gates will be opened for us rather than closed. I predict that important new deposits of gems and minerals as well as many new kinds of fossils will come to light in the Midwest. Won't you join the fun?

HOW TO USE THIS BOOK

If this book is used properly, you undoubtedly will find lots of good rock. However, it is not a guarantee. The book will guide you to the proper area and tell you what to look for, but bear in mind the following facts.

First, roads, bridges, fences, and other landmarks are being changed constantly. If things do not appear to be as described, inquiry may be necessary. All of these places have been checked and were accurate at the time of writing.

Second, remember that you are not the only one using this guidebook. In a matter of time all the stones nearest these locations will be picked over. It is up to the alert collector to look for the identifying marks of the locality and find similar outcrops or deposits in the vicinity. A little careful study will reveal whether to go upstream or down, to the hills above or the plains below, whether to wade, dig, or pound.

Third, there is no doubt that luck plays a part in spectacular finds. More often than not, great finds are made not in the old well known area, but in the fringe area. They are made by collectors who have "boned up" on whatever they are hunting for and who have the good fortune to be hunting soon after heavy rains, melting snows, new excavations, new blasting, or other natural or mechanical aids.

There are several ways you can make your trip more interesting and more productive. Plan your trip carefully in advance, whether it be a one-day or a one-month long excursion. I usually try to visit a museum or private collection first in order to study the materials I hope to find. If your trip is to be a long one, here are other sources which will help you plan:

1. The state chamber of commerce or tourist bureau of the state you plan to visit.

2. The state geologist or geological survey of the states on your itinerary. The state

publicity director also may have information for you.

3. The department of mines of the state, or the college of mines or mining engineering. This address may be obtained from the Department of Education at the state capitol.

4. The U. S. Geological Survey, Washington 25, D. C., has publications about many areas, as well as detailed quadrangle maps of each state. Index maps are free.

5. In many areas, the highway department can give you information about new road cuts, active gravel quarries, proposed construction, etc.

6. Most towns or cities in a good mineral or gem area will have someone at the chamber of commerce who can put you in touch with local dealers or collectors. Read the hobby magazine ads for names of dealers in the places you will visit.

7. Chances are that someone else from your home town has made a trip similar to the one you plan. To find out, get in touch with your nearest rock club. If you are a newcomer to the hobby, you may not know that there are over 600 rock clubs in the United States affiliated with regional federations and the American Federation of Mineralogical Societies. There probably is a club near you. Most metropolitan areas have gem or rock shops or lapidary equipment dealers who can put you in touch with local clubs or collectors. Consult the yellow pages of your phone book for dealers.

8. The many excellent field guides and rock hobby magazines are full of accurate information about many areas. Study all issues for possible help.

9. Get county maps if available, or Geological Survey Quadrangle maps. I find the **Rand McNally Road Atlas** of 1959 indispensable. Why 1959? Because the newer editions show fewer of the small towns, minor creeks, and country roads a collector is interested in. The oil company maps are a big help. I get lots more clues by getting maps from several different companies, as different maps include different details.

Where I have given exact directions to a spot on private property does not automatically give collectors the right to enter. Considerable instruction has been written about how to get in. Bearing gifts or silver offerings are accepted methods, but the best way is to think a little more of the people involved and a little less of the rocks. If you genuinely like people and are friendly, thoughtful, and honest, you will seldom have trouble convincing property owners that you can be trusted.

The author examines a pile of Pierre shale concretions.

More and more areas are open on a fee basis. Often, nearby clubs have special arrangements at local collecting localities. In some places guides are available with four-wheel drive vehicles, canoes, horses, or whatever transportation is best.

In describing the huge, twelve-state area, I have taken each state separately and started with the northwest corner and worked down to the southeast corner. Wherever feasible, I have given gems of each section first, followed by minerals and fossils. However, each section does not always have collectable amounts of every category.

Where exhausted or closed localities have been particularly famous, I have described them, knowing that new discoveries often turn up in old areas and closed places sometimes open suddenly.

Rock collectors have an obligation to science. The sciences of geology, paleontology, paleobotany, and mineralogy are comparatively new. Every collector should be well informed on aspects of the hobby other than his own pet interest, because any field trip may turn up a new species of fossil, a new mineral, a new meteorite — something to add to our knowledge of this earth. It is up to us to be alert enough not to step over such things.

As I said before, I've tied down no rocks for you. If I knew exactly where a big Fairburn or rare cycad was, I'd be out there loading it up right now. I've tried to give you the best localities and tips that I know, and I am sure if you follow much of this book, you will have more rocks than you know what to do with.

SOUTH DAKOTA

New Finds

Since South Dakota is at the extreme western border of the Midwest, it combines elements of the mountains and the deserts with the prairies, the plains, and the woods. These natural advantages make it the most important state mineralogically in this region. The Black Hills and the Badlands, particularly, are so covered with interesting rock deposits and outcrops that hundreds of tourists each year are inspired to become collectors.

For the past few years there have been rumors of fabulous new agate beds in the Hills where you could dig for and find in profusion South Dakota's most colorful agates, the Fairburns. The rare and beautiful Fairburn agate has been found in badland areas for many years, while in the Black Hills a similar agate called Park agate has been found. Near Custer is a deposit of agate nodules in limestone, called Tepee Canyon agate, which also has many of the characteristics of Fairburns. Collectors theorized that there must be some relationship somewhere in these similarly colored fortification agates in such proximity. Could the Fairburns have weathered out of a formation like the Tepee agate or Park agate?

Fairburn Type Agate

Rumors persisted of 40 to 100 pounds of Fairburns dug in a day. Occasionally I saw a large, beautiful specimen of highly polished agate. It was shown to me as a Fairburn, and since there is a wide variation in Fairburn types, I had no reason to doubt this nomenclature.

Then one day I saw a box of maybe a hundred pounds of bright, tumbled, fortification agate. Many of the larger ones (up to 3 x 4 inches) if examined separately would pass for top quality Fairburns. On the whole, though, there was too much similarity, the bands were too fine, too uniform, for these agates to be true Fairburns.

Then the whole story came out. This box of agates and many more were part of the results of one day's bulldozing in a rocky pine-clad area not far from Wind Cave Park. Some of the agates were huge in size when first found, but with most there was a lot of grey matrix. The agates did not occur as nodules in limestone as do the Tepee Canyon agates. Rather, they were of assorted sizes and shapes often attached to a limestone layer and sometimes coated with white lime. Once freed of their matrix, these agates contain intricate bands of spectacular reds, pinks, and blues. They have some clear bands, some quartz centers. In short, most of the characteristics of true Fairburns are present.

These agates are obviously a step closer to Fairburns than the Tepee Canyon agate. They seem to furnish further evidence that Fairburns found in alluvial deposits have come from a similar formation not far from this area. Some of these agates are equal to good Fairburns and some can be classed with lower grade Fairburns. To distinguish these agates from other types found in South Dakota, I have named them "Fairhills agates" for the Fairburns they resemble, and the Black Hills which are their home.

I hope that some rancher in the area with a bulldozer will open his land to collectors on a fee basis. In the meantime, the best way to find this agate is to follow side roads between Hot Springs and Custer and walk along various limestone ridges in hopes of spotting an outcrop. I am sure literally thousands of acres of the Hills are underlain with brilliant fortification agate, but right now it takes a bit of luck as well as persistence to get some. Agate outcrops extend from near Buffalo Gap to the Wyoming border. The best are between Pringle and Minnekahta.

Blue Chalcedony

Blue chalcedony is another South Dakota gem almost unknown a few years ago. There are miles and miles of chalcedony of all colors and qualities in the Badlands near Scenic. The late Tom Friet of Scenic told us years ago that there was some chalcedony near Rockyford which was a light sky-blue. He laughed at the fact that some collector from the East had shipped home a ton of it. Once in a while in the high mesa region of Red Shirt Table we saw some chalcedony of good quality and desirable color which was almost blue. Then a few years ago Mr. Krueger of Cedar Pass began to advertise a true blue chalcedony from the Badlands. We saw some of this material in the rough as well as cut and polished. There was no doubt about it, the color was blue.

The area given here is the easiest to get to with a car. However, like the agate, there are vast areas of the blue chalcedony. It is interesting to note that the bluest seems to be the veins associated with an almost white

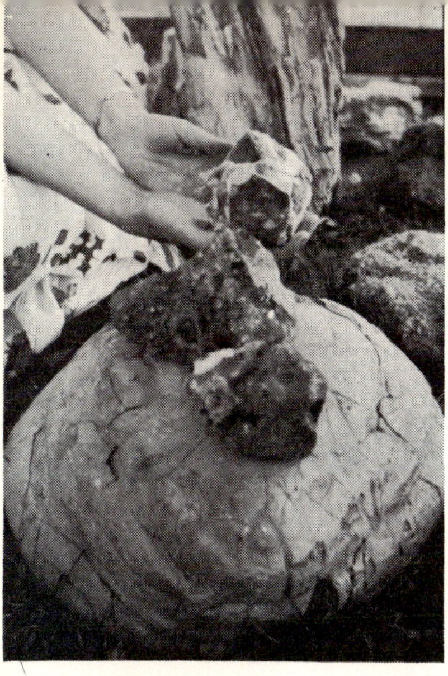

A Pierre shale concretion.

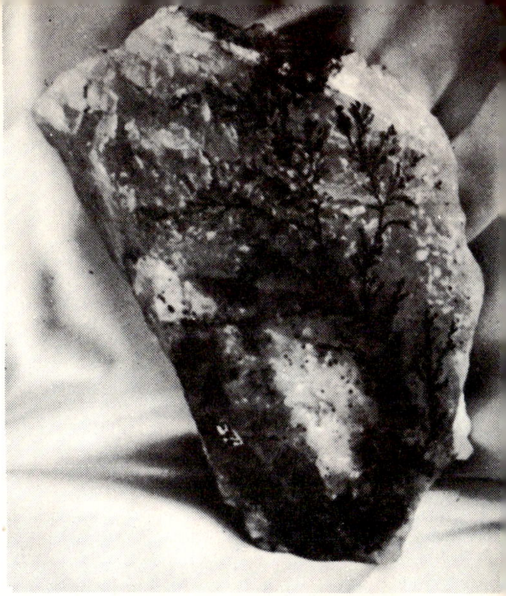

South Dakota's rose quartz sometimes has delicate dendrites.

Pale yellow and green, opaque beryl is often found in large crystals in South Dakota's pegmatites. When cut or tumbled it often has a pleasing chatoyancy. Photo — South Dakota School of Mines.

clay. Also, the chalcedony you dig for, while fracture free, is not quite as blue as the surface material.

There is a layered pink and blue chalcedony present, also, which is very attractive when cut cleverly. Occasionally you will find a piece of blue chalcedony with a red fortification pattern in it. Most of this chalcedony is highly fluorescent.

Leave Highway 18 at Batesland and follow the gravel and dirt trail through Wounded Knee, site of the last Indian battle in the United States, and continue a total distance of 42 miles where you cross the White River. From this point on, the blue chalcedony beds are in the badlands breaks to the west. From the road the chalcedony deposits may be spotted a long distance off as grey white areas on otherwise tan and yellowish soil. After crossing the river, continue north until you spot a likely bed and **get permission to enter. This is all private ranch land and is fenced.**

Incidentally, most tourists who wish to see the Badlands, take U. S. Route 16 through the National Park, but to me the untouched badlands along this remote road and the even more spectacular ones on the parallel rock route north of Oglala from No. 18 are far more intriguing. These badlands areas north of U. S. 18 are mostly unexplored by rock collectors. No find from this bizarre land would surprise me.

Tourmaline

Watermelon tourmaline is found in Maine, California, and Brazil. Why not in South Dakota? I wondered. We have visited the pegmatites of Maine and found such similar material that we could only hope in time someone would discover watermelon tourmaline in our State. Then, in 1958, in the Dixie Mine near Custer where miners were recovering spar and mica, a fortunate blast opened up a small cavity lined with real watermelon tourmaline crystals, juicy pink in the center, shiny green for the rind. The miners collected all that were in this pocket, possibly a hundred pieces. Unfortunately, the crystals were fractured by the blasting. Although no more have turned up to date, many mines are not operating, and I am confident that more of this fine tourmaline awaits determined collectors.

Selenite

Winged selenite roses are a new discovery from eastern South Dakota. You will notice on the map that the Missouri River bisects South Dakota. As you travel through the State, you will see that this division is even more definite than the map suggests. The western side of the Missouri is rolling ranch land, flat-topped mesas, cedar draws, pine canyons, eroded badlands, majestic mountains. The area east of the Missouri is mostly flat farm lands dotted with lakes. In recent years the old lake beds have produced some of the most unusual as well as most perfect selenite roses ever found. These roses have come from road cuts near Wagner and Scotland, from river banks, and from such excavation projects as digging basements or stock dams, particularly in the Armour-Corsica area.

Four miles west of Yankton, on the Gavin's Point road, on your right you will see an abandoned brickyard. In the clay pits of this yard are selenite crystals and roses.

Again, I am sure most of this entire region is underlain with these fantastic selenites but it takes a lot of digging and an alert collector to recover them. The best place was a stock dam near Corsica. I am sorry to say it is completely full of water so that collecting is impossible there.

The well formed roses are honey-colored, transparent, and have one or more large terminated blades which remind one of wings. If you find a road cut where there has been digging, look for evidence of broken selenite. Then with a tilling spade dig straight down and you will hit something hard. Carefully lift out the shovelful of dirt and you will see one or more roses in it. The best kind of soil in which to find good roses is very sticky, black gumbo.

New Discoveries

Tiny crystals of emerald green beryl have been found in an outcrop near Mount Rushmore. Just specimen material so far, it is likely that larger crystals will be uncovered with the development of new mines in the area.

Chuck Hull of Rockerville showed us some lively smoky quartz crystals newly discovered in the western Hills. They are of the black variety called **morion.** Chuck also reports that chert and jasper nodules locally called "Black Hills thundereggs," may be found in many canyons in Pennington County.

HOT SPRINGS AREA

Mines in the Hot Springs vicinity are producing rich uranium ore (carnotite). The mines of the Custer and Keystone areas are rich in lithium, a vital strategic mineral, as well as beryl, mica, spar, and tungsten, and also have most of the tin reserves of the United States. In Lead is the Homestake, the largest gold mine in the western hemisphere. In Belle Fourche is a booming bentonite enterprise, yet the entire distance from Hot Springs to Belle Fourche is less than 125 miles.

One of the most interesting things in the Hot Springs area is tufa, commonly called "petrified moss." This natural oddity is found in the banks and beneath the waters of the Cascade and Fall Rivers.

Stop at a rock shop — there are many in and around Hot Springs — and examine a piece of this moss turned to stone. Calcite, or sometimes silica, is deposited by the hot mineral waters on algae, moss, twigs, and other plant life in the stream. The formation builds up much as a lime deposit gradually accumulates in the bottom of a teakettle.

Of course the moss disintegrates, but its external coat of durable mineral remains, often preserving minute details of the pattern of the plants over which it formed.

Several types of the moss are found. The best and rarest is the "fern" moss. Others are the medium coarse "reed" and "water cress" varieties and the coarse "twig" or "cattail" varieties.

If you would like to try to dig out a piece for yourself, take a good pick, hammer, chisel, and some burlap in which to wrap your specimen.

Follow Highway 89 south of Hot Springs about 7 miles. You will pass on your left the ghost town of Cascade, once a fashionable spa. When you pass the empty stone buildings you will notice Cascade Creek to the right of the highway. Soon you will see an old picnic ground by the river. Park your car there, follow the stream, watching the banks. You will soon find some moss that appeals to you.

Another good area is along Fall River on U. S. 18 east of Hot Springs about 3 miles. If you don't want to bother to dig it out, there are several places which sell it reasonably. About 2 miles out you will notice one house on the farther bank of the river. It is the Haley home. Eve Muchow, a landscape gardener, designed and built the most beautiful fireplace in this house that you can imagine, entirely of tufa.

When you come to the first bridge east of Hot Springs, find a place to park and take some pictures of the great rock deposits of the old falls area. You will find tufa and travertine here as you leisurely explore the smooth, worn terraces.

Rockhounds are not always lucky. Sometimes one has to make many trips to find a good specimen.

Our luck is about average. However, the first and only time we went after tufa, we had such exceptional luck we have never dared to tempt fate again. We simply drove our pickup to a spot along Fall River, got out our tools, and started digging. The piece we dug up was fine lifelike "fern" moss, with every bit of the detail of the lacy fern perfectly preserved. Never before or since have we seen a piece quite like it.

Cycad

If you refer to your map you will see west of Hot Springs the words, "Cycad National Monument." These are as meaningless words as ever appeared on a map! The barn was locked after the horse was stolen. Few natives and fewer tourists know anything about cycads, but at one time this part of our State was a forest of this earliest form of flowering plant life.

We are often asked what there is to see at Cycad National Monument. The answer is, nothing! There is no sign, no "monument," no museum, no buildings and certainly no cycads — not even a picture of one. The land is all under lease to private individuals as grazing land.

Though much of the area is now densely covered with ponderosa pine, it was in a balmy, tropical climate similar to that of Florida that the cycads grew. Indeed, relatives of the cycad ornament beautiful parks in Florida today.

There were several species of cycads but the most common one preserved in this region resembled a pineapple in shape, though several times as large, as a rule. Out of the pineapple-shaped trunk at the top grew long fernlike fronds. The bark was irregular with the scars of fronds of previous years just as you see on many palm trees where the old leaves have dropped off.

The cycads found in South Dakota are highly agatized. Some have been preserved so completely that buds, crowns, and fruit development can be observed plainly. None has been found yet with the imprint of a dinosaur's teeth but since these ancient reptiles and plants were contemporary and many dinosaurs were herbivorous, such a specimen is not impossible.

Over one thousand completely fossilized cycads have been taken from the National Monument and surrounding area. During the W.P.A. and C.C.C. days, the Monument area was thoroughly combed for cycads. It has been reported to me many times that a large eastern university has more than 300 of the best specimens.

It is prohibited to hunt for cycads in the Monument but even if it weren't, your chances of finding one would be almost nil.

The wonderful petrified forests of Arizona were preserved before it was too late, but as far as I can find out, in owning the Cycad National Monument the public owns only another tract of fairly scenic land.

Don't go away, though. There are still cycads to be found and places where you can look for them to your heart's content.

Here is what we think is the best locality, but it isn't the only one. Cycads have been found on the Wyoming side of the Hills and as far away as the Badlands.

A word of warning to the novice: The roads in this region are rugged to non-existent, and the cycads are not grouped in plain sight waiting to be picked up. Of course such words only serve to spur a real rockhound.

Follow U. S. 18 west of Hot Springs to the railroad siding of Minnekahta. This is 12 miles from the city limits. The long, high tablelike mountain to your left is Parker Peak. Take the Forest Service trail through the farmyard on your left. This trail leads to the top of the mountain where the road splits. The right fork goes to the ranger station. You take the other fork.

One woman who got the directions from a friend in Hot Springs, thought she was supposed to turn toward the ranger station. Almost beside the station she picked up the best cycad to leave the Peak that summer. So if you can't follow my directions, it may be to your advantage.

We follow the main trail as long as it is navigable. This leads past a dam and through three gates. There is one trail branching to the left. Don't take it! Later you will see a short trail to a farmhouse. Don't take that, either. When the trail comes to a large open flat area after you have gone through the third gate, you will wonder whether your car will make the abrupt turn to the right and the steep rocky hill. Well, don't try it. We don't any more. Park on the inviting piny flat and get out your equipment.

Better have plenty of water. The elevation is high, and you will tire faster than you expected.

Cycads are found generally near other petrified wood. There is much petrified wood to be found on and around Parker Peak. The low hills to your right are liberally strewn with fossil palm wood.

Sometimes cycads are found barely sticking above the surface. Sometimes they are found on the slope of the Peak and sometimes they have eroded out and are found at the foot of the Peak on the opposite side from the highway. From any high point you can see the highway to the north looking like a comfortable reminder of civilization, and surprisingly close, since it took you well over an hour to get to your "lookout."

Don't neglect lichen-covered rocks or an area which seems to be just a lot of hunks of limestone. A cycad can be sitting anywhere, under any guise. If you find one, you will know it. If you wonder whether what you see is one or not, it isn't. They are entirely different from any other stone. Almost always well shaped and symmetrical, they are also very hard and heavy. The lime and sandstone of the mountain are soft.

Charlie Frank of the Forest Service was working on a Forest Service dam on Parker Peak. He and his co-workers had a favorite spot where they stopped for midday lunch. In the shade of some pine trees was a convenient circle of stones, each big enough for a man to spread out his lunch and have a comfortable seat. One noon Charlie happened to glance at the base of his "stool," and was struck by the grace of its line, the uniformity of its tapering curves. Quickly he glanced at the rest of the "lunch room."

Sure enough, every "stone" in the group was a splendid cycad! These men had been eating their lunches on seats so valuable that the most expensive seat in the richest of night clubs would be a wooden bench in comparison.

Cycad as a gem material is a beautiful beige or amber color with various shades of rich brown markings. A clear, diamond-shaped pattern is one of its characteristics. Not all cycad is suitable for gems, however, and even if a large one of solid gem material is found, it is far more valuable as a specimen than cut up for gems.

We did find one cycad in all these years. That is, my husband, Albert, did. Before World War II he and John Covey took the truck and drove to Parker Peak to find a cycad for our museum.

After scouring the mountain for two days in nearly 100-degree heat, Albert decided to try the foot of the mountain instead of the top. This, too, was unproductive so he started to short-cut to the top, through a patch of wild plum briar, instead of around it where the path was. Right in the middle of the plum brush was a cycad. Not a little one either, a veritable giant of a specimen with several beautiful buds.

Finding a cycad is simply the first step

of a chain of events. The specimen Albert stared at in grateful bewilderment weighed at least 300 pounds. The pickup was on top of the mountain a steep 1,000 feet or more, and there is no road to the valley. You can hardly roll such a specimen up a rocky hillside.

Albert called Johnny and it was soon apparent that the two men could not budge the huge cycad. Then they saw that there was a fracture of considerable size toward the top where the best of the buds were clustered. They decided to take this part of the cycad and return in another week with proper equipment to get the rest.

The piece broke off cleanly and weighed about 70 pounds. They placed it on a length of heavy burlap and each took an end.

It was almost dark when the cycad section was loaded into the truck. Both men were exhausted but due to go to work the next day about 200 miles away. So they kept moving.

All this happened the summer of 1940. John was in the R.O.T.C. and was summoned to active duty. Albert felt sure that by the next summer he would find someone to go with him for the rest of the cycad. The remainder was well hidden by branches and weeds plus a few rocks that the two had rolled around it.

Hundreds of collectors have asked me why I never finished the story of the lost cycad. It is one of those sad tales without an end. As you know, the war started in 1941 and no gas was allotted to cycad hunters. After the "duration" we eagerly returned to the site of the cycad only to find the area changed beyond recognition. We have combed the locality many times in vain. To be sure, we have since acquired a couple of other cycads, but none as marvelous as the one still beckoning us to the Hills.

Sand Barite

Everett Hill of Cascade, on his ranch on Highway 87 southwest of Hot Springs, thought he had discovered a new locality of sand calcite crystals. After members of the Hot Springs Mineral Club and the Rapid City School of Mines staff examined this new find, it was determined that the deposit was not sand calcite but sand barite. Some of the pieces I looked at had diamond-shaped crystals. Other specimens were more like the barite roses of Kansas. I mention the Kansas roses rather than the Oklahoma variety because the South Dakota ones are beige white like some from Kansas, instead of red like those in Oklahoma. Also, the Oklahoma roses have sharper details than any Kansas or Dakota specimens so far. There are singles, twinned crystals, groups, plus all sorts of clusters. Massive barite is also present on this property.

ARDMORE AGATE BEDS

One of the best one-day field trips in the Hot Springs district is to the rock deposits near the town of Ardmore. These rock beds are often referred to as the "Nebraska beds." Some of the deposits are on the state line and some stretch a few miles into Nebraska.

Follow State Highway 87 south of Hot Springs to the town of Ardmore, a distance of 33 miles. From here there are several ways to get to the rocks.

While it is always tempting to be the first to examine the newly washed stones after a rain, we no longer hunt in this area if the roads are wet. Once we got stuck in the gumbo and had a tractor pull us out.

If the roads are dry the easiest way to reach your destination is to follow the country road east of Ardmore for seven miles. You will come to a ranch on the south side of the road, owned by a man named Flemming who is interested in rocks and will tell you how to get to the badland breaks you are seeking. The trail leads south and east for several miles across his land, and due to erosion the trail is not always in the same place.

You will see groups of these jagged rocky breaks stretching for miles, and one place is as likely as the next to yield a good crop of gems.

The first time we hunted the Nebraska beds we were with our friends, Lou Miller and Frank Soresnsen of Hot Springs. Lou had the Agate-Wood Shop, and Frank has the Agate Court. Louis said he was a "grass hunter" — that is, he found most of his agates in the grassy edges around the rock beds. I tried this system and had the best luck I have ever had agate hunting. I picked up two large agates and eight small ones that day.

The agates are the brightly colored fortification agates known everywhere as Fairburns. However, anyone who has handled many Fairburns usually subdivides the agates according to area. The agates from the Nebraska area seem to tend to a brown matrix which is often soft and badly fractured. The agates from the Oelrichs area are often black and white. The agates from Fairburn are often brighter in color and have less matrix. However, there are no hard and fast rules. We have seen black and white ones from Fairburn, brightly colored, matrix-free ones from Oelrichs, and agates without a trace of brown from the Ardmore or Nebraska location.

I was so thrilled with my first day in the Ardmore breaks that I told Albert we should take our trailer to the spot and camp for the summer. Albert was less enthusiastic. Hours of careful searching had yielded him exactly nothing. I did manage to get him to take me back to the area three more times but in all of those times he never found one, and I found only one more small one.

The agatized wood of this area is very acceptable cutting material. Lou Miller has some polished pieces of wood from this region which holds its own with wood from anywhere.

You will also see beautiful cherry-red, lavender, yellow and even rare green jasper. Much of the jasper is black on the outside, and when chipped reveals striking color combinations inside. There is also a clear chalcedony with black markings, which makes fine tumbled stones or cabochons similar to moss agate.

The waterworn nodules of rose and white quartz are of superior color. Occasionally you will find a piece of pudding stone or conglomerate with many colors of jasper pebbles connected together by quartz. This is a surprisingly different cutting material.

If you have never hunted for agates, you will wonder how to be sure that you have one. Almost every Fairburn has a definite pattern plainly visible on some part of the exterior. If you see any hint of a pattern, do not use your hammer. The value of a whole Fairburn type agate from any one of these localities ranges from $5 to $200 but will be considerably less if the specimen is broken or chipped.

I know of only one good Fairburn which showed no pattern at all on the outside. That was found by MacFaddin of Custer, and was an almost spherical black rock.

OELRICHS AGATE BED

There is a delightful rumor that somewhere in the Oelrichs area is a basement full of Fairburn agates. Of course such a treasure trove would be like finding a gold or uranium mine. The story goes that after years of hard luck, the family who had collected these agates moved to California, leaving the agates stacked in boxes in the basement. Whether the house is still there is a question, but undoubtedly the basement is — if it ever was!

There is a persistent theory that somewhere in this sparsely settled part of western South Dakota there are virgin agate beds so remote that they have never been seen by white man. There is talk — the wishful thinking variety — of finding a spot where big perfect masterpieces of banded agate are waiting to be picked up by the bushel, like the "old days" at Fairburn.

So regularly each fall or winter we hunt this entire area. No, it isn't our hopes that keep us warm, either. Summer visitors like to imagine that to compensate for being surrounded by so much beauty in the summer, we huddle by our stoves all winter waiting for spring to open our snowbound roads.

Most of our winter is mild, and the roads always open. Part of each winter month is warm enough to melt what little snow we get. The winter months provide ideal hunting for us. It's my guess that native South Dakotans do most of their productive agate hunting in the winter. For one thing, with the ground frozen you can drive places that are often impassable in the spring or summer, and more important, the grass and weeds are down so you can hunt areas that are overgrown in the warmer seasons.

The town of Oelrichs lies just south of a new section of Highway 18. Starting at the intersection of 18 and the road leading into town, here are the directions to a few rock spots.

One mile east is a side road which leads south toward the nearby buttes and others farther on. There is no gate in the fence here, so you will have to park and walk.

One and a half miles east is another place you can stop and walk over to the large landmark buttes a few hundred yards south.

The new highway cuts through a badlands area 7.4 miles east of the Oelrichs junction. Most of the rock is widely scattered in the eroded areas adjoining the highway to the north.

Nine miles east of Oelrichs is a stock dam in a ranch field on the south side of the road. There is a gate near the dam. A ranch trail through this pasture leads south to numerous breaks well covered with rocks.

Another small section of badlands is bisected by U. S. 18 at 18.4 miles from the starting junction. Here again the best hunting is on the north. Albert picked up a dandy black and white Fairburn here. It was only a few feet off the road.

The largest and most important of the Oelrichs bed, however, is not on Highway 18. To find this excellent agate locality go south through the town of Oelrichs and turn east on the first country road. Drive east one mile, then turn south two miles. You will pass an old rural school on this stretch. At two miles you will see a large farm to your right and the road turns sharply east again here. Follow this winding trail east 4 miles. You will have to be careful of washouts and particularly the rickety bridge. Incidentally, a collector from Illinois found a splendid big Fairburn right beside the bridge when she and her husband stopped to inspect it.

After 4 miles the trail grows dimmer and soon the main trail makes a sharp turn south again. This time you do not take the south turn. Look instead for the faint tracks leading north. Take this north route which roams over the pasture following a fire break and heads one and a half miles northwest to the gigantic alluvial rock beds of this badlands area.

You can find virtually any quartz family gem in this area, plus interesting fossils. Two types of jasp-agate found in these rock fields are often confused with Fairburns by the uninitiated. These are locally called "water agates" and "prairie agates." Both are very different from Fairburns to the experienced collector. They are colorful and seem to have wavy lines and swirling patterns. But the pattern of a Fairburn is intricate, bold, precise. A prairie agate's patterns may appear almost symmetrical, almost parallel. The symmetry of a Fairburn's parallel bands does not have to be imagined. These patterns are very definite. The contrasting bands in sharp hollylike fortifications, the distinct alternating colors, should leave no doubt of the identity of a Fairburn. If you wonder whether it is or not, my guess is that it isn't.

The water agates run mostly to yellows, browns, blacks, and whites, while the prairie agates are in wild gypsy colors. Both cut and polish well and as the true Fairburns are being depleted, the substitutes are gaining in popularity.

First-grade wood and rare exotic fossil plants are also present in these fields. There are concretions, cone-in-cone calcite, and fluorescent specimens just for variety. When you get tired of walking here, sit down in the middle of a tempting rock pile and start turning them over one by one. I have found several Fairburns this way, as well as a piece of cycad.

THE CUSTER AREA

From Hot Springs to Custer is an easy 30 miles. Soon after you leave Hot Springs you will no longer see the red coloration in the Hills. This attractive red area is known as the Red Valley and entirely surrounds the Hills.

Wherever you enter the Black Hills you will see first the outer wall of Hogbacks, then the Red Valley, then the Limestone Plateau, and near the heart of the Hills the true mountain or crystalline area.

The limestone plateau area is the home of many beautiful, famous caves. The largest and best known is Wind Cave National Park nine miles north of Hot Springs. This is one of the largest caves in the United States. It has never been fully explored, although about twelve miles of passages have been mapped. There is a well lighted guided tour through the most interesting part of the cave which is worth the time of anyone interested in geology.

The largest room covers several acres. The most famous formation in the cave is the boxwork, best seen in the section dubbed the "Post Office." These well formed aragonite boxes have calcite foundations. They are of varying tints and textures. Some look like chenille or candlewick, some like tiny bunches of raisins, some like delicate frost formations.

The cave is mostly dormant and does not contain the beautiful sparkling crystals many of the Hills caves have.

The strong drafts which give Wind Cave its name are probably due to a higher opening somewhere in the Cave. Cool air will settle and a system of circulation comes about which blows cold air out of the Cave when the weather is warmer outside, and warm air if the outside air is cooler.

Many caves in the limestone plateau have not been explored, and only a handful has been developed. Onyx Cave three miles southwest of Wind Cave is not open to the public and we have never visited it. However, we have found some beautiful chalcedony in the adjoining area. This chalcedony is of a bluish color and often has lacy patterns.

Custer lies in the mountainous crystalline part of the Hills. It is surrounded by granite peaks which house the pegmatites where the rich mineral and gem veins are found.

The past of this interesting mountain town is steeped in gold. Gold was first discovered in French Creek just east of Custer in 1874. Rumors of gold in those days traveled fast even without radio, and it wasn't long until this Sioux Indian country was swarming with so many prospectors that the United States ordered General Crook to remove these miners from the Hills by

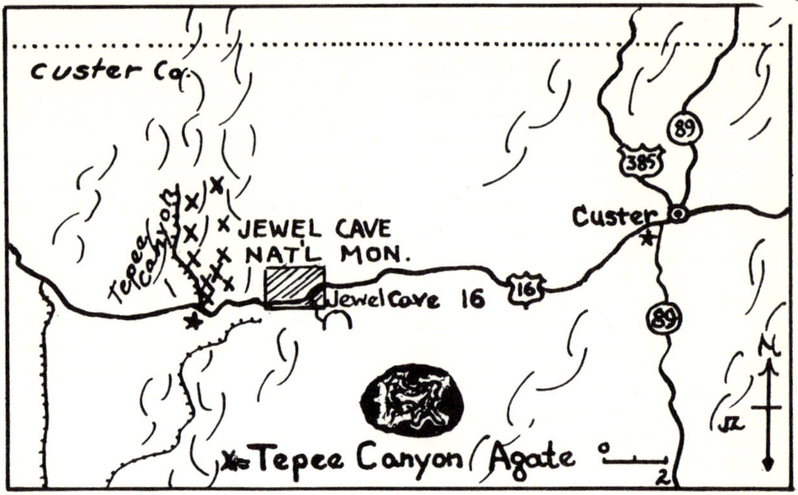

force in order to prevent an Indian war.

In 1876, a new treaty was negotiated with the Indians, and the miners were back thicker than ever willing to take their chances.

Even to this day the yellow metal is sought and found in the Hills. Gold-bearing sands underlie much of the town of Custer. In many places nearby, the old method of panning will show "color."

It is feldspar, not gold, that has made Custer a mining town. Each year around 50,000 tons of spar are mined in this area. One spar processing mill is on the edge of Custer. Lighted up like a skyscraper at night, it is a symbol of an enterprise which is vital to modern industry.

There are gems in the spar family, such as the turquoise-colored amazonite of Colorado and Virginia. However, the Black Hills spar tends more to the rose and reds, and although it tumbles well, cannot properly be called a gem.

The gems we went to search for in the Custer vicinity are almandite garnets, Hells Canyon agate, Park agate, beryl, lepidolite, staurolite, tourmaline, and the famous South Dakota rose quartz.

Perhaps the first thing you will want to do is acquaint yourself with the minerals of the area by visiting some of the rock shops.

You will find the owners of most of the Black Hills rock and mineral shops friendly and cooperative.

Albert and I were driven away from one location in the Hills (where we were only taking pictures) by an irate rock shop man who cursed loudly and long about "rockhounds taking everything out of South Dakota."

We're thankful to say that most of the rock men in the Hills agree with the dealer who told us, "After all, our business depends on people being interested in rocks."

Tepee Canyon Agate

Bright and early the first pine-scented morning in Custer we started for Tepee Canyon where the agate formerly called "Hells Canyon" agate is found.

Don't be confused; no matter which term is used you will recognize the agate as a jasp-agate embedded in limestone.

On your way to the location west of Custer on U. S. 16, you will pass Jewel Cave which is also operated by the National Park Service. If you have not seen one of the crystal caves of the Black Hills you will enjoy this one. There are shimmering miles of crystal-lined passages. Much beautiful material from this cave was taken out years ago for the noted Crystal Grotto of West Bend, Iowa.

Even if you aren't collecting rocks, this is a fascinating place to visit. It is part of the limestone area of the Hills. If you climb the hill and investigate the agate mines, you will see numerous hard, round concretions in the limestone. These concretions can be broken out whole.

Sometimes they will be solid jasper, sometimes they will have fanciful patterns of pinks, reds, yellows in measured concentric bands. If you are very lucky, you will find one like Chet Archer of Custer has, one of the most colorful agates in the world, a veritable Joseph's coat of the agate world.

Some of the prized specimens are lined with purple amethyst crystals.

Each nodule is different. You need heavy hammers and strong picks to work here.

Tepee at its best is very similar to Fairburn. One cannot help but wonder whether some such formation was not the original home of the Fairburns.

One night at Archers we tried a test, laying out pieces of South Dakota agates from many localities and trying to tell what distinguished each. Really, slabs of Nebraska agates with their brown matrix and Tepee with its brown matrix were all but identical. And many of the others could have been from one place as well as the next.

Tepee Canyon is 14 miles west of Custer on U. S. 16. The diggings are to your right or north of the highway. You can see the holes made by hand or blasting up toward the hilltop. An unimproved trail leads to the right. Turn along this trail to park. Other agate spots are scattered all along the Canyon. Tepee is a place where collectors must be extremely cautious. Do not dig in spots with an overhang above, or in places where the rock is loose.

The Black Hills area is noted for beautiful rose quartz. The best of the South Dakota quartz compares favorably in color with that of Brazil. However, much of it is fractured due to the fact that there is a large market for it as an ornamental stone, so it is blasted.

One of the well known rose quartz areas is the Scott Mine near Custer which is private property and closed to the public.

There are many spots in the Hills, though, where you are likely to run onto a vein of rose quartz. One of our favorite areas for rose quartz and other pegmatite minerals is the gravel road behind Mount Rushmore, which connects Alternate U. S. 16 with State 89. Tourmaline, mica, staurolite, garnet, spar, epidote, apatite, are other minerals you will find along this scenic byway.

Another rose quartz outcrop is east of Pringle on U. S. 385, a few yards off the road on the north side. The point is about halfway between Pringle and the Wind Cave Park boundary. A pegmatite showing rose quartz is near Highway 79 a few miles north of Custer.

Many times we are asked why rose quartz fades. We have boulders of South Dakota quartz which have been lying in our yard for 25 years and have not faded a bit. When you buy quartz, look it at in both sun and shade and remember that when you cut it for cabs, you will be working with thin pieces and so the color will seem less dense. Also, if you let a piece of quartz knock about for a few years, it may become more fractured. This, too, would give it the appearance of having faded.

Garnets

The best gem garnets are found seven miles west of Custer in an area known locally as Tin Mountain. The road you take is on the right (assuming that you are coming from Custer). There is a small government sign pointing to various ranches and ending with "Deer Camp – nine miles." You need only follow the trail about a quarter of a mile where the rocky uplift to your right becomes steeper and closer to your car.

You have your choice of hunting for the garnets in the old stream beds or climbing the rocks where there are liberal deposits of them.

There are several types of garnets found in the Hills. If you are new to the study of rocks, you will be surprised to learn that there are at least nine types of garnets. They are not all the same shape and the formulas are different. The range of color is from red to black, from clear to yellow, and even purple and green. However, garnets do have some family characteristics in common. They are all hard (about 7) and the crystals are isometric, mostly dodecahedrons, trapezohedrons, and combinations of the two forms.

The almandite garnets you find near Custer are red and contain iron, aluminum, and silica, the gem-forming mineral. The garnets are commonly found in metamorphic rocks such as mica schist. However, in this particular spot the biggest and best gem garnets are associated with quartz and perhaps a small amount of mica.

In the School of Mines Museum we had seen some big gem garnets from the Hills, and we had read of the thousands of beautiful gems recovered and cut by the Marion Company near Custer at the turn of the century. We had little hopes of finding any garnets big enough to cut.

Albert told me laughingly that he'd find me a garnet as big as the end of my little finger. I laughed, too. It was a good joke.

We scrambled among the steep rocks like goats and finally discovered that the garnets found with a sort of iron-stained quartz seemed not only slightly larger, but also had brighter faces.

In trying to climb a particularly steep rock Albert noticed a streak of mica under-

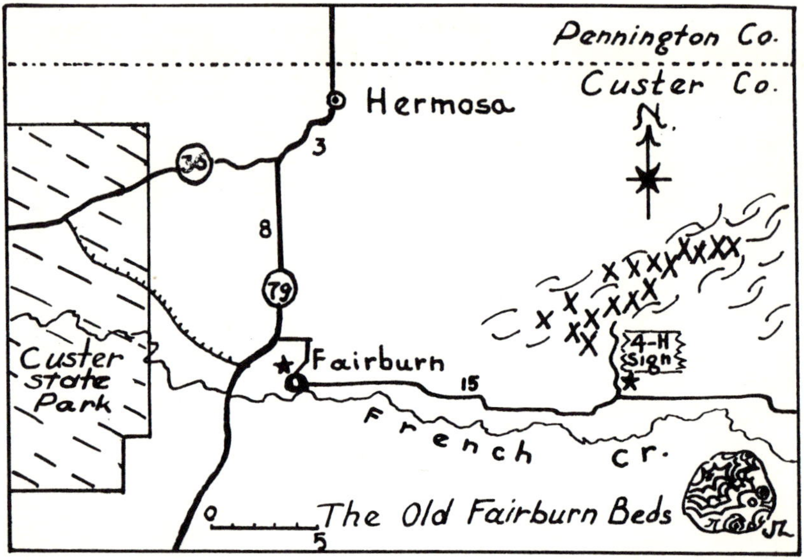

neath. Following this streak, he found several fine large garnets. The largest was not only bigger than the end of my little finger, but it was bigger than the end of my thumb!

The smaller garnets sticking out of their sparkling dark mica make attractive specimens. The larger ones because they are found partially embedded in the hard quartz are harder to get out whole or to take out with matrix all the way around.

Fairburn Agates

There is some question in my mind whether to include the original Fairburn agate location in the Custer or the Rapid City section. Actually, the distance from Custer to Fairburn is 36 miles and from Rapid City it is 32 miles. We always make Custer our headquarters when we go to Fairburn because we like the mountain scenery, the pine air, and the cool nights Custer has to offer. Since Rapid City is the natural gateway to much of the Badlands and all of the northern Black Hills, there will be plenty of places for that section.

An old tale tells of a wealthy agate fancier from the east who came to the Fairburn agate fields in the early days and hired children to mark off every bit of the land in foot squares with ropes. Then each child was paid to turn over each individual stone in a certain number of square feet. The collector was supposed to have taken in a haul of several bushels of agates.

It's a good story and I suppose I should go along with it. However, I doubt very much that it actually happened. In the first place, the Fairburn agate fields cover thousands of acres of very stony land. In the second place most of this land is straight up and down and well decorated with cactus, weeds, cedar trees and cow chips.

When Fairburns were discovered on the old Kern ranch near Fairburn, it was an easy matter to walk around in a fairly normal posture and spot a dozen or two brilliant beauties in a day. I don't think anyone ever scooped them up in truckloads.

Jack Zasadil of Hermosa, who had a splendid collection of Fairburns, recalls that the first time he went agate hunting. Grandma Kern chased him off with a shotgun. In late years Grandma was to become more cooperative. She was losing her sight and could not find the agates she had grown to love. So she followed agate hunters around in the fields, wearing a nail apron full of coins which she eagerly exchanged for agates.

It is said that one of the Kelloggs of Battle Creek, Michigan, offered her a real fortune in those days for her agates. There was nothing money could buy that she wanted more than she wanted her precious agates, so she turned down the offer.

When Grandma went blind many of her best gems were stolen so she eventually did sell what was left of her collection.

Jack Zasadil has a Fairburn which weighs over 25 pounds. How much over he does not know as that is the limit of his scales.

Fred Hammerquist of Rapid City had a

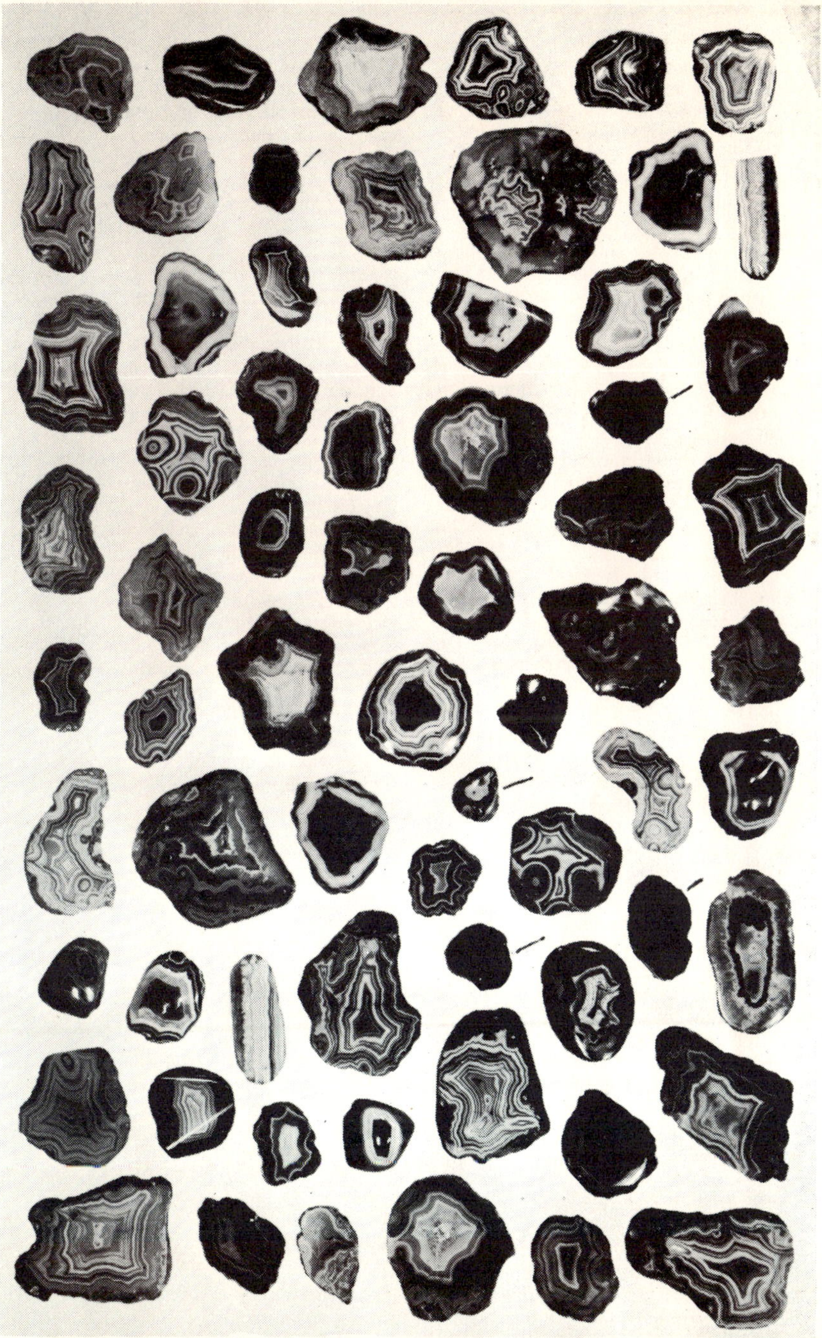

Varieties of South Dakota's famous Fairburn agate.

14-pound Fairburn, Niles of the Custer Cycad Shop a 12-pound one, and MacFaddin a 10-pound agate. Mrs. Harvey Schliep, Hot Springs, has a large beauty. Art Bunce and Lou Miller have some prizes. Of course there are probably many others of the big class I have not seen.

As in most gems, the big Fairburns are not always the best. The largest one I know of weighed nearly 40 pounds and was found by an Indian from Pine Ridge. Its fortifications were few and far between, and the agate was broken to see whether the pattern inside was larger. No such luck!

Some gem hunters have tried to invent drags to pull behind a Jeep to turn over the stones. This didn't work; both the ground and the sizes of the rocks were too uneven. One friend invented a sort of a sled on rollers, on which he intended to lie on his stomach and be pulled over the ground only inches away from the agates. This didn't work either.

The gates to the Kern beds are closed and padlocked. However, there is a way for agate hunters to get to the same rugged area the original Fairburns came from. Turn into the town of Fairburn from Highway 79. The principal route going east of town, French Creek Road, is the one to follow. This is a county-maintained dirt and gravel road. When you pass a sign on your right reading, "McDermond Ranch," you are nearing your turn-off. The turn-off is 15 miles from Fairburn and is on the left. There is a big sign which says, "4-H Wranglers Picnic Ground." Follow the trail through the picnic ground and drive north toward the badlands buttes as far as you can. This depends on trail conditions and weather, but when you cross the picnic grounds you are within easy walking distance of the eroded agate beds. You will find the agates scattered among the stone-covered hills. Every year finds are made in this old area. Look, too, for high quality red and yellow jasper and agatized wood, particularly palm.

In order to find a Fairburn you may have to slide onto a cactus as I did. You may wear holes in your jeans rubbing the dust off stones to look for signs of fortifications. You may stare holes through your glasses, too. You may let out a yelp at a discarded rattlesnake skin, and get lost in a ravine.

There's something about it all that makes a real rockhound consider this fun. He wouldn't work as hard for anyone for even the best wages, but to do it for fun—that's different. It's this willingness to keep trying that makes us feel companionable toward the old gold prospectors who opened up this country and most of the west for us.

Fairburns are constantly going up in price, so if you find one, hang onto it. It will draw good interest for you.

Perhaps you wonder what makes the Fairburn so important, and how it was formed.

A lot of agates on the market are dyed. They have bands of pleasing lines in grey, brown, black, white, and clear, and they are treated by chemicals and heat to give them color. But the coloring they are hoping to equal is that which nature has given the Fairburn. The true colors of the Fairburn can never be reproduced successfully by artificial means. A dyed agate may succeed in getting bands of pink alternating with bands of brown, but here are the colors, in order, of a Fairburn in front of me: brown, clear, pink, white, black, wine, pink, penline band of wine, pale blue band, raspberry-red — quite wide — white band set off by red, narrow black penline band outlining center which is yellow gold with a wine-colored triangle in the middle. Since these colors are produced by different means which often cancel one another, only nature can get them all together successfully.

There are many theories about how agates form. The chief mineral in their composition is the versatile silica which is responsible for all the varied quartz-family gems. You hear a lot these days about silicones being added to car polishes, dust cloths, furniture and floor finishes, glass cleaners, and many other things. Silica is also found in corn stalks and bamboo. It is used for abrasives, glass, castings, cement, plaster, water filtration. You can't get away from silica. It is everywhere, the most universal element.

The manner in which the Fairburns were formed may be that water carrying silica flowed in and out of small pockets in the earth or soft stone formations. Each time the waters left a small deposit of silica stained with minute amounts of different minerals. Finally, the entrance and exits were themselves plugged with silica and the agate was finished. This theory is called the duct theory and fits the Fairburns well as they all show these pipes or ducts quite clearly.

Another theory is that of silica gel which the German chemist, Liesegang, showed by laboratory experiments to be capable of producing most kinds of agate patterns. In this case the cavities would have held silica in a liquid state, and a dissolved metallic salt followed by an acid solution, which caused the liquid to turn to a solid.

So far I have mentioned the Fairburn beds of Oelrichs, Ardmore, and Fairburn. These are not the only places. Fairburns have been found near Crawford and Harrison, Neb., near Wasta and Scenic in the Badlands, in canyons almost on the Wyoming line, in hills on the Pine Ridge Indian Reservation, and in the beds of streams draining thousands of acres of hills, badlands, and prairies.

If you wish to look for a new area, there is much unexplored (from a rockhound's viewpoint) land in the north and west part of our state. These magnificent agates appear widely scattered.

Maybe I should add a word or two here about the clothes to take for rock hunting in South Dakota.

After years of begging on our part, our friends, Willard and Orla Olsen from Florida, finally came to South Dakota one spring to go rock hunting. They had sleet, rain, snow, and a dust storm all in one day.

We take the entire blame, though. That kind of weather greets us wherever we go. The weathermaker merely wanted to show that his greatest efforts went out to our friends, too.

In over a hundred thousand rocky miles, we have hit no spot where the weather wasn't, according to the natives, unusual. We willingly take the blame and are seriously considering hiring ourselves out to bring rain, snow, ice, or whatever else is in demand.

As a rule, if you are a summer visitor, you will find the weather hot and dry in the Badlands but comfortably cool in the mountains.

Many wear boots in the fields as a precaution against snakes. Boots are too hot and uncomfortable to suit me in the summer, and I happily wear soft-soled Indian moccasins. I have never seen a rattlesnake on any of our trips. As a matter of safety first, I never reach onto ledges I cannot see, and I don't walk places where I cannot see the ground.

A cool hat with a brim to protect your eyes is better than dark glasses. As it is very easy to get legs scratched up with cactus, weeds, and thistles, I usually wear lightweight slacks. A long-sleeved cool shirt will protect your arms from sunburn. You won't have to worry about mosquitoes. They don't like our rocks.

Take plenty of water, and even if it is 100 in the shade of the sagebrush, take sweaters along in the car. One never knows!

Pegmatite Minerals

The novice in the rock world will secretly wonder for some time just what a pegmatite is. The abandon with which rockologists throw the word around suggests that it is altogether too common to risk displaying one's ignorance by asking about it.

Pegmatite is a coarse granite occurring in the form of small or large dikes, and cooled slowly enough to form coarse crystals. If you are driving along a highway cut through the massive rocks of the Hills, you may notice that suddenly in the middle of an otherwise gray formation there will be a wide slanting streak of white quartz with black pencils of tourmaline. This is a pegmatite dike. Such dikes commonly hold large crystals of feldspar, beryl, mica, spodumene, topaz, garnet, and many other minerals and gems.

One of the minerals rockhounds learn to seek in pegmatites is tourmaline.

It is surprising to know that tourmaline, like garnet, is not one mineral but a family of minerals. Tourmaline has more variations in color than most gems. There are sparkling rose-red stones called **rubellite,** blue, called **indicolite,** and incredible numbers of red and green dubbed **watermelon tourmaline.** There are all tints of red, blue, green, plus black, brown and clear.

All tourmaline is hard and the chemical formula varies according to color, always containing silica and aluminum, with small amounts of iron, chromium, lithium, or magnesium. In many places in the Custer or Keystone area you will be able to collect tourmaline crystals. It is important in collecting crystals to find good terminations.

Black tourmaline is the easiest to find. Take the road back of Mount Rushmore, a gravel road connecting 16-A with 87. Almost any spot where the rock formations are near the road you can see the shiny black tourmaline sticking out of the white quartz.

In the mine dumps near Keystone you will find the blue and the red varieties. Good tourmaline may be found associated with the mica of the Hills, also. In the area around Harney Peak you will find some of the prized green tourmaline. Crystals of tourmaline up to a foot across have been found in this region, unfortunately badly shattered. Since tourmaline is so fine a gem, many pieces suitable for tumbling can be collected. Facet cutting quality is more valuable.

Permission should be sought before search-

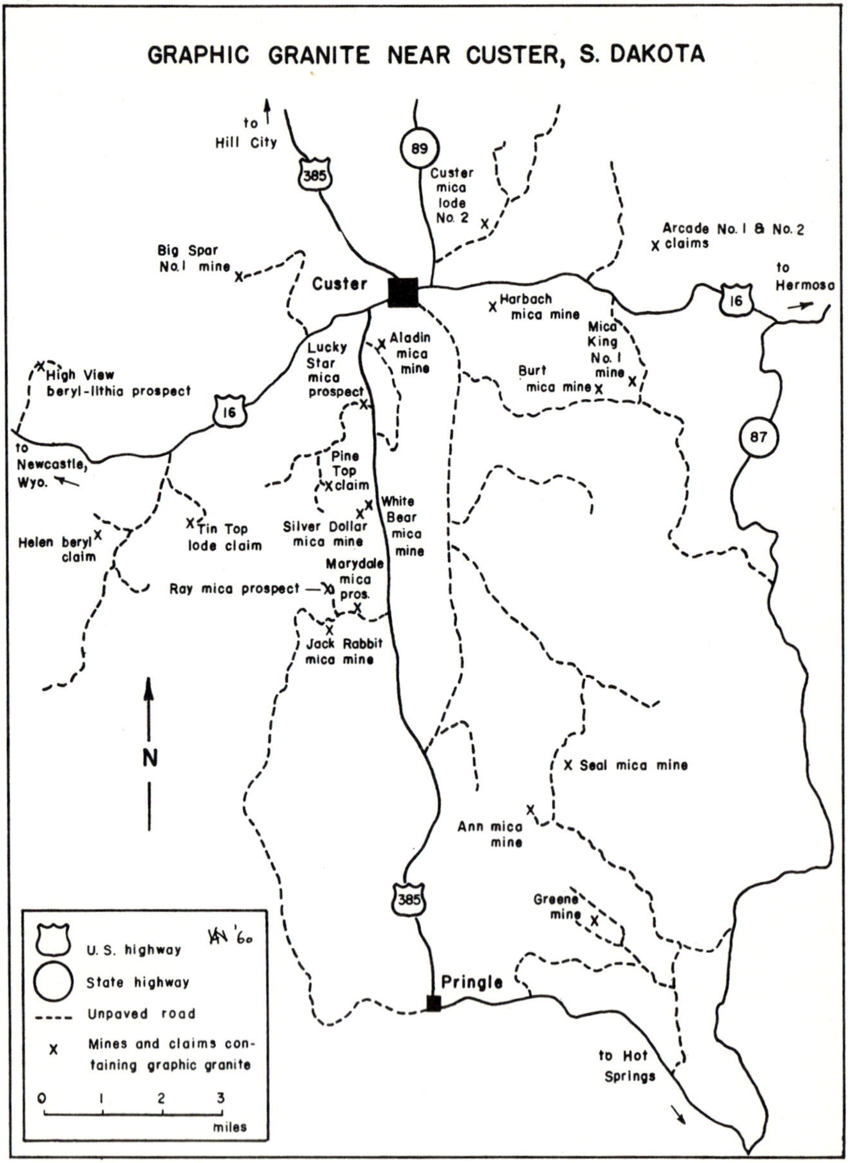

ing mine dumps. Some of the mines are still operating and often the operators themselves reprocess the dumps to retrieve certain minerals not previously considered desirable.

Beryl is another gem found in the Black Hills. Gems of the beryl family include the green emeralds, blue aquamarines, and lesser known stones of other colors.

Gem golden beryl (heliodor) has been found in several Hill mines.

There is also gem quality aquamarine beryl found in the Keystone pegmatites. We have a few specimens of the aquamarine in our museum in Mission, but potentially the finest we have seen was a sadly ruined specimen which had 36 perfect crystals of aquamarine standing in white quartz until someone got the idea of trying to dig them out—a priceless specimen completely ruined.

Green beryl suitable for tumbling may be found, but not the precious emeralds.

Apatite is another gem found near Keystone. It is an hexagonal blue crystal similar to beryl in appearance though usually smaller and always of inferior hardness.

One of the famous old mines of the Hills is the Etta. This is a lithium mine where spodumene crystals over 40 feet long have been found. One 36-foot crystal from this mine weighed over 50,000 pounds.

The gem kunzite of the spodumene family has been found in a limited quantity in the spodumene mines. There is perhaps more of it there than is recognized, as mine operators can seldom be bothered to search through large masses of ore for gem crystals of small size and thin distribution.

Pastel lavender lithium mica, or lepidolite, is found in the Etta Mine as well as the Bob Ingersol, another noted mine of the region. The Ingersol has produced some of the largest beryl crystals in the world. A ten-foot plank used as a scaffold barely covered the width of one.

The Ingersol Mine also has small amounts of gummite, autunite, uraninite, and other radioactive minerals.

Some zircons have been found in the Hills, notably in a district known as Nigger Hill, almost on the Wyoming line.

You can scarcely drive a few miles in the Black Hills without seeing an active or abandoned mine of some kind.

The uranium mines opened in the Hills will bring knowledge of new species not identified before in this area.

A good spot near Keystone in which to look for garnets, tourmaline and staurolite is the tunnel on U. S. 16-A between U. S. 16 junction and the town of Keystone. Instead of going through the tunnel, take the gravel trail around it. In the rock piles on both sides of this short stretch you will find plenty of pegmatitic minerals.

Another rewarding road to take is the short cut from Hill City to Keystone, an unmarked gravel trail.

The first mine dump along this route is an old tungsten mine. Your eyes will light up with pleasure if you find some of the scheelite of this area known for its electric blue fluorescence.

Along the trail are old tin mines. One of the major tin reserves of the United States is in the Black Hills. The high cost of handling cassiterite at the present time keeps this area from commercial production. Foreign markets, because of their cheap labor, now supply our needs.

A collector looking for specimens of tin, tungsten, columbite, and tantalite in this region will do well to follow the streams and search the gravel beds. The high specific gravity of these minerals hold them in such deposits.

RAPID CITY AREA

Rapid City is appropriately called the Gateway City. Boasting superb tourist facilities, it is situated on Rapid Creek at the foot of this ancient mountain range known to the Indians as Paha Sapa.

If you are a casual tourist somewhat interested in the rock formations before you, or if you are an ardent rock hobbyist, your first stop in Rapid City should be the School of Mines Museum.

Many of the wonders so well displayed in this fine, modern museum, come from the area you are visiting.

Of particular interest at this time is the exhibit of radioactive minerals complete with counter ticking off its findings. Another eye-stopper, particularly to the uninitiated, is the dazzling fluorescent display.

At first you see as uninteresting a bunch of rocks as you ever beheld. Then—click! A marvelous transformation is wrought! The whites and greys are suddenly fiery pinks and reds. The tans are an almost blinding chartreuse. A pale beige may be in turn a fairly screaming orange. There are rocks dotted with royal purple. There are rocks of pure sky-blue, of vivid yellow, of cerise, carmine, ultramarine.

This crazy-quilt of colors is a phenomenon produced by exposing otherwise drab specimens to a long- or short-wave lamp.

Not all rocks are fluorescent, by any means. We have a fluorescent collection in our museum in Mission, of perhaps 200 specimens. Every rock we bring home we try for fluorescence. Out of tons and tons of rocks to find their way to the Zeitner rock piles in over forty years, these 200 are the only ones with good fluorescence.

Do they contain minerals and combinations of minerals different from other rocks? No. As an example, one type of stone, calcite, sometimes will fluoresce red, sometimes blue, sometimes pink and often not at all.

Science does not completely explain the dramatic change you see. However, it is thought that trace amounts of certain elements in a certain combination serve to activate each other. Many radioactive minerals fluoresce.

Another exhibit that will make you stop and wonder in the Mines Museum is the case of hexagonal sand calcite crystals piled helter-skelter on top of each other like so many jackstraws. They are arranged here just as they grow in South Dakota's famed Rattlesnake Butte, an area unique in the world.

You will see the giant cycads as well as fossil woods and plant remains of many kinds. You will be stunned to see the huge fossil fish hanging on the wall, one of the best of its kind anywhere. Other fossil animals from the lowly corals and mollusks, to huge vertebrates long extinct, will fascinate you.

Most of the exhibits are from South Dakota; however, some specimens from other states and foreign localities are included for the sake of comparison.

From Rapid City west and north on Highway 14 are some interesting stops.

There are several caves as well as petrified forests. These petrified forests are not in place. There is a lot of petrified wood all right, but it is not always where it originally grew. There are places in the Hills where you can see petrified wood only partially uncovered, lying in great sections no doubt where they once grew. These areas are remote from the main highways.

If you have seen the splendid petrified forests of Arizona you will be disappointed in the South Dakota examples. The bulk of our wood is not colorful or well agatized or opalized.

Old Crystal Cave is a well known cave and contains a wide variety of formations such as stalactites, stalagmites, box work, calcite crystals, spacious vaulted ceilings, and narrow, crooked passages. This cave was opened in 1890.

Three miles southeast of Piedmont, rare fossil shellfish called "belemnites" are found. These resemble cartridges in shape and are grey in color. Near Piedmont also one may find fine selenite, the clear variety of gypsum. This location is three-quarters of a mile east of town.

If you continue on Highway 14 another 17 miles you will reach the town of Sturgis. Turn right here and drive out toward the inverted cone named Bear Butte. This is the classic example of a geological formation called a laccolith. This is a dome-shaped mass of igneous rock which was forced while in a hot, doughy state, through the existing older formations. Bear Butte shows the effects of erosion, so one can clearly see the edges of the formations turned aside by the rising magma.

From Sturgis it is only nine miles to Whitewood. Along the banks of the stream here amethyst geodes have been found. Geodes are round crystal-lined stones. Many geodes are hollow in the center and some are completely filled with crystals. Usually a good geode is easy to recognize because of its shape and the fact that due to its hollowness it is lighter than other stones its size. When these geodes are filled with the sparkling purple or lavender crystals of quartz they are among the most spectacular of specimens.

Spearfish Canyon is another place where amethyst geodes have been found. Even if you find no amethyst, the trip up Spearfish Canyon is one of the most memorable trips in the Hills.

The road through the picturesque canyon is State 89.

There are two waterfalls along this 17-mile stretch, both well marked and worth a view. Then there are rugged cliffs in contrast to the tall dark Black Hills spruce trees. Spearfish Creek which runs along the road the entire distance, is one of the best streams in the Hills.

The wild flowers you will see here are fireweed, bee plant, thistles, penstemon, wild roses, and bluebells.

This is a paradise for birds, too. The Black Hills seem to be a natural meeting place for both western and eastern birds. I have seen humming birds here and eagles. I have watched cliff swallows and listened to warblers. I watched a dipper and a gallinule, and was thrilled by the glimpse of a scarlet tanager and his somber mate.

Jasper Conglomerate

One day I received a letter from Dr. Frank Fleener, one of the three fathers of that standby rock book, "Quartz Family Minerals." He wanted to know about the occurrence of jasper conglomerate, in place, in western South Dakota.

All we knew at the time about this famous pudding stone was that after seeing polished specimens in several out-of-state museums we tackled a piece ourselves and found it to be excellent cutting material.

We determined to make a trip to Buffalo Gap in order to study the deposit and give Dr. Fleener a first-hand account.

We took Highway 79 from Rapid City to Fairburn where the conglomerate occurs on the land of some ranchers named Gregorson who live on Highway 79 – first farm on the east side of the road right north of town. We went to ask permission and directions from the Gregorson's and found them to be much interested in rocks. They sell their conglomerate to dealers for reasonable prices.

We turned west at Fairburn on an unmarked country trail. Then we turned south for a few miles and entered a hilly field to our right through a cattle gate. Gregorson's will give you exact directions when you stop for permission.

We wound around in the foothills until we came to an old windmill where we parked. The conglomerate occurs in the form of enormous waterworn boulders in and near the beds of a dry creek known as Lame Johnny. Some of the boulders are barely visible while others line the banks or jut from cliffs.

Conglomerate is a mixture of small pebbles, mostly rounded, which have been cemented together by nature. This particular conglomerate is more desirable than most because the pebbles are of gay red, yellow, tan, orange and lavender jaspers, and the cementing agent is a durable, beautiful hard quartzite. Both the jasper and its matrix take a good polish.

A slice of this jasper conglomerate is not unlike a slice of rich fruit cake in appearance. It comes in four predominating colors (I almost said flavors) — chocolate brown, spice tan, plum, and cherry. It is the matrix that furnishes these colors. The pebbles themselves vary in every specimen. The lavender and red backgrounds are preferred. The brown matrix seems crumblier and not as finely grained as the others.

Lame Johnny must have been quite a river when it deposited all these Badland pebbles. This may have been its delta, and the Badlands may have been covered with the shallow seas into which it emptied.

It is no easy matter to pound off suitable samples for your collection. My little prospector's hammer failed to make any headway on them. However, with a chisel and a sledge, Albert was able to obtain a specimen of each color.

You will find excellent waterworn specimens of this same material many miles away in the rock beds of the Badlands. The main part of the deposit stretches for about 100 yards, but following the dry creek bed one sees scattered pieces for many miles.

I am especially fond of the samples which have quite a few pebbles of white quartz to furnish a contrast to the rainbow jaspers.

A totally different material is sometimes found in alluvial deposits in the Badlands and mistakenly called "jasper conglomerate." It is really a brecciated jasper. The pieces which compose it are sharp and angular. They are crushed and broken sections of jasper instead of the smoothly rounded stream pebbles of true conglomerate. The recemented fragments are in a quartzite matrix, very often off-white in color, with the pattern all of one tone, sometimes reds, often yellows. This, too, makes an attractive cutting material.

Golden Barite

The rarest and most sought mineral crystals South Dakota has to offer are the transparent coffee-colored golden barite found in all concretions in the alkali beds of some of the Badlands and foothill streams.

These sparkling crystals occur with well formed yellow calcite crystals and often a drusy fluorescent matrix. No wonder they are so popular with all who have seen them. It is hard to imagine finer cabinet specimens.

You can see the huge concretions in the road cuts and on the hillsides between Rapid City and Wall.

Although these specimens were described as early as 1900, it is only in recent years they have been collected extensively.

It gives one a lot of food for contemplation to break open one of these massive concretions and find huge fossil shells in it, encrusted with crystals of calcite and barite. It is not every concretion that holds both fossils and crystals. The formations containing the crystals are the same as those containing the well known Pierre shale cephalopods.

We drove from Rapid City to Wasta on U. S. 14-16. From Wasta we drove north on the gravel route shown on the South Dakota Highway Department's free map. Elk Creek, the best locality for the specimens, is the second stream you cross on this road.

We turned off the road to our left and went through the farmyard (with permission). We followed the dry stream bed for a short distance and parked on a hill overlooking the peaceful summer scene.

The concretions were lying everywhere. I could hardly wait to start opening them. Each one was to me an unopened Christmas package.

Many of these concretions contained nothing but mud-stained calcite of inferior color. We were surprised at the number which had been broken open. New concretions keep weathering out of the eroded cliffs and hillsides so there will always be a new supply.

The rockhounds who had preceded us

were obviously looking for nothing but barite. I was able to collect exquisite calcite groups and drusy fluorescent specimens with no pounding.

In about an hour I caught up with Albert. He had really been only a few hundred feet beyond me around a bend. He was armed with a crowbar and was working gently at a giant round concretion.

I peeked into an open vug in the heart of the stone and there delicately perched on a ledge and clinging by a hair to another, was the specimen of specimens — a group of big perfect golden barite crystals with no matrix and all perfectly terminated.

I sat on another boulder and didn't even watch. I was trembling with anxiety because I had collected enough barite to know that the crystals may break off at a mere touch, and that Albert's chances of extracting the specimen intact were less than 50-50. Only patient prying to enlarge the incision enough to get his hand under the specimen, would help him now.

In a short while he told me to come and hold the box he had lined with cotton. He laid in it the undamaged group of crystals. We have since counted them and there are 65 crystals, many of them doubly terminated.

I also collected one thumbnail-sized specimen on this trip, and one baculite of miniature size full of drusy calcite crystals.

On the top shelf of our fluorescent collection is a row of matrix hunks of the barite. It fluoresces under long-wave lamp, and few materials can equal its rich apricot and forest green combination.

Once at a national mineral convention a dealer begged me to tell him where to get the South Dakota barite. He said if he knew he'd be there next day with three trucks.

I didn't tell him. I am quite positive that he could not collect one truckload, to say nothing of three, of the barite specimens. They are not easy to find, they are difficult to work out, and they aren't a truckload type of merchandise.

Black Agates

The area around the Badlands town of Scenic on State Highway 40 is covered with interesting gem material. One of the most unusual is black agate.

Picture, if you can, a stone coal-black on the outside and snow-white on the inside. When cut, these stones have a wide black frame around a white agate filling. They are best cut in thin slabs, and polished on both sides and the edges, but retaining the original outlines. This gives a unique gem and has the advantage of showing strikingly against most fabrics.

Take the graveled trail west of Scenic, an unmarked country road. About two miles west of town the buttes are near the road on the right. Find a place to park and hike up the eroding ravines of these gumbo structures. Sometimes the gems will be covered with sticky gumbo, but usually they are a shiny smooth black and easy to recognize. They are from ½ to 3 inches in length on the average, and of irregular shape.

Chalcedony

One of the most interesting minerals is chalcedony, the reason being that chalcedony in most of its forms is real gem material. We have searched for chalcedony on the deserts of the west in a form known as "fire agate." We have dug for chalcedony in Tampa, Florida, in its exotic agatized coral form. But by far the biggest chalcedony deposits we have seen anywhere are in South Dakota.

Not far from the town of Scenic on State Highway 40 is the town of Imlay. That term **town** is used loosely here, but there is a railroad track and a building or two. The distance from Scenic to Imlay is practically one huge field of chalcedony. Just before we crossed the railroad to go into Imlay we stopped and climbed a hill on the right of the highway. In every direction were piles and veins of chalcedony.

Much of this chalcedony is well suited to lapidary uses. The best of it shows carnelian (red) spots and sometimes plumes. The pale blue is also a desirable color. Lots of it is grey which is an undesirable shade, and some of good color is too thin.

Often chalcedony in this locality is in huge sheets. If you pick one up and examine it you will see it resembles a sandwich. There is a smooth, even layer and a topping of another smooth layer. The characteristics of the deposit change rapidly from hill to hill, from ravine to ravine.

The area is by no means limited to what you can see. It stretches for many miles on both sides of the highway and railroad.

Not far to the south and almost directly in line with these huge fields is the strange fossil area of Crawford, Neb., where the bones of a multitude of prehistoric animals have been preserved in fine detail by this hard chalcedony.

The specimens most sought in the Scenic-Imlay area are chacedony geodes, often locally called "rattle stones."

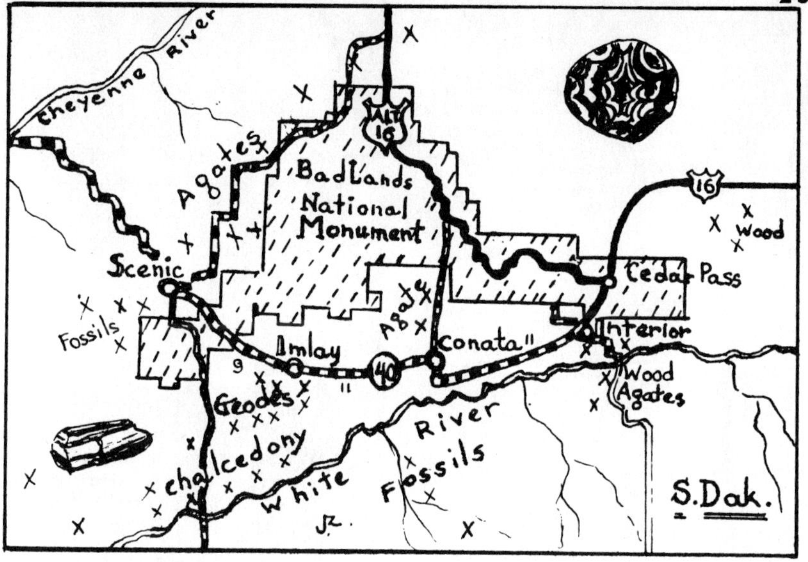

Some of the choice geodes are lined with shiny, bladed crystals of clear selenite. Often the crystals are snow-white quartz like the popular milk glass in appearance. Some of the crystals are a pale pink tint, and some are lavender. One red clay butte has many geodes which are polka-dotted, white chalcedony with red spots. Near a farmhouse to the east of the highway and a little nearer Scenic we found a deposit of almost transparent geodes with lacy patterns of a more translucent white.

There was one disgusting thing: the poor ones were almost impossible to break, and the good ones fairly popped open. We have tried opening them with our diamond saw but they are extremely hard on the saw because of the loose, sharp quartz crystals which become wedged in the saw and cause it to bind.

In size the geodes vary from a pea to a basketball. Large ones, the size of an orange or better, are rare. The average is about the size of a small egg.

We have one small one with crystals of dolomite, several with botryoidal chalcedony, and one with small white cubes which I cannot identify. Perhaps they are pseudomorphs.

We have not found "fossil" water in these geodes as we did in the chalcedony geodes of Florida. Nor have we found oil in them as in the geodes of the Warsaw formation in Illinois.

In one spot where there were many cracks filled with chalcedony, we found the forms or casts of these cracks clasping small geodes in the spokes.

THE BADLANDS

Tourists from the East at their first sight of the Badlands of the White River gasp in astonishment. The miles of weird formations stretching into the distance before them gives them a landing-on-the-moon feeling. "Look," I have heard them say with a 360-degree sweep of their hands, "as far as you can see, not a living thing in sight."

That science-fiction feeling is always with you to some extent, because although you soon will see all kinds of life, much of it will be strange to you.

Your main feeling will be of awe and wonder at the beauty and variety of the panorama you see. You will also experience a great curiosity as you pick up such things as shark's teeth, corals, and sea shells thousands of miles from the sea.

As you venture, cautiously at first, away from the main traveled roads you will be astonished by showy and fragrant wild flowers. The white satin blossoms that fold up to a blush pink are the gumbo lilies that have roots that go to China. The odd three-petalled flower is the mariposa lily. The tall lavender bell flowers are penstemons. The creeping red ones are crimson wings.

If you spend much time scouting around in the Badlands you will see antelope, deer, and perhaps even coyotes or bobcats.

But all these healthy signs of life forms

are as nothing compared with the tales you will see of life of the past. No geological formation in the world offers a greater chance to study the history of our earth than does this area, the great White River Badlands.

Here the master sculptors, wind and water, have combined to erode away great masses of land, leaving excavations where the scientist can study rocks and fossils of the earliest eras to the latest periods of the development of the earth.

The Badlands were once a part of a vast salt sea which stretched from what is now the Gulf of Mexico to the Arctic Circle.

During the early period of the Badlands development the king of beasts was the titanothere, a large ungulate. It was the fossilized jaw of one of these animals that was brought out by the American Fur Company in 1846. This fossil, at first misnamed, was the first to be studied from an area which soon came to be known as the world's greatest storehouse of fossils.

Among other animals which have roamed the Badlands during some period of its development are the tiny ancestral horses, the fierce sabre-toothed tigers, early camels, rhinoceroses, wild dogs, wild pigs, and even great turtles three feet across.

Almost every summer you may see in the Badlands parties of students from the big universities, seeking new knowledge of the past and new specimens for their museums. Hardly a museum of importance is without White River Badlands specimens.

One of the intriguing gems of the Badlands is agatized coral. Locally it is often called "agatized sponge," because the rough tan exterior and the general size and shape are much like the real sponges.

If you find one of these spongy looking masses you have a real treat in store when you cut it in two. I know how you hate to load up with useless material so if you have to chip it to see if it's worth taking, make it a very little chip. Don't pound it open. The saw is best.

Your chip will reveal that the sponge is really a chalcedony variety of agate. Your saw will reveal a radiating pattern with tints of peach, rose, pale gold, brown, and white. The pattern in no way resembles the coral which the agate replaced. This is truly one of the fine gems of the Badlands.

Another rock you may run across is the picture agate. This like some of the other Badlands rocks should really be called "jasper."

The specimens with the best pictures are of a fist size or larger and are an opaque yellow brown with mottling of white. When cut longitudinally there is often a scene resembling a sepia print, of rolling hills and cloudy skies.

The Badlands around the town of Interior abound in many kinds of hard gem rocks. In two places I scooped up a couple of handfuls of rocks and counted them, then counted the number I knew to belong to the quartz family. In the first spot 87 out of 98 stones were quartz family, and in the second 68 out of 72. This high proportion of gem stones with the variety of colorings, is the reason for the fame of the Badlands rock piles.

In the area east and north of Interior, you will run into pockets of what we call "eye agates." They aren't agates but rather jasper. We cannot properly call them orbicular jasper because the eyes don't carry far inside. The rounded, smooth, usually walnut size pieces have a beauty that is only skin deep. The patterns greatly resemble an old-fashioned calico print. The color combinations, however, are straight from Paris, the latest thing. They are of a cream or beige background with orange and green print, or a rose background with black print, or grey with red.

These stones are well suited for jewelry if tumbled. Fine cabs can be made from them also, if you remember that most of their beauty is on the outside and plan the size and shape of your cabochon accordingly.

Some of the chalcedony of the interior Badlands is of a prized red color, far prettier than most carnelian on the market. You will find only scattered pieces, usually botryoidal (grapelike) in shape.

You will find pebbles or rose quartz, too, ground to a smooth finish by nature and ready for their final polish.

Other stones worth keeping are the red or yellow jaspers, black and white chalcedony, and the spotted agates named by the late Tom Friet "fish-egg agates."

The so called fish-egg agates can be found almost anywhere in the Badlands, at least I do not recall visiting a spot where I have not picked up at least one. The matrix is clear and unmistakably agate. The fine oolitic spots are red and yellow jasper. Tom had many first-quality ring stones of this material which takes a high polish and has few flaws.

You have a good chance in the Badlands of running onto a Fairburn or a stray piece of cycad or palm wood. You even have a fair chance of discovering a new type of gem material.

PIERRE SHALE FOSSILS

To amateur collectors perhaps the best known of the Badlands fossils are the Pierre shale cephalopods. These Cretaceous shellfish distinguished by their ornate, many-chambered shells, grew to unusual sizes here, and are extremely well preserved. Most popular are the ammonites, baculites, nautiloids, and scaphites.

The fossils are found in large concretions weathering out of the hillsides, road cuts, and creek banks of most of the Badlands area. The trick, of course, is to find an unopened concretion. The Cheyenne River and its tributaries have been exceptionally good for fossil-bearing concretions, but the Bad River and the Moreau River farther north are also productive. You will have to park and walk along the river.

From Wicksville on Highway 16 east for many miles you will see the black Pierre formation with characteristic concretions weathering out. This is a prominent formation and evident along most of the side roads leading either north or south.

Open the giant concretions with care. We use a maul to take a small "lid" off the top, and then proceed with pry bars. Calcite and barite crystals occur in these concretions, too, Fossil clams are quite common. Even if your concretion turns out to be nothing more than oddly shaped pieces of drusy or velvety limestone, you will have brilliant fluorescent material, especially under long wave.

Fossil turtles are also found in the Badlands. Many people mistake a somewhat flattened concretion for a turtle. However, if you should find a turtle it would look so nearly like a live one except the color that you would not have to guess.

In various rock beds of the Badlands there are fossil shark teeth, cup corals, horn corals, and occasionally brachiopods. Some of these fossils are limestone but many are chalcedony or jasper. You will even find fossil imprints on some of the prairie agates.

It is imperative in fossil collecting to write down exactly where the fossil came from and get a complete, accurate identification of it. Otherwise, it becomes quite valueless.

Invertebrate fossils are numerous throughout the Midwest, but well preserved vertebrate fossils are not easy to find. Since the science of vertebrate paleontology is based on the evidence of past life through the study of such remains, it is imperative that these fossils be collected by experts. A federal law, the Antiquities Act, makes it a punishable offense to remove vertebrate fossils from all federal land, not merely national parks or monuments. Dr. Robert Wilson, Director of the Museum of the South Dakota School of Mines, points out that even public institutions with trained personnel have to apply for permits to collect vertebrate fossils. Specimens collected illegally are turned over to the National Museum.

Inasmuch as most of the big Badlands of South Dakota is federal land, if you happen to find a vertebrate fossil while looking for gems or minerals, the correct procedure is to notify the School of Mines Museum of Geology in Rapid City. Then you will be assured that your discovery will be collected scientifically and used for educational purposes. Furthermore, you'll stay out of jail!

THE MISSION AREA

Near our home in Mission, there are few gems to look for. We find some interesting fossils, and the fossil mastodon ivory can be classed definitely as gem material. This opalized ivory is often colored green, grey, yellow, or blue by mineral inclusions and is even often dendritic. It is found in gravel or sand pits of the southern section of South Dakota. The best ivory is usually in small solid pieces but we sometimes find complete tusks or large sections.

Our best known gem material is also a fossil. It is coal-black opalized wood. We do find agatized brown wood and even some almost white wood, but by far the best is the black. True black stones are not easy to find as most so called black stones, even black jade, usually exhibit some tendency to another color, but not the best of the local wood. It is really black, and is easy to cut and polish. Hunt for this along the banks and hillsides of the Little White River 12 miles west of Mission.

The Mission area is well known for vertebrate fossils, particularly three-toed horse, camel, mastodon, and rhinoceros. Fossils are found in sand and gravel pits of Todd County as well as in road cuts and stream banks. The fossils can be found only when the pits are operating. The sand and gravel are used in road construction.

Arrowheads, many of them beautifully detailed gem points, used to be plentiful in sandy "blowouts" produced by erosion. There are still fine artifacts to be found

Sand calcite crystals from South Dakota.

but now it takes many patient hours to come up with one perfect point.

Perhaps the most famous locality in this part of the state is the sand calcite crystal classic location, Rattlesnake Butte. This is private property and at the present time is absolutely closed to all collectors. So many people ask about this site that I will give a short description.

Sand Calcite Crystals

There is something so wild-west sounding about the name, "Rattlesnake Butte, South Dakota," that one expects to arrive there clad in chaps and spurs on a bronc and perhaps see Indians crouched behind the flat tops. That impression isn't far wrong, at that.

This landmark owes its undying geological fame to one of nature's strangest crystal formations, the showy hexagonal sand calcite crystals.

A formation similar to this is reported in the limestone beds near Fontainebleau, France. I have seen some of these specimens and although chemically they may be the same as those of South Dakota, their physical appearance is quite different.

There are two large barren buttes standing almost alone. The butte to the north, although similar in apperance, had no sign of any crystals.

The abrupt slopes rise over one hundred feet above the surrounding field. The top of the butte was paved with crystals, pieces of crystals, and the shiny sand of which the crystals are composed.

Part of the hill was a wall of this silica sand cemented solidly by nature. The composition of these crystals is 60% of this shiny, finely grained quartz sand and 40% calcite, which is the cementing agent. In the dipyramidal class many of these crystals have perfect terminations at both ends. The crystals have six sides.

Perfect small single crystals seem quite common. Many clusters of crystals have quite large pebbles of quartz, spar, or some other mineral as inclusions. Most of the crystals are of a beige color.

The small loose crystals can be readily found by screening the sand in which they occur, while the larger ones are from two to three feet under the surface of the butte. The larger crystals are often 6 to 8 inches in length and up to 2½ inches in diameter.

Many of the specimens we have seen in collections across the country, as well as in rock shops, are not of first quality. Some are badly weathered and have lost the characteristic sharp outlines of the freshly dug material.

Petrified cones and sequoia wood from North Dakota.

This tourmaline specimen from the Black Hills, South Dakota, has black crystals but blue, pink, green, and watermelon are also found. Photo — South Dakota School of Mines.

NORTH DAKOTA

North Dakota leads the nation in lignite production. Sand and gravel, clay and shale also rank high in the State's natural resources. The eastern part of the State belongs in the central lowland division of the plains while the more rugged western half lies on the Missouri Plateau. With this variety, collectors would expect gems, crystals, and fossils, and it is true that all are found in the State.

WESTERN NORTH DAKOTA, Badlands and Buttes

Since oil was discovered in the Williston basin a few years ago, petroleum has been a leading industry of North Dakota. Prominent topographic features in western North Dakota are the flat-topped buttes and mesas and the weirdly eroded Badlands. The scenic beauty of the North Dakota Badlands is an unforgettable sight because of the brilliant colors of the various strata. The exceptional coloring is due to contrasting scarlet red bands of scoria which were produced by the underground burning of the lignite seams. The heat of the burning coal "fired" the high quality clays and fused the sands into a clinkerlike mass. Some of these burning coal seams still may be observed. One is northwest of Amidon and another at Theodore Roosevelt National Park near Medora. These scoria clinkers make colorful and unusual specimens.

Gems and Fossils

Gems may be found in western North Dakota in alluvial gravels, along rivers, in Badlands, gravel seams, and other rough, eroded areas. Quite a few excellent moss agates of the Montana type are found along the western border, especially gravel bars in McKenzie County where the Yellowstone and the Missouri unite. Cartwright is the center of the most favorable moss agate sites. Agates are scattered also along the Little Missouri in the southwestern section. Agates can be spotted quickly by their white lime coating. Scenic agate, tube agate, and iris agate are some of the types you may find.

Western North Dakota has a considerable amount of well agatized wood. Much of this wood can be found in huge sections. The Little Missouri River in McKenzie County is exceedingly productive. Not only does this River have agate and wood, but jasper, sard, and plasma.

Petrified wood is also found northeast of Searing, McKenzie County. A splendid location is 11 miles northwest of Mott in Hettinger County. This is along the rugged hills carved by the Cannonball River.

There is also good wood along the Cedar River in Adams County. A petrified wood city park in Lemmon, South Dakota, was built almost entirely of North Dakota wood.

The southwestern part of North Dakota is the highest part of the State. Black Butte near the Cedar River north of Bowman at 3468 feet is the State's highest point. But the lack of really towering altitudes of the western states belies the truly rugged nature of western North Dakota.

Grant County's Cannonball River breaks are also full of petrified wood, most of it well silicified and of exotic nature.

The Sequoia cones and wood found here by John Bunting of Mandan are of scientific value as well as being adapted to lapidary use. The rare type of sequoia was identified by the noted midwest paleobotanist, Dr. Chester Arnold, as **Sequoia dakotensis.** The dark brown silicified cones are about walnut size. Details of preservation are astounding.

Another find in this Cannonball country was silicified pods of the extinct Katsura tree. **Tempskya** fern, and **Osmundites** also have been identified from North Dakota's fabulous petrified wood piles.

Exceptionally detailed teredo wood is another of Mr. Bunting's recent discoveries. This was found in a Mandan gravel pit. Commonly called "worm-bored" wood, it is full of borings replaced by chalcedony or calcite, giving the wood an abstract, modern look. Actually the teredos which bored the fantastic designs were not worms but tiny wood-boring pelecypods. Species of these little mollusks thrive in oceans today and may be found boring their way into driftwood, pilings, and even ships.

Any collector hunting petrified wood in North Dakota and other midwestern states, should be conscious of the opportunity to find rare fossil seeds and cones. Besides the usual field trip equipment, a set of screens and a shovel will be helpful. Wherever there is an abundance of fossil wood, the seeds of the trees also may be present, although sometimes it takes a fine-toothed comb to locate them. Also, if any unusual wood is found it should receive professional attention, for alert amateurs can make lasting contributions to science.

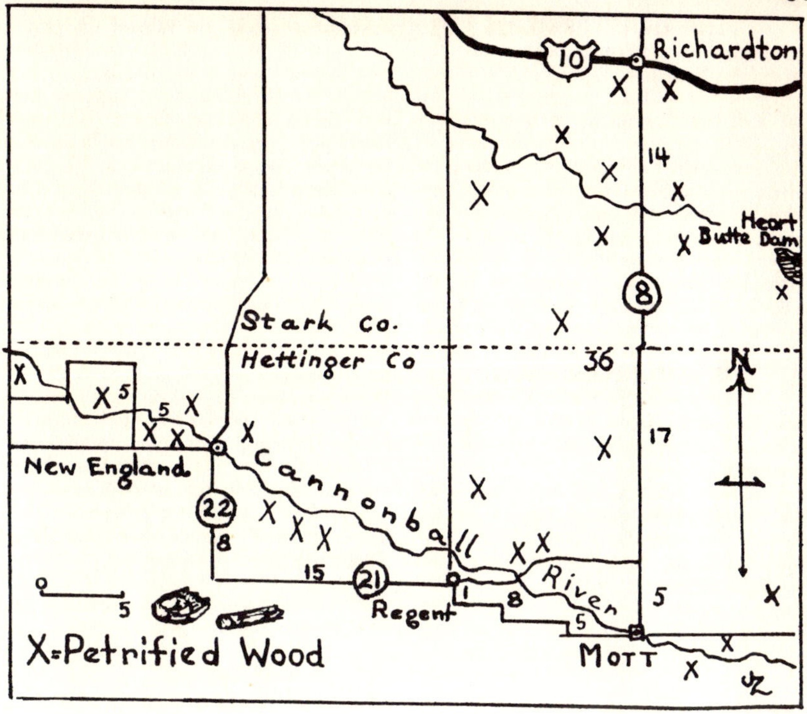

State Route 8 between Richardson and Mott takes the collector through country rich in chalcedony, jasper, and other quartz gems.

Six miles north of Dickinson in Stark County is a large gravel deposit which has yielded silicified wood, jasper, and other stones which will take a good polish.

Crystals and Specimens

Pyrite and marcasite are common in the strip coal mines of western North Dakota. The major lignite beds are in the Paleocene Tongue River formation. This formation is about a thousand feet thick in the southwestern section of the state. Uranium is also associated with the lignite here. The highest uranium content is from Sentinel Butte in Golden Valley County. There are several mines near Hazen in Mercer County.

The Pierre formation which in South Dakota bears the giant fossil-filled concretions can be seen in several places in North Dakota, also. Concretions in North Dakota have yellow calcite crystals, sometimes cave-like aragonite structures, sometimes siderite, seldom barite, but as far as I know, none of the big cephalopods. Concretions are found in eroded buttes and badlands pinnacles and cliffs. Some are weathering out near Medora.

Selenite crystals are found in the Mott area and in isolated areas northwest as far as Williston. North and west of the town of Stanley in Mountrail County are a number of lakes which are highly saline. At one time glauberite was an important product here. The mines are not being worked at present. Glauberite crystals can be found where the water is evaporating; thenardite, halite, and other salt crystals also may be found.

THE CENTRAL PLATEAU

Gravel pits along the Missouri River near Bismarck have agates. There are a number of excellent gravel deposits east of Tappen where quartz gems may be found. Since most of North Dakota was glaciated from two to four times, the many gems and fossils may have been carried tremendous distances, so it is possible to find a great variety of interesting materials.

Minot is another location with some of the state's finest gravel deposits. The pits are a few miles south of the city.

Dunsieth on the edge of the Turtle Mountains in Rolette County, has a large operating pit. The Turtle Mountains have large manganese reserves.

THE DRIFT PRAIRIE

Much of eastern North Dakota was once covered by huge Lake Agassiz which is now extinct. The gravels of this extinct lake and the gravels of modern lakes such as Devils Lake, contain gems as do the gravel bars of the two major rivers in this section, the James and the Sheyenne. This area is bordered by the Altamont glacial moraine which roughly parallels the James about to Harvey and then veers toward the northwest. The gravels most interesting to the collector are around Devils Lake. Quite a number of Indian artifacts have been picked up in this area.

THE RED RIVER VALLEY

The fertile valley of this backwards River (the Red River flows north) also has the deltas of the Pembina, the Elk, and the Sheyenne.

The town of Concrete on the Tongue River in Pembina County has an outcrop of fine blue grey limestone where fossils and crystals may be found. This limestone was quarried about the turn of the century but quarries are no longer in operation. Teredo wood and quartz family gems have been found along the lower Sheyenne River near Lisbon in Ransom County. The wood found here is well silicified, jet black, with the teredo boring filled with amber-colored chalcedony. Gravels of all three river deltas have both gems and fossils. Lake Superior-type agates have been reported from Grand Forks and Wahpeton.

Although not much is known about the gems of North Dakota, it is not because North Dakota doesn't have them. The population of the entire state is less than the population of Milwaukee, Wisconsin. With only 600,000 people and one rock club in a state of 70,000 square miles, this is truly a marvelous frontier for collectors who like to do a little prospecting of their own. All signs are present pointing to unlimited fine materials for collectors but so far there simply hasn't been enough exploration to pinpoint them.

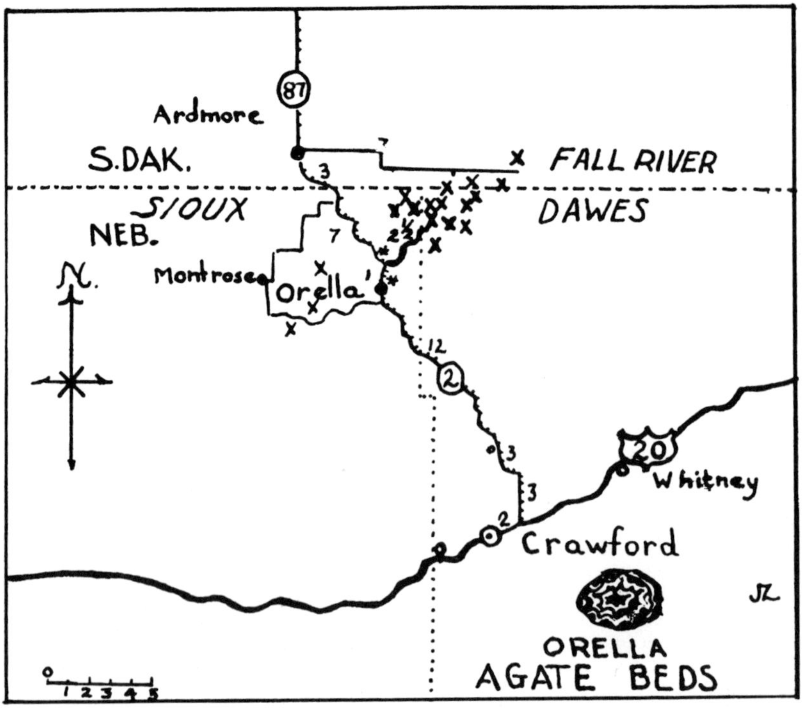

NEBRASKA

NORTHERN NEBRASKA

Early in the spring, after the snow has gone and before the prairie grass is too high, is a good time to visit the gem fields of northern Nebraska. Both the Black Hills of South Dakota and the Badlands have spurs in northwestern Nebraska. It is in these rough areas that you will find the elusive Fairburns, the absolutely gorgeous jaspers, and the gaily fluorescent chalcedonies which are Nebraska's chief contribution to the gem world.

The gentler southern slopes of South Dakota's Pine Ridge escarpment are in Nebraska. Here along the White Clay Creek near the Indian town of the same name you will find the first small agates. From here west to Wyoming the entire Nebraska-South Dakota border is good rock country.

Among unusual things found in northern Dawes and Sioux Counties are concretions with calcite-coated pillars, chalcedony rosettes, celestite crystals, rare fossil plants and vertebrate remains, and occasionally very small brown barite crystals. There is no end of interesting things to look for, just as there is no end of places to look.

Claude and Dot Sheffner of Hay Springs found some of this region's best material, thick chunks of chalcedony with swirling patterns of brown and black with white and cream radiating lines along the edges. The lines are not sagenite but give that appearance. Some of the pieces of chalcedony have a botryoidal cavity reminiscent of Florida's agatized coral.

Bill Zeig of Alliance, who has over 2000 Fairburn agates, found most of them in the hills and badlands of northern Nebraska.

The breaks of the White River north of Crawford have yielded choice agates. There are many dirt and gravel ranch trails in this rugged, sparsely settled area. Most of the trails lead through private property. Many have numerous gates. It is hard to get blanket permission for all rock collectors to use a specific private trail, so seeking local permission is the only way to get in. Generally speaking, the ranchers of this area are more or less interested in rocks, themselves, and are friendly and cooperative if convinced you don't mean to abuse any privilege granted you. If you are refused point blank, it is usually because someone before you has created a poor impression by leaving gates open, being a litterbug, or carting off a ton of material.

There are some places which are federal grazing land where theoretically anyone may collect. However, these federal lands are leased by local ranchers, and only a trip to the Forest Service office will help you discover which tracts these are. Very few areas are not fenced. These are usually in the most inaccessible and hazardous places. Though most of the northern Nebraska rock beds are easily reached by passenger car, a few call for a Jeep.

One of the best collecting areas for the gem hunter in Nebraska, or in the entire Midwest for that matter, is around Orella. There are several ways to get there. From Crawford, take State 2 northwest to the Orella rail station. One mile beyond this, turn east on a ranch trail. There is a gate here as this is grazing land. Follow the trail northwest two miles to the lone butte. Another way to reach the Orella agate area is to go 7 miles south of Ardmore, South Dakota, and take another ranch trail which winds east and south to the extensive rock beds.

Rocks are scattered for miles in the Orella area. Some are in concentrated spots, some distributed through the grass, others in eroded ravines and gullies. The dense patches of rock appear red brown or whitish in the distance. It has been my experience that one seldom finds many agates in the spots which appear too white from a little way off. Much of the rock in such beds is quartz of a crystalline nature.

The darker patches will have a variety of cryptocrystalline quartz gems such as jasper, jasp-agate, agatized wood, and chalcedony. So attractive is this material that you easily can load up more than you will ever use. A little skillful chipping is called for, as many of these gems are altogether different in appearance on the interior than the exterior. For example, the coal-black jasper is usually cherry-red inside.

Of the many kinds of agate found here, the best known as well as hardest to find is the Fairburn. On the average, the Fairburns found in this area run larger than those from most other localities, but when there is matrix attached, which there frequently is, it is of a brown tone and poor quality.

If the collector can get his mind off

searching for the world's record Fairburn, he may find some of the rare agatized plant life for which this region is noted. The well named **Tempskya superba** is found here as well as two other species of colorful, well agatized **Tempskya** fern. Agatized bog is another fine fossil found here. It is exactly what it sounds like – bits and pieces of agatized plant life cemented together in hodgepodge fashion and replaced by silica. **Pteridosperm**, palm, teredo wood, and even cycad frequently are found in this region.

Many of these rare plants resemble wood. Others look like chunks of jasper, and only upon close examination will you notice the orderly arrangement of symmetrical patterns which indicates the fossil nature of the rock. Jaspers, anyway the best jaspers of the region, are in the form of nodules, so chunkier, irregular pieces are more likely to be fossils.

Some of the jaspers are brilliantly colored. Much of the chalcedony has pleasing patterns and can be heat-treated successfully if more color is desired.

Bill Zeig found something new in this well hunted Orella area – chalcedony nodules that are certainly pseudomorphs. The chalcedony shows definite hexagonal crystal faces on the exterior. The interior is agate, often bright carnelian.

Another thing to remember in this area is that many of the rocks are fluorescent. Some of the chalcedony fluoresces almost an emerald-green. Some nodules in these rock beds will fluoresce pink and green, some almost red. Some nodules resemble geodes but are quite solid. Some with small openings are lined with blue grey opal. Cecil Vickers of Alliance first discovered the remarkable fluorescence of these nodules. Another fluorescent find is selenite encased in chalcedony. The fluorescence is orange under short wave.

This is the area of a collector's dreams where you literally can scoop up interesting material. It is a rare collector who doesn't load up with a hundred pounds or more. The area is being combed constantly, yet although every time I go there it looks virtually the same. I always find something new and interesting.

For another good area near Orella, go one-half mile south of the railway station and turn west. Cross the tracks and follow this narrow ranch trail to the badlands canyons 3 miles away. This is steep terrain, as good for fossils as it is for gems. You may wind up with anything from a Fairburn to a titanothere. As eroded as this area is, there are mesas covered with rich native grasses, so this, too, is cattle grazing land.

A road 3 miles south of Ardmore, South Dakota, leads 9 miles south and west to Montrose on Hat Creek. Any trails leading west from this road will take you to rock and fossil beds. Two miles south of Montrose there is a good trail leading east into the Badlands.

Charles Bass of Jay Em, Wyoming, reports some interesting specimens from this region of Nebraska. On Highway 20 about halfway between Crawford and Harrison, is an extensive sandy road cut. When stopping here to look for arrowheads, he found a considerable number of elongated sand spikes similar to those found along the Colorado River in California.

The fabulous gem field of northern Nebraska covers well over 80 square miles and you can walk all day without looking at the same rock bed twice. Each year something new turns up in this area and with careful, well informed collectors I am sure new finds will continue.

Fossils

One of the most remarkable deposits in the world of Tertiary fossils is the James Cook ranch. Southeast of Harrison, Nebraska, 23 miles, is the post office of Agate. Looking east from the post office, you will see two prominent flat-topped buttes. A Miocene stream once flowed here, but the present river is the Niobrara.

One slab of the buff-colored sandstone contained 4300 bones of early Miocene life. Not only are the bones abundant, they are extremely well preserved. Complete skeletons are not uncommon. Fossil quarries have been operated at Carnegie Hill and University Hill and later, 2 miles east at Amherst Hill. They are known as the Agate Springs fossil quarries.

Of the various types of rare mammals found in this productive "old bone" bed three are especially well known. One is a small, early member of the rhinoceros family called **Diceratherium.** Another is **Dinohyus**, a tall, piglike animal. The third was an ugly beast resembling a moose, a rhino, and a tapir but having claws instead of hoofs. His name was **Moropus.**

Dr. Harold Cook, son of the famous pioneer who originally owned this ranch, was a professional geologist and had a remarkable collection of vertebrate fossils on display. Paleontologists from all over the world are regular visitors at the Cook Ranch. Mainly they are professional scientists who collect

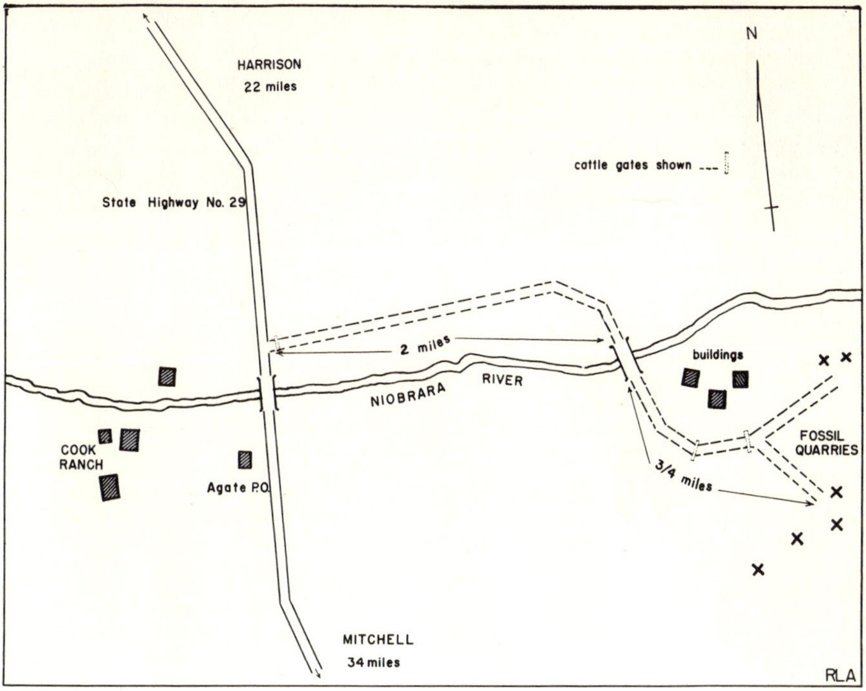

vertebrate fossils, but since fossil teeth and other partial vertebrate remains are widespread in southern South Dakota and northern Nebraska, amateur collectors often become fascinated by this branch of collecting and seek to learn more about it. But if you collect vertebrates, remember the Antiquities Law.

NORTH CENTRAL NEBRASKA

Another section of northern Nebraska which draws many collectors is the Sand Hills country near Valentine. This is also ranch country, and with its ponderosa pine-covered hills, steep canyons, and swift streams the Valentine country also looks like a spur of the Black Hills.

Along the Minnechaduza Creek and the Niobrara River are high hills where cuts and draws reveal fine quality petrified wood, often in huge logs. The wood is mostly black or almost so, and often has an outer rind of sandstone. There is dark opalized wood as well as agatized. Once in a while an opalized log will have minute spots of "fire." This seems to fade readily after the wood is weathered. In fact, the only time to catch the precious gleam is when you have a large opalized piece which you are attempting to break up in order to carry. So brittle and saturated is this opalized wood that as you whack off a conchiodally fractured section a thin film of water will be visible momentarily.

To find this wood follow the streams, with permission of course from local ranchers. The Keya Paha River and Spring Creek are other tributaries where this wood is available.

Gravels here also have sections of agatized or opalized mastodon tusk. Tusk sections are frequently taken for petrified wood because of the rounded shape and obvious concentric rings. While most of the wood is very dark, the tusks are pastel. The fossilized ivory will sometimes have dendrites, the wood never. The ivory has a tendency to be fibrous and does not break like the wood. Wood of this region seldom shows growth rings, and if it does, the rings are not as symmetrical as those of the ivory.

Incidentally, this region was a favorite Indian hunting ground and many exceptional arrowheads and other artifacts are found here. We have found a number of sharply flaked points of the gem wood of this district.

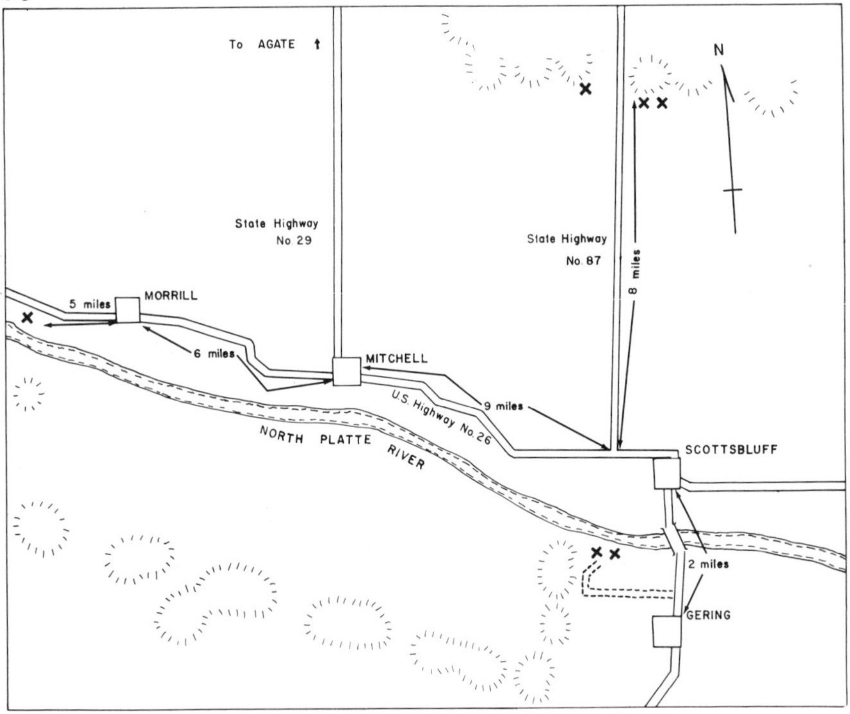

WESTERN AND CENTRAL NEBRASKA

Near Scottsbluff in western Nebraska is another area of rugged buttes, spires, and pinnacles where gem and specimen material may be found. In a road cut on a new portion of Highway 87 north of Scottsbluff, Bob Morris of Mullen found some gem wood entirely replaced by pure white opal with well formed black dendrites. The material fluoresces green under short wave. A considerable quantity of this wood has been found in recent years but it is by no means plentiful.

Fossils and concretions are found in the Scottsbluff Badlands. The area south of Scottsbluff is the highest in Nebraska, with the highest point 5424 feet in the extreme tip of the panhandle.

Near the small town of Angora in Morrill County on U. S. 385, is an abandoned mine of fluorescent moss opal. The clear to milky opal nodules have a snowy white calcium coating and fluoresce a light green. Indians knew of this opal, as opal arrowheads have been found on these hills. The mine is two miles east of Angora Hill on a gravel trail. It was worked considerably around the turn of the century and at present one ledge is being worked spasmodically.

The area between the two Platte Rivers produces many interesting things. Lodgepole Creek, a tributary of the South Platte, is noted for many varieties of good agatized wood. John Bergstrom of Chappell has found many large pieces of gem quality wood in this region. Fred Beltner of Bayard has found so much wood here that he believes there is an extensive ancient forest buried under these rolling hills. He says Big Springs on the South Platte is especially good, but that the wood may be found from south of Sidney to Ogallala. Along the north banks of the South Platte and the south banks of the North Platte are many sand pits where sand for road construction is obtained. These pits and gravel deposits are productive but some of the best material comes from grassy hillsides or farmers' fields. A particularly fascinating wood find of Mr. Beltner's is a well agatized cottonwood twig with the typical five-pointed star of the poplar family in the twig's center.

Wood, jasper, agate, and chalcedony may

be found near Platte Center at the confluence of the Loup and the Platte Rivers. Any gravels along the Platte from Kearney west are the likeliest places to seek quartz gems. Highway 30 follows the Platte closely through most of the State so that the river spots are readily available to anyone who cares to spend time searching the gravels for gem material.

EASTERN NEBRASKA

The Queen Hill Quarry 7 miles south of Plattsmouth on the west banks of the Missouri River is noted for both fossils and crystals. The Pennsylvanian limestone is rich in marine fossils, particularly invertebrates. Over 25 species have been identified so far. The rarest of these was an unusual trilobite. The exception to the fossils classed as invertebrates is the presence of fossil fish in this quarry.

Credit for the quarry's rarest specimen goes to David Brown of the Omaha Mineral Society. David split a piece of shale and was surprised to find inside a rare and perfectly preserved fossil split-tailed fish. Another club member, John Hufford, on his lucky day uncovered the impression of a giant shark. Both of these notable scientific discoveries are now on display at the excellent and famous museum of the University of Nebraska at Lincoln.

Horn corals from this quarry are exceptionally hard and detailed in preservation. Local collectors dye and polish them. Bright pyrite, some good small calcite, some sphalerite and marcasite crystals have been found. There are also nodules of chert of a polishable quality in the Queen Hill Quarry.

The Snyderville Quarry between Weeping Water and Nehawka has an interesting assortment of brachiopods, horn corals, and crinoids.

A quarry 3 miles southeast of Wymore, which belongs to the Gage County Road Department, has geodes with rare inclusions of blue celestite. A quarry on the Blue River immediately southwest of Holmesville also has a geode layer. Still more are to be found in the quarry 5 miles south of Blue Springs on the east bank of the river. Most of the geodes are quartz-lined and quite small. All these quarries have fossils also.

Huge concretions near Rock City, Kansas. Photo — Ada Swineford, State Geological Survey of Kansas.

KANSAS

The Kansas scene is varied. From 700 feet above sea level in the southeast, the elevation rises to over 4000 feet in the high plains of the west. The state is easily divided into eight geologic areas, all of them of interest to collectors.

THE HIGH PLAINS

By far the largest section of Kansas is occupied by the rolling and often rugged High Plains. Mineral resources of the area are oil and gas, sand and gravel, limestone, volcanic ash, chalk, clay, and diatomaceous earth.

Moss Opal

Most interesting to the gem collector is the fine quality moss opal of Kansas. A road cut 5 miles south of the town of Wallace in Wallace County is one of the best known of the many opal localities. The manganese dendrites in this clear to milky opal often create scenic effects similar to Montana agate. The opal has an opaque white coating when weathered.

Opal also may be found in Logan, Gove, and Trego Counties. These counties are traversed by the beautiful Smoky Hill River and afford some of the most spectacular scenery in Kansas. The mesas, buttes, pinnacles, and spires remind me of the South Dakota Badlands. To look for opal as well as for fossils, follow the famous chalk bluffs of the Smoky Hill River. Opal is found in either direction from the town of Elkader.

Another opal deposit in the High Plains region is in Clark County, north of the town of Ashland in the steep hills of Bluff Creek.

Fossils

Many of the fossils of western Kansas are opalized. The chalk beds of the Smoky Hill River valley constitute one of America's greatest fossil warehouses. Over 200 species have been found from Trego County to the Colorado border. Crinoid and shell fossils are comparatively easy to find, but many extremely rare, valuable fossils have been collected in this area.

A fossil collector really should start with the museum at the Fort Hays State College, Hays, Kansas. Here you will see the noted fossil of a six-foot fish inside the fossil of a 15-foot fish. Other notable finds from this area include **Pteranodon,** a flying reptile; **Hesperornis,** a giant bird; plus plesiosaurs and mosasaurs.

Concretions

Though septaria are found in several Kansas locations, those of Osborne County in the upper High Plains are particularly well known. One-half mile south of Hobbie Lake, one may find the septarian concretions filled with yellow calcite veins which often are sawed in two for bookends. Another location is two miles south of the town of Osborne. Calvert in Norton County, and Quinter in Gove County have volcanic ash concretions cemented with calcite.

Geodes can be found in the valleys of Trego and Wallace Counties. These are usually quartz, chalcedony, and calcite.

THE SMOKY HILLS

The Smoky Hills of north central Kansas is another region which will appeal to the rock collector. The western part of this area is called the **Blue Hills.** The whole area is rolling, with many natural outcrops of clays, sandstone, and other minerals of economic importance. An unusual feature of this area is its fences. There are miles and miles of fences where the fence posts are of a quarried limestone, called, naturally enough, "fence-post limestone." Sawed when freshly quarried into giant post shapes, this limestone fills a need in an area where wood is scarce.

Gem Material

The Republican River in Cloud County is a source of agate, jasper, and petrified wood. One good area is north of Concordia. An area called the **Old River bed** is especially good. There are several types of agate—clear, mossy, and banded. The wood occurs in small solid streamworn chunks. Petrified wood is found northwest of Ada, Ottawa County.

Ellsworth County at one time produced amber. Lignite is common in the Cretaceous banks of the Smoky Hill River. Five miles south of the little community of Carneiro, George Jelinek found a deposit of yellow to brown amber. The sizes were up to 4 inches in diameter. The Kanopolis Dam now covers this area but it is a distinct possibility that amber will be found in other lignite beds of this region.

Barite Roses

Odd concretions of sand and barite are found in several places in Kansas. Some of these are locally referred to as "barite roses" and others are called "walnuts." These "walnuts" are abundant in a quarry in Saline County. Go west of Salina about 7 miles. Your destination is the old Saline quarry, 2 miles east of the town of Bavaria.

Most of these roses are lighter in color than the bright Oklahoma barite roses. To make really good specimens, dig for fresh roses and clean them well by soaking and using a good stiff brush.

Barite roses are also found around Lake Kanapolis, Ellsworth County.

Concretions

The largest concretions in Kansas are 2½ miles southwest of the town of Minneapolis, Ottawa County. These 200 or more concretions ranging from 8 feet to 28 feet in diameter are a big tourist attraction of the Smoky Hills area. Of course these giants are not collectable, but are interesting to see as you travel to Mitchell or McPherson County where the right size occurs. In the Blue Hills of western Mitchell County, many of the best type of septarian concretions have been found. There are two locations in McPherson County for the cuttable type of concretion. One is at Roxbury Hill just out of the town of Roxbury, and the other is at Freemount south of State Route 4.

Fossils

North of the town of Hunter in extreme southwest Mitchell County, State Route 181 will lead you to an area marked on the map, "Blue Hills." Here you will find such pelecypods as clams, oysters, and mussels.

There are vertebrate fossils also in the Smoky Hills section. Often teeth of saber-toothed cats, elephants, and three-toed horses are uncovered. To find such fossils takes time and patience. Best bets are eroded banks of rivers, lakes, or dams, or in the chalk bed area.

Fossil leaves may be found in the sandstone of the hillsides 5 miles northwest of Brookville, Saline County.

Other Collectors' Items

Interesting pyrite concretions are found in the area known as "Mushroom Rocks" near Carneiro, Ellsworth County.

At Great Spirit Spring, Mitchell County, is a good deposit of banded travertine and some tufa. Celestite crystals are found near Kanapolis Dam. Good crystals of celestite also occur along Mill Creek in the Permian formation northeast of the town of Washington, Washington County.

THE RED HILLS-WELLINGTON AREA

The next part of Kansas that holds interest for the gem, mineral, or fossil collector is a colorful, mesa-butte area where badlands, running rivers, sink holes, rock quarries, and even a natural bridge vie for attention. Collectors particularly enjoy the scenery of the area known as the Gyp Hills (short for gypsum) where striking red Permian shales are capped with snowy white gypsum.

Gems

For the gem collector there are agate, jasper and wood near Aetna, Barber County. Along the Medicine Lodge River and the buttes and terraces associated with it there is lots of good gem hunting. This productive area stretches toward Kiowa. Then in the adjoining Harper County, north of the town of Harper, the Chikaskia River also affords gem collecting areas.

Good calcite crystals are found near Sun City where gypsum is mined. The natural bridge is six miles from here. Some of the country's largest gypsum deposits occur in Barber and Comanche Counties; in fact, the buildings of an entire business block of Wellington were constructed of gypsum.

THE FLINT HILLS

The Flint Hills, a land of rolling grass country, wooded valleys, and dramatic escarpments, is of particular interest to the collector. The outcrops of rock revealed by rivers and streams of the area show the layer of flint for which the region was named, as well as limestone of Permian age.

Gems

Agate and jasper are found in the gravels of the Republican River in Geary County. Moss opal is found in adjoining Dickinson County on the Smoky Hill River. Petrified wood, some of excellent quality, is also found in the sand and gravel pits of Geary County.

Robert Kruger of Linsborg who personally checked many of these Kansas areas, knows of at least 13 gravel quarries in Geary County; however, he emphasizes that they are private property. Although local inquiry will lead you to these quarries, you must get permission before attempting to explore. Bob also suggests that you not overlook the road cuts of Geary County. He has found many quartz and calcite geodes in road cuts.

Geodes

Although geodes are found in a number of places in Kansas, perhaps the best ones come from Chase County. These well-formed geodes with their lively crystal interiors compare with the geodes of Iowa and other classic localities. They range in size

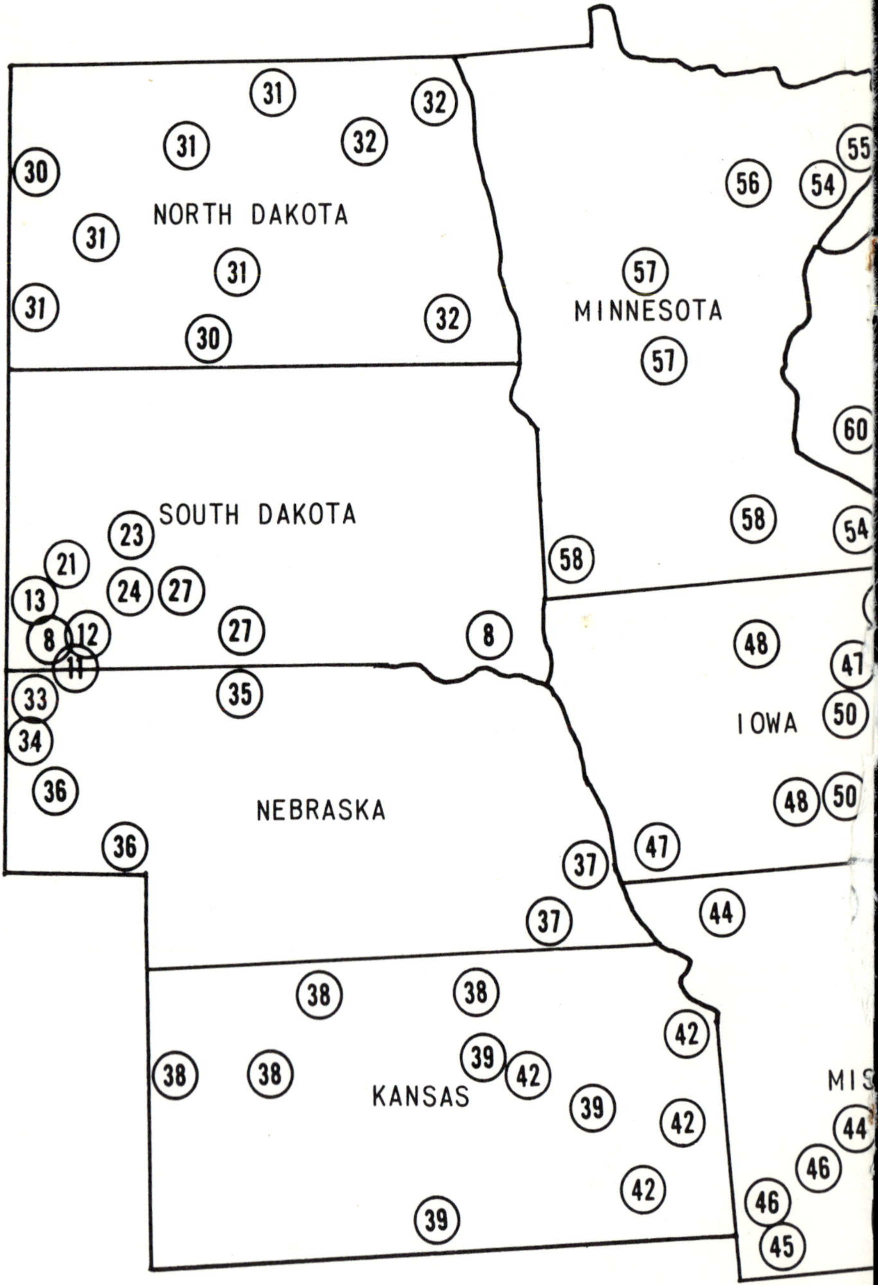

Each circled number is the page number on which you will find descri
localities in the general area on which the number is placed. Co
standard road maps to plan routes and assess specific areas.

Index Map and Trip Planner to MIDWEST GEM TRAILS

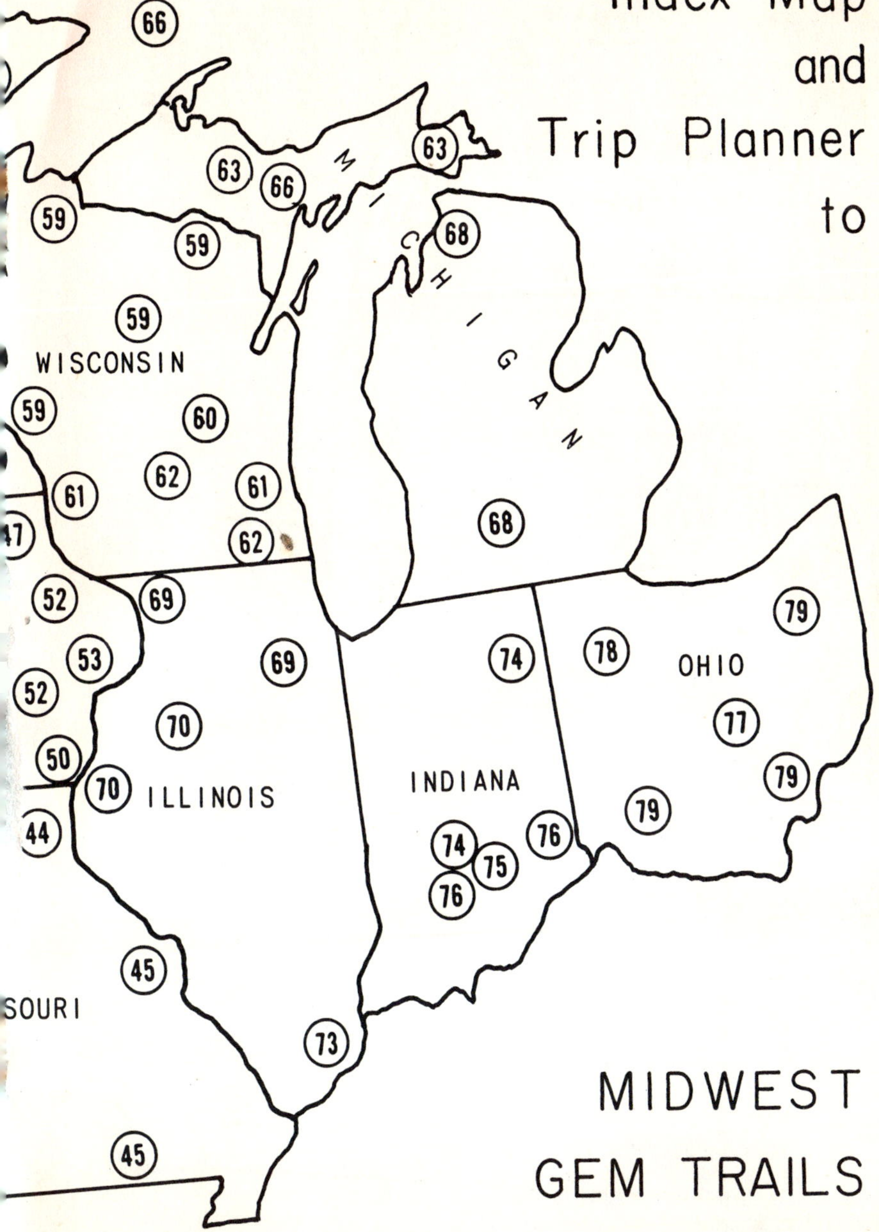

tions of the collecting
rdinate this map with

from that of a walnut to about the circumference of a softball. The locations are near Strong City, Chase County, and Florence. Another good geode locality is along the Walnut River in the southern section of the Flint Hills, both in Butler and Cowley Counties.

Fossils

In the region known as the Black Hills of Dickinson County lies a world-famous deposit of fossil insects of Lower Permian age. Although this is an old and well known collecting area, it is extensive. One of the amazing insects to come from this place is a giant dragonfly with a 30-inch wing spread. The community of Elmo is on State Route 4 in southern Dickinson County. The Wellington shale outcrop where the fossils are found is 3½ miles southeast.

Limestone quarries of Moline, Silverdale, and Cottonwood Falls also produce fossils, primarily marine. The quarry at Moline is especially known for cephalopods.

THE GLACIATED REGION

The Kansan glacier, the second of the Great Ice Age, advanced into northeastern Kansas as far as the Kaw Valley and the Little Blue River. There are limestone quarries, gravel quarries, and caves in this area.

Gems

Chalcedony, agate, jasper, and petrified wood are found in the glacial drift of this region. The agate is of the Lake Superior type. Rivers, rocky hillsides, and gravel pits are the places to hunt. Try the glacial deposits near McLouth, Jefferson County.

Good quartz crystals are found at the Lone Star Quarry at Bonner Springs, Wyandotte County.

Celestite

The best celestite collecting in Kansas is in northern Brown County. Here, masses of pink crystals occur 2 miles northwest of the town of Morrill, in the banks of Pony Creek. The crystals are large and well developed and are found in veins in the Permian shale. This site has been abused by collectors and if it is not closed it will take lots of work to uncover new veins which are there, undoubtedly.

THE OSAGE CUESTAS

This hilly, mineral-rich region has eroded areas showing both hard limestone and soft shales, but because of the characteristic outcrops of Pennsylvanian rocks the region has particular appeal to the fossil collector.

Gems

Agate, jasper, chalcedony, and wood are

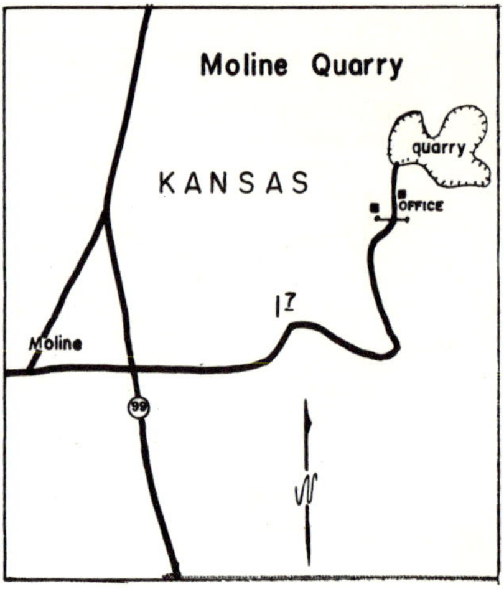

found along the Verdigris River near the town of Buffalo, Wilson County.

Fossils

The famous plant fossils of Kansas, so often seen in museums and fine private collections, come from near Ottawa, Franklin County. The Buildex Quarry 4 miles south on U. S. 59 has produced detailed fossil ferns, rushes, club mosses, horsetails, and prints of bark, leaves, and seeds. These fine fossils are in the form of impressions both concave and convex, in a fine buff-colored sandstone. They range in length from less than an inch to over 6 inches.

Two other good quarries in this part of Kansas are the Rose Quarry of Ottawa and the Railroad Quarry 3 miles north of Garnett. Fossils and crystals are found in both.

THE CHEROKEE PLAIN

The last section of Kansas is a large coal producer and the home of the Kansas share of the noted zinc-lead Tristate mining district. The dominant feature of the area is the huge waste piles of the mines. These piles, often over 100 feet high, are called "Chat Mountains." "Chat" is a corruption of the word, **chert.**

Crystals

Fine pyrite crystals are found in the strip coal mines of Cherokee County. The excellent calcite, dolomite, marcasite and sphalerite crystals for which this region is noted, are almost impossible to get except by purchase or trade.

Meteorites

Kansas has reported more meteorites than any other state west of the Mississippi. Meteorites are on record from 44 counties. Contributing factors to the unusual number of meteorites are the lack of heavy vegetation or vast wooded areas, the predominance of sedimentary rocks, and the widespread plowed fields. However, the biggest factor by far is that Kansans are meteorite-conscious as a result of publicity given the famous "Meteorite Farm."

The Kimberly ranch between Greensburg and Haviland first gained fame when a meteorite was discovered there in 1885. Since then well over 6000 pounds of meteorites have been recovered. The latest masses have been located by the use of metal detectors. H. O. Stockwell of Hutchinson is credited with record finds from this locality. The meteorites of this farm are of the quite rare stony-iron variety called **pallasites.**

Any collector in Kansas, as well as in other parts of the Midwest, should familiarize himself with the appearance and characteristics of meteorites. To be able to recognize a meteorite and bring it to scientific attention is another obligation of the devoted rock and mineral hobbyist.

This large plate of crinoids shows why Iowa is famous for its fossils. Photo — Iowa State Department of History and Archives.

MISSOURI

NORTHWESTERN MISSOURI

Most of the State of Missouri above the Missouri River was glaciated, and northwest Missouri is no exception. Most of the rock outcrops of this wooded, hilly country are Pennsylvanian. There is an abundant fossil record in the marine limestones of this period. Shales, clays, sandstone, and coal also are present.

Gems

Lake Superior-type agates are found in the glacial drift, particularly in Gentry, Daviess, Grundy, and Livingston Counties. Also in these deposits are other quartz family minerals of polishing quality such as jasper, petrified wood, and agatized coral and bone. However, such gems are not abundant, and all the hunting is on private property. Fred J. Call of Jamesport, Daviess County, finds the nearby Grand River best, but he points out it is much easier to find fossils than gems in this area.

Fossils

The West Grand and East Grand Rivers and their tributaries in northwestern Missouri have a multitude of fossils. There are brachiopods, crinoid stems, gastropods, also teeth and bones of vertebrate fossils such as mastodons. There are also gravel pits and limestone quarries in these northern counties where fossil hunting is good.

NORTHEAST MISSOURI

Gems

The favorite agate locality in Missouri is La Grange on the Mississippi River. Gravel operations here are constantly dredging out a fresh stream of stones. The agates of the La Grange gravels do not run large but many are of high quality. Naturally, there are other quartz gems present.

Geodes

The Missouri geodes like those of southern Iowa, are from the Warsaw formation. The Fox River near Kahoka, Missouri, has shale outcrops which are actually crowded with geodes. The little streams flowing into the Fox also reveal geode-studded banks. At some farms you will be allowed to collect on a fee basis, while other don't mind your exploring their lovely streams as long as you remember the Golden Rule. Weaver's Branch near St. Francisville also has plentiful geodes. Fox City, Wayland, and Alexandria are other geode locations.

The geodes of the Fox River differ somewhat from the geodes of the Des Moines River. A higher percentage of them are hollow and there is a greater chance of finding pink calcite crystal inclusions. Goethite, millerite, fluorite, and pyrite inclusions are choice.

It is interesting to see the geodes in place, neatly arranged as though a master stone mason had started an important building. There are several geode-bearing ledges. Although you may dig them from the surrounding rock, it is easier to pick them up from the stream beds or gravel bars after they have weathered out. Some like to wear boots for this, but personally I can think of nothing pleasanter than wading in the clear, geode-filled waters on a bright spring day, now and then stopping to admire the redbud trees or the big, blue violets, or to listen to the demanding whistle of the cardinal.

Fossils

Both silicified and calcified corals of several species can be found in this region. Other marine fossils are found in streams and quarries.

North of New London in Ralls County is a road cut near the Salt River bridge where fossil conodonts are plentiful. Conodonts are a toothlike fossil about which little is known.

CENTRAL MISSOURI

Gems

A colorful compact chert is plentiful in central Missouri, especially in Benton and Hickory Counties. A road cut near the town of Lincoln originally revealed the material and it wasn't long until local collectors realized its potential as a gem material.

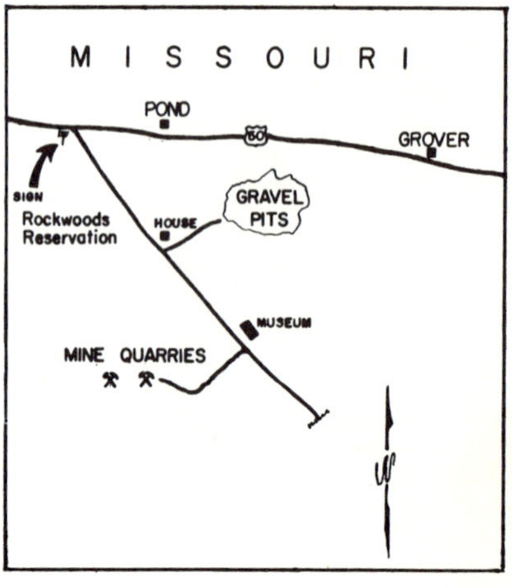

Locally called "mozarkite," this chert varies in color from pink to lavender and blue. It varies in pattern from cloud effects to dense swirls giving a banded effect. It varies in quality from rather fractured colorless material to fine jasper and chalcedony. To me, the most pleasing color combination is chocolate brown with pink patterns reminiscent of a marble cake.

By far the largest deposit was unearthed during dredging operations for an artificial lake in Benton County. Road cuts or excavations in any direction from Lincoln will produce specimens. Turn east at the blinker light on U. S. 65, go through town and stop at the first road cut east to reach one good place. A rock shop in Lincoln owns land where collecting is much better. It charges a modest fee for this privilege.

The huge gemmy chert boulders are weathered out of dolomitic limestone. Some of the nodules weigh as much as 500 pounds. It is necessary to be extremely selective in picking the material.

William Patt, Kansas City, reports that he has seen yellow and green material from this area and even better material from near Heritage in adjoining Hickory County. The Heritage material runs more to chalcedony, and the colors lean toward blue. Undoubtedly further deposits of this chert will continue coming to light as this entire portion of the state is probably underlain with it.

Fossils

Central Missouri also has several well known fossil localities. Most of these are near the Missouri River which bisects the state. Some fossils are found in the stone quarries at Kansas City. The valleys and rock quarries of Callaway, Boone, and Montgomery Counties have many species of Devonian marine fossils. A popular spot in Callaway County is a shale outcrop along the gravel road 2 miles east of New Bloomfield.

Excellent brachiopod casts may be reclaimed from the boulders scattered over the hillsides 8 miles west and north of Owensville, Gasconade County. The abandoned clay pit at this spot reveals many of these blue grey quartzite boulders.

St. Louis in east central Missouri is a classic locality for rare fossil echinoids. Fossils of the genus **Melonechinus** have been shipped to museums the world over, from various quarries in and around St. Louis. One of the richest finds came from an excavation for a new brewery.

Highway and railroad cuts near Eureka,

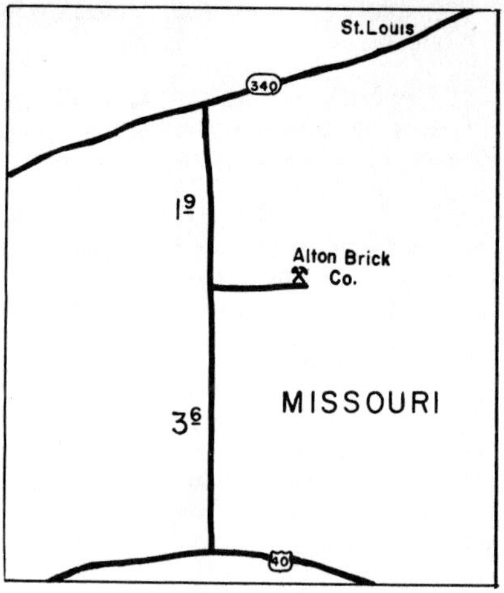

west of St. Louis on Route 66, have some of the best trilobites of the state. The shaly limestone in which they occur is also noted for bryozoan fossils.

The Alton Brick Company near Creve Coeur, east of St. Louis, has a limestone formation which has produced exceptionally fine masses of crinoid stems, called "Indian beads."

Fossil plant remains are found in the spoil piles of almost any coal mine in central Missouri.

THE OZARKS

The Ozarks are a domed uplift of igneous rock of which the summit is the St. Francois Mountains. As with other mountain areas, rocks of several different geological periods are evident. The Ozark region is one of the most heavily mineralized areas in the world. Lead, zinc, hematite, barite, and clay from this area constitute some of Missouri's greatest natural resources. Numerous subsurface streams and enormous springs have helped form the famous caverns of the region.

Gems

Along the Current River of Ripley County are more of the giant chert nodules similar to those of Benton County. This chert, too, has extreme variations in color, pattern, and quality. Being very brittle, it fractures readily.

Cutting quality chert is also found at Bee Bluff near Powell, McDonald County. This runs to blues and has numerous drusy quartz pockets and vugs. Banded yellow and white chert is found north of Gainesville, Ozark County, on State Route 5 at Timbered Knob.

Crystals and Specimen Minerals

Large deposits of crested barite are notable in St. Francois County. Missouri is a principal producer of barite. The best barite for collectors comes from around Potosi, Washington County. There is a village called "Old Mines," on State Route 21 north of Potosi, where barite is plentiful. Some high-grade chert and drusy quartz also are found in dumps of this region. A good collector's item is massive barite encrusted with transparent, sparkling barite crystals.

The gorgeous crystals of the zinc-lead mines near Joplin are the most sought of Missouri's crystallized specimens. For over 20 years I have heard that the mines are below the crystallized zone and that there will never be more of these dramatic cabinet pieces. Nevertheless, every year more of these rare beauties reach the market and the current crop is some of the best ever.

The prized crystals of the area are the brilliant dicelike cubes of lead, the distinctive bronzy cockscomb marcasite, the deep ruby-colored crystals of sphalerite, often with peacock-colored iridescent sphalerite, the showy honey calcite, and the delicate, curved crystals of flesh-pink dolomite with iridescent chalcopyrite. Although there are vast waste piles from the mines throughout this part of the state, you will find none of these famous crystals here. The mines are underground operations and the crystallized minerals, being rich in lead and zinc, are not thrown on the dumps. The country is wonderful to see but you will have to purchase your crystal specimens. There are many rock shops in the area as well as many fine private collections.

Fossils

Well preserved fossil leaves are found in the Clay Pits of Stoddard County. The plant fossils are from the Eocene and resemble many modern plants such as hickory, sycamore, and walnut.

Marine fossils of the Devonian are found along Little Saline Creek of Ste. Genevieve County. Quarries at Springfield and Carthage have Mississippian marine fossils.

Kings Butte just north of Springfield, has been a favorite fossil ground for many years.

The Old Sweeney Quarry at Clifton City, Cooper County, has yielded a large number of excellent specimens.

Fossils preserved in the chert of southern Missouri are finely detailed and very hard. Brachiopods, gastropods, cephalopods, and occasionally trilobites are associated with the chert.

The Elephant Rocks

Most tourists in Missouri find the mammoth Elephant Rocks intriguing to visit, but rock hobbyists will find this area even more interesting. Gigantic granite extrusions which form the greater part of the Saint Francois Mountains have weathered into massive boulders near the appropriately named town of Graniteville.

Missouri Caves

There are 25 caves open to the public in the State of Missouri. Four of them are in MacDonald County while Stone and Camden Counties have three each. Since there is an unusual flow of ground water in the Ozark region many of these caves are still classed as "live," that is, such forms as stalagmites and stalactites are currently being formed. Delicate crystals of calcite and aragonite also occur in these caves. Many when first explored contained pottery, arrowheads, and other evidence of early man.

Jasp-agate from Crowley Ridge, southern Missouri.

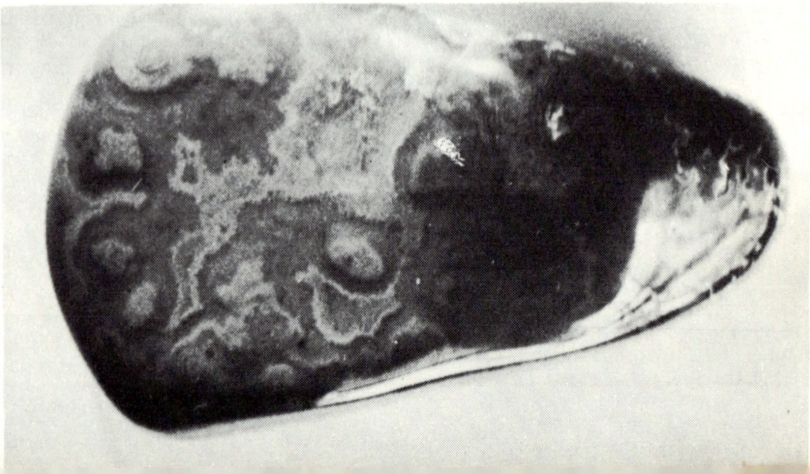

IOWA

Iowa, like other midwestern states, has gravel pits, stone quarries, and coal mines dotting a varied terrain. Any which grant permission to enter may be considered of interest to collectors. However, as a state, Iowa is not well mineralized. Its chief mineral resource is the wide expanse of America's most fertile farmland.

WESTERN IOWA

Although western Iowa is not an extensive gem area, there is a deposit of polishable chert known as "protozoa agate," near Red Oak. The material is tan to black with white to blue tiny shells replaced by agate. It takes a very high polish and does not undercut.

The bedrock is limestone used for road building but a layer in the quarry about 30 feet from the top reveals this dark silicified stone varying from 2 inches to over 2 feet in thickness. Because there has been blasting, a collector will have to be selective and look for small, solid, fracture-free pieces.

Margaret Yanasak of Des Moines, who has had excellent results with this stone, gives exact directions to the quarry but emphasizes that as with other private property, permission must be asked and rules of safety and courtesy obeyed.

Take Highway 34 west from Red Oak. One mile from town there is a motel on the north side of the road. Here you turn north on the unpaved side road. In a short distance you will see some large buildings on the east, or to your right, and the huge quarry will be on your left. Ask permission at the weighing station. Park your car out of the way of truck traffic. The topsoil here is slippery gumbo clay so this is no place to be in wet weather.

NORTHERN IOWA

Gems

Fayette County in northern Iowa has many creek beds with high quality and above-average sized Lake Superior agates. A new find in this County was a 6-pound carnelian agate frosted with drusy quartz.

"Coldwater" Agate

Specimens from a major agate discovery in northern Iowa were shown for the first time at the Midwest-American Federations show at Des Moines in 1962. The resemblance of these agates, found in a limestone matrix, to some from the limestone areas of South Dakota and Tennessee is interesting. Ted Vanasse, who has made a study of Lake Superior agates, called a similar variety, found in Wisconsin limestone, "Coldwater agate." The Iowa agates have been given this name though there is enough difference between them and the Wisconsin variety to make this a misnomer. The Iowa variety should not be called "Coldwater" any more than they should be

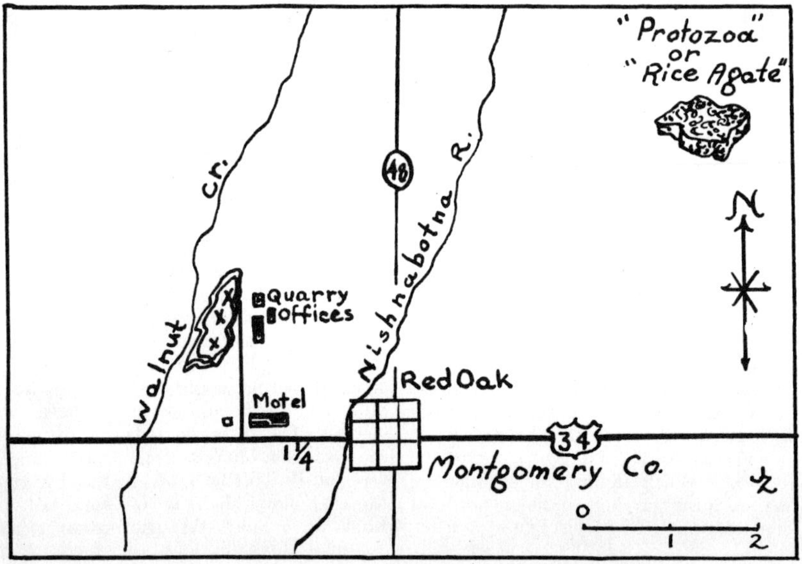

called "Fairhills" or "Teepee Canyon."

The agates are usually in fortification patterns and nodule form. They vary in color through most tones of blue, grey, and other neutral shades. Some have a dramatic black and white contrast. A few are an ivory or pale yellow, and even some pink and amethystine varieties have been found.

The exteriors are similar to some geodes. Some of them actually have crystalline centers. Plume or lace agate fills some of the nodules.

Look for this type of agate in northern Iowa in Black Hawk, Bremer, and Benton Counties. Any limestone quarry, road or stream cut, or gravel pit is a likely spot.

Fossils and Specimens

Mason City has some good quarries for collecting marine fossils of many species. Prospecting is allowed with permission, and the collector will be rewarded for patient searching with fine pelecypods, gastropods, corals, and perhaps even trilobites and crinoid stems.

The most unusual specimen material of northern Iowa comes from near Webster City, Hamilton County. This is an exceptionally attractive, well developed cone-in-cone calcite. This strange kind of calcite which resembles tiny cones nested one inside another, occurs in veins or layers in certain sedimentary rocks. Its usual association is with gumbo, clay, or shale. Though there are several explanations of this unique structure, no theory has been finally accepted. Much cone-in-cone is unspectacular in appearance and of no interest to any but the scientific mineral collector. However, the Iowa material, coal-black in color, the graceful flared cones stacked up to 12 inches high, appeals to almost every rock hobbyist.

The exact location is near the small community of Stanhope. The place is known as Bells Mill. Go north from Stanhope on Route 60 to the second crossroad. Turn west until you come to the end of the maintained road. Here you will see a well traveled trail heading north. Follow it until you reach a bridge. Cross the bridge and park on the right side of the road. From where you park, look back across the bridge and you will see the veins of cone-in-cone. Do not visit this spot in wet weather. Handle the fragile specimens with extreme care.

There are fossils and geodes along the little creek which flows through Brandon, Iowa. A quarry a short distance north of Maquoketa on U. S. 61 has lots of brachiopods.

Geodes

Northern Iowa, too, has geodes. A limestone quarry at Chapin, 6 miles north and ½ mile west of Hampton, has a formation of geode-bearing limestone. Most of the crystals in these geodes are small and sparkling. The average size is about that of a baseball. The exterior is smooth and almost snowy white, with the cavity usually a little off center.

Another locality is near Hubbard. Five miles south of Hubbard on Highway 65, turn west on a hard-surfaced county road. After 4 miles, leave the hard-surfaced road and turn south to the next intersection and proceed 6 miles. At this point take another jog to the south and you will see the quarry just west of the next intersection. The spherical geodes are in the same brown limestone formation as the geodes of the Hampton area.

Eldora and Union are two other communities from which geodes have been reported. Many streams flowing into the Iowa River in this area, as well as the Iowa itself, have exposures of geodes.

Gem Grotto of the Redemption

At West Bend in northern Iowa, the late Father Paul Dobberstein constructed a grotto of gems which is unmatched. From the outside, this grotto appears to have been formed naturally in that very position. Inside are glistening passageways leading to the top of the shrine. Each passage is a virtual treasure house of exquisite gems and crystals from all over the world. Nine grottoes portray scenes from the life of Christ, each scene a masterpiece in gems and precious stones. A marble replica of Michelangelo's "Pieta" is at the top of the shrine. Father Dobberstein spent 50 years creating this amazing garden of the flowers of the mineral kingdom. Every collector regardless of faith is awed by this magnificent display.

CENTRAL IOWA

Crystals and Fossils

The concretions of the Knoxville region are large and full of surprises. Several choice crystals are found here. The most unusual is calcite in sharp, white, crystal bundles arranged like pineapple tops. Siderite, dolomite, and barite also occur in these concretions. The places to look for them are the coal mine dumps of the entire region. One of the better spots is the Pershing Mine. Follow Highway 60 southeast of Knoxville 8 miles, then turn straight east ¾ mile. Unusually long calcite crystals as

Examples of the variety found in Iowa's Coldwater agate.

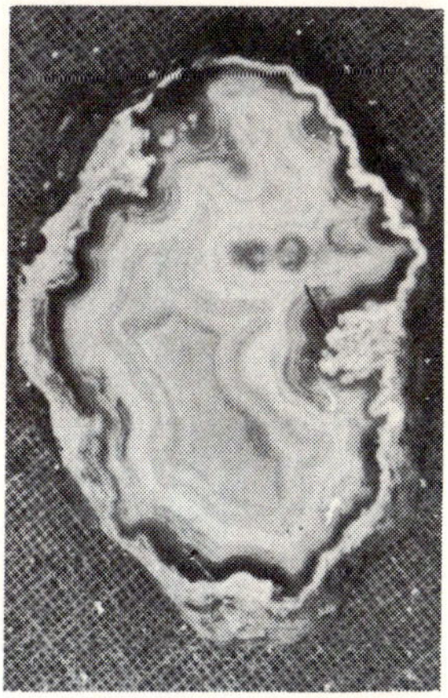

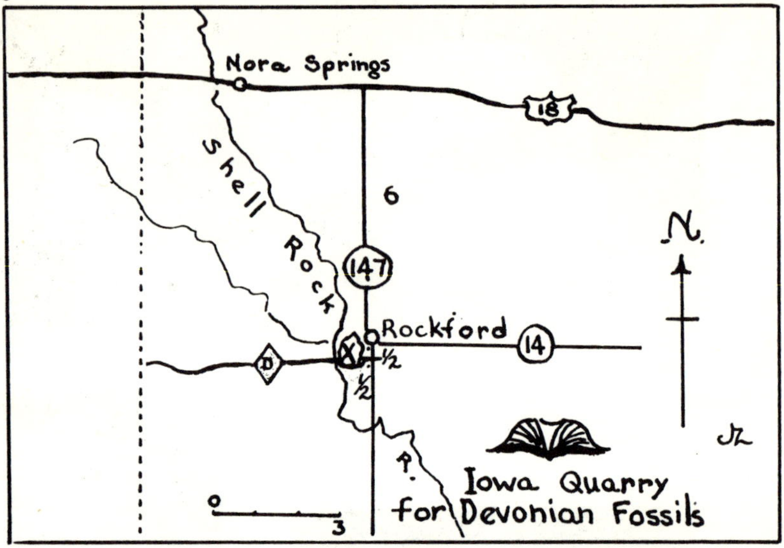

well as a rare kind of pyrite may be found here.

Oskaloosa is another place where wonderful crystals occur in concretions. The crystals are dolomite, but instead of being off-white or flesh-pink they are iridescent and vary from a rich bronze to a jet-black. They are decorated with clusters of the typical white calcite of the area. Unfortunately, the original locality has been worked out, but there is always the chance of a new discovery.

Exotic fossil woods, many of them polishable, are associated with the coal mines of the region. Finding one of these prized pieces now, however, is mostly a matter of luck.

The quarry at Pella has some of Iowa's finest fossils. There are dainty, complete brachiopods, blastoids, horn corals, and the tiniest trilobites I ever have seen. At present the quarry is closed. Other quarries with fossils are located at Ames, Winterset, and Earlham.

Iowa's most famous fossil quarry is the one at Le Grand. Here, Dr. B. H. Beane has discovered and prepared some of the most splendid fossils ever found. Outstanding are the complete flowerlike crinoids of several species, but truly exciting is a great slab of limestone with 183 perfectly preserved fossil starfish in bold relief. Dr. Beane worked off and on for 26 years on the cleaning and preparation of this rare museum piece. Forty species of echinoderms have come from this quarry. Though this quarry is now closed, the Concrete Materials Company has opened a new quarry across the Iowa River. The State of Iowa has purchased some of the outstanding fossils from Dr. Beane and has them on display at Des Moines at the Iowa State Historical Museum. This was accomplished largely through the efforts of the Des Moines Lapidary Society.

SOUTHERN IOWA

Crystals

The area around Centerville in southern Iowa is another coal mining region. There are countless mine dumps for many miles. Mines are scattered all the way from Albia to Coal City on the Missouri border. A great number of these mines, especially around Centerville, have selenite crystals. Pyrite is often found in these mines, also.

Keokuk Geodes

The best known geode formation in the United States is the Warsaw formation and though the city for which the formation was named is on the Illinois side of the Mississippi River, so many of these geodes have been found in Iowa that they are quite commonly referred to as "Keokuk geodes."

Virtually every stream in southern Iowa from Ottumwa to Keokuk, and the Des Moines River into which they flow, will have a harvest of geodes. Geodes are sometimes in banks and cliffs, sometimes on gravel bars, often in the streams. Commercial gravel operations and quarries also have their share of geodes. Road cuts and construction excavations yield a new supply.

Mississippian age coral, similar to Petoskey stone, is also found in Iowa. The stones and jewelry were made by members of the Des Moines Lapidary Society.

(Below) Brown "rice" agate, cut and mounted by the late Gus Brown of Iowa.

The best time to hunt is after the high water has receded in the spring.

Another geode-bearing stream is the Skunk River, especially south of New London. The gravel pit at Farmington has geodes. There is a state park called "Geode," near Burlington. You may not collect there, but it is an interesting park. Many farmers in the region permit collectors to hunt for geodes; a few may charge a modest fee. You will have little trouble finding geodes in this rock-rich area; however, not all the geodes are good. Many are solid quartz inside and hence, strictly speaking, not geodes inasmuch as geodes are defined as hollow concretions.

The geodes which collectors prize are those with inclusions of something other than the usual clear to white quartz crystals. Of course, any interior showing crystals of unusual beauty is a welcome addition to a collection, but the following are some of the inclusions which make some geodes even more highly prized: dolomite, goethite, marcasite, pyrite, sphalerite, ankerite, aragonite, chalcedony, kaolin, limonite, calcite, and millerite. the rarest is millerite which occurs as dark green, hairlike inclusions in calcite. To me, the two prettiest inclusions are pink calcite and glittering pyrite. Amethyst is also rare and lovely. The Smiths of New London have several of these.

The variation in size is tremendous, many of these round rocks being smaller than a golf ball and some of them larger than a beach ball. The baseball to softball size seems commonest. You will see geodes used for everything from stone walls to bird baths, from doorstops to planters.

Some collectors prefer to saw their geodes but I like to see them broken open carefully so the larger part is a little natural cave and the rest merely a lid to close the cave. They are easily broken with hammer and cold chisel — that is, if they are good ones. The solid quartz variety is very difficult to open. You soon learn by the heft of the geode whether or not it is likely to be hollow.

Calcified and silicified corals of the genus **Hexagonaria**, the same type as Michigan's Petoskey stone, are also found in southern Iowa in the same streams and banks as the geodes. The best of the Iowa coral is well silicified, often brightly colored by iron oxides, and takes a perfect polish. The color of one piece I found is almost a true coral. The gravel of Cedar Creek in southern Iowa is likely to contain coral. The silicified variety is also found in quarries at Coralville, a suburb of Iowa City.

Crystals and fossils also may be found on mine dumps of southern Iowa. On the coal mine dumps at Lovilia, there are honey-colored calcite crystals with inclusions of dark, hairlike goethite needles. Lovilia is on State Route 60 in Monroe County.

MISSISSIPPI RIVER BORDER

Gems

Most of Iowa's gems are found in eastern Iowa along the entire length of Iowa's stretch of the Mississippi River. Collectors think first of Lake Superior agates when Iowa gems are mentioned, and rightly so. Any gravel bar, commercial gravel operation, or tributary stream of the whole region has agate. Of course, they are not all good. A collector may pick up pounds of agate in a day but many will be broken or fractured or lacking in acceptable color or pattern. A few agates from every lot, however, will be so desirable that once a collector tries this region he will be lured back again and again.

Dubuque, Bellevue, Burlington, and Muscatine lead the list of places to try, with the last perhaps ranking first. Several companies dredge gravel along the River at Muscatine — the Acme Company, Hahn Brothers Gravel Company, and Northern Gravel Company. Permission must be obtained. Agates are easier to find if the belts are in operation so that there is a continuous flow of new stones. I have tried picking agates from the moving belts and to me this is the same as a ride on a roller coaster. Gravel is screened for size. You can find more agates in the smaller sizes but the possibility of a great big "raving-rock" keeps most eager pickers on the larger piles. It is easier for some to find agate if the sun is shining, but of course a little rain makes the agates easy to spot, too.

C. S. Morris, Dubuque, says many visitors to this area can't see the forest for the trees. He refers to the fact that these gravels carry coral, jasper, moss agate, petrified wood, "moonstone" spar, and many other fine gem materials, all of which are overlooked in the search for Lake Superior agates. A delicate pale blue oolitic agate is found sometimes. Clear or swirly agates of the Montana type are quite common. Various types of Petoskey corals are found which are polishable. Another interesting limestone is dark grey with dramatic white geometric designs or cross sections of crinoid stems, blastoids, and corals.

There is a good rock shop in Muscatine

and you may have the chance also to get a bargain in agates from local people who spend much time agate hunting.

To get to the famous Muscatine agate piles, follow U. S. 61 south through town past a big pearl button factory and a sprawling millwork plant. The millwork plant ends at Oregon Street where you turn left. In a few blocks you will see Musser Park, a nice spot for picnics. There are also public rest rooms. Climb the levee for a breathtaking view of the wide and busy Mississippi. Continue on Oregon to Stewart Street which angles right and is the main thoroughfare to the gravel operations. You will soon see gravel piles of all sizes on both sides of the road. The road you are on takes you to the Hahn Brothers' dumps, while a fork to the left after you see the first gravel will take you to the Acme Company property.

Don't forget that it is possible for a sharp-eyed, well informed collector to find a diamond in these Iowa gravels.

A gem quality green diamond was found in the gravel deposits at Dubuque. Crystal faces were prominent on two sides. The gem was between the size of a pea and a small hazelnut. It brought in excess of $1500 to the lucky finder who sold it to a Chicago jewelry firm.

A grey banded vein agate as well as cave onyx is found in limestone bluffs along the Mississippi in northeastern Iowa. Pieces of the agate can be found in washes both north and south of Guttenburg. A black jasper as well as several other colors also is found south of Guttenburg.

Iowa Pearls

No discussion of Iowa gems would be complete without some account of the pearl industry of the Muscatine area. The mussels of the Mississippi River are dredged from the bottom and used for the manufacture of pearl buttons. Baroques, slugs, and a few high-grade gem pearls are found in these mussels. The fancifully shaped but lustrous slugs and baroques are sold by the ounce, while the real gems are sold by the grain and command steep prices. Muscatine was for many years the center of pearl button manufacturing. Many of Iowa's best gem pearls came from the Mississippi as far north as McGregor, while others have come from swift streams which flow into the Mississippi.

Pearls still are being found. An iridescent 28-grain pearl was found at Harpers Ferry, Iowa. A solid pink 48-grain beauty was claimed from the Mississippi near McGregor. Many of the pearls of the Mississippi are of desirable colors — soft pinks or golds, and once in a while a pigeon-blood red. Blemished outer layers, particularly of oddly shaped pearls, often are carefully peeled until a layer of superior sheen and color is uncovered.

Three things have brought about a decline in the pearl industry. One is the growing use of plastics and synthetics for buttons. Another is the numerous flood-control dams along the great river systems, which create lakes of relatively quiet water. The third is the increasing pollution of streams and rivers by a rapidly expanding population. In spite of all these, in swift streams of rural areas many species of pearl-producing mussels are re-establishing themselves, and many freshwater pearls remain to be discovered by future collectors.

A large calcite crystal surrounded by quartz crystals in the cavity of a Keokuk geode.

MINNESOTA

Lake Superior Agate

The most widely distributed and justly popular of Minnesota's gem stones are the Lake Superior agates. That is not to say that these beautiful agates are plentiful, but there is a good chance of finding at least a few in almost any gravel pit or stream bed in the state.

Lake Superior agates are distinguished primarily by their fine parallel banding and rich colors. There are several varieties of Lake Superiors. A few are eye agates, some have straight onyxlike bands, some are true fortification agates like Fairburns, while others may present a picture or scenic effect. A typical Lake Superior, though, is a rather small, semitranslucent agate of a carnelian-brown color pattern with a multitude of fairly uniform bands in a harmonizing color.

Most Lake Superiors range in size from ½ inch to 2 inches. Often a lucky collector finds a beauty in the over-one-pound category, but a large agate of high quality is extremely rare. Oiva Maki of the Mesabi Rock and Mineral Club found a 17½-pound Lake Superior near Gilbert. It is reassuring to collectors to know such finds are still possible.

Agates are found in the basalt flows of the north shore of Lake Superior. Gooseberry River, Beaver Bay, and Grand Marais are well known shore locations.

Your best best is gravel-pit hunting. A visit to a gravel operation which is active is vastly better than searching old gravel pits. If the commercial gravel companies will allow you to pick agates from the belt, picking will be very good indeed. You will find that spotting the agates becomes easier with practice. There is a translucent glow to agates. The sun shining through them calls attention to them immediately.

New road construction or dam construction, new excavations, shifting sand bars, lake shores — all these are havens for the agate collector.

Some of the towns in Minnesota near which you can find agate, start in the north as you follow a Minnesota map, and end in the southeast: Hibbing, Cloquet, Brainerd, Little Falls, Appleton, Montevideo, Mankato, Red Wing, Blue Earth, Winona. Remember these are well known areas and there are plenty of other spots that are just as good.

One of the best areas for agate is in and around Winona. Several years ago, some construction dredging took place both in the river and in Lake Winona, where many specimens were found.

In Goodview, a western suburb of Winona, there is a large active gravel pit right along Highway 60 where you are welcome to search the stockpiles for agate. The best picking is usually found on the medium-sized gravel pits rather than the larger ones.

Along the right-of-way for the section of Highway 60, many old gravel beds have been exposed by the road work. Right back of the Northwestern shops a small boat harbor was dredged, so all of the gravel along the shore is exposed and well worth examing closely.

Several years ago the river threatened the city when it flooded the airport and some of the western parts of the city, so a large dike was built of gravel in which agates can be found.

If you want more hunting grounds, drive up Highway 60 to Wabasha, Minnesota (30 miles). Stay on the highway all the way through town until you see the railroad station off to your right. Park your car at the depot and walk down into the huge gravel pit where they take a great deal of gravel out for use in railroad construction. You may have the pleasure of picking a nice Superior agate right out of a wall of gravel. The gravel deposit is 30 feet thick in spots along here.

The Lake Superior agate is found widely scattered in the gravels of Wisconsin,, Iowa, and Minnesota. Many of the original localities were along the shores of Lake Superior, hence the name. In "The Agate Book," by Dake, sixty or more varieties and subvarieties of agate are described. More than half of these have been found in the Lake Superior agates.

Most Superior agates are in distinct bands of red, red brown, tan, beige and white. The brighter colors are wanted most, and of course the more complicated the pattern and more fracture-free the stone, the finer it is. Some of the agates have great clarity while others tend to be nearly opaque.

While most of the smaller Lake Superior agates, like the one- and two-inch sizes, will be found free of checks, cracks and incipient fractures, the larger sizes tend to present these defects. As a general rule, a large Lake Superior agate, found, say, in an Iowa farm field, will have these defects. The agate may present a colorful and interesting pattern, but unfortunately "checks" are likely to be present. However, as a rule, a specimen of this kind may be sawed and the surfaces polished without parting company. As with most other agates, the saw cut is usually made parallel to the greatest diameter.

There are some new gravel pits for agate hunters west of Osseo, in suburban Minneapolis, a little northwest of the metropolitan district. Take Route 110 ¼ mile south, then turn west. This road dead-ends at three gravel pits. George Rickert of the Geological Society of Minnesota, says to ask permission from Mr. Barton at the first pit on your left. Mr. Anderson is in charge of the second pit which lies to the north. There is a third pit on the right belonging to the county, and at the time Mr. Rickert was there, permsision was not required. Lake Superior agates, chalcedony, and jasper are among the cutting materials here. Some of the agates resemble those from Montana except that they are not dendritic.

THE NORTH SHORE

Thomsonite

Minnesota's most unusual gem is thomsonite. Found on the north shore of Lake Superior in a matrix of basalt, these dainty zeolite nodules are so individual in their markings that no other gem can be mistaken for them. The sunbursts and eyes seem to be part of the radial habit of the stone. The pink, red, and green are brilliant against the creamy white background. Black accents make some stones unusually showy. When polished, thomsonites appear to have the texture of fine porcelain.

Thomsonites are found mostly in an area of approximately a mile square. Though Thomsonite Beach is known best, the thomsonite-bearing formation stretches about a mile inland, and extends a mile from Terrace Point. Since most of the shoreline is private property and is fenced, it is not easy to find a spot to look for waterworn pebbles. However, some motels and tourist homes in the area can help you find a place to look along the shore, or you may find an outcrop north of Highway 61 and with a hammer and a chisel work out the gem nodules, or pieces of the hard rock encasing them.

Lintonites are the translucent, solid color, olive-green nodules found in the same area. They are really a variety of thomsonite with the fibrous structure not apparent. Both lintonites and thomsonites are small; sizes of an inch or more are quite hard to find.

There are many other places to look for gems along the beautiful North Shore drive. Following are some which G. M. Schwartz figured, using Lake Avenue in Duluth on U. S. 61 as point zero:

Agates at French River on beach 12.2 miles.

Agates at Knife River 18 miles.

Agate beach at pole 1385. (The telephone poles are plainly numbered in this area and since distances between towns are great, the poles make excellent markers.)

Agate beach at 28.2 miles.

Agates in stream and on beach at 34.6 miles.

Pole 1915. Gem gravels.

Pole 2120. Gull Rock agate beach. Ask permission.

Zeolite collecting starts at about 62.5 miles.

Good zeolites at mouth of Little Marais River (64.5), Manitou River (65.9), Cross River (79.4), and Temperance River (80.7).

Thomsonite Beach is at 103.2 miles.

Special Note

In 1962, the entire area along Highway 61 was closed to collecting because too many people had thoughtlessly dug and left holes along the right-of-way until the situation was dangerous. Also, the Omega Land and Mineral Company claim mineral rights on the public areas.

The Minnesota Mineral Club (Minneapolis) has petitioned the State Conservation Service and State Legislature to allow supervised collecting, the same as it does for hunters and fishermen. Collectors are being asked to be especially careful in this area so as not to jeopardize the negotiations

There are places to collect on private property providing permission is obtained. Local inquiry is required. At least one motel in the area has access to a thomsonite locality.

The thomsonite (a member of the zeolite family) is a secondary mineral formed in cavities of lava rock. The process isn't known, but it's believed that ancient, subterranean water percolated through the solidified, spongy looking lava rock, dissolving minerals which gradually settled to fill the small cavities and fissures with crystalline material.

The split thomsonite is interesting to study. Generally, each stone has several centers from which hair-thin needles radiate in all directions like quills from a riled-up porcupine's back. Many colors may be found — white, pink, salmon-red and gray green — and these are arranged in spheres within spheres.

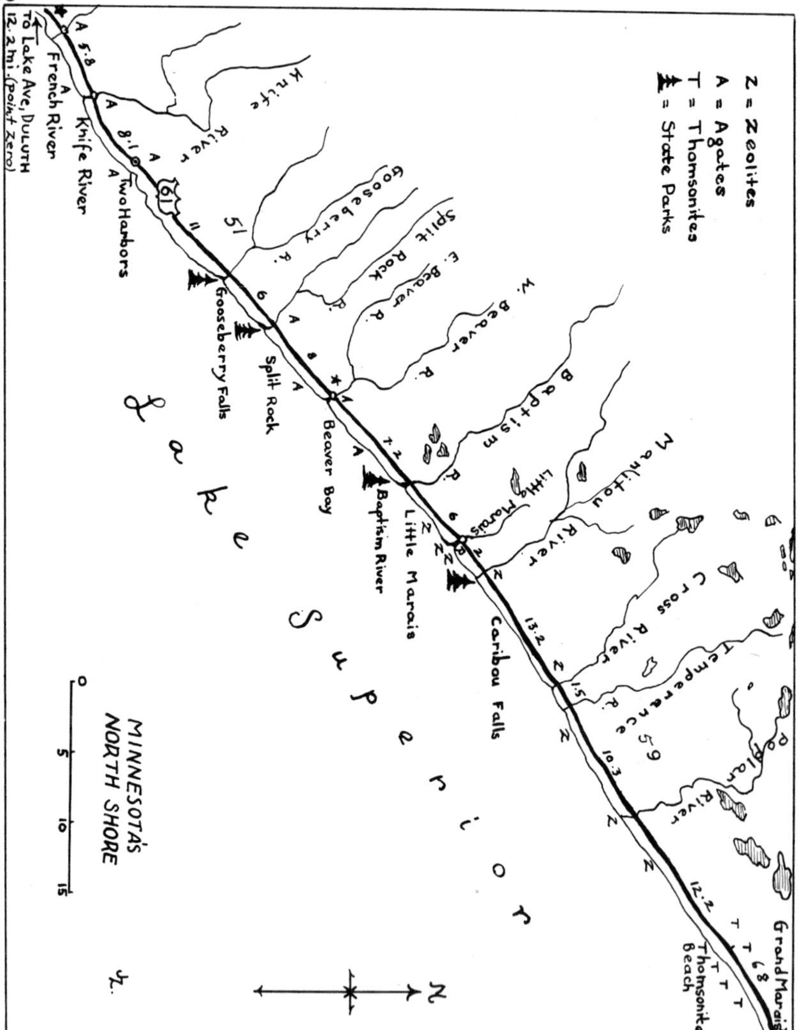

Thomsonites have a hardness of 5 to 5.5. The green circles may be scratched with a nail. As they are also brittle, they are easily crazed. Stones which fall free from the eroding matrix and collect in the rock basins are covered with an earthy pink skin.

The value of a thomsonite for jewelry depends on how artistically Nature arranged the "eyes" and how subtly she blended the colors. And, of course, they must be fairly free from fractures.

THE MESABI RANGE

The world's largest open-pit iron mine is at Hibbing, Minnesota. The mine-studded range surrounding it is known as the "Mesabi." The best grade of iron ore is scarce but there are tremendous amounts of lower grade ores all of which are commercially valuable because of modern industrial processes.

One of the gems of this area is an attractive jasper called "Mary Ellen jasper," for the mine in which it was first found. It is a colorful, red, algal jasper of swirling designs. Some of it has metallic-appearing inclusions, probably hematite.

The Mary Ellen Mine is 1 mile west of Biwabik. The Corsica Mine is another location. If these mine dumps are closed to the public, try the roadsides, stream beds, and abandoned waste dumps of the area. I cannot emphasize too strongly that collectors must have permission before hunting on active mine property.

Since Mary Ellen jasper appears so similar to some of Minnesota's other fine jaspers, you may find pieces of it or material quite like it long distances from these mines.

The goethite of the Mesabi range is also a polished mineral. At first thought to be hematite, the goethite when polished resembles the so called Alaska black "diamonds." The hard compact massive goethite is suitable for tumbling. Fine specimen material is the botryoidal and stalactitic variety. The best goethite comes from Hibbing and Chisholm.

Agates may be found on the mine dumps at Eveleth, westward to Grand Rapids. Floodwood, Cloquet, Carlton, and Moose Lake have all produced agates of finest quality.

Crystal and mineral collectors will find much of interest in this area. There are garnets, maganite, minnesotaite, magnetite, greenalite, pyrite and marcasite. These were reported by Richard Lake of Chisholm.

Fossils also are found in the Mesabi, with shark teeth and mollusks predominating. Grand Rapids is the center of the fossil area.

Jerry Huber of the Mesabi Rock and Mineral Club, advises one to inquire locally before attempting field trips in this area. Hibbing Junior College has a display of Minnesota minerals provided and arranged by members of the active Mesabi Club.

The beautiful Vermillion Range near Ely, north and east of the Mesabi, has gem jaspers in a myriad of showy colors. Excellent quartz crystals also are found in the mines of this lake-studded Range. At present, the most popular material from the Vermillion is a deposit of gem green jasper known as "Evergreen jasper," found near Winton.

THE CUYUNA RANGE

Minnesota's Cuyuna Range is in a picturesque north-woods setting of pines and lakes. Although the principal product of the range is iron ore, this district also is known for unusual gems.

It was near Crosby in 1936, that a new American gem, "binghamite," was discovered. William Bingham of St. Paul, and his son were looking for Lake Superior agates in the strip mine dumps when suddenly they noticed a pile of silicified material. Noting that freshly broken surfaces showed pleasing yellow and red colors, Bill stuck a couple of pieces in his rock bag. The following winter when Bill got around to polishing some of the material, he realized that it was a fine new gem material.

"Binghamite" is a vein material, a crystalline quartz replacement of fibrous goethite. The fibers are straight and colored red by hematite, yellow by limonite. The material resembles tigereye. The dumps of the Arco and Portsmouth Mines are the likeliest places to hunt but permission must be obtained.

Later, a very similar gem was discovered in this same range. Named "silkstone" by Ray Lulling who discovered it, this material differs in that the fibers are not straight. Silkstone also has less silica.

Agates also are found in this area. Those who are interested in thumbnails and micromounts will enjoy searching the dumps for small crystal vugs of various iron and manganese minerals.

CENTRAL AND WESTERN MINNESOTA

Near Little Falls, Minnesota, you may look for staurolites, the interesting, twinned crystals commonly called "fairy crosses" or "fairy stones." Together with garnets, they are found in the sands of Elk Creek near Little Falls and the Mississippi near Royalton.

Not all the dark brown to red brown staurolites are perfect crosses. You will find the crystals twinned at several different angles as well as some singles. To find the crosses you should have a shovel and a screen of about one-half-inch mesh.

Staurolites are found on both sides of the river downstream from Blanchard dam. Con Peterzen of Hibbing gives the following directions: Go south of Little Falls on U. S. 10, setting your speedometer at the St. Gabriel Hospital as you leave town. At 6.3 miles, turn right on the asphalt township road. Drive 1.2 miles and turn left, then 1.6 miles to a dirt road which takes you 0.4 of a mile to the dam parking area. The property belongs to the Minnesota Power and Light Company. Please respect their rights.

I think there are other staurolite localities in the area. We found some in a stream near Charles Lindbergh State Park by wading the stream and sifting the sand, particularly under the bridge.

Southwestern Minnesota is the home of the catlinite, the sacred pipestone of the American Indians. This lovely, historic area is now a national monument and collecting is forbidden. The place is well worth visiting. The stones as well as hand-carved artifacts made from it, are available from local Sioux Indians.

The catlinite from Pipestone National Monument, Pipestone, Minnesota, comes in several colors, the most prized being a deep red. When first quarried, it is softer and easier to carve than after it has hardened in the air. It is classed as a hard, finely grained clay which grades into red shale. Red Sioux quartzite also can be seen in this area. The red color of both kinds of stone is due to small amounts of iron. The National Monument is a scenic area as well as being of historic interest. Waterfalls, a lake, steep canyon walls, and Indians at work in the quarry combine to make a visit memorable to the collector.

Fossils

Marine fossils are numerous throughout Minnesota. A productive area is a quarry 5 miles east of Rochester. Road cuts in the Rochester area will also add to your fossil collection. Red Wing is another good area for fossils, as well as the agates mentioned previously. Actually, most of the agate areas have fossils of some kind also. Any gravel deposit may have teeth, tusks, or other Pleistocene fossils as well as earlier marine fossils in the form of imprints in harder rocks which the glacier often transported great distances.

There are many types of coral fossils at the quarries around Kasota which is just west of Highway 169 between Mankato and St. Peter. The quarries are along the Minnesota River.

"Kidney ore," hematite, from the Carey Mine, Hurley, Wisconsin. Photo — Dr. Oliver Lohr.

WISCONSIN

Wisconsin has several claims to fame in the gem, mineral, and fossil fields. The Mississippi River area has produced pearls, the glacial moraines have yielded diamonds, gravel pits boast the fine Lake Superior agates, and many mines and quarries are the homes of fossils of rare varieties as well as choice crystals.

LAKE SUPERIOR-GOGEBIC DISTRICT

Wisconsin's upper border is on Lake Superior and Green Bay of Lake Michigan, connected by the border of Michigan's iron country and by the Menominee River. The Gogebic Range is an iron-producing area stretching through Iron County, Wisconsin, and Gogebic County, Michigan. Upper Wisconsin is a land of pine forests, clear lakes, and swift streams.

Gems and Specimens

This part of Wisconsin is not particularly noted for gems; however, it is a rocky and often rugged country so more prospecting may uncover all sorts of gems. I base my high hopes for this area on three finds. A family from near Superior, Wisconsin, found a large number of beautifully banded pastel agates which look more like Mexican nodules than like Lake Superiors. None of the bands could be seen on the outside of the agate. The nodules were waterworn and about 1 to 2½ inches in diameter.

The second discovery was a deposit of beryllium with some fine large crystals of beryl, on the Embarrass River near Tigerton, Shawano County. It was reported by William Tom Zuehlke of Milwaukee, an advanced crystal and fossil collecter. Then before long a letter from Joe Phetteplace of Wauzeka, who specializes in intarsias, reported corundum of both ruby and sapphire varieties from near Seymour, Outagamie County, near Green Bay. These corundum gems were of faceting quality.

Upper Wisconsin is of more interest to the mineral and crystal collector. Near Gordon, Bayfield County, on the banks of Ounce Creek, there is an abandoned copper mine where epidote, diopside, and native copper may be found. Some native copper also has been found at Copper Falls State Park, Ashland County.

The most famous location in this area is the Montreal Mine at Hurley, Iron County. This mine is the deepest iron mine in the world, with shafts over 4000 feet down. Good quality crystal specimens from this mine are bladed barite, bladed selenite, radiating stalactitelike columns of goethite, calcite crystals, manganese crystals, rhodochrosite, and the first vanadinite to be found in Wisconsin. A mile east is the Cary Mine, another active mine.

An exceptional marble has been quarried in Bayfield County near Grandview. Kyanite and garnet are found near Powell, Iron County.

Where Marinette, Oconto, and Forest Counties join is a giant guartz outcrop about 20 miles long and 4 miles wide. This rugged forested area is called "McCauslin Mountain." Wisconsin State Route 32 borders this mountain on the west while County Road F lies to the south and County Road C to the north. Fine quartz crystals are most noteworthy, although the specular hematite is also worth collecting.

The crystal area is on the west end. From Townsend on Highway 32, drive 2.5 miles north. Check your speedometer at the bar to your right. Continue north on No. 32 only .8 of a mile more. Park your car by the old trail on your left. You can walk to the ledge 500 yards to the right.

CENTRAL WISCONSIN

Gems

The bluffs of the Mississippi River and its tributaries have Lake Superior agates. Agates have been found at Chippewa Falls, Menomonie, Durand, and LaCrosse. Any gravel pit in the state is likely to produce colorful agates.

Wood County in central Wisconsin has a large, varied quartz deposit of cutting quality. Some of the material is aventurine, some merely colored quartz. Some of the roads of the county are even paved with this material. The color of the aventurine is orange to red brown. Gem material is found in the numerous sandstone quarries, in contact zones of pre-Keweenawan igneous rocks and upper Cambrian sandstone.

The Wausau area, Marathon County, is known chiefly for its choice quality, bright red granite, but gem collectors also find this area one of the State's best. Just north of Wausau is an intersection known locally as the "Little Yellow Schoolhouse." Here you will find large amounts of the so called Wisconsin "moonstone" and "labradorite." This is really a type of rock known as albite peristerite. It occurs in pegmatite dikes.

The type called "moonstone" is a cream to peach color and when properly cut has

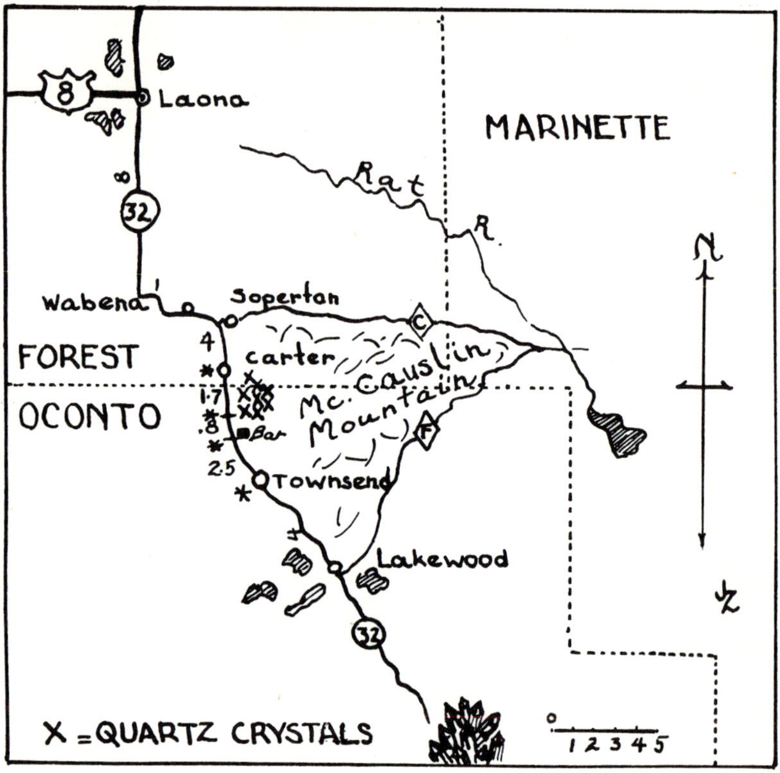

a shimmering chatoyancy not unlike true moonstone. That called "labradorite" has a dark grey background and when polished, exhibits flashes of blue and green. Much of this material is fractured but persistence always turns up some high cutting quality.

Rib Mountain, with an elevation of 1941 feet, is the highest point in the State and is in a well mineralized area. Quartz crystals may be found on the road leading to the peak. Massive rhodochrosite has been found in this area. Epidote and unakite are found one mile north of the junction of State Route 153 and Road H, a county road.

It is also from this area that jade was reported. However, well known Wisconsin collectors agree that the jade deposit has not been verified.

Crystals and Specimens

Catlinite (pipestone) can be found 5 miles east of the town of Rice Lake, Barron County. A red and white banded quartzite also may be collected in this area.

For many years the Lutz Quarry of Oshkosh has produced fine crystals of marcasite, sphalerite, galena, pyrite, and calcite. The specimens are on a grey limestone matrix. They are iridescent and remarkably sparkling. Sometimes fossils lined with drusy crystals are found in this quarry. At the present time the Lutz Quarry is not open to collectors, but in the same region another excellent quarry does allow visitors. This is the quarry of Marblehead, 7 miles southeast of Fon du Lac. This quarry has an abundance of brachiopods and other fossils at the south end. It is located on County Road V, ½ miles west of Eden. Herman Hollub of Oshkosh says the fossils are in the Niagara formation. He adds that there are active limestone kilns at the site of the quarry.

Fossils

Good fossil collecting is possible throughout central Wisconsin in road cuts, cliffs and banks, rivers and streams, and quarries.

A quarry at Colfax in Dunn County exposes 30 feet of fossiliferous rock. At Mt. Washington in Eau Claire, is a quarry with abundant trilobites and brachiopods in the upper 70 feet.

Road cuts in the upper Cambrian sandstone north of Whitehall, Trempealeau County, are full of marine fossils.

The quarry at Tunnel City, Monroe County, has several types of fossils in a layer near the quarry floor. Also road cuts in this county along Trunk Highway Z, southwest of the town of Wilton, reveal strata containing fossils.

Road cuts along Highway 82, 6 miles west of Mauston, Juneau County, have brachiopods, while fossil worm borings may be found in the same County, 6 miles north of Elroy.

In the vicinity of Green Bay, near the town of Wayside, fossil bryozoans are found in road cuts and stream banks. In fact, there are similar outcrops all the way to Lake Winnebago.

SOUTHERN WISCONSIN

Gems

The Mississippi River and the Wisconsin River gravels are the chief sources of agate in the southern third of Wisconsin. Muscoda, Prairie du Chien, and Cassville are well known localities. Since the best known localities tend to be overworked, the alert collector will remember that any gravel operation in the State is a possible agate producer. Inquiry is the only way to find locations where collectors are allowed.

At Devil's Lake, south of Baraboo, Sauk County, is a deposit of quartzite some of which will cut lovely gems. The deposit stretches east toward Columbia County. There are still active quarries in the Baraboo Range.

Many of the famous Wisconsin pearls came from the southern section of the state. The Grant River at Potosi and the Wisconsin River at Boscobel are important areas. The $20,000 pearl which is part of the English crown jewels came from the Mississippi River at Prairie du Chien. Any unpolluted stream of this section of the state may have pearl-producing mussels. A license is required for collecting pearls.

Most of the diamonds of Wisconsin have come from the southern part of the state, especially the southeastern counties near Milwaukee. The earliest diamond discovery was in Waukesha County. The largest find, a 21-carat stone, is from adjoining Washington County. Racine County, Ozaukee County, and Dane County, all in this region, have each yielded one of the rare diamonds of the Great Lakes area. The only other part of the state to produce any number of diamonds is Pierce County on the Mississippi River in the central part of the state. Here, small stones were found near Diamond Bluff. The Kettle glacial moraine is the source of these diamond finds, but where the glacier found them is anybody's guess.

Crystals

Southern Wisconsin also has some good spots for crystal collectors. In an area known as the Ableman Narrows, just north of Rock Springs, Sauk County, are several road cuts which reveal vast quartzite deposits. Here are some fine quartz crystals with a pleasing light red color probably due to the presence of iron. These crystals are usually rather small, about 1 inch long, but cover huge pieces of quartzite with a dense mat. The matrix is reddish brown grading into off-white. Some crystals are doubly terminated. Heavy equipment and much patience are required to extract them. William Zuehlke and Henry Kluk of Milwaukee worked out one piece weighing 85 pounds entirely coated with perfectly terminated crystals.

In southwstern Wisconsin, the zinc-lead mines of Grant, Iowa, and Lafayette Counties long have produced fine crystals for the discriminating collector. There are many mine dumps in the vicinity of Mineral Point, Shullsburg, Tennyson, Benton, Hazel Green, and Platteville. Careful hunting in the old mine dumps will reveal crystals of calcite, smithsonite, sphalerite, barite, marcasite, pyrite, and galena. The dog-tooth calcite of the mine dumps near Werley is particularly fine.

Rare millerite crystals in calcite were found at Estabrook Park along the Milwaukee River in Milwaukee. This area is closed now. However, just outside of the park area on the west side of the River are some small but exquisite geodes.

The Ives Quarry of Racine, noted for large blades of marcasite and high quality calcite crystals, is also closed.

Fossils

The Hartung Quarry of Milwaukee has long been famous for magnificent specimens of Silurian trilobites. The Quarry has been purchased by the city and will be filled in as a city dump. Members of the Wisconsin Geological Society were allowed to collect in this locality in 1963. Local inquiry about the status of the quarry is necessary. Some of these trilobites are up to 3 inches long and are fully extended.

The Franklin Quarry, also in Milwaukee, has produced fine fossils as well as some exceptional calcite crystals. Collecting is allowed sometimes, but again, permission must be obtained.

The Halquist Stone Quarry of Sussex still yields crinoid stems, brachiopods, and cephalopods.

Quarries near Lannon, Waukesha County, are noted for cephalopods.

The Niagara dolomite of the Cedarburg-Grafton vicinity is rich in fossils. Look particularly along the Milwaukee River and the quarries north of Saukville.

Quarries in Racine, Racine County, have crystals and crinoids. Quarries along Highway 83 between Burlington, Racine County, and Waukesha have excellent crinoids and sometimes rare, large trilobites.

The Niagara dolomite of the entire region of southeastern Wisconsin constitutes the most important collecting area of the state to fossil hunters. Since this is also a heavily populated region, many people examine the road cuts and quarries. There are always new fossils weathering out and new spots to collect. Treat each spot you visit in such a manner that others may be welcomed after you leave.

As crystals are among the most likely finds in Wisconsin, if you are a newcomer to the hobby you may be interested in knowing a little about collecting them.

You will find crystals in pockets and vugs and seams, in rock outcrops, or in quarries. Most crystals are in or on a hard,, resistant matrix. If the crystals are scratched, banged up, or the terminations broken, the specimens are ruined.

Tools such as chisels should be sharp. A heavier-than-average hammer or pick is desirable. Pry bars often help. We take a piece of foam rubber with us to lay over the crystals while we chisel away at the matrix. In a pocket in my rock bag I always have a supply of cleansing tissues or paper napkins so I can wrap each specimen individually. Under the front seat of the car I have a large flat box where I lay crystal specimens in a single layer.

Start your actual work by locating a fracture, a porous section of matrix, or an uncrystallized spot. Be sure to work down deep enough so the layer of crystals doesn't flake off the top. Patience and perseverance are required but bring their own reward.

Don't neglect even small pieces with crystals or tiny singly terminated crystals. With a magnifying glass or a microscope you will be amazed at the perfection of these jewel-like small bits. Many hobbyists specialize in thumbnails or micromounts and if you decide this branch of the hobby is not for you, at least you will find that good quality small crystals are popular trading stock.

Many collectors start with agates, but those who stay with the hobby eventually become entranced with the wonder of crystals. Good crystal specimens are often worth far more than a piece of cutting material of equal size.

Crystal collecting in mines or caves should never be undertaken without expert help. They may be full of hazards such as poisonous mineral salts, deadly gases, snakes, and loose rock and dirt.

When you arrive home with your crystals, they may be cleaned with soap and water, and for stubborn stains, a little chlorine bleach. Trim as much matrix from the specimen as possible without running the risk of breaking it. Display or store with a label giving correct name and locality of each piece.

A delicate sphere of calcite crystals from the Montreal Mine, Hurley, Wisconsin. Photo — Dr. Oliver Lohr.

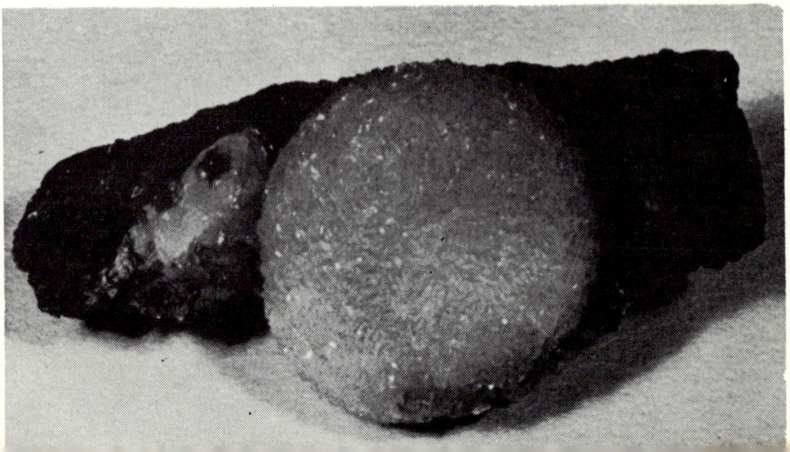

MICHIGAN

THE KEWEENAW PENINSULA

Michigan's fabulous copper country, cool and green in the summertime, is justly a collector's Mecca of the midwest. The copper deposits, known and worked by ancient Indians, have produced the world's largest masses of native copper. One mass was over 420 tons. A suitable introduction to the gems and minerals of the copper country for the collector visiting the area is the splendid museum of the Michigan College of Mines and Technology at Houghton.

Beaches

There are two general types of collecting in the Keweenaw – the beaches and the mine dumps. The beach gravels have agate of the Lake Superior type. Violet Miller of Ahmeek reports a prize find of 17-pound agate at Keweenaw Point. Most of the agates found on the beaches are quite small but those dug from the basalt banks range larger in size.

Many of these agates are called "Keweenaw agates," as in some respects they seem to be a separate subdivision of the Lake Superiors. For instance, the predominant color is brown. They tend to be opaque, and the patterns are tone-on-tone bands.

The best agate beach for quantity and quality is the stretch which reaches from Maclain State Park to Five Mile Point. Another interesting beach is near Ontonagon. Still another is at Eagle Harbor.

Thomsonites also may be found on these Lake Superior beaches. They are pastel pink and green with radiating sunburst patterns. They seem to be denser and pinker than the Minnesota variety. Some local authorities suggest that these thomsonites are a type of pink prehnite. The best beaches are from Ahmeek north to Eagle Harbor. Ontonagon beaches are fruitful.

Other gems of the beaches include a variety of colorful jaspers, chalcedony, chert, and the colorless orthoclase feldspar called **adularia** which sometimes cuts a moonstone.

Mine Dumps

The entire peninsula is loaded with mines and old mine dumps. The materials to look for on the dumps are many. Most sought is the massive form of datolite, a gem unique to this region. The datolite nodules often have native copper inclusions. Others have mottled scenic effects. When polished, the quality is like rare porcelain. The average size of these gems is about 2 inches though specimens have been found up to 7 inches and more in diameter. The colors are mostly pastel but there is a fantastic array of tints, with green and yellow being the rarest. One color I have never seen is a true violet. The exterior is dark with a cauliflowerlike shape. Another rare zeolite gem, chlorastrolite, is sometimes found in the dumps.

Gems, however, are not the only things for which these old copper dumps are noted. There are beautiful specimens and crystals. Choice collectors' gems are the nuggets of native copper and native silver known as "half-breeds." Attractive calcite crystals, some with native copper inclusions, are another collector's delight. Then there are fine specimens of epidote, quartz, domeykite, prehnite, tenorite with chrysocolla, ankerite, and laumantite. No wonder this area is a magnet to collectors.

Favored dumps have been the Delaware, Mandan, Central, Cliff, Star, Clark, and Phoenix, all of Keweenaw County. The best dumps of Houghton County are the Arcadian and the celebrated Quincy, the most prolific datolite producer. The mines at Rockland and Mass in Ontonagon County are possible hideouts of gems and specimens.

The Wolverine Mine of Kearsarge has epidote crystals, agate, and chrysocolla. The Copper Falls Mine has zeolite crystals. Amethyst occurs north of Copper Harbor.

Of the innumerable mines of the area, the treasured datolite has been found in at least twenty-two. Harry Sprague of Saginaw has datolite nodules from eighteen mines in his matchless, personal collection. However, the greatest number of his came from the Delaware in the northern part of the Peninsula.

You will notice as you look at a map of the Keweenaw, that many of the mine names are the same as the names of the towns where they are located. All these Keweenaw towns are mining centers, though tourism is now the leading industry of many.

Local information may be obtained from the rock shops of the Keweenaw and the southern part of Michigan's Upper Peninsula.

UPPER PENINSULA IRON RANGE

The Kona dolomite which burst onto the lapidary horizon in a blaze of glory is in reality a very ancient rock, having started with algae of the Huronian period. The fact that the rock could be cut and polished was

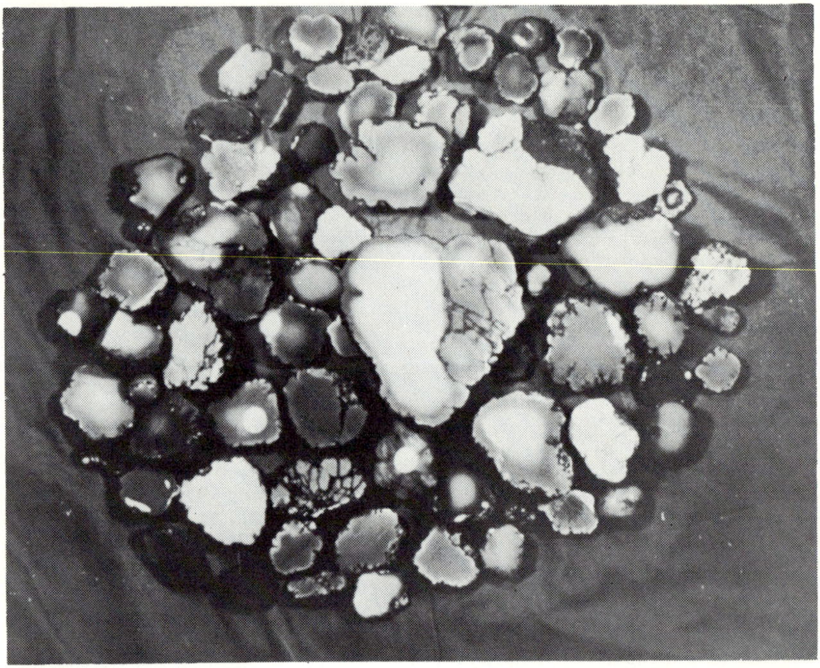

Prize-winning specimens of datolite show black and copper veining against a soft, glowing pink. From the Harry Sprague collection. Photo — Dr. Oliver Lohr.

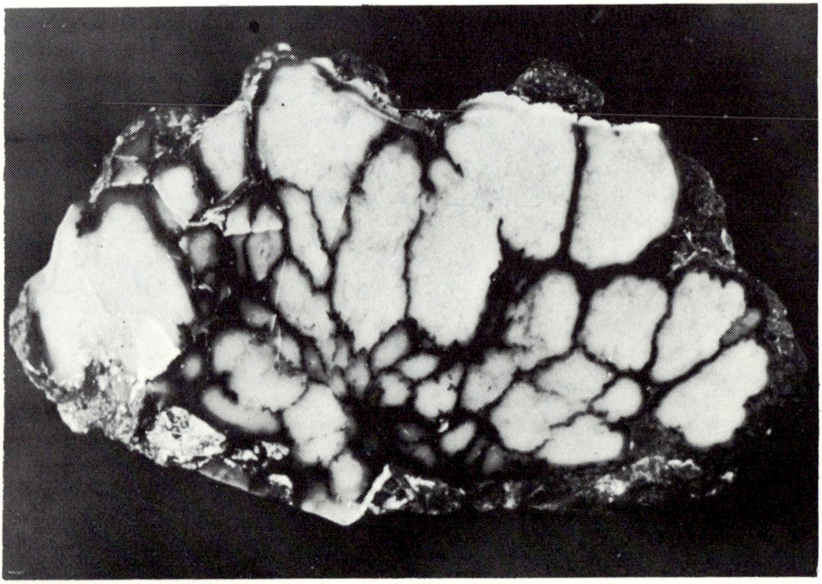

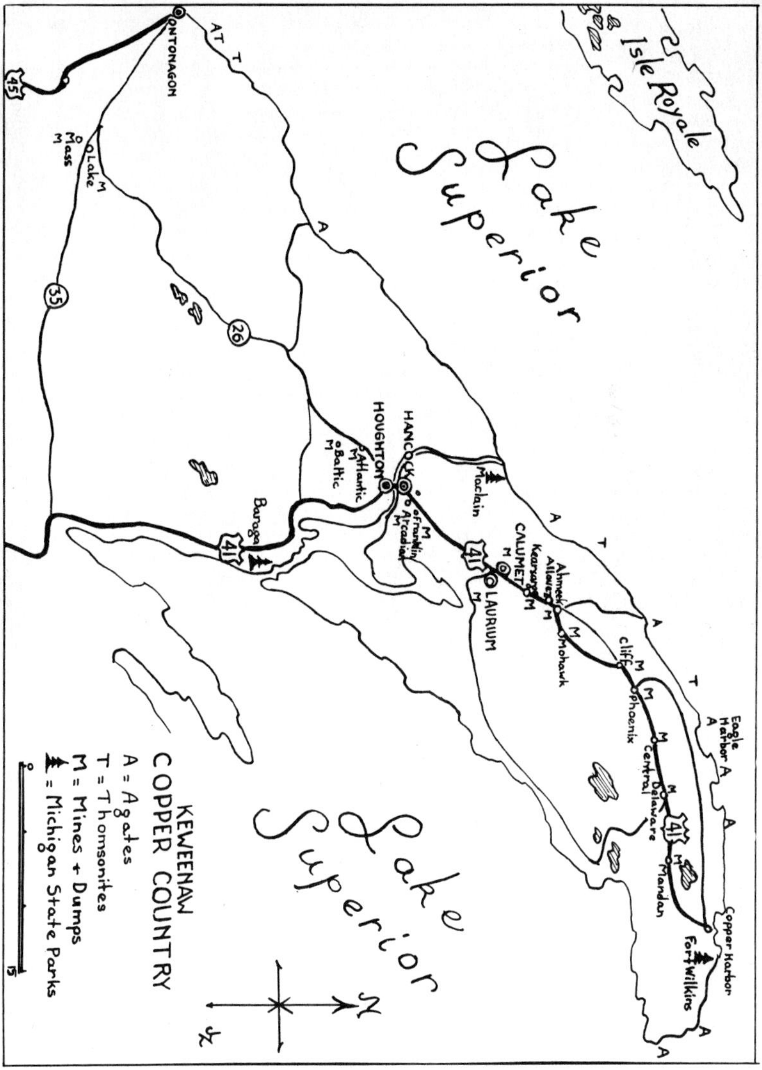

also known a long time ago. However, the 700 collectors who attended the Midwest Federation Field Trip Convention in Ishpeming in 1960 were so pleased with the material they gathered that the gem suddenly zoomed to popularity.

The rock, named for the Kona Hills at Goose Lake, is not pure dolomite, but has more silica present and grades into chert and quartzite. The strata were subjected to intense folding, resulting in a breccia cemented with quartz and hematite.

The colors of the dolomite are red, pink, orange, and brown in many shades and tints with some spots of cream color and plenty of black lacing for contrast.

The Lindberg Quarry near Ishpeming, where the most spectacular dolomite has been found, is now closed to the public. The collecting privileges were so badly abused, not by the convention group, but by a few unscrupulous individuals, that the quarry owners had no choice. Inquire locally for current information.

Jaspilite, a red jasper with hematite, is another gem of upper Michigan. Jasper Hill in Ishpeming is a famous example of this distinctive gem, but there are plenty of other outcrops for the collector in the surrounding country. Michigamme and Republic, also in the vicinity, have abundant jaspilite.

Garnets are found at Beacon Hill near Champion, and at Mt. Shasta near Michigamme. Beryl, tourmaline, and quartz can be found in pegmatite outcrops near Republic and specifically at the quarries at Randville, Dickinson County.

A new gem for northern Michigan is corundum, variety sapphire. These blue gems from the Champion Mine were identified by Robert Markert. They occur in pegmatite with sericite. The sapphires brought to light so far are small, but there is hope of larger ones as exploration of the vein continues.

One of the most interesting specimens from Michigan was brought up by a skindiver. At the bottom of a deep lake in northern Michigan a diver found an old axe handle completely covered with beautiful, sharply bladed, selenite crystals. The clear sparkling crystals were up to three inches in length and among the most perfect I have ever seen. But the axe handle, still wood, and old crumbly wood at that, is plainly visible. In the historic lumber country of Michigan, an axe handle in a lake has no significance, but the astonishing build-up of crystals in the time the axe handle had lain in the water is a major discovery to rockhounds. The haft broke in four crystal-encrusted pieces after being exposed to the air.

A considerable amount of collecting has been done in the mine dumps around the iron mining city of Ishpeming. One can spend some time here, for this is not a region of quick results. A. Joseph Alessi has visited some of these localities, and has given us the following information without any guarantee of results. One may well spend a pleasant vacation here.

Old Lake Shaft (abandoned), Ishpeming — quartz, greenstone, hematite, and jasper.

Section Seven Mine (abandoned), Ishpeming — hematite, jasper, hematite with quartz, mica, milky quartz, greenstone, limonite, magnetite, quartz crystals on hematite and magnetite, siderite and specular hematite.

Section Sixteen Mine (operating), Ishpeming — hematite and limonite ores in various forms including massive, specular, kidney, grape, needle and stalactitic, small quartz, crystals, jasper, soapstone, pyrite crystals on limonite, and calcite concretions on hematite.

Holmes Mine (operating), Ishpeming — hematite, hematite with jasper, ferruginous quartz with mica, limonite, calcite filling cavities in hematite, specular hematite, magnetic crystals.

Cliffs Shaft Mine (operating), Ishpeming — hard specular hematite, jasper, pyrite and iron-stained chert.

Morris - Lloyd Mine (operating), North Lake — hematite with blue jasper, and various iron minerals.

Cambria Mine (operating), Negaunee — "kidney ore," massive hematite, soapstone, and specular hematite schist.

Archibald Mine (operating), Gwinn — large gypsum crystals on hematite, specular hematite and magnetite.

Beach at Presque Isle — brown sandstone showing veins of calcite, small fragments of agate and chalcedony geodes.

Much specimen material for beginning and advanced collectors is abundant in this part of Michigan. Barite is found at the Lucy Mine at Negaunee. Actinolite, biotite, asbestos, dolomite, and wollastonite are found at Rian's Quarry near Felch, Dickinson County.

Massive rhodochrosite is found on the Baltic dump at Negaunee. Pyrite, pyroxene, fluorite and phlogopite are among the many minerals of the varied zones of the Metro-Nite Quarry at Randville.

All of Upper Michigan is forested and hilly with numerous deep clear lakes and trout-filled streams, but the opportunities for an energetic rock collector are virtually endless.

ISLE ROYALE

I have purposely left until last in the Keweenaw Peninsula, the fabled Isle Royale and its unique gem, chlorastrolite, or "greenstone." Isle Royale is a national park and collecting is prohibited. Nevertheless, these chatoyant gems constitute a major gem deposit in Michigan and should be mentioned, at least.

This rocky island with its dense pine woods is the world's one major locality of the tiny "green stars." The gems are found both in the lava flows and as waterworn pebbles on the shore. They seem to be related to the zeolite gems such as thomsonite or lintonite, but their exact classification has not been determined.

Beyond doubt there are many chlorastrolites under Lake Superior, and occasionally

Kona dolomite.

Copper crystals, Houghton, Michigan.

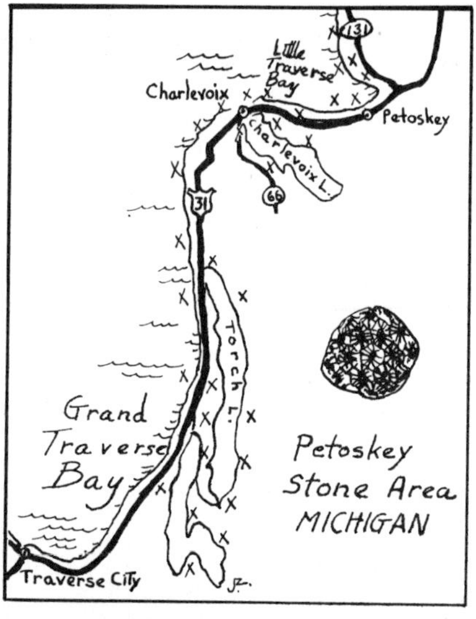

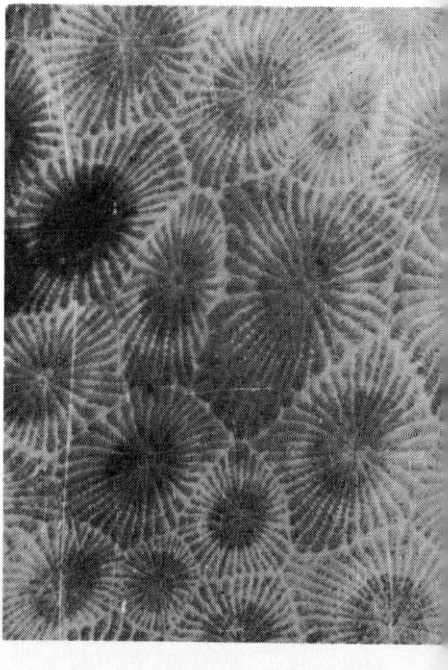

The designs in Petoskey stone are formed by fossillized polyps (Hexagonaria percarinata).

one is picked up on a northern Michigan or northern Minnesota beach.

Scuba diving expeditions under the direction of Arthur Vierthaler of the University of Wisconsin have recovered chlorastrolites of record proportions. Spectacular big thomsonites have been found in this manner. The new roads in Canada north of Isle Royale also may result in new discoveries.

LOWER MICHIGAN

Though Lower Michigan ranks annually among the top states in the production of gypsum, marl, salt, and sand and gravel, it is not noted as a gem area. The one exception is the distinctive and popular fossil gemstone known as "Petoskey stone." However, there are numerous deposits worth while for the specimen or crystal collector.

Crystals and Specimens

Of the many quarries with crystals in southern Michigan, the France Stone Company quarry at Monroe has been exceptionally popular. Crystals found here are golden calcite scalenohedrons and dolomite. In the quarry at Rockwood, south of Detroit, yellow calcite with celestite is found in geodes. This is the Sylvania Sandstone Quarry.

Brilliant marcasite comes from the Cheney Quarry at Bellevue. Pyrite and calcite also are found here. Sphalerite and calcite are found in a quarry 1 mile west of the town of Grand Ledge.

There are several alabaster quarries at National City. In fact, a town in the vicinity is named Alabaster. Gravel pits north of Tawas contain some of the best quartz gems of the state.

Fossils

Petoskey stone is a term commonly used to identify the calcite-replaced corals of the genus **Hexagonaria.** However, there are several other types of corals and marine fossils similarly replaced by calcite in the same area. These like the **Hexagonaria** may be cut and polished successfully, so it seems that the term "Petoskey stone" could cover them all as far as the lapidary is concerned.

These fossils are found as weatherworn, sand-polished, specimens along Traverse Bay from Petoskey to Charlevoix. Burt Lake, Torch Lake, and Crystal Lake as well as many other inland lakes in the area have abundant Petoskey stones on the beaches.

Your first difficulty will be in recognizing the stones as you see them on the beach. If you are lucky enough to find the water very quiet, you will see the turtleback-patterned fossils glistening underneath. Or if it has just rained you will be amazed at the high proportion of beach stones that are Petoskey stones. If the stones are dry, you will have little to guide you. They will be limy white on the outside but the structural lines of the weathering may give a clue to their fossil origin. After you have carried a hundred or so to the water's edge to wet them, you will gradually acquire an "eye" for the material and accumulate all you need rapidly.

The best of the Petoskey stones are those with the most distinct patterns and most contrasting colors. A combination of medium beige with dark brown markings is most interesting when cut. Other colors range from grey to almost black.

Unweathered specimens of Petoskey stones are easier to recognize. These can be found in quarries south of Petoskey or gravel pits in the vicinity of Charlevoix. Quarries near Afton, Onoway, and Alpena also have Petoskey outcrops.

One of the prolific producers has been the Rockport Quarry near Alpena. Follow U. S. 23 nine miles north of Alpena and turn east on the county road 1½ miles.

Bryozoans, cup and horn corals, favosites (honeycomb coral) and even occasional shells, are among other polishable specimens of the same replacement and same locations.

John Wilhammer of Gary, Indiana, found a method of polishing Petoskey stones using a velvet lap which puts a true mirror finish on them and gives them a higher status among midwestern gem stones. Because of their intricate and regular patterns, Petoskey stones also are used for imaginative carvings.

The following counties afford particularly good fossil collecting: Monroe, Alpena, Presque Isle, Charlevoix, Chippewa, Schoolcraft, and Delta. Collectors who want to see what may be found in Michigan should visit the Cranbrook Institute of Science at Bloomfield Hills.

Some of the brachiopods of lower Michigan have crystal-filled cavities, making them part fossil, part geode. The crystals are usually calcite.

Fossils occurring abundantly in Michigan's southern peninsula are brachiopods, pelecypods, cephalopods, gastropods, crinoid stems, and corals.

ILLINOIS

Illinois has much to offer the mineral and fossil collector even if the gems of the state are scarce. Northern Illinois with the sand dunes of Lake Michigan is a vivid contrast to southern Illinois where bald cypress trees grow in the swampy valleys of the Ohio and Mississippi Rivers. The general collecting areas of the state are the zinc-lead mines in northwestern Illinois, the coal mines of northern Illinois, the glacial drift of the Wisconsin glacier, the bluffs and cliffs of the Ohio and Mississippi, and the fluorspar region in the south.

Gems

The glacial moraine and drift of northern Illinois is a source of a few quartz family gems. A few years ago diamond was discovered in a drill core in the oil fields. Alluvial diamonds also have been reported.

One type of geode found in west central Illinois has concentric layers of variegated blue grey to white chalcedony. I have seen gems cut from this. These geodes are found at Hamilton.

Bishop Hill north of Galva in Henry County has some jasper and agate. Several places along the Mississippi have yielded quartz family gems. One such spot is Moline, another Hamilton. Thebes and Fayville, two small towns set in the rugged hills of Alexander County on the Mississippi, have gravels with occasional gems coming to light.

Some of the fluorite from Rosiclare can be faceted or adapted to gem carving. However, it is really not in the gem field that Illinois has become a famous goal for collectors in the Midwest.

NORTHERN ILLINOIS

Minerals

Galena near the Mississippi River in northwestern Illinois, is named for the famous ore from its mines. Many fine groups of zinc-lead mineral crystals have come from this mining district. Some of the galena cubes have been of exceptional size. One once used as a paperweight in President Grant's home at Galena has crystal faces six inches across. It is completely coated with marcasite.

An unusual type of crystallization is found here, known as "plume marcasite." Groups of elongated cubes create the plume effect. Analysis has disclosed that the plumes are in reality pyrite, and the mineral is now called "radiant pyrite." It represents the youngest deposition of pyrite in the area.

There are still some productive mine dumps about 20 miles northeast of Galena. There are cockscomb marcasite, lead and zinc specimens, and calcite to be found here if one can get permission.

Galena deposits in this district were known and worked by ancient Indians, as were so many other mineral deposits of the Midwest. Patient craftsmanship and true artistry are seen in the pipes these aborigines carved from catlinite and inlaid with lead.

Another northern Illinois location of interest to the mineral collector is the strip coal mine district near Wilmington. Pyrite and marcasite are found in association with coal seams in many spots. A favorite spot is at the small town of East Brooklyn. Turn east at Gardner which is 7 miles southwest of Braidwood on Alternate Road 66. East Brooklyn is three miles southeast on this paved county road. It adjoins the equally small community of South Wilmington.

Fossils

Some of the best fossil flora of the world is to be found at the strip coal mines of Wilmington, Braidwood, and Coal City. Often called "Mazon Creek fossils," these perfect impressions of Pennsylvanian ferns, seeds, reeds, leaves and stems are found in flattened oval concretions in the overburden of the coal seams.

Usually one-half of the fossil imprint is indented while the other is in bas relief. One part is characteristically darker than the other. The concretions vary in size from 1 to 8 inches, with 5 inches or more being rare. Many of these concretions have to be split open carefully to find a few prizes. Ferns of many species are found. Such fauna as fossil shrimp sometimes turn up. Particularly beautiful are the delicate, graceful leaves of **Annularia** and **Asterophyllites** which belonged to the scouring rushes but look like delicate flowers.

The State Museum at Springfield has a remarkable collection of the fossil plants collected by George Langford and his son who spent 140 days on the mine dumps and split 250,000 concretions. Mr. Langford, though starting as an amateur, has contributed extensively to the knowledge of plants of the past. His book, "The Wilmington Coal Flora," has been published by the Earth Science Club of Northern Illinois, which further shows the help our hobby can give science.

The coal fossils were first available in Grundy County, in the banks of the Mazon Creek. Strip mines of the Northern Illinois Coal Company in the Wilmington area began to reveal vast numbers of the fossil-bearing nodules in 1928. Some collectors in the past were also able to gather fossils from road or railway cuts.

Some collecting still may be done in the area. This usually is on the club field trip plan. Waivers must be signed before entering the mines. The Peabody Coal Company on Alternate U. S. 66 south of Braidwood is one company which has allowed collectors.

Due to vandalism by a scientific organization (not organized rock collectors), the Mazon Creek area is in danger of being closed to collecting. Other parts of the fossil collecting grounds are due to go into private hands, though this may not mean closure.

The best way to collect in this area is to belong to a mineral club in the vicinity and join its field trips. Permission to collect is usually easier for a club to arrange.

The doubtful status of this old and popular area makes it imperative that every collector redouble his efforts to build an excellent reputation for the hobby by observing the rights of landowners, obtaining permission, and avoiding damage to installations.

Special caution is called for, also, in the Terre Haute fern fossil area, the only other known locality of similar fossils.

A famous fossil fauna of northern Illinois was found in the Western Quarry of Lemont, Illinois. The intricately detailed Silurian trilobite fossils from the Niagara dolomite were this Quarry's chief magnet for collectors. The replacements are glistening white silica. The Quarry has been flooded, so collecting there is now impossible.

Numerous Pennsylvanian fossils are found around Minonk on Route 51 in Woodford County.

The Modusa Quarry of Dixon, Illinois, is another well known limestone quarry famous for marine fossils. Another is the Garden Prairie Quarry 5 miles west of Marengo, McHenry County. Buffalo Rock, Oglesby, and Ottawa also have quarries where collectors have been allowed with permission.

The glamour fossil of the snail family was discovered in a strip coal mine at Farmington, Illinois, in 1960. When first found, these dark pyritized shells in their black iron sulphide matrix are anything but spectacular. However, the gastropods, **Shansiella carbonaria,** gleam like gold when a patient collector cleans them.

Of course, these Pennsylvanian marine fossils have been known to paleontologists for years, but their recent popularity, amounting almost to a fad, came about when they were brought to the attention of the Illinois Valley Rockhound Society of Pekin.

Pyritized fossils are not found promiscuously throughout the coal measures, according to Dr. Frank Fleener of Joliet, but are localized in specific areas of very black shales rich in organic matter. Pelecypods, crinoid stems, and brachiopods are also found in the Farmington seam.

The Farmington fossils vary in size from less than an inch to well over 2 inches in diameter. They may be cleansed with acid, but a brass brush also does a good job. Some collectors protect them with clear lacquer.

The mine, Rapatee No. 5, is located on Route 116, 6 miles west of Farmington. It belongs to the Midland Coal Company. You must obtain permission to seek the 160-million-year-old fossils. Work in the strip area near the stripping shovel. Friends warn me that this is very dirty work, so go dressed for the occasion. It is best to schedule your trip on a Sunday or holiday as much massive machinery is used on working days.

CENTRAL ILLINOIS

Geodes occur abundantly in Illinois in the Warsaw formation at the type locality at Warsaw. Hamilton, Nauvoo, and Niota are also in the geode region. The Warsaw formation is a calcareous shale of the upper Mississippian. Outcrops are in a narrow band along the river and tributary streams of the region. Quarries, cuts in the side roads, gravel bars, or excavations, are all geode hideouts.

In general, inclusions in the Illinois geodes are like those of the nearby Iowa and Missouri geode areas. However, at Tyson Creek, 2 miles south of Niota, there is a strange and rare occurrence of geodes which are full of liquid petroleum. Some of these oil geodes contain up to a quart of oil, others only a few drops. The geodes have the usual crystal linings but of course the sticky black oil covers every crystal face and fills every crevice. Oddly enough, there is no petroleum field in the immediate vicinity, and the surrounding shale shows no evidence of oil stain.

Dr. Wells Sinotte of Keokuk, Iowa, collected many of his notable geodes right in Hamilton. One of his sparkling giants measures 21 x 27 inches.

The Niota area is also a noted fossil locale. The Burlington limestone is almost

Fluorite,
Cave-In-Rock,
Illinois

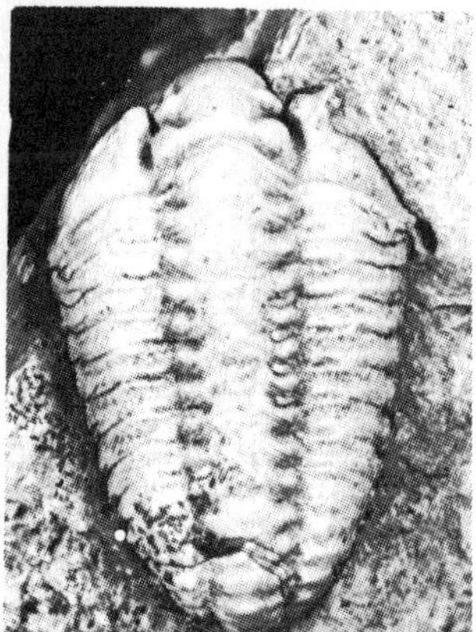

Trilobite,
Kankakee,
Illinois.

Pyritized
snails,
Farmington,
Illinois.

Calcite
crystals,
Rosiclare,
Illinois.

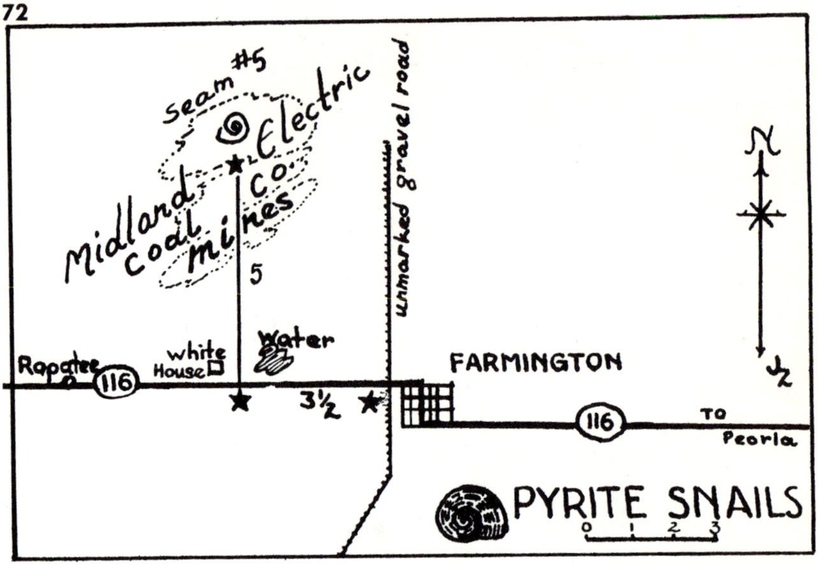

entirely a mat of brachiopods and crinoids. Mr. and Mrs. Maurice Lamb of Niota dug out a 500-pound piece of limestone covered with a crinoid root system with individually preserved roots over 12 inches long.

There are a few places where a fee is charged for hunting geodes. Fees range from nominal near Nauvoo, Illinois, to $10.00 at Wayland, Missouri. As far as we could discover the fees were justified by the amounts and quality of material available.

Now about the time element. We were there in early spring and it was so delightful that I hope every rockhound can visit the location under identical circumstances.

True, the water was a bit high in places and there was some mud on the side roads, but we found all the geodes we needed — and unless you want to make geodes your business, so will you.

The scenic drive along the river to Nauvoo, Illinois, was worth the time even if we hadn't been so lucky with the geodes.

Near a big old farmhouse there was one bank which was literally studded with geodes. The good ones shattered too easily with a blow of the hammer and the solid ones were so hard that I might as well have tried breaking up anvils.

The other locality we visited was near Hamilton, Illinois, south of the Keokuk bridge. Here we found geodes with more inclusions. The geodes of the Warsaw formations are noted for their variety of inclusions.

SOUTHERN ILLINOIS

Crystals

The fluorite mines of southern Illinois were first opened for galena over a hundred years ago. The fluorspar was then considered a waste mineral. Some of the mines reported as many as 20 ounces of silver per ton of galena. After new uses for fluorspar were developed, the Rosiclare Mine was the leading fluorspar producer in the world for more than a century.

The fluorspar deposits are in fissure veins of the Mississippian sedimentary rocks. Although modern industry depends upon fluorite for such things as steel, aluminum, refrigeration, chemicals, insecticides, lenses, etc., the famous mines are now closed.

Fluorite can be faceted, cabbed, or carved. However, because of its softness it is usually preferred as specimen material. Ancient Indians used fluorite for carving and ornamental uses.

The splendid crystals from these southern Illinois mines are translucent cubes of blue, violet, yellow, amber, and lilac. The crystals are often two-toned. Some are less than an inch square while some have crystal faces of 5 inches or more. The really breathtaking specimens are those partially frosted with glittering quartz or calcite crystals, or combined with crystals of zinc, lead, barite, or pyrite.

A type favored for cutting is a banded variety called locally "coon tail" spar. The rarest colors are green and pink. Ben Clement of Marion, Kentucky, who has probably the ˌırgest and best fluorite collection in the country, discovered a pocket of a new type of fluorite crystallization. This is tetrahexahedral fluorite. The amazingly intricate crystals are a color between lilac and mauve. The pocket was near Rosiclare.

Attractive cleavage octahedrons of assorted sizes and colors are always popular with collectors and are used for modern nugget-type jewelry.

Inasmuch as most of the mines are closed, it is difficult for the collector to find an area where he can do a little hunting. Persistent inquiry may result in a lead or two. One dump we were told of is north of the Route 146 junction on Route 1. Eight-tenths of a mile north, you will notice a narrow gravel road. Turn west and follow this trail 2 miles to Mahoning No. 3. You may find other spots, but if not, there are numerous places where you can purchase almost any kind of specimens.

Near Sparta, Randolph County, radiating pyrite disks are found. They are thin and slightly larger than a dollar. When cleaned they are dazzling cabinet pieces.

Fossils

Valmeyer, 25 miles south of St. Louis, has an Ordovician limestone quarry containing a variety of marine fossils. Brachiopods, corals, bryozoans, and fragmentary crinoids are the chief types. The Columbia Quarry Company Plant No. 3 is of special interest.

Red Bud and Grafton, also in the St. Louis vicinity, have well known quarries. Blastoids are common at Red Bud, while Grafton area quarries have trilobite casts and molds.

Blastoids of the Belleville area are excellent. They can be found in the Paderbon fault. Property owners where this fault occurs, so far have admitted collectors.

There are fossils in the shales of the strip coal mines at Sparta, Randolph County. There are several large mines west of town, where Mississippian fossils are abundant.

Brachiopods found in quarries at Danville are replaced by marcasite and make exceptionally interesting specimens when cleaned. The fossils occur in dark shale and are similar in appearance to the marcasite brachiopods of Silica, Ohio.

The largest of these geodes from southern Indiana weighs 300 pounds. Photo — Indiana State Geological Survey.

INDIANA

Gems

Since there are no igneous or metamorphic rock outcrops in Indiana, the few gems which do occur are found in the glacial drift, principally of the Wisconsin glacier which covered well over two-thirds of the state. The gems are mostly small ones of the quartz family. Jasper, agate, wood, and polishable fossil coral have been found in the gravels of the Maumee River in the vicinity of Fort Wayne.

Pebbles of quartz, topaz, and even corundum are found in the glacial moraines of Morgan County, a thrice glaciated area. Highland Creek near Wilbur has glacial gravel bars.

The big exception to Indiana's lack of gems is diamonds. Over thirty diamonds have been recorded in this state over the past hundred years. Again, heavily glaciated Morgan County produced most of them, but adjoining, rugged Brown County also produced quite a few. The diamonds were recovered by gold prospectors panning the streams of these Counties for the precious yellow metal known to occur there.

CENTRAL INDIANA

Because there is little of interest to the crystal, mineral, or fossil collector in northern Indiana, I will go directly to central and south central Indiana where almost every road cut, stream bed, mine and quarry is worth intensive exploration.

The western portion of the region is dotted with many coal mines. Pyrite, marcasite, goethite, sphalerite, and selenite are some of the minerals of the coal mining district. They occur on the dumps, in the seams, banks, and cuts of the entire region.

The Enos Coal Mine pit 2 miles northwest of Spurgeon in Pike County, is a typical pyrite-marcasite locality. Another is the Morgan Company Pit No. 2 northeast of Kingman in Fountain County.

Limestone quarry hunting is convenient for all collectors in central Indiana.

The France Stone Company quarry 2.5 miles east of Logansport in Cass County, has apatite, calcite, glauconite, marcasite, pyrite, and quartz.

Celestite, rather rare in Indiana, is found 3.5 miles northeast of Spencer in Owen County in the Dunn Limestone Quarry. Barite and siderite are also found in the Spencer area. The location for these is 4 miles east at the junction of Indiana Route 46 and a small secondary road leading toward Gosport. There are numerous quarries in Owen County in the area around Spencer and Gosport. Not only these, but the creek banks and railroad cuts of this region have produced a nice variety of specimen materials.

Dolomite, marcasite, and pyrite can be found at the Erie Stone Company quarry in Wells County. The quarry is 1.5 miles north of Bluffton. A number of minerals occur in the Debolt Quarry 3 miles southeast of Richmond in Wayne County.

The most fascinating of central Indiana specimens are the geodes of Brown County. It is hard to know whether to class them as geodes or fossils. Locally they are called "geodized fossils." These quartz geodes come literally in all shapes and sizes. The unusual fact is that the shapes are almost exact replicas of such fossils as brachiopods, pelecypods, corals, and crinoid heads. The colors are from off-white to buff. The exteriors are knobby or lumpy as geodes from many localities are inclined to be. Resemblances to known fossils are so remarkable that most paleontologists of the area insist that these unique geodes are, indeed, of fossil origin. A few disagree but I see no reason to, as I have spent much time hunting other geodes of proven fossil origin — the agatized geodes of Tampa, Florida.

The fossil-geodes of Brown County occur in road cuts, cliffs, and banks of streams, washes, and dry stream beds. Although they are found in several parts of the County, the best known locality is at Bean Blossom Creek. The town of Bean Blossom is 5 miles north of Nashville on State 135. Another locality is along the beautiful Yellowwood Trail of Yellowwood State Forest. This is a steep rugged area of deep woods, especially colorful and breathtaking in the fall. Trail information may be obtained at Nashville.

Incidentally, you may pan for gold also and get some fair results in Greenhorn Creek, Brown County. Another Indiana gold locality is Gold Creek in Morgan County. A third is Highland Creek.

Fossils

Central Indiana has plenty of fossils to keep collectors busy a long time. The area around Crawfordsville, Montgomery County, is the state's best for crinoids.

Ordovician fossils may be collected along the railroad cuts near Weisburg, Dearborn County. This has been a prolific area for

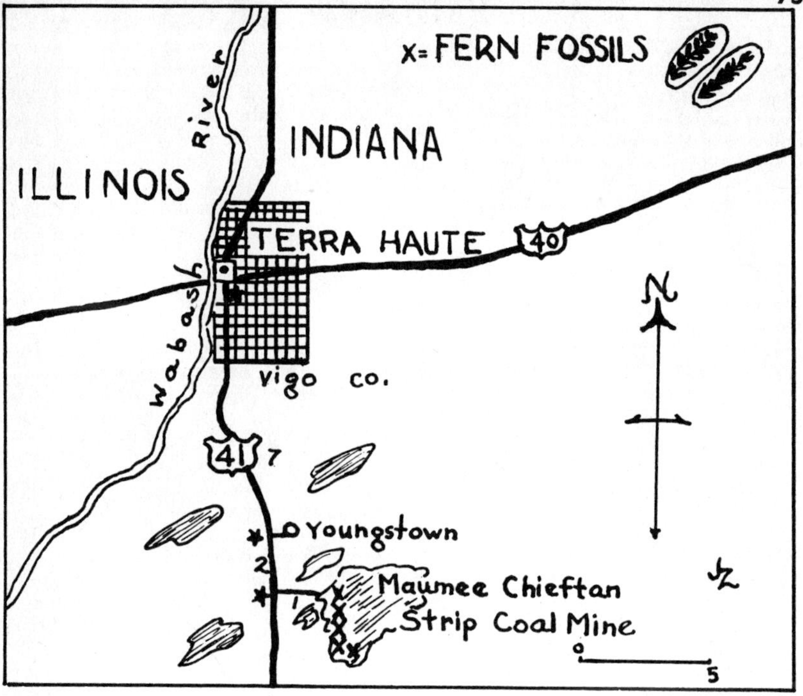

50 years and is still the chief locality in Indiana for trilobites.

Hartsville, Bartholomew County, has abundant Silurian brachiopods, blastoids, and corals. Marine fossils are numerous in quarries at Delphi and Logansport. A quarry at Mecca, Parke County, is a classic locality for fossil fish.

The most popular of Indiana's fossils are the fern fossils of the Pennsylvanian found near Terre Haute. Until this discovery was made there was no known deposit of fossil flora in concretions similar to those of Mazon Creek, Illinois. The Terre Haute fossils are exceptional in their detailed preservation. The concretions are grayer in tone than those of Illinois, but the many species of ancient ferns and other plants are much the same.

The fossils are found at the Maumee Chieftain Mine operated by the Peabody Coal Company. It can be reached from U. S. 41. Eight miles south of Terre Haute is the community of Youngstown just off the highway to the east. Proceed 2 miles south of the sign pointing to the town and turn left on a county maintained gravel road. You will see the spoil banks in less than half a mile. The best hunting is half a mile east of the west edge of the mine. Washes and eroded areas make hunting easier.

Merton Young of Michigantown says that so far, collectors have been treated very well here. It is his hope and mine that abuses will not close this area. Do not park where you will obstruct trucks or mine equipment. Do not go into dangerous areas. In other words, obey the rules of safety and common courtesy.

Marine fossils of numerous varieties are found near Waldron a mile west of Middletown on Route 421 between Shelbyville and Greensburg.

SOUTHERN INDIANA

Lawrence and Monroe Counties in south central Indiana probably have more mineral localities than any other counties in the state. Barite occurs in several places in Lawrence County. One spot is the Webster Quarry 3.5 miles southwest of Springville. Another is the Nally Quarry half a mile west of Georgia. Dolomite and strontianite are present here, also.

The type locality for oolitic limestone in the United States is at the town of Oolitic north of Bedford. The so called Bedford limestone is carboniferous and has found great popularity as a building material.

An abandoned quarry 2 miles southeast of Buddha also has barite and strontianite plus calcite, sphalerite, and celestite.

Barite is also common in Monroe County. It can be collected from a quarry half a mile east of Unionville on Indiana 45. With it are goethite, dolomite, glauconite, and pyrite.

The Bloomington Crushed Stone Company quarry half a mile north of Bloomington, has a great variety of minerals. Fifteen have been recorded from this quarry. A new iron mineral, smytheite, was recorded from a quarry in Bloomington a few years ago. The dark acicular crystals are inclusions in white calcite on peach-colored dolomite. The attractive crystal pockets are in a greenish matrix.

Road cuts near Harrodsburg yield many interesting specimens. One of them just north of town on Indiana 37 has some good aragonite.

Marcasite and pyrite are found in the Quimby and Stephen Quarry 2.8 miles south of Stanford. Marcasite and pyrite are also the chief minerals for collectors in Knox and Pike Counties where they are found in association with the coal veins. The Enos Coal Mine pit 2 miles northwest of Spurgeon, is one spot. The coal and shale of southwestern Indiana have the state's largest pyrite and marcasite concretions.

Fluorite, not common in Indiana, is found in some of the Bloomington quarries and in an abandoned quarry 1 mile west of Pekin. The Pekin quarry also has sphalerite, calcite, and selenite.

Harrison County has fluorite in quarries at Corydon operated by the Corydon Stone Company. Calcite and quartz are also found in these quarries. Attractive pink dolomite crystals are among Corydon's choice, collectors' items.

Crawford County in the hilly Ohio River border area, has several caves with beautiful aragonite, calcite, and travertine. Collecting is illegal in commercial caves but there are many undeveloped caves. Cave collecting generally is dangerous for amateurs, unless professional guides are available. However, I have seen so many ruined caves that were centuries in the making that I cannot help but wish all cave collecting could be done in rooms too far from the entrance to be viewed by the public, or rooms too small in which to stand up.

South central and southern Indiana also have deposits of geodes of the Keokuk type. Six miles east of Bedford, geodes are numerous in the creek and banks. The knobby greyish quartz geodes up to 15 inches in diameter, are found all through the Bedford vicinity in Lawrence County. Salt Creek and the East Fork of the White River are the main streams. Four miles east of Medora is a creek filled with geodes.

Towns with geodes nearby are Guthrie, Heltonsville, Erie, Zelma, Pinhook, Clearspring, and Buddha. Robert Giltner of Eminence, Kentucky, has found several Indiana geodes east of Bedford with traces of crude oil. Geodes are also found in the Ohio River area. In fact, these hard, round stones are so common in southern Indiana that one often sees stone walls and building formations with geodes used as a construction stone. Incidentally, don't ask natives of the area about geodes. Inquire instead about "niggerheads."

Other inclusions in Indiana geodes besides quartz and calcite are sphalerite, siderite, goethite, dolomite, limonite, kaolin, celestite, fluorite, and chalcedony.

Fossils

Ordovician trilobites and brachiopods are found in quarries near Versailles on Laughery Creek in Ripley County.

There are fossils near Corydon, Harrison County. The entire Bedford vicinity is rich in fossils.

Several species of fossil shells have been found at the Louisville Cement Quarry in Milltown, Crawford County.

OHIO

Ohio, bordered on the north mostly by Lake Erie, and on the south by the great Ohio River, was for long periods of geologic time a sea, then a dense forest swamp. Ohio was glaciated four times. Its present mineral wealth makes it rank second among all states in the production of limestone and dolomite. and first in the production of clays and clay products. It has, of course, thick beds of coal as well as gas and oil.

Gems

Since even Ohioans brag about no other gem than flint in their state, I shall not divide Ohio into gem hunting districts but go directly to Flint Ridge. This area covers a distance of about 8 miles with an average width of ¾ mile in Licking and Muskingum Counties. From only a few inches thick at the edges, the deposit thickens to depths of 6 to 10 feet toward the center. In some places the vein of flint is practically on the surface and in other spots it is buried beneath several feet of rich soil. The deposit begins southeast of Newark and ends northwest of Zaneville.

Collecting is restricted in the area. The State Park does not permit collecting within its boundaries. However, there are road cuts in the area as well as spots on private property where collecting is allowed. Permission must be obtained before attempting to collect on private property. Some farmers charge a fee.

The area is a beautiful, rolling, wooded country known and beloved by rock collectors since the days early Indians from many tribes and areas came here to gather material for their choice weapons and tools. Ohio flint artifacts found their way to many states. Choice Ohio flint arrowheads are highly prized by collectors of gem points.

The hilltops are now strewn with flint scraps so deep as to make walking difficult. There are hundreds of pits of varying depths and sizes.

The late Audrey Ackerman of New Concord, Ohio, summed up the appeal of the Ohio flint in these words, "It is my favorite gemstone because the search is always fascinating and endless. One piece will be a breccia designed by a modern artist. The next may be scenic dendritic patterns in translucent chalcedony. Swirly banded jasper will give way to clear fortifications, and then to brilliant drusy crystals. Truly, there never are two alike."

Many collectors who are not familiar with Ohio flint change their preconceived notions about it in 60 seconds when they see the beautifully polished slabs and cabochons of Floyd Ackerman's. Some of his imaginatively cut pieces could easily pass for Arizona wood, Mexican crazy lace, California flowering jasper, or Kansas moss opal.

Chemically, the flint is impure silica varying from crystalline to cryptocrystalline and amorphous. It has a hardness of 7 and is tough and resistant. Flint seems to be a misnomer as the material does not have the nodular form of other noted flint deposits, while other characteristics such as color and translucency tend to class it as a mixture of jasp-agate, chert, chalcedony, and common opal.

Two types of flint are considered quite rare – green and amethystine. The Indians discarded the pieces with pockets and vugs of drusy quartz crystals, but collectors now seek these for both cabinet specimens and jewelry.

Fossils

Few areas ars as universally rich in fossils of many eras as Ohio. All 88 counties have fossils. Even the walls of the State House in Columbus contain fossils. There are places where you can actually scoop up the fossils, and other spots where a day's work may reward you with a rare, complete speciment of **Phacops rana,** the prized Devonian trilobite. There are fossils so small it takes a microscope to discern them, and fossils of mastodons which you can't possibly unearth yourself. The fossils range in age from Ordovician to Pleistocene.

Fossil Collecting

Ohio is literally dotted with quarries. All of them are possible sites of a fossil bonanza. However, quarries are private property and not all of them allow collectors. Many are hazardous because of loose rock, blasting, active machinery, or water. In some cases you will be asked to sign a waiver releasing the company from responsibility in case of accident.

Strip mines in the coal areas are fertile collecting grounds. Highway or byway cuts are worth investigating. Don't forget the railroads, either. Stream or lake banks, eroded hills or cliffs, gullies or ditches – all are havens for the fossil hunter.

Besides your prospector's pick, you will find cold chisels of several sizes, a knife, a shovel, a screen, and a pry bar useful.

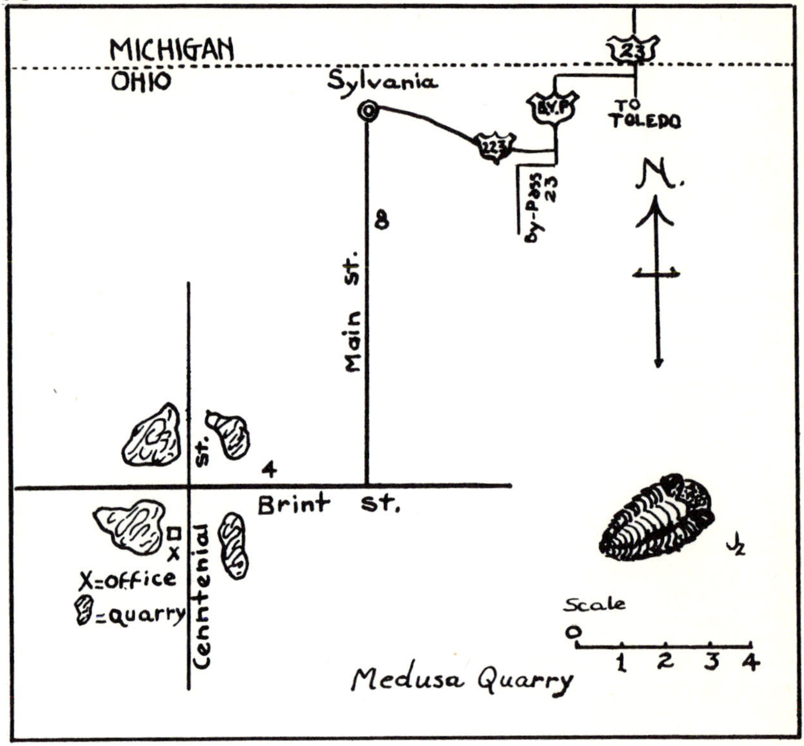

NORTHWESTERN OHIO

Most of the fossils of northwestern Ohio are Silurian with a few Devonian areas. Perhaps the most famous quarry in Ohio for the amateur collector is the Medusa Quarry of Sylvania. This is the Devonian silica shale formation and as a type locally it is shown as "Silica" on many maps.

The quarries are located at the junction of Brint Street and Centennial Road southwest of Sylvania. The best hunting is in the southwest quarry, but the other quarries are worth investigating. The Medusa Quarry office is a mile south of the quarries. Get permission and sign a waiver there before doing any collecting.

The fossils of these quarries are too numerous to mention in detail. There are brachiopods, pelecypods, gastropods, corals, crinoids, and most important, the finest trilobites imaginable of the species **Phacops rana.**

The limestone is finely grained, very hard, and a pleasing grey color. The fossils are in bold relief in dark grey to black. Some of the most interesting are the graceful **Spirifer** brachiopods which have been replaced by marcasite, the hollow shells lined with crystals of calcite and marcasite, or the "doublets" where one fossil is perched upon another.

For many years the great limestone quarry at Clay Center, Ottawa County, has been a celebrated locality for crystals as well as Silurian fossils. The common fossils are corals and gastropods.

The crystals of this quarry are celestite of exceptional beauty, fluorite, dolomite, marcasite, and calcite. They occur in cavities in the massive limestone and must be worked out with a great deal of patience. The fluorite from this quarry fluoresces and phosphoresces. The crystals are brown under natural light, green under short wave ultraviolet light. The delicate blue and white radiating fans of celestite crystals are especially prized. There are tiny brilliant pyrite crystals as well as other small crystals suitable for thumbnails or micromounts.

When and where collecting is permitted will have to be determined by inquiry locally. There are many other good to excellent collecting spots in this area, as well as Ottawa County as a whole. Two other good spots are the quarries immediately to the west and to the southeast of the town of Genoa. Woodville, 5 miles south of Genoa, is another collecting area.

Seneca County is a likely spot for finding Silurian marine fossils. There is a quarry at Maple Grove about 5 miles northwest of Tiffin. Follow Highway 53 to Fort Seneca and turn 2 miles west on the section line road. Then turn north again for half a mile.

Wyandot County has a number of quarries where gastropods, cephalopods, and brachiopods may be collected. Just northwest of the town of Crawford on Highway 23 is one quarry. Another productive locality is nearby Carey.

The Pugh Quarry to the west and south of Bowling Green is another place famous for crystals. This popular spot for collectors has some superb celestite crystals. Pyrite, barite, calcite, and fluorite also may be found in veins and cavities in this Quarry.

NORTHEASTERN OHIO

The Lake Erie border of northeastern Ohio is Devonian with the zone just south of it Mississippian. Then the area from Portage County south and east is Pennsylvanian.

Some outstanding fish fossils have been found in the black shales of northern Ohio. Carbonized fish fossils were discovered near Cleveland. Some of the Devonian fossil fishes were of enormous size, such as **Dinicrthys** ("terrible fish") which grew to 25 feet in length.

In the Pennsylvanian outcrops of northern Ohio, footprints of reptiles and amphibians have been found. However, the plant fossils are better known representatives of the Pennsylvanian period. Many famous plant fossils are associated with the coal seams and their accompanying shales and sandstones. Outstanding are the detailed ferns preserved in the black shales. The lycopod tree, **Lepidodendron**, which sometimes grew one hundred feet tall, is often found. This is a relative of club mosses. Another odd plant of the Pennsylvanian forest now found in Ohio is **Calamites.** This also grew in treelike proportions but otherwise resembled our horsetails or scouring rushes. **Cordaites,** a distant ancestor of the pine, is also represented in the Ohio coal fossils.

The Ohio coal fields are bituminous. Coal-bearing rock occurs in thirty counties in Ohio, most of them in the eastern part of the state. There are countless mines, dumps, and road cuts in the coal area of the northeastern section of Ohio in Carroll, Columbiana, Coshocton, Harrison, Jefferson, Mahoning, Portage, Stark, and Tuscarawas Counties.

SOUTHWESTERN OHIO

The Dayton-Cincinnati area alone has yielded over 700 species of Ordovician fauna. One of the most famous fossils anywhere is the giant trilobite, 14½ inches long, found in Dayton. Other fossils to look for in this area are brachiopods, crinoids, pelecypods, and corals.

There are plenty of both active and abandoned quarries in this area. One good quarry is just off the campus of the University of Miami at Oxford, Butler County. Many river banks and road cuts in this county and adjoining Preble County are loaded with fossils. Fossils can be picked up even in the stream beds of the area.

Rock exposures in an area locally known as "Stony Run" at Fort Ancient, Warren County, have abundant fossils. Fort Ancient is 7 miles from Lebanon on State Route 350. Blanchester in southwest Clinton County has an exposure rich in fossils. There is a quarry noted for fossils at Piqua, Miami County. Near the campus of Antioch College at Yellow Springs, Greene County, is another fine quarry. The whole city of Cincinnati is a fossil bed. Any quarry, excavation, ravine, or stream bed of the vicinity may be the source of prize finds.

SOUTHEASTERN OHIO

This part of the state is entirely bordered by the Ohio River. It is mostly Pennsylvanian with some Permian. Perhaps the best plant fossils of the state occur at mines and road cuts in Cameron and Carrington near the Ohio River in Monroe County. Excellent plant fossils also are found at Becket, Crabapple, and Vallonia in neighboring Belmont County. **Psaronius,** an unusual type of tree fern fossil, has been found near Athens. Large sections of silicified trunk were found, some of polishing quality.

Brachiopods and pelecypods of the Mississippian come from Licking County. A prolific region is around Granville and Newark. Some of the fossils of this region are in iron concretions.

At several localities in Ohio, large masses and clusters of pyrite crystals are found in the seams of "blue clay." One locality is given as a "few miles" west of Chillicothe. Inquiry may be made at local farms. While not a gem material, the pyrite specimens make magnificent cabinet pieces when carefully dug from the blue clay.

The pyrite specimens have been found also in the blue clays of Delaware and Franklin Counties as well as Ross County. The Ross County nodules generally show good cubic crystallization but are so close and flush on the outside of the sphere that they look almost like golden mosaics. In another location in Delaware County they are sharply cubical and more or less spherical in shape. In another they are rough with fully completed cubic crystals sharply defined all over the outside of the nodule.

In some of the beds, particularly those in Delaware County there appears to be a concentration of low-grade pyrite in layers, generally on the lowerside of the seam of blue clay and just above the shale. Where this type of base is found, the little nodules rest very closely to the concentration and the stems seem to point down.

Gem hunting and mineral collecting in the midwest region, as in other parts of the country, have their characteristics. Again, we enumerate the best places to search in the Midwest: (1) gravel pits, including commercial gravel diggings and any exposures or outcroppings of glacial outwash, (2) quarries where economic minerals are mined, including limestone, (3) stream beds and exposures cut by water, (4) mine waste dumps, (5) road cuts and any excavations made in building or construction work, (6) rocky hillsides, (7) pegmatite outcrops.

Trilobite (Phacops rana) from Silica, Ohio.

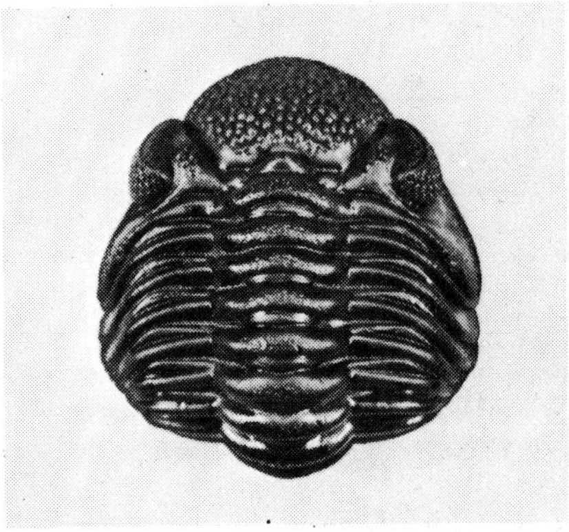

Cone-in-cone formation found near Conneaut, Ohio. Photo—Murray's Studio.